REVVED

NEW YORK TIMES BEST SELLING AUTHOR
SAMANTHA TOWLE

**OTHER CONTEMPORARY NOVELS
BY SAMANTHA TOWLE**

Trouble

THE STORM SERIES

The Mighty Storm
Wethering the Storm
Taming the Storm

**PARANORMAL ROMANCES
BY SAMANTHA TOWLE**

The Bringer

THE ALEXANDRA JONES SERIES

First Bitten
Original Sin

Copyright © 2015 by Samantha Towle

All rights reserved.

Cover Designer: Najla Qamber Designs

Editor and Interior Designer: Jovana Shirley, Unforeseen Editing, www.unforeseenediting.com

No part of this book may be reproduced or transmitted in any form or by any means, electronic or mechanical, including photocopying, recording, or by any information storage and retrieval system without the written permission of the author, except for the use of brief quotations in a book review.

This book is a work of fiction. Names, characters, places, and incidents either are products of the author's imagination or are used fictitiously. Any resemblance to actual persons, living or dead, events, or locales is entirely coincidental.

Visit my website at www.samanthatowle.co.uk

ISBN-13: 978-1508776208

*For Trishy and Sali.
My adoration for you both is immeasurable.*

contents

Prologue 1
Chapter One 5
Chapter Two 29
Chapter Three 39
Chapter Four 53
Chapter Five 61
Chapter Six 83
Chapter Seven 97
Chapter Eight 107
Chapter Nine 115
Chapter Ten 123
Chapter Eleven 129
Chapter Twelve 147
Chapter Thirteen 167
Chapter Fourteen 187
Chapter Fifteen 205
Chapter Sixteen 223
Chapter Seventeen 237
Chapter Eighteen 249
Chapter Nineteen 265
Chapter Twenty 277
Chapter Twenty-One 287
Chapter Twenty-Two 305
Chapter Twenty-Three 317
Chapter Twenty-Four 329
Chapter Twenty-Five 335

Chapter Twenty-Six	347
Chapter Twenty-Seven	359
Chapter Twenty-Eight	367
Chapter Twenty-Nine	383
Epilogue	389
Acknowledgments	397
About the Author	401

prologue

▰ MONTE CARLO, MONACO

I LOOK UP AT MY MUM. She looks worried, and she's holding my hand tight. She always does this when Dad's racing, but I don't mind. I know she gets nervous, so I let her squish the life out of my hand because I know holding it makes her feel better.

I don't know why she gets nervous though. I don't get nervous, ever, simply because my dad is the best driver in the world. He's the champion, and he's about to be the champion again.

I wriggle my fingers a little as they start to feel funny.

"Sorry, darling." Mum smiles down at me. It's a tight, worried smile.

I wish she wouldn't worry so much.

I smile up at her, trying to make her feel better.

She's really beautiful, my mum, and very tall. She used to be a model, but she gave it up when she had me.

I'm going to be tall like her. I'm already tall for my age. I hate it. I'm ten and taller than most of the boys in my class. I'm all limbs and gangly. *Ugh*. I wish I were small and petite, like the other girls in my class.

Everyone says that I look just like my mum though, which is a nice thing because she's the most beautiful person in the world.

My dad says I look like her, too, and that he's in for a nightmare when I grow up. Apparently, he's going to keep a cricket bat by the front door to beat away any boyfriends I might have.

He's crazy. *Like I'll ever have a boyfriend.* I won't have time for boys when I'm older.

I want to race like Dad does or maybe even be a mechanic like Uncle John. He's not my real uncle, but I always call him that. He's my dad's best friend and my godfather.

I love when Uncle John lets me work on the cars with him, and I get all covered in oil and dirt. Mum gets mad though when I get it on my clothes, but I don't care.

Mum doesn't say it, but I know she doesn't want me to work on cars, and she definitely won't want me to race. I think she'd be happy if I did what she used to—be a model.

But I'm not into pretty things like her. I'm like my dad. I love cars.

And Dad says I can do anything I want as long as I put my mind to it and work hard in school.

"And he's set to do it! Coming in on the final lap!"

At the sound of the announcer's voice, I look up at the screens and see that my dad is on the last lap, leading and heading for the finish line.

I get that excited feeling in my stomach like I always do when I see him racing, and I start jigging on the spot.

"Our reigning champion, William Wolfe, is set to take home the trophy again. Wait—something's happening. Wrong…oh God, no. There-there looks to be a problem with the car. Fire's coming from the back of his car…"

I watch helplessly as my dad's car tailspins out of control, the back end on fire, and he crashes into the barrier.

I feel his impact like it's my own body hitting that barrier.

Then, everything happens so fast yet so incredibly slow.

I can hear Mum screaming. And people are yelling. On the screens above, I see the marshals running to his car.

I can't move. I don't want to move or look away from the screens in case I miss anything.

Please be okay, Daddy. Please.

Then, without warning, I'm being picked up from behind and carried away.

Uncle John.

He turns me in his arms, pressing my face into his chest, so I can't see anything. He moves quickly through the garage, taking me away from the screens, away from the track.

Away from my dad.

I'm yelling, "No!"

I'm trying to fight him. I have to be here. I have to see that my dad is okay.

Then, I hear the bang. It's so loud that it hurts my ears through my headphones.

Uncle John stops moving.

He slowly turns with me in his arms. Every muscle in his body goes rigid.

Fighting free, I look at the screens, and that's when I see it.

My dad's car is gone.

Replaced with flames. And smoke.

Thick black smoke, billowing up into the sky above.

FOURTEEN YEARS LATER

🇧🇷 SAO PAULO, BRAZIL

"I'M GOING TO MISS YOU SO MUCH, DARLING."

The emotional edge in my mother's voice has my lips wobbling and my eyes misting with tears.

"I'm going to miss you, too." I hug her tighter.

Leaning back, she takes my face in her hands, staring into my eyes. She's crying. I hate seeing her cry.

"Are you absolutely sure you have to go?"

We've had this conversation a lot over the past few weeks. I know I'm hurting her—I hate that I am—but I have to do this. If I don't, I know I'll regret it for the rest of my life.

"Mum, this is an amazing opportunity for me," I say softly. "I know you're worried, but I'll be fine. I'll be with Uncle John, and it's not like I'm actually getting in the race cars and driving them."

"I know…" She sighs.

It's a worrisome sigh, and I know where it comes from. I know my leaving is hurting her for many reasons—mostly because she's going to miss me, but largely because of where I'm going. It's stirring up painful memories for her.

"I'm not trying to hurt you," I say softly. "I just…I have to do this."

"I know." She kisses my forehead. "You are so much like your father. He would be so proud of you, you know."

Well, that just sets me off, and a tear spills down my cheek.

Mum wipes it away with her thumb. "I'm just being a silly clucky mother. I don't want to let my baby girl go."

"I'm coming back," I reassure her. "I'm not leaving forever."

"I know. Just take care of yourself, and be careful. You're going to be in a lot of strange countries. You have that rape alarm I bought for you?"

"Yes. It's in my bag."

"And you won't walk anywhere alone, especially at night."

"I won't."

"And if you must take a cab, then check that it's a city-approved cab."

"I will."

"And you'll check in with me every day?"

"I will. I promise." I give her another tight squeeze. "Don't worry." I pick up my bag from the floor, hanging it on my shoulder. "I'm going to go. Otherwise, I'll miss check-in."

"Okay." She stifles her tears. "Bye, darling. Have a safe flight."

"I'll be home for a visit as soon as I can. I love you."

I start walking backward toward the check-in gate, my chest heavy with emotion.

"I love you, too," she says, wiping her face with a tissue.

"I'll text as soon as I land."

"Okay. I'll miss you, darling."

"Miss you, too."

Then, I turn and walk away. Swiping a tear from my face, I hand my ticket to the guard and go through security.

SIXTEEN HOURS LATER

✈ LUTON, ENGLAND

I think I'd be exhausted after hours in an airport, waiting for my flight, which was delayed, before taking a twelve-hour flight from São Paulo to Luton, and now, it's one p.m., UK time. My body clock is a little all over the place, but as I drag my suitcase along, pushing through the door into Arrivals, I'm filled with a sense of excitement that's been building the whole journey here.

I'm thrilled to be back in England, buzzed at the prospect of starting my new job. But most of all, I just can't wait to see Uncle John. It's been a while since I last saw him.

I do a quick scan over the horde of people, looking for Uncle John, and then I see him. He's a hard guy to miss—built like a bear with a head full of salt-and-pepper hair.

He catches sight of me, his face breaking out into a huge smile. He waves a hand. I pick up speed to him as he moves toward me, his arms opening wide for a hug.

I jump into that hug like a little kid.

Uncle John has always had that way of making me feel like I'm ten years old again.

"Hey, kiddo." Releasing me, he smiles down at me, his eyes showing their age at the corners. Uncle John is in his late forties, but he looks good for it.

"Hey." I beam.

"How was your flight?" He bends to take my suitcase from me.

"Good. Long."

We start heading toward the exit.

"I'm just parked in the waiting area, so not far to walk."

"Thank God."

I shiver as the door opens, and a gush of good old English cold air hits me. I wrap my leather biker jacket around me, not that it's providing much warmth. I'm just glad that I thought ahead and changed in the airplane restroom, out of the shorts and tank that I left Brazil in and into the skinny jeans and T-shirt that I'm now wearing. I'm also glad I freshened up with wet wipes and spray of deodorant. There's nothing worse than feeling stale after a flight.

I forgot what it's like to live in England, how chilly it is here in February. I used to be acclimatized to it, but it's been fourteen years since I was last here.

I was born in England. I lived here until I was ten. After we lost Dad, Mum and I moved to Brazil, her home country.

"I'd offer you my jacket if I were wearing one." Uncle John chuckles while he walks along in a short-sleeved shirt.

"I'm okay. Don't worry."

"Sure, but I'll get the heat on in the car as soon as the engine warms up."

I adore Uncle John. After Dad died and Mum and I moved away, he stayed in our lives with regular phone calls and emails, and he visited every time he was in Brazil.

Uncle John is the chief engineer for Rybell's Formula 1 team—well, Carrick Ryan's team. Each Formula 1 team has two drivers. Rybell's other is Nico Tresler, a seasoned driver from Germany.

And Carrick Ryan is the playboy from Ireland, but he's one insanely talented driver.

He's way too handsome for any woman's good. He's a total womanizer and party boy. He's in the press more for his late-night antics and bedroom play than he is for his driving abilities. He acts more like a rock star than a Formula 1 driver.

He doesn't seem to have a sense of discipline that can be seen from other drivers. But his talent is unmistakable. His advancement in racing was so quick that he was making his debut with Formula 1 at twenty and taking home the trophy that same year. Now, five years later, he's only lost one championship.

I'm going to be working on Carrick's team, thanks to Uncle John. One of their mechanics quit suddenly a few weeks ago, and Uncle John offered me the job.

If you haven't guessed, I'm a mechanic.

Ever since I started working for the Brazil Stock Car team three years ago, Uncle John has been saying that I should come and work in Formula 1, and the minute he got an opening, it was mine.

He wasn't kidding, and here I am.

Formula 1 jobs don't come up easily, especially not on Carrick's team. He keeps everything close-knit, so I know how lucky I am to get the position.

"How's your mum doing?" Uncle John asks.

"She's okay…struggling with me leaving. Worried. You know how she is."

"Yeah." He chuckles. "I know how Katia gets."

"Uncle John…you haven't told anyone at Rybell who my dad was, have you?"

"No. You asked me not to, so I haven't. I get why you want to keep it a secret, but honestly, I don't think it's necessary."

For me, it is. My dad is regarded as one of the greatest drivers of all time. He was like the Messiah of Formula 1. People in the industry worshiped him—they still do—especially here in the UK. And I don't want people thinking that, as a twenty-four-year-old female mechanic, I got the job off the back of my father's name. I'd rather them think I was hired for my looks than that. So, while I'm here, I'm using my mother's maiden name, Amaro, and telling no one that I'm William Wolfe's daughter.

"I just want to prove myself without people knowing who my dad was."

"Not necessary," he reiterates.

I give him a look. "It is necessary. People will think I got the job because of my surname."

"No, they won't. You got the job because you're one hell of a mechanic and no other reason."

"You know that, but other people don't. I just want the chance to prove myself before everyone knows who my dad was."

"Okay." He lets out a defeated sigh. "It's your call. I'll keep my mouth shut until you tell me I can open it."

"Thank you." I smile appreciatively at him.

Uncle John knows almost everyone in Formula 1, so asking him to keep this a secret is a big ask.

Uncle John has been with Carrick since he started karting when he was fourteen. That's how Uncle John ended up back in Formula 1.

After my dad's accident, Uncle John left Formula 1 and went to work in karting. I think being there, after my dad, was too hard for him. It was hard for everyone.

But when Carrick progressed and Uncle John saw the talent in him, Carrick and Owen Ryan—Carrick's father and manager—persuaded Uncle John to move back to Formula 1 with them, so he did.

Working for Carrick is going to be such an honor.

Am I concerned about his reputation? Sure I am. But lucky for me, I'm used to horny drivers. Being a woman in a man's world, I have to be. I've worked around men for long enough to know how to put them in their place. Getting involved with a driver is not an option for me.

After seeing what losing my dad did to my mum, I'm not exactly a relationship person. I tend to date here and there—a couple of months, maximum. It's not that I'm averse to having a boyfriend. I just haven't found anyone who I want to spend a lot of time with. And with my job, I travel around a lot, so it's not really viable.

I'm either with other mechanics, who are all male—and I don't get involved with coworkers, too messy—or I'm around drivers.

And I definitely don't ever get involved with drivers. Ever.

They're a slippery slope to heartbreak.

Uncle John comes to a stop outside a car I recognize instantly because I spent a lot of time driving around in it as a kid.

"Is that…your old Ford Capri?" I smile wide.

Uncle John had this car when I left for Brazil. A 1987 black Ford Capri with a red racing stripe down the side. I can't believe he still has it.

"Yep, I still have her." He grins. Popping the trunk, he hauls my suitcase into it.

"I can't believe she's still running."

"You doubt the master." He gives me a cheeky look before climbing into the driver's side.

I get in the passenger side, putting my belt on. "No, I just thought you'd have upgraded by now."

"You can never replace your first love." He lovingly pats the steering wheel. Then, he turns the ignition, and she hums to life. "Okay, so where are we going?"

I give him a questionable look. "I thought you'd know that."

"Well, I just thought I'd check and see if you'd changed into a normal person, one who just arrived here after traveling for the better part of a day and might want to go to her new apartment and get some rest."

Uncle John has rented me a little furnished one-bedroom apartment, near Rybell's headquarters in Heath and Reach, which is a little village in Bedfordshire.

"But if I'm guessing right and you're not normal—like me—then I'm taking it, we're going straight to Rybell?"

I look at him, a grin sliding on my face. "You guessed right."

On the drive to Rybell, Uncle John talks to me about work and what I'm going to be doing when I start tomorrow.

He's telling me the names of people I'm going to be working with, and I'm not remembering one of them, but I'm sure they'll stick once I have a face to put with the name.

I see the Rybell building up ahead in the distance, and I start to bounce in my seat with excitement.

I'm not weird. This is just my thing.

You know how some girls get excited at the prospect of going shopping for shoes? Well, I get that way around cars, especially race cars.

I spent the better part of my life around a Formula 1 garage and the second half of it with my cousins back home, working on their cars.

I was practically raised in garage, a Formula 1 garage to be precise, so to me, this is like coming home.

"Andi...,"

Uncle John's voice pulls my attention from the view to him.

"I haven't asked this yet, and I just want to check...are you feeling okay about this?"

"Yeah. Sure I am." I give him a confused smile.

"I just...I know my first time being back in the garage after losing your dad...it was hard."

Ah, right.

My smile fades a little. "I'm okay. It was a long time ago, and it's not like I haven't been back to the tracks since it happened."

Each time Uncle John was in Brazil for the Grand Prix, he got me tickets to go and watch. Granted, it was a little different, being a spectator in the stands than being a part of it, but I'm sure I'll be fine.

"I know. I just wanted to make sure that you're okay before we go in."

"I'm okay." I give his arm a reassuring pat.

Uncle John pulls down the private road, taking us to Rybell.

"Here we are." He pulls into the parking lot outside the building. It's a big white purpose-made building. Rybell itself is owned by a few major shareholders and headed by CEO Pierce Vose. He was a driver himself back in the day, not for Rybell though. Pierce and my dad drove on the same team in the early days of their racing careers.

Uncle John parks his car, and I follow him inside the building, walking through as he holds the door open for me.

"Morning, Liz." Uncle John lifts a hand in greeting to the forty-something blonde-haired lady behind the reception desk.

I see the way her eyes light up when she sees him. I think someone has a thing for Uncle John. Understandable. He's a good-looking guy and in great shape for a man approaching fifty.

"Liz, this is Andi Amaro, our new mechanic."

"Oh." Her brow lifts to her hairline. Then, she stands from her seat, reaching over the desk to greet me. "Well, hello, Andi. It's nice to meet you." She tilts her head to the side, hands going on her hips, as she assesses me with her eyes. "So…you're our new mechanic?"

"I am." I give a tight smile.

"Well, you're definitely not what I was expecting."

Huh?

I see her give Uncle John a look, and he frowns.

"Come on. Let me show you around," Uncle John says, trying to usher me away by the elbow.

"Andi, can I just get you to sign in before you go through?" Liz says to me.

"Of course." Picking up the pen from the desk, I scribble my name down on the sign-in sheet.

"Bye, John," she says in a saccharine voice.

He lifts a hand as he walks toward the door.

"Nice to meet you," I say to Liz.

I follow through the door that Uncle John is holding open. "What was that about?" I ask him as soon as the door's closed.

He gives me a confused look. "What was what about?"

"The you're-definitely-not-what-I was-expecting comment."

"Nothing." He looks away, shifty.

"Uncle John." I put my hand on his arm, stopping him.

"Fine," he huffs out. "I might have failed to mention to people that you're a…well, that you're a girl."

What?

"I'm not a girl. I'm a woman. And why would you do that?"

"Because I knew Pierce wouldn't give you the job if he knew you were a woman."

"Why not?" Jesus, I know Formula 1 can be a little on the sexiest side, but not hiring someone because of their gender would be unethical and a little on the illegal side.

Uncle John blows out a breath. "Because of Carrick. God knows, I love that boy, but…he has an eye for the women."

"I'm aware of that, as is any other person who reads the news. But just because I'm female doesn't mean I'm going to shag him."

"I know that, but Pierce doesn't. And because of a little incident that happened a few weeks ago, and is still burning up the tabloids here, Pierce will want to keep all forms of possible temptation away from Carrick."

"What kind of incident?"

"Well, you know how your job suddenly became open?"

"Carrick shagged the last mechanic? No, hang on. Wasn't he a guy? Does Carrick swing both ways?"

"No, thank God. Otherwise, he'd be a worse bloody nightmare to control than he already is. No, Rich—the guy who had your job—had been with us for three years. When our front-of-house girl left to have her baby, Rich's girlfriend, Charlotte, got the job."

I can see where this is going.

"Rich caught Carrick and Charlotte here one night, having—" Uncle John stops short of the word.

"Sex. You can say it. I'm not ten, Uncle John." I laugh.

His cheeks redden as he chuckles with the discomfort that only a person who still sees you as a kid can.

"So, yeah, Carrick was at it with Charlotte in the director's suite, Rich caught them, and it was a bloody nightmare. They got into a fight. Thankfully, Owen—Carrick's dad—and I were still here even though it was late at night. Rich quit, and he dumped Charlotte. She didn't seem too cut up about it since she thought she was going to get more from Carrick."

"But she didn't?"

He lets out a rumbling laugh. "Carrick doesn't give more. She was lucky to get more than one time with him."

"So, they were having an affair?"

"Not an affair in the real sense of the word. I think Carrick slept with her a few times, and she thought there was more going on than there actually was. Anyway, Charlotte didn't take being tossed aside too well, and she sold her story to the tabloids. Safe to say, Pierce hit the fucking roof at the bad press right before the season is about to start. Also, Charlotte is suing Rybell for losing her job. Total bloody nightmare. And I knew Pierce and Owen would be uncomfortable at the thought of having a female mechanic, especially one as pretty as you, working so closely with Carrick."

"I can understand that. But you know me, Uncle John. That's not how I work."

"Of course I know, and that's why I wanted to get you here, so there's nothing Pierce or Owen can do about it. I'm not having you miss out on your dream job because Carrick can't keep it in his pants."

"But…you've put me in an uncomfortable situation here, Uncle John. I appreciate why you did it, but I kind of don't want to go in there and meet everyone now, considering what might happen."

"Nothing will happen. Pierce isn't here at the moment. He's away at a meeting. And I'll talk to him before you meet him. Don't worry." He puts an arm around my shoulder, giving me a squeeze. "It's gonna be fine. Now, do you want a tour of the building or the garage first?"

"Garage. I might as well get the inevitable over with."

I'm feeling less than excited now, knowing I'm going to be a shock to my new employers.

Come on, Andi. You can do this. So what if you get some stares and whispers? That'll be nothing new. Pull your big-girl knickers on, and woman the hell up.

With a renewed sense of purpose, I follow Uncle John in the direction of the garage.

The moment he pushes the door open, I hear the sounds of machinery and engines revving and music playing on the radio along with the smell that can only come from cars, especially racing cars. And all my nerves disappear into thin air.

It's been a long time since I've been in a Formula 1 garage.

Nostalgia sweeps over me, and I feel a lump in my throat.

"So, what do you think?" Uncle John asks from beside me.

"I think it's amazing." I push a smile onto my face.

"Come on. Let me introduce you to the people you're going to be working with."

I follow Uncle John over to one of the cars that a couple of guys are working on.

"Ben." Uncle John touches his hand to the guy's shoulder.

The guy lifts his head from the car, turning to us. He's moderately attractive with light brown hair and green eyes, and he's just a little taller than me. Not my type though.

"Andi, meet Ben. Ben is the head mechanic, so you'll be working mostly with him. Ben, this is Andi Amaro."

I see Ben's eyes widen at the sight of me.

"Hi, Ben." I step forward, holding my hand out to shake his. His hands are covered in oil, but that doesn't bother me. "Nice to meet you. I'm guessing you're one of the people Uncle John failed to tell that I'm a girl."

Ben's eyes flicker past me to Uncle John and then back to me. "He did." Ben clears his throat. "But not that it's a problem. Nice to meet you, too, Andi. I'm looking forward to working with you. John's told me impressive things about your way with a car." He wipes his hand on his overalls and shakes mine. "This here is Robbie." He kicks a foot on the leg of a body underneath the car. "Robbie, get your arse out from under there, and come say hello to Andi."

"He's here?" The guy pushes out from under the car before getting to his feet. He looks at me and then glances around.

"This is Andi." Ben gestures a hand to me.

"Hi. Nice to meet you." I smile at Robbie and then offer my hand to him.

Robbie stares at my hand like it's alien. Then, he looks back to my face, a little stunned, but there's also harshness in his eyes.

Uncle John clears his throat behind me, snapping Robbie to his attention.

Robbie wipes his hand on his overalls and shakes mine. "Good to meet you…Andi." Then, he turns to Ben. "I gotta go get that…thing. I'll be back in a few."

Then, he walks off.

Ben shakes his head. "Don't mind him," he says to me. "He lacks this thing called a personality. Great mechanic though."

"So, it's not just because I'm a girl then?" I grin.

Ben chuckles. "No. He's like that with everyone. But when he sees that you're just one of the boys, he'll warm up in no time…or maybe not." He laughs, again.

I like Ben more and more as the seconds go on. I think we're going to get along just fine.

"John, you got a minute?"

I turn to the sound of the voice to see a man about the same age as Uncle John, I'd say, wearing a smart black suit. He's very handsome in that older, distinguished way with short dark blond hair mixed with flecks of gray and piercing blue eyes.

"Owen, yeah, sure. Just let me introduce you to Andi first."

Owen's eyes land on me, fix, and then widen, and something settles into his expression that's not altogether pleasant.

An uncomfortable knot forms in my stomach.

I follow Uncle John over to Owen. All the while, Owen's eyes are watching me like a hawk.

"Owen Ryan, meet Andi Amaro, our new mechanic." Uncle John says the word *mechanic* very pointedly.

Owen Ryan—this is Carrick's dad.

Well, this is going to be interesting if the expression on his face is anything to go by.

"Hi, it's really nice to meet you, Mr. Ryan," I say, forcing confidence into my voice. I hold my hand out to shake his.

He just stares at my hand, like Robbie did, but with a more pissed off look on his face.

Ignoring me and my hand, which I awkwardly pull back, he turns to Uncle John. "This is Andi?" Owen points a finger at me. His accent is pure Irish.

I love the Irish accent, and I would normally be thrilled to hear it, but not when it's coming from a man who clearly has an issue with me.

Uncle John frowns. Through tight lips, he says, "Yeah, this is Andi."

"And she's female," Owen says through gritted teeth.

"Clearly."

Am I invisible?

"And," he growls, "she looks like that." He wafts a hand up and down in my direction.

I look like what?

"Careful, Owen. You're close to crossing a line."

"I am? You hire a mechanic who looks like a fucking supermodel, and I'm crossing a line? Fucking brilliant, John. Has Pierce seen her yet? Even worse, has Carrick seen her?"

Uncle John's voice cracks out like a whip as he says, "Knock it off. You and me, out there. *Now.*" Uncle John jerks his head to the door behind them.

With a face like thunder, Owen storms through the door with a furious Uncle John right behind him. It slams shut. Then, I hear the low rumble of angry voices coming from the other side.

Well, that went well.

I'm standing here, like a bloody lemon, feeling the most uncomfortable that I've ever felt in my life.

What is the problem here? Sure, I'm female, and no one clearly knew that. But what is Carrick? A dog in heat with uncontrollable urges?

Aside from sleeping with his mechanic's girlfriend, I'm sure he can keep himself in check around me.

But now, I'm having visions of a horny Carrick Ryan, dry-humping my leg, and I start laughing to myself.

My laughter promptly stops when the door opens, and Owen reemerges with a red-faced Uncle John behind him.

Owen comes over to me. I tense, not sure what to expect. Maybe my marching orders.

"Andi," Owen says gently, his voice a hell of a lot different than it was a few minutes ago, "I'm sorry about before. I spoke out of turn. You were just a surprise to me." He takes a deep breath. "Things have been a little...*tense* here for a while. But that doesn't excuse my behavior. Please accept my apologies."

"Accepted." I smile lightly.

Relief flickers across his countenance. But his eyes say something entirely different. They're lined with suspicion. And I know this apology isn't for my benefit, and I also know that I'm not going to have an easy time with Owen Ryan.

"From your resume, I saw that you're very experienced for such a young age."

"Mmhmm, I grew up with my head under the hood of a car."

"And you have a degree in mechanical engineering?"

"That's right. After I graduated I took a job working for a stock-car racing team back home."

"Of course, you worked for Ingo Serra's team."

"I did."

My answers are guarded, because if I've learned anything in this business and about people like Owen Ryan, give them just enough, but not enough to hang me with.

"I've seen Serra race. He's incredibly talented."

"Yes, he is." I give a genuine smile at the thought of my old boss. Ingo was such a nice guy. "I enjoyed working for Ingo very much."

"Fabulous." Owen nods, smiling through tight lips. "Well, John speaks highly of you, and I'm sure you'll fit in here, no problem."

He doesn't mean that. He's worried that I'm going to shag his son. But it's nice he said it I suppose.

"I'm looking forward to getting started."

"Great. Well, I must get on, and I'm afraid I'm going to have to steal John for ten minutes."

"Will you be okay on your own?" Uncle John asks me, moving closer.

"Fine." I smile softly at him.

Uncle John stares at me for a moment. Owen is by the door, holding it open for him now.

"Go on ahead, and I'll be there in a minute," he says to Owen.

On a nod, Owen lets the door close.

Once Uncle John's sure he's gone, he says quietly, "Not that I'm excusing Owen's behavior, but with what happened with Rich and Charlotte, it all fell on him. He's Carrick's manager. He's been left to clean up the mess that Carrick created. Pierce was seriously pissed, and the sponsors didn't like the bad press. It was a nightmare all around. The last thing they want is another scandal. That's why he reacted like he did when he saw you."

"And that's why you should have told them that I'm a woman." I give him a disapproving look.

"If I had, you wouldn't be standing here right now. And I'm glad you're here."

I smile at that. "Yeah, me, too, barring insta-hate from one of the bosses."

"Owen's fine. And he doesn't hate you. He just has concerns. But once he gets to know you and sees that Carrick is the last thing you're interested in, he'll be fine."

"Yeah, you're right. Anyway, go. You're needed, remember?" I shoo him away with my hands.

"You sure you'll be fine?" he says, taking a step back.

"I'm sure. I'm just going to take a look around here."

"Okay. I'll see you in ten minutes or so, and then I'll show you the rest of the place."

I watch Uncle John leave through the door, and then I turn around to the car that Ben and Robbie were working on, but Ben is no longer there.

The engine cover is still up on the car so I decide to go take a look, see what I'm going to be working with.

As I wander over to the car, David Guetta's "Dangerous" starts to play on the radio. Humming along to the song, I take my jacket off, laying it over the cockpit. I run my fingertips over the blue-and-silver paintwork as I walk toward the back end. Bending over, I start poking around, taking a look at the engine.

"Please tell me that you're my birthday present."

The Irish drawl has the hairs on the back of my neck standing on end.

I turn my head to find Carrick Ryan standing behind me.

Oh. Wow.

He's definitely better looking in the flesh than on television. I knew he was attractive. But blonds aren't usually my thing. I'm more of a dark-hair-and-dark-eyes kind of girl.

But his dirty-blond hair, blue eyes laced with sin, and full lips—the kind of lips you spend hours sucking on—and that chiseled jaw decorated with stubble...yep, it all seems to be working for me. Well, my body anyway. Definitely not my head. Man-sluts are not my thing.

My eyes meet with his as he lifts them from blatantly staring at my arse. The look in them hits me straight in the gut, surprising the hell out of me. His eyes are profoundly blue and filled with heat. My skin starts to prickle as his intense stare burns me up.

I've never had such an instant visual reaction to a man before.

Fuck.

Take it easy, Andi. This isn't a problem. You've met good-looking men before. You can turn this off. Drivers are a no-go area, especially ones you work for.

My job is too important to lose over a man.

Straightening, I turn to face him.

"Hello," I say in my most confident and formal voice.

I get nothing back, and that's because he hasn't heard me. He's too busy staring at my breasts.

Typical man.

I have the sudden urge to punch him in his handsome face.

But I won't because I'm a professional. I'll handle this in the best way I know when it comes to dealing with pervy dickheads like him.

"It's your birthday?" I say sweetly, my smile a little on the flirtatious side.

He grins. "It sure is, and it's definitely looking up now that you're here. Are you going to make it extra special for me, sugar?"

He thinks he's about to get lucky.

Far from it. Smarmy twat.

I tilt my head to the side, keeping the flirty smile on my face, as I walk up to him until there's very little space between us. I press my fingers to his chest. *God, that's firm.* I can feel the ridge of his muscles underneath my fingertips.

He's tall, too, a good few inches higher than my five-nine. I'd say he's six-one, which is tall for a driver, but he's lean. He needs to be to fit into those cars. I bet, under those clothes of his, there's nothing but toned muscle. Drivers have to be seriously fit, and Carrick Ryan certainly ticks that box on both counts.

Now, I'm imagining him naked. *Great. Just fucking great.*

I force my focus back to the now. "Well..." I lean in closer to him, hearing him suck in a sharp breath. I lower my voice as I whisper, "If you ever call me sugar again, you won't see your next birthday. That's for sure."

He tilts his head back in amusement. "Feisty. I like it."

I take a step back, dropping my hand from his chest. "There's nothing here for you to like."

His eyes run the length of me, lingering on my legs, the lusty look firing in them again. "I see plenty to like. Jesus…your legs go on forever."

I wish I had something to hide my legs behind. Instead, I fold my arms to bring his focus up. "I'm not your type."

Lifting his eyes back to mine, he gives me a confident smile. "Amazing arse. Great stems. Awesome rack. Beautiful face. Yep"—he nods—"you're definitely my type."

"I would have thought stupid, gullible, and willing—of which, I'm none—would be more your style."

He lets out a laugh, which shivers through me, leaving my skin covered in goose bumps. "We'll see—on the willing part, that is."

On a sigh, I turn and pick up my jacket off the car before pulling it on.

"You're leaving?"

"Looks like it."

"Give me your number."

"Nope."

"At least tell me your name?"

Pausing, I glance back at him. "Andressa."

"Surname?"

I smile at his persistence.

Just at that, Ben comes back into the garage. "Ah, cool. You've met Andi," he says to Carrick as he passes by.

Carrick's gaze hits me full-on. Confusion flickers over his face. "Andi?"

"Mmhmm."

"But isn't Andi my—"

"New mechanic? Yeah, that's me."

"You're Andi…my new mechanic?" His eyes are wide with surprise.

I have to suppress the smile I feel. Tilting my head to the side, I put my hands on my hips. "I am."

"Well, fuck me. I was expecting someone—"

"With a penis and a deep voice? Sorry to disappoint."

His face blanks, and then deep laughter bursts from him.

At that moment, I realize that I just said *penis* to Carrick Ryan.

I said penis.

Fuck.

Kill me. Kill me now.

He's staring at me with a sexy smirk on his face and deep curiosity in his eyes. He's looking at me like I'm his next meal.

He takes a step closer to me. His voice lowers as he says, "I'm far from disappointed. You're beautiful, smart, feisty, and good with your hands. All my favorite things wrapped up in one hot package." His eyes draw the length of me.

I hear a throat clear and turn to see Uncle John standing behind me with a pissed off look on his face.

"Carrick, your dad wants to see you in his office."

He frowns at Uncle John. "Why?"

"I don't know. Why don't you go see him and find out?"

He lets out a sigh and starts backing up. His eyes are still on me. "We're all going out, the team and a few of my friends, for birthday drinks tonight. You should come."

"Oh." I'm taken aback. "Thank you, Mr. Ryan, but—"

"Carrick. Actually, call me Carr. That's what my friends call me."

"Carr. Original," I deadpan. I can't seem to help it. He naturally brings the snark out of me.

He grins. It's a real panty-dropping grin. "Yes, you are."

Oh, he's good. But I'm better. "I'll stick with Carrick. Thanks. And I appreciate the invitation, but I already have plans for tonight."

His brow furrows. "With?"

Rude much? My new bed, if he must know.

"Me," Uncle John imparts with a fatherly tone in his voice.

Carrick's eyes flicker between the two of us, settling on Uncle John. "What are you doing?"

"Dinner."

Guess I'm going to dinner tonight with Uncle John.

"Well, you can come for a drink after. It'll give me a chance to get to know my new mechanic better." He gives me a pointed look. "I'll see you tonight."

I watch as he walks away, his confident stride moving through the garage.

"So, that's Carrick," Uncle John says, letting out a huff of air.

"Hmm."

"He's a good kid. Smart as shit and one hell of a driver, like nothing I've seen since your, erm—" *My dad.* He breaks off and clears his throat. "Anyway, unfortunately, Carrick's pretty much led by his dick." Realizing what he said, Uncle John goes bright red in the face. "Shit. Sorry, Andi."

I laugh. "Uncle John, I'm a grown woman, and I work around men all the time. I've heard worse words than *dick*."

"Sure, sure." His cheeks flush red again. "So, was Carrick okay with you? I heard him say—"

"Yeah. No problem at all." I brush him off.

I decide against telling him that Carrick was very much trying his luck with me. I handled it, so no need to worry Uncle John with it.

I suddenly feel a wave of tiredness and have to stifle a yawn.

"You sure you're gonna be okay for tonight? You don't have to go, you know."

"No. I'm fine." A yawn escapes. "It'll be a good way to get to know my new coworkers. But would it be okay if you take me to the apartment now? I can get a shower and some shut-eye. Then, I'll be fine for tonight."

Another yawn escapes me, and Uncle John chuckles.

"Come on, sleepyhead. Let's get you to your new home."

✈ BEDFORDSHIRE, ENGLAND

"WE DON'T HAVE TO STAY LONG. An hour max, and then I'll get you home."

"Okay." I smile at Uncle John and then climb out of his car.

We had dinner at this nice Italian restaurant, and now, we've arrived at the pub where Carrick's birthday party is going on, but I'm already starting to lag a bit.

When Uncle John took me to my new apartment, I barely looked around. He got me settled, and I fell facedown on my bed. I woke up hours later with only thirty minutes to spare before Uncle John was coming back to pick me up.

It was a quick shower and hair wash. With a halfhearted attempt at blow-drying my hair, after I dug the dryer out of my suitcase, I ended up putting it up into a messy bun. I rarely wear my hair down.

I threw on a clean pair of skinny jeans, and a long-sleeved emerald-green sweater with some little diamantes along the neckline. My mum bought it for me. After putting on my ballet flats and slicking on some lip gloss, Uncle John was knocking at my door.

I follow Uncle John into the pub, weaving through the throng of people. A lot of people are here, but then I guess Carrick's a popular guy.

"Hey, you made it. I'll get you both a drink," Ben says as we approach him at the bar.

"Don't worry. I'll get them," Uncle John tells him. "Beer?" he checks with Ben.

"Yep." He lifts his bottle, draining the last of it.

Uncle John turns to me.

"I'll have a beer, too, please," I say.

Uncle John leans up against the bar, waiting to be served.

"Did you have a nice dinner?" Ben asks me, pulling my attention to him.

"Yeah, it was good. Thanks. Nice to catch up with Uncle John."

"How long have you known John?"

"All my life."

"Cool." He smiles. "So, how are you finding England? I heard you're from Brazil."

"Yeah. Good." I decide not to regale the fact that I was born and lived here for ten years. "How long have you worked for Rybell?" I ask him.

"Four years."

"You like it?"

"Love it. It's long-arse hours and shitty hotel rooms, but I get to see the world, and nothing beats the buzz of race day."

"I hear you." I smile.

"Here you go." Uncle John hands my beer over to me and then gives one to Ben.

"Well, welcome to Rybell." Ben lifts his bottle to mine, so I chink it against his.

"Thanks." I take a swig of beer.

Perfect. Just what I needed to pick me up.

"You want me to introduce you to some more of the staff?" Ben asks me. "The rest of the pit crew guys are here and some of Nico's team along with the front-of-house girls."

"Yeah, that'd be great."

I tell Uncle John where I'm going, and he tells me that he's going to go find Owen – business to discuss. Uncle John is always working.

I follow behind Ben through the pub to a table in the back. While I'm walking, I glance around for Carrick but no sign yet.

Ben stops before the table. "Everyone, this is Andi, our new mechanic. Not that you'll remember their names, Andi, but this is Amy, Petra, Damon, Paul, Mike, Davis, and you know Robbie."

I follow Ben's finger around the table.

"Hi." I lift a hand in greeting.

A pretty girl with blonde hair and huge blue eyes, who I think is Petra, gives me a big smile. She's shorter than me, I'd say, but it's hard to tell with her sitting down.

"Shove over, Amy. Come and sit down with us," she says.

I slide onto the bench beside her and put my beer on the table.

"So, you're from Brazil?" Petra asks me.

I'm guessing Ben must have told her. "I'm from England originally, but I've lived in Brazil since I was ten."

"Wow. You're so lucky. I would love to live somewhere hot."

"You spend more than half of the year in hot countries," the other girl, who I think is Amy, says. "God, I can't wait to get out to Australia. Never been before."

"Amy's newish, like you," Petra tells me. "Been here a few weeks. She works front-of-house with me."

"So, you're the girls to see when I want some really great food." I smile.

"For sure," Petra says.

Amy just stares blankly at me, which she's kind of done from the moment I came over here. I can tell she's doing that bitchy girl assessment of me. I hate that.

I take another swig of my beer, and I'm thankful when one of the guys asks me a question.

I'm there for a while, chatting, and my beer is quickly empty. *I should probably go find Uncle John.*

"I'm going to the bar," I say to no one in particular. "Can I get anyone anything?"

I get a few noes from the ones who were listening around the table. The others luck out because I'm not asking again.

Picking up my bag, I head in the direction of the bar. I'm still surprised that I haven't seen Carrick yet. The pub doesn't look to be that big, and he's not exactly a guy you can miss.

I actually want to wish him a happy birthday, which I failed to do earlier. That was kind of crappy of me.

With no sign of Uncle John or Carrick, I slip into a spot at the bar and wait to be served. I decide on getting a drink and then going to look for Uncle John. He's probably with Carrick.

I feel him before I hear him.

His heat presses up against my side. "You came."

Carrick.

Turning to him, I smile. *God, he looks good.* His eyes are bright, and his cheeks flushed, like he just came in from outside.

"I did. I got here a while ago."

"Hmm. Did you now?" He cocks an eyebrow. "You should have come and found me."

"I thought maybe you were busy as you were nowhere to be seen."

"I was cornered. Couldn't get away."

"But you're free now?"

A mischievous glint appears in his eyes. "Yeah, I'm most definitely free."

Feeling that tension run over my skin, I look back out at the bar.

"So, Amaro—that's Brazilian, right?" He leans closer to me.

I slide a glance at him. "Right."

"Dad told me that you just arrived in today from there."

"I did."

God, aren't I full of the vocab tonight?

"Not to be offensive, but you don't sound Brazilian. Your accent sounds a little diluted."

"I'm from England originally. I was born here. My mother's Brazilian. We moved there when I was ten."

"Ah, right. Explains the dilution then." He smiles.

"So, I didn't wish you a happy birthday earlier," I say, changing the subject from my history.

"No, you didn't." His stare on me is suddenly direct and intense.

"Well…happy birthday," I say awkwardly.

His stare relaxes, and a smile lifts his eyes. "Thanks."

"Let me buy you a drink. Beer?" I check, nodding at the bottle in his hand.

"Mmhmm."

He downs his bottle, and I can't help but watch his lips around the rim or the way his throat moves as the alcohol slides down.

"What can I get you?" That's the bartender.

Feeling like I've been caught staring at Carrick, my face flames.

"Um, two beers, please."

The bartender deposits two bottles on the bar just as Carrick puts his empty one down.

I'm digging in my bag for the money to pay when I see Carrick handing a twenty over.

"Hey, I was supposed to buy you a birthday drink." I frown.

"Call it a welcome-to-the-team drink from me."

"Well, thank you. But that kind of defeats the purpose of me buying you a birthday drink."

I lift my bottle to his and chink it, and then I take a drink.

"So, Andi—what's that short for?" he asks me.

"Andressa."

I did tell him my full name before in the garage, but clearly, he's forgotten. Then again, he probably has a lot of women's names to remember.

"Andressa..." He rolls my name around his mouth.

I love the way it sounds in his Irish lilt, the way his tongue rolls on the S. It sends shivers hurtling down my spine.

"Of course, you did tell me earlier. So, why Andi instead of Andressa?"

"Because Andressa is a bit of a mouthful, and it's just what everyone has always called me." My dad started calling me Andi. It apparently drove my mum mad until she finally gave in.

Carrick raises his eyes, and I can read the sexual innuendo all over his face.

"A mouthful can be a good thing." He grins sexily. "Andi is a boy's name, and you're far from a boy. No, Andressa...that's a beautiful woman's name. It's perfect for you."

Oh, he's good.

I feel him move in even closer to me. My heart starts to beat harder and faster than I've ever known it to do before.

What the hell is wrong with me?

Unable to look at his face, I keep my eyes on his chest. "You're pretty rich in lame pick-up lines."

"That's not all I'm rich in."

As I look up, I see him flash a glance down, causing my eyes to focus on the very prominent bulge in his pants.

Good God.

And that breaks the spell he was weaving over me.

I turn back to the bar, leaning into it, I put my bottle down and rest my elbows on it. "You really shouldn't talk to me like this."

He rests his back against the bar, but I can feel his eyes on me. "And how exactly should I talk to you?"

I slide my eyes to his. "Like you would speak to any of your mechanics."

"How do you know I don't speak to Ben like this? And Robbie? He and I have something special going on." He winks cheekily before taking a swig of his beer.

A laugh escapes me.

Cutting it off, I stare ahead. "Seriously, we need to draw a line here. So, let me just lay it out for you—"

"Perfect. Your place or mine?"

"Jesus, can't you be serious for one minute?"

He angles his body toward mine. "I am being serious." The tone in his voice screams a totally different kind of serious to mine.

"So am I." Straightening my spine, I turn to face him. "Exactly how much have you had to drink tonight?"

His brows pull together. "Not enough that I can't get it up. And even if I was wrecked, I can guarantee I would have no problem getting it up for you."

Then his eyes do that thing they do, running the full length of my body, giving a lazy perusal. And it irks the hell out of me. He wouldn't treat his male mechanics this way, so he definitely doesn't get to do it with me.

"Let's just cut the comedy. You need to stop with the flirting and the sexual innuendos. You and me – not going to happen. I don't go with drivers. It's a rule of mine."

He frowns. "You don't *go* with drivers?"

"I don't sleep with them."

"What I was suggesting wouldn't involve sleep."

"Yeah, I got that memo. But if you're wanting sex tonight or any other night, it's not gonna be with me. Drivers are off-limits for me, especially ones I work for. Now, thanks for the drink." I pick my bottle up. "And have a great rest of your birthday." I turn to leave.

"That's it?" he says, his voice pulling me back to him.

I give him a strained smile. "Yeah. That's it."

"So, we can't even be friends?"

I give him a suspicious look. "You want to be friends?"

"Why do you sound so surprised?"

"Um…because less than thirty seconds ago, you were trying to get into my pants."

"Look"—he scratches his cheek—"the flirting…it's just the way I am. I don't mean any offense. But I like you. I think you're cool. I'm guessing, as you're new here, you don't have many friends—aside from John—so I'm saying, let's be friends."

I ponder on it for a minute. *Is it a good idea to be friends with Carrick? Probably not.* But I'm going to be working for the guy, so friends seems logical. Not good friends. Just work buddies.

"Friends…okay, I can do that."

"Good." He smiles winningly.

"Carrick? You ready to go?"

My eyes swing to the voice calling his name, and I see a group of guys and girls all by the main door, looking like they're about to leave. I notice that Amy and Ben are with them. Amy is looking at me less than favorably. A definite frown is on her face. I get the impression the frown is because Carrick is talking to me, and she likes Carrick, which isn't surprising.

In this moment, I find myself comparing my looks to hers, not something I usually do. She's pretty, womanly. She has definite hips and a bum and plenty going on up top. Me…well, my figure's more boyish. I'm slender with no hips and very little arse. My cup size is generous but not too generous. I know my face is nice because people always tell me how much I look like my mother, and she is beautiful. And I have nice dark-brown hair—long, thick, and with a natural wave. I don't wear it down often though as it's always tied up because of work.

"I'll be there in a sec," Carrick says to the group.

"Well, the cabs are here, so hurry up," someone calls out.

I watch as they pile out the doors before I bring my eyes back to Carrick, who's already looking at me.

"We're going clubbing. Do you want to come?" he asks with a tilt of his head.

"No, but thanks for asking. I'm tired. The jet lag is catching up with me. I'm gonna head home soon."

He stares at me for a long moment, before he starts backing away. "Okay…cool. Sleep well, and I'll see you soon, friend."

He gives a cheeky grin, one that I can't help but return in the form of a soft smile.

"Good night, Carrick."

One last dazzling smile, then, he's gone, and for a split second, I regret not going with him even though I know that I did the right thing. Nothing good could have come of me going clubbing with Carrick.

That becomes even more apparent in the morning when I go out to get some food from the local shop and see the newspapers in the stands. They are filled with pictures of Carrick leaving a club, looking the worse for wear, with a couple of girls hanging off of him, and I recognize one as Amy, the front-of-house girl.

I'm guessing Carrick hasn't learned his lesson about sleeping with coworkers.

Seeing this picture and going by the icky feeling in my stomach at the knowledge that Carrick quite possibly had sex with both of those girls, probably at the same time, I'm starting to think that it's maybe not a good idea for me to be friends with him.

Because, if after a day of knowing him, I feel icky over a picture, then it can only go downhill from there.

🇦🇺 MELBOURNE, AUSTRALIA

I'M IN MELBOURNE for the start of the season.

It's my first time in Australia. We've been busy since we arrived, preparing for the first race of the season at Albert Park, so I haven't seen a lot of the sights, but what I have seen is amazing.

What, or I should say whom, I haven't seen is Carrick—for two weeks now.

The last time I saw him was the morning after his birthday. He came into the garage, wearing sunglasses and a ball cap pulled low.

When he saw me, he stopped and stared at me in a way I couldn't decipher, but I felt that look all the way down to my bones. Then his eyes cleared, he lifted a hand in a wave, and was gone.

I felt rattled for the whole day after that, but then I quickly sorted myself out.

Carrick is a player. And a driver.

Drivers equal bad.

And my little whatever it was—my-body-wants-his-body crush—is gone. Done with. Finito. It has to be because the racing season runs from March to November, and Carrick and I will be seeing a lot of each other. Nothing good could come of this my-body-wanting-to-jump-his-body thing for the next eight-plus months.

Carrick is due to arrive in Australia today. We're a few days out before practice sessions start, but Carrick needs to be here early to acclimatize to the weather.

Nico's also arriving. I have yet to meet him, not that I'll have a lot of interaction with him as he has his own mechanics, but I'm still looking forward to it.

From what I can tell of Nico from the press, he's the complete opposite of Carrick. Very focused and dedicated, he's never seen out partying, and he is very much a family man, married with children.

I wonder how he and Carrick get along—if they get along at all. It's not unusual for teammates not to like one another. Drivers might be paired under the same banner, but it's a solitary sport and incredibly competitive.

It's coming up to dinnertime, and I'm in my hotel room, the room I'm gonna be sharing with one of the hospitality girls, Petra. She'll be getting in soon. I haven't seen her since I met her on Carrick's birthday.

To be honest, I'm surprised to be sharing a room with her. I thought she would have been sharing a room with the other front-of-house girl, Amy, the one who was photographed leaving that club with Carrick. I expected to be rooming alone. But it's not a problem. I'm sure it'll be fine. I guess it'll be strange at first, sharing a room with someone I barely know, but I'm sure we'll get on no problem,

I don't have a problem getting along with women. I just tend to get along better with men. I guess my interests, cars, aren't that of a usual woman.

I'm sprawled out on my bed, deciding what to do for dinner, while watching TV when I hear the door open. Petra comes in, dragging a suitcase behind her, sounding out of breath.

"Hi." I sit up, turning the volume down on the TV.

She closes the door and props her suitcase up against the dresser. "Hey. Andi, right? We met at Carrick's birthday?"

"Hi. Yes, we did."

"Sorry. I was a bit drunk that night. My memory sucks when I've had a drink. So, we're gonna be roomies for the next eight-plus months." She drops down on the other bed, her bed.

"I guess we are." I slide my hands under my thighs, sitting on them.

"Well, I don't snore apparently. And it doesn't matter if you do. I'm a heavy sleeper." She shrugs.

"Okay. Erm…well, I don't think I snore. I mean, I've never had anyone tell me that I do."

"Awesome. So, what's the plan tonight?"

"Plan?"

"Are the guys going out?"

"Um, I think so." I shrug. "Ben said something about going out for a beer later."

"Cool. We'll text them and see what the plan is. Have you eaten? 'Cause I'm starving."

"No. I was just thinking about dinner."

"Fabulous. We'll get something to eat, either here or out. Then, we can meet up with the guys for a drink."

"Sounds great." I cross my legs on the bed, so I'm sitting Indian-style. "Are you not tired?" I ask her.

I was zonked when I first got here. I'm still trying to adjust to the time zone now. I'd only just got used to being in England.

"Nah. I had a good sleep on the plane, and I'm used to all the traveling around. Been doing this for years. I'm easily adaptable." She kicks her flip-flops off. "And anyway, who needs sleep?"

"People." I grin.

"Yeah, but I'm not most people. And in the wise words of Bon Jovi, 'I'll sleep when I'm dead.'"

I laugh lightly. I'm starting to like this girl already.

"Yeah, I guess you've got a point. I'm not usually one for lying in. But I was knackered when I first got here."

She chuckles. "You'll adjust to it all soon enough."

"Yeah, I'm sure I will. Has the other girl, Amy, arrived, too?"

Petra's face frowns at the mention of Amy's name. "No, she got let go."

"Let go?"

"Sacked."

"Oh. Why?"

"Because she shagged Carrick. I bloody told her not to, that no good would come of it, especially not so soon after what happened with Charlotte, but she didn't listen."

"Oh, right. Yeah, Uncle John told me about the Charlotte thing, not that we were gossiping or anything." I'm quick to clear it up. "Uncle John was just telling me how my position came up."

"Yeah, it was all a bit of a mess, to be honest."

"So, does every girl who sleeps with Carrick get fired?" At her expression, I clarify, "Not that I'm asking because I want to sleep with him. Purely asking out of nosiness."

She shrugs. "He's never really bothered with staff before. I mean, he never tried anything with me, not that I'd let him. He's not my type. But before Charlotte, it was Lea, and she was married. Then, she left to have a baby, and Rich got Charlotte the job, and we know how that ended—a big fucking tabloid mess. So, when Amy got the job, she had her eye on Carrick straight away, and I told her it wouldn't be a good idea as Pierce is still prickly about the whole mess. Then, she goes and gets herself photographed with him and another girl. I mean, seriously!" She laughs, throwing her hands up in the air. "So, Pierce had my boss, David let her go, which David did easily as she was brought in only as a temp because Pierce didn't want to risk any future problems arising, like what they had with Charlotte—you know, her suing them and all."

"Hmm. Not that it's nice, but yeah, I guess I can understand Pierce's point of view."

"Yeah, but now, I'm stuck working on my own. Pierce won't let David hire anyone else because he's worried that Carrick will shag the next one. And it's not like David can hire a guy because you know it's all about appearances in this business. So, he's brought in Franco to add more hands in the kitchen to relieve me of that, but I'm up front, serving on my own." She pulls a face.

"Sucks," I sympathize.

"Yeah, but never mind. It is what it is." She climbs up off the bed. "I'm gonna go shower the flight off me and get ready to go out. Text Ben, will you, and find out what they're up to?"

"Sure."

I grab my phone off the nightstand and begin typing out a text to Ben as Petra disappears into the bathroom.

As it turns out, the guys are already out, so Petra and I catch a quick bite at the hotel.

Now, we're walking down to meet them on Fitzroy Street in St. Kilda. It's a hive of activity. The street is lined with bars and restaurants. Petra told me that this is the best place to come drinking while we're in Melbourne, not that I know how much drinking I'll be doing while I'm here.

The air is hot and humid, so I'm wearing jean shorts, a short-sleeved T-shirt, and flip-flops.

As we arrive, we see the guys seated outside the bar, and Carrick is with them. At the sight of him, my heart does a little bumpity-bump in my chest. He's wearing a team ball cap, a T-shirt, and jean shorts. He looks good. No, better than good. He looks gorgeous. Not seeing him for two weeks while trying to dull my memory of him has only made seeing him now fresher, like I'm seeing him for the first time, and my crush comes back with a loud bang. I feel that bang in all my girl parts.

Crap.

His eyes meet mine as I approach, and he smiles.

I swoon. I actually fucking swoon. I'm so pathetic.

"Ladies," he drawls.

His voice hits me in all the right places.

"Hi," I say to him.

Casting my eyes around the table, I greet the rest of them.

"I'll go get us a drink," Petra says. "What do you want?"

"Beer would great. Thanks."

"I need another," Ben says, getting up from his seat. "I'll come with you."

"Sit down, Andressa." Carrick reaches over and grabs Ben's now empty chair and pulls it next to him.

"Won't Ben need that when he gets back?"

Tilting his head, he smiles. "He can get another."

"Okay." I slide into the chair, and I try not to be aware of him, but I am.

"So, you missed me then?"

I turn my face to look at him. "With every fiber of my being," I deadpan.

A smile tips up his lips. "A simple yes would have sufficed."

"Why be simple when you can be amazing?"

"True." His eyes smolder at me.

And I love the smolder too much, so I look away.

"So, how has my new best friend been? Aside from being amazing, of course."

Moving my eyes back to him, I raise my brows. "Best friend?"

"Oh, yeah. We're best friends. Did you not know?"

"Apparently not. So, how are we best friends again exactly?"

"We're best friends because"—he leans in close, moving into my space, with his lips next to my ear, and his hot breath makes me shiver—"you won't let me shag you. Now, we're going to be the next best thing, and that's best friends because I don't do things by halves, Andressa. I'm an all-or-nothing kinda guy." He sits back in his chair, staring at me.

I feel a wobble deep inside of me. I swallow down. "Um, yeah…I'm kind of getting that impression."

"So?" He's still staring at me.

"So…what?"

"How have you been?"

"Oh, good. Great. You?" I tuck a loose strand of hair that fell out of my ponytail behind my ear.

"I've been good." He shrugs. "Better now that I'm with my best friend."

"You really need to stop saying that. It makes you sound weird. And a little tragic."

He lets out a loud laugh, his eyes bright with mirth. I feel that smile radiate inside my chest.

Petra comes back with my drink.

"Thanks," I say, taking it from her. I put it down on the table. "Do you want your chair back?" I offer to Ben, lifting my bum from the seat.

"Nah, don't worry. I'll grab another." He gets a couple of spare chairs from another table and carries them over, putting them next to me.

Petra sits by me, and Ben takes the chair next to her.

Reaching for my beer, I take a welcome sip.

"How are you finding Australia?" Carrick asks me.

"It's great. I haven't seen much of it yet, but I plan on doing a little sightseeing when I get the chance."

"I plan on doing some shopping," Petra imparts. "Namely a pair of Uggs. So much cheaper here than back home."

"I might tag along when you go, if that's okay?" I love Ugg boots.

"Sure it is." She smiles. "It'll be good to have another shopping buddy, seeing as though I lost my last one." She leans forward and pointedly looks at Carrick.

I see him shift in his seat, and then he's standing. My eyes follow him up.

"I'm going for a piss," he says to no one in particular.

I watch his back as he heads into the bar, feeling oddly bad for him.

"Pet…"

I hear the chastising low tone of Ben's voice.

"Go easy on him with the Amy thing."

"I know. I know." She lifts her hand. "I'm just pissed off 'cause I'm serving on my own."

"I know, but that's not his fault. That's on Pierce. Carrick feels like shit about it. Told me himself. And I was there that night at the club. Amy did all the chasing. She wouldn't leave him alone. He was hitting it off with this other bird, and Amy was in there. It was her idea for the three of them to leave together. Seriously, any guy would have had a hard time saying no to that. It was his birthday, and he was hammered. You know Carrick. He wouldn't have touched Amy if he knew it meant she'd get sacked. He's not exactly challenged for women." Ben picks his bottle up from the table and takes a drink. "You know, he argued with Pierce about it the next day."

"He did?" Petra sounds surprised.

"Yeah, I heard him and Pierce going at it in Pierce's office." That's Robbie. "He said that Pierce was out of line for sacking her. Carrick tried to get her job back, but Pierce wouldn't budge."

"And the job she's got now—who do you think lined that up for her?" Ben adds.

"Carrick? Did he really?" Petra asks.

Ben takes a sip of his beer, nodding his head. "He's not a bastard, Pet. You know that."

"I know he isn't. Just…Amy never said," she mumbles into her drink.

"Yeah, well, she wouldn't, would she? She was after more than the one night—like they all are. She's gonna paint him in a bad light."

I see Ben's eyes lift, and I turn my eyes to see Carrick heading back to the table. He drops into his seat and picks up his beer.

"So, are we staying here all night or moving on?" Carrick asks.

"Moving on!" says Petra and Ben at the same time.

We've worked our way down a few of the bars, and I'm starting to feel a little tipsy and tired and ready for my bed.

Petra looks nowhere near done. She and Ben are at the bar, getting some more drinks.

I wait for her to come back to our table, and then she takes her seat next to me.

"Petra, I'm gonna head back to the hotel. I'm knackered. You don't have to come," I say at the disappointed look in her eyes.

"Nah, I'll come. I don't want you walking back on your own."

"I'm ready to go, so I'll walk you back." That's Carrick.

I see Petra's eyes swing to him.

"Um…okay. As long as you don't mind," I say to him.

"We are staying in the same hotel, so it's not a massive chore." He grins.

"Of course. Yeah," I reply, feeling a little stupid.

He gets up from his chair. Getting his phone from the table, he slips it into his pocket. I grab my handbag from the floor before hanging it on my shoulder.

"I'll see you back at the hotel," I say to Petra.

"You sure you're okay with going back with Carrick?" she says quietly.

"I'm fine." I laugh a little awkwardly, knowing what she's thinking. "I'll catch you later."

I give a wave to the table and walk around to Carrick.

"Ready?" he asks.

"Yeah." I follow him out of the pub and onto the street.

It's late, but the temperature is still high, not that I'm not used to it. Living in Brazil, the weather can get a little heated.

For a while, we walk side by side in silence until Carrick breaks it. "Whereabouts in Brazil do you live? Or *did* live until you moved to the UK."

"Santos. It's in São Paulo, on the coast."

"Yeah, I know Santos. Beautiful beaches."

"I spent a lot of time on those beaches." I smile fondly at the memory of spending time at the beach with my mum. "I lived in central São Paulo for a while, too."

"Oh, yeah?"

"I went to the university, lived on campus, saved traveling back and forth. My mum wasn't so keen on me living away from home though." I laugh lightly, remembering how stressed she was about me moving out that first time.

"You ever go to watch the Prix back home?"

"A few times. Uncle John got me tickets."

"You saw me race?"

"I did." I smile. "And you were awesome, especially that year when you beat Leandro Silva taking that corner on the Bico de Pato. It was outstanding."

Staring at me, he blinks. "How did I never meet you before a few weeks ago?"

"Because Uncle John probably didn't trust you around me." I give him a knowing grin.

"Yeah, good point—not that I can be trusted much nowadays either. Kidding." He holds his hands up, laughing. "We're best friends, and I don't shag my best friend."

"You really need to stop saying that."

"What? That we're best friends?"

"Yeah."

"Why?"

"Because it makes you sound weird, like you're a five-year-old boy."

"I'm definitely no boy. And I was going more for charming than weird. Clearly, that's not working."

I laugh at the mirth in his eyes.

"So, John's not your real uncle, right? But you call him Uncle John?"

I instantly tense at the question, worried about the direction it might take. "Yeah." I swallow down. "He's a close family friend. He's known me since I was a baby. He's my godfather."

I think Carrick senses my discomfort because he changes course. "So, what did you study at university?"

"Mechanical engineering."

"Figures." He smiles warmly. "I never went to university."

"Too busy racing?"

"Yeah. I think I would have liked it though."

"Hmm…yeah, the student life would definitely have suited you," I tease. "Parties, women, and booze."

He laughs lightly. "I'm not as bad as the press makes me out to be, you know."

"But you're not far off…"

He gives me a sobering look. "Not too far, no."

Looking up, I see that we've reached the hotel.

Carrick holds the door open for me, letting me in first. We walk through the lobby and get into a waiting elevator. I press the button for my floor, noticing that Carrick doesn't press the button to his floor.

"Which floor?" I ask him.

"Penthouse."

Figures.

I press the button for the penthouse and then move back to stand beside him.

We're silent as the lift starts to ascend, the tinny elevator music playing in the background.

Carrick shifts his stance and pushes his hands in his pockets, his arm knocking against mine. "Sorry," he murmurs.

"It's okay," I reply. God knows how I managed to get the words out because I'm feeling all kinds of weird and wired due to this intense blaze of heat now licking its way across my skin from where his arm just touched mine.

The space in here suddenly feels a hell of a lot smaller.

I take a deep breath, trying to be unaffected, but it doesn't work.

I'm totally aware of him next to me. All I can smell is his sexy-as-sin aftershave, and it's making my head feel dizzy. I'm starting to burn up.

What the hell is wrong with me?

I fix my eyes on the digits, watching the numbers climb. I need to get out of this elevator and soon, but the counter seems to be slowing down to a snail's pace.

Goddamn it!

Carrick exhales. It's a soft sound, but I feel like he's blowing in my ear.

I shudder. I actually fucking shudder.

I wrap my arms around myself, trying to take control of my raging hormones, but I somehow manage to knock my arm with his this time.

Well done, Andi.

Now, all I've succeeded in doing is to set off the lick of heat again, and it's quickly heading south.

I can *feel* Carrick's eyes on me, but I don't dare look at him. And I definitely don't dare to speak, for fear of saying something stupid, so I pretend not to notice that I just touched his arm.

Instead, I press my thighs together and beg to the gods to get me out of this elevator fast.

What the hell is going on with me? And is this elevator ever going to reach my fucking floor?

Come on…come on…

Finally!

It reaches my floor with a ping, like the timer on an oven, and like the chicken, I'm done.

"This is me." My voice sounds unnaturally high. I slip out the door before it even has a chance to fully open. "Thanks for walking with me," I say, backing away.

He steps outside the elevator, hand holding the door. "Anytime. Good night, Andressa." His voice sounds different—deeper, husky.

"Good night, Carrick." I turn on the spot and walk as fast as I can to my room. My heart is beating up a storm in my chest while my head is wondering what the hell that was all about.

🇦🇺 MELBOURNE, AUSTRALIA

TODAY IS RACE DAY. The garage is a hub of activity. And I'm beyond excited. I've been on countless tracks for races, especially when I was working in stock cars back home. But being here, being part of the Prix, is amazing.

The noise of the engines revving, the smell of the cars, and people all around prepping for the race, it carries like a buzz of energy in the air. There's nothing quite like race day.

It's electric, and I feel privileged to be a part of it.

I'm slingshotted back to when I was a kid, and I would come to watch my dad race.

I did wonder if this first race would feel strange for me. I guess it does a little, but I'm more focused on the excitement of Carrick's upcoming race, and all the work that needs to be done beforehand is keeping me busy. And it's not like I haven't been to the Prix since my dad died.

But being here in the midst of it all…totally different feeling from standing on the sidelines watching. It's amazing.

I spy Nico Tresler coming into the garage. I haven't seen him at all during practice sessions. If he's been here, it's when I haven't been.

Right, this is it. I'm going to stop being a wimp, and I'm going to go over and introduce myself.

I cross the small distance over to Nico's side of the garage. Coming up behind him, I shift to the side, so he can see me in his peripheral.

He's currently talking to Damon, his chief mechanic. When Nico notices me, he stops his conversation and turns his head to me. "Can I help you?"

"Hi, Mr. Tresler. Sorry to interrupt. My name is Andi Amaro. I'm Carrick's new mechanic, and I just wanted to come over and introduce myself. I'm a huge fan." It's not a total lie. I prefer other drivers over Tresler, but buttering up a driver is always the best way to go.

He turns to face me, so he's giving me his full attention. "Oh, yes. Ryan's new mechanic. I've heard all about you." His eyes rake over me in a less than comfortable way.

I shift on the spot.

"Not surprising that he gave *you* the job."

He didn't actually. "I was hired by John, not Carrick." I keep my tone even, professional, and definitely nonconfrontational.

Drivers can be difficult at times, especially on race day. They're tense and stressed, so it's best not to stoke the fire. *Keep it courteous.* He might be acting like a bit of a tool, but he's a driver, and I need to respect that.

"Of course you were," he says dismissively. Then, he leans in close. "You might be naive enough to think that Ryan hired you based on your skill set. He didn't. He hired you because of your bra size. The guy has no class and treats this profession like a joke. He's a selfish bastard who doesn't give a fuck about anyone but himself."

Wow. Okay.

I flicker a glance at Damon, who gives me a look of sympathy before turning away.

"I wouldn't say that—" I start to defend Carrick.

"Everything okay here?" Carrick cuts me off.

I spin around to him. His stare is on Nico. Carrick's face is perfectly blank, but in his eyes is a world of anger.

"Everything's fine." Nico smiles, baring teeth at Carrick. "I was just letting Andi know what she's gotten herself into, working for you."

Carrick lets out a sardonic laugh. "I'm sure you were. Andressa, do you have a minute?" His fingers press against my upper arm.

Even through my coveralls, I feel his touch, like it was on my bare skin.

"Yes, of course." Feeling a little deflated, I follow Carrick as Nico turns away from us.

When we've reached Carrick's side of the garage, I stop and ask, "So, what do you need me for?"

"Nothing. Just getting you away from Nico. He's a pompous prick with a massive chip on his shoulder."

I cover a laugh.

I want to agree, but I don't want to be seen dissing a driver, especially of Nico's caliber. It would be unprofessional of me.

"He's definitely interesting," I say, choosing my words carefully.

"He's a twat. And I can guarantee whatever he said about me was probably only about sixty percent true. He just hates me because I won more races in my first two years than he has in his whole career. Fucking tosser."

I laugh. I can't stop this one.

I've noticed that Carrick does that a lot—makes me laugh.

I like it.

"My advice, don't talk to Nico unless you absolutely have to."

"Okay. Got it, boss." Grinning cheekily, I give him a salute.

I see a light flicker in his eyes. "Boss? Hmm...I like that."

"Carrick?"

He turns at the sound of his dad's voice, who looks a little less than pleased when he sees Carrick is talking to me.

"Coming." He lifts a hand to Owen. Looking back at me, Carrick says, "Catch you before the race, yeah?"

"Yeah."

He gives me one of his heart-stopping smiles, leaving me feeling a little breathless, and then he turns to go with his dad.

I don't really get a chance to talk to Carrick when he comes back down as we're all busy as hell getting his car ready, and he goes straight outside, having photos taken, meeting people—sponsors most likely—and doing interviews. I notice how he laps up the attention of the grid girls and brolly dollies.

But I'm…whatever. It doesn't bother me in the slightest.

When Carrick finally comes back in, it's time for him to get in his car. I have my helmet on as do all the mechanics since we're in the pit. But somehow, he manages to lock eyes with me.

He gives me a cheeky wink and then grabs his helmet, pulling it on over his fireproof balaclava. He climbs in the cockpit and gets strapped in. Ben fits his steering wheel, and Carrick's good to go.

We all head back into the garage. I pull my helmet off, so I can watch the race on the screens.

I cast a glance at Uncle John, who is sitting at the control desk with Pierce and Owen.

Then, my eyes go back to the screens, and I watch as Carrick sets off on his warm-up lap. The roar of the engines vibrates through me.

God, I love this.

I watch as the cars zigzag from side to side along the straights, warming up their tires. But my eyes are mainly focused on Carrick's car. The bright blue of his helmet glints in the sun.

Finally, all the cars file around the pit straight and take positions on the grid. Carrick is in pole position as he qualified first yesterday. It's a great start to the season, and I know Carrick is happy with it.

Then, the atmosphere heightens, and I find myself holding my breath as the five traffic lights above the starting line glow red, red, red, red, red. Then, they go out…and it's GO!

Carrick has a great start, taking the first corner like the pro he is.

As the laps go on, he starts to pull away from the pack, taking a good lead.

When he comes in for a tire change, the vibe is good all around. The pit crew gets to work on changing his tires.

Carrick stays in his car, watching the race on the screens above his head. When the tires are done, he's heading back out onto the track.

He picks up his position in no time.

There are a few tense moments in the race, like when he drops down to second as Leandro Silva, a Brazilian driver, passes him.

I would never say this to Carrick—as it's well known that Leandro and Carrick have a serious rivalry going on—but I love Leandro. Not in a creepy way, but in a hero-worship way. He's an amazing driver. He's not better than Carrick. He's just different.

I hold my breath as Carrick nips up on the inside of a corner and takes his place back from Leandro.

Yes!

The race is pretty much that way the whole time. It's edgy and thrilling with Carrick fighting Leandro for pole position.

We're on the final lap, and Carrick's now in the lead, but there's still that nervousness that he could lose his place in that last moment as Leandro is not one for giving up easily.

Carrick needs to win this. It'll set his whole course for the rest of the season.

Crossing my fingers, I will him on.

Come on, Carrick. You can do it. Come on...

I'm counting down the last seconds, my heart pumping in my chest and my veins alive with adrenaline.

Then, he crosses the finish line, the checkered flag dropping.

He won! Yes!

I let out the breath I wasn't even aware I had been holding and do a little happy jig on the spot.

I'm beaming from ear to ear—not just for Carrick, but also for the whole team and myself, too. I didn't just get to watch, but I got to aid and be part of a Carrick Ryan win. This is only the beginning. There's more to come. I feel an overwhelming sense of privilege right now.

I'm watching everyone in the garage, all clapping and cheering. The atmosphere is electric.

And I'm catapulted back to all the times I was with my dad when he won and how we would all celebrate in his garage.

I feel a pang in my heart, a painful ache for things long gone.

Dragging myself from the past to the present, I see Carrick climbing out of his car. Removing his helmet and fireproof balaclava, his hair is all stuck to his head, but he still looks amazing, beautiful.

He's being congratulated by all our team, his dad, Uncle John, and Pierce. Carrick's grinning and laughing.

Just watching him makes my heart swell, my chest filling with happiness.

Then, Carrick's face tilts my way, his stare finding mine, and the look he gives me—the depth in his eyes, the smile on his face—leaves me feeling breathlessly staggered, and exhilarated.

In this moment, I realize that I'm massively screwed.

Because I fancy him. Big time.
And now, I have to find a way to deal with that.
Trust me to get a crush on the one man I can't have.
Pulling in a deep breath, covering my feelings for him, I smile and make my way over to congratulate him.

🇲🇾 KUALA LUMPUR, MALAYSIA

"I'M BORED." Carrick drops down into the chair in front of me.

He's looking as gorgeous as ever, dressed in khaki shorts and a white polo shirt, which shows off the deep golden tan of his skin.

I'm trying really hard not to stare at his arms. They're just really good arms. Unblemished smooth skin, muscular, sexy veins running along them—they're the kind of arms you want to lick.

As you can see, my crush is going extremely well. The stopping-it part? Not so well.

We're in Kuala Lumpur for the second leg of the season. It's my first time in this country, and I've got to say, it's amazing.

"How can you be bored? It's only nine thirty in the morning." I take a bite of my toast.

I'm eating breakfast alone as Petra is still in bed, sleeping off last night's hangover. Surprisingly, I'm feeling bright this morning, considering how much I drank last night. Carrick came out last night, but he didn't stay long as he had an early morning training session.

"Yeah, well, I've been up since six. Feels like half the day's gone already."

"You just left the gym?"

"Yep."

"Your new trainer kicking your butt?"

Carrick was complaining last night about his dad hiring a trainer for him while he's here.

Because he's taller than the average driver, he naturally weighs more, so he has to be careful not to tip the scales.

Carrick might win his races, but he likes to drink, and his diet isn't exactly healthy. If he's not careful, he'll gain weight, putting him at a disadvantage on the tracks—hence, the new diet and training regime.

"The guy is a fucking drill sergeant. I'm bloody starving as well. Muesli was what I was allowed to eat for breakfast. Fucking muesli," he grumbles.

"Poor baby," I tease.

That earns me a grunt.

My phone alerts a text from Mum.

Good night, darling.

The time zones are really starting to mess with her. Chuckling to myself, I text her back.

> *Mum, I'm ten hours ahead of you, so it's nine thirty in the morning here. I'll call you tonight, so it'll be morning your time.*

She messages back straight away.

I love you.

♥

Then, I look up from my phone to see Carrick eyeing my bacon with what can only be described as longing.

"You all right?" I laugh.

"No, I'm dying of starvation." He looks up at me. "Are you going to eat that bacon?"

Our hotel is one of the only places in Kuala Lumpur that serves proper bacon. I was looking forward to eating it, and I kind of don't want to share it with him. I'm greedy like that.

Leaning back in my chair, I pick up my coffee cup. "Do you really think it's a good idea for you to eat bacon? You're on this health kick for a reason."

He lets out an exaggerated sigh. "Jesus, I'm not exactly overweight, am I?"

He flexes the muscles in his arms, and I have to resist the urge to stroke them—or lick them.

"And one piece of bacon isn't gonna turn me into Jabba the fucking Hutt."

"I'm pretty sure when Lucas created him, it was just Jabba *the* Hutt. Not Jabba the *fucking* Hutt. And if your dad sees me giving you bacon, he'll have my job."

"No, he won't. Come on...just one piece of bacon."

"No." I move my plate toward me and away from him.

"Aw, come on, baby. You know you wanna give me some."

Baby?

I feel that word wash through me like an erotic cleansing.

Pressing my thighs and lips together, I shake my head. "Nope. Your smooth Irish charm won't work on me."

Grinning, he gives me a look straight from the sex devil. "Aw, Andressa, *baby*, if you give me some...I'll make it worth your while. It can be our little secret. I won't tell anyone. I promise."

"How do you manage to make a conversation about bacon sound dirty?"

"I'd say it's a talent...but maybe it's not me who's dirty. Maybe it's you. After all, you are the one interpreting it that way." He lifts a brow.

And my face goes bright red.

His fingers creep over the table toward my plate. "So, am I getting that bacon?" He flutters his eyelashes at me.

Bastard knows how good-looking he is.

"Fine." I give in. "One piece, and that's your lot."

I pick up a piece of bacon and hand it to him.

"Have I told you recently how awesome I think you are?"

"Nope."

I watch as he puts it in his mouth, the way his eyes close on the taste.

"Well, you are. So fucking awesome. God, that's some good bacon." He moans, chewing it.

I start squirming in my seat at the sounds he's making.

Who knew a piece of bacon could be such a turn-on?

I have a vision of me naked in bed with him above me, inside me, making those same noises—

"Okay, I need more." His voice breaks into my sex thoughts.

"Hmm? What? Yeah." I pass the plate over without even thinking.

Then, a second later, I realize what I've done. "Wait! Give that back! You're gonna get me in trouble!"

I try to grab the plate, but Carrick scoops up all the bacon and shoves it in his mouth.

"Oh my God! I can't believe you just did that!" I slap my hand over my mouth, laughter escaping.

"Never underestimate what a starving man is capable of," he says, munching his way through his mouthful of bacon, a glint in his eyes.

I can't help but stare at him as he swallows, his Adam's apple bobbing, it's oddly sexy.

"God, that's so much better. I feel like a normal fucking human being now." He leans back in his seat, pressing a hand to his stomach.

"You have issues," I quip. "Do you want the rest of my breakfast?" I gesture to what's left, my coffee and half-eaten toast.

"Sorry." He gives me a cheeky grin. "You want me to get you some more?"

"Nah, don't worry about it." I wave him off.

"So, what have you got planned for today?"

"Nothing much. Probably just gonna laze around the pool."

"Even though the thought of you lying around in a bikini is awesome—"

I cut him off, "Who said I'd be wearing a bikini?"

"My imagination. Why? You going topless? Skinny-dipping?" His eyes spark like a struck match as he sits up straighter in his seat.

"No, perv. I meant, I might be wearing a bathing suit for all you know."

"Way to take the fun out of it." He pouts.

Shaking my head, I laugh. "I'm your friend, remember? You don't perv over your friends."

"Says who? As long as I'm not touching, I can do what I want up here." He taps a finger on his head.

"And if you want me to keep being your friend, then you'll knock it off." I give him a smug smile.

"Fine, spoilsport." He rolls his eyes. "So, instead of hanging by the pool in your old lady bathing suit, do you wanna come have some fun with me?"

The previous part of our conversation and the cheeky glint in his eyes have me asking, "What kind of fun?"

"The fun kind."

"The fun kind of fun?"

"Exactly." He tilts his head, his lips teasing a smile.

It's such a charming boyish smile that I find myself saying, "Okay, I'm in."

After breakfast, Carrick goes back to his room to get his wallet, and I pop back up to my room to grab some money. Carrick told me to put some trainers on, so I've got a feeling we're going to be doing some kind of sports activity.

Petra is still in bed, but she's awake, sitting up and watching TV. "Hey, have I missed breakfast?" Her voice is all croaky.

"Yeah, they stopped serving at half past nine, but I grabbed you these." I hand over a muffin and banana.

"Ah, you're a star." She pulls the wrapper off the muffin and starts nibbling on it. "So, what we doing today?"

I sit on the edge of my bed and kick my flip-flops off. I'm pushing my feet into my trainers when I answer. "Oh, I'm going out with, er…Carrick."

That raises a brow. She knows Carrick and I get along well, and she hasn't said anything, but I know what she thinks.

"Just as friends," I add.

"Yeah, I got that."

"You did?"

"Mmm." She has another bite of muffin. "If you were going to shag, you would have done it by now. Carrick's not one for messing around. It's about time he learned how to be friends with a member of the opposite sex. I think it's nice that you guys are friends."

"Yeah," I say on a smile.

"So, what are you both doing?"

"I don't actually know." I get my bag from down the side of my bed, checking my wallet is in it. "He won't tell me, but apparently, it's fun."

"Well, have fun having your fun."

Picking my sunglasses up from the dresser, I put them on my head and stop at the door. "Hmm. Do you want to come with us?" It's not exclusive to him and me. I don't think.

"Nah, all I'm up for today is lounging by the pool."

"Catch you later." I pull open the door.

"We going out tonight?"

"Definitely."

Leaving Petra, I head back to the elevator to meet Carrick in the lobby.

He's already waiting for me when I get there. His lips lift into a smile when he sees me. "Ready?"

"Ready."

I follow him out through the hotel to the parking garage.

Lifting his key, he unlocks the door to a sleek black Mercedes SLS AMG Roadster.

"Nice," I comment.

"Loaner." He shrugs. "The dealers like to give me cars when I'm here for races."

"Must be awesome being you." I let out a little dreamy sigh as my fingers run over the shiny paintwork of the car.

"It has its benefits." He grins. "You wanna drive?" He holds up the key.

I feel a frisson of excitement, and then my face drops. "I don't know where we're going."

"Ah, yeah, right. You can just drive back then."

That lifts my smile right up.

I climb in the car, buckle in, and drop my sunglasses over my eyes. Carrick turns the engine on, the car filling with the sound of Clean Bandit's "Real Love." He puts his shades on and drives us out of the garage into the gorgeous sunny day.

"You want to go karting?" I stare up at the sign above the entrance, my hands going to my hips.

We're standing outside the Sepang Kart Circuit, which is adjacent to the track he'll be racing on in a few days.

"Yep," he says from beside me.

"But you race for a living."

"So?"

"Okay, so you want me to race against you, the previous karting and current Formula One champion of the world. Well, I guess at least I won't feel too bad when I lose."

"If it makes you feel better, I'll let you win."

"Ugh, a pity win? No, that's even worse." I nudge my shoulder into his, ignoring the pang of attraction I feel at the contact.

He chuckles.

"Actually, should you be doing this? What if you get hurt?" Disconcerted, I look at him.

If he hurts himself and can't race and Owen and Pierce find out I was with him, my head will be on the chopping block.

He gives me an insulted look. "You know who you're talking to, right? I'm Carrick Ryan, god of the tracks."

"Ha!" I laugh. "Should I bow at your feet, oh godly one?"

"Not necessary, young grasshopper."

He pats me on the head with his hand, and I bat him away, causing him to laugh.

Then, his face sobers. "But…what I do need from you is your silence."

"Silence?" I cock my head in confusion.

"Mmhmm. My dad doesn't know I'm here, for the prior mentioned reason, so to save me a month of earache from him about my irresponsible behavior, it'd be great if you kept this little karting thing a secret."

"Ah." I fold my arms. "So, I'm your dirty little secret."

"Well, I wouldn't go that far, but you can be my dirty secret if you want to be. You only have to say the word."

Tutting, I shake my head in mock disgust, which earns me a filthy sounding chuckle. I pretend not to feel it in every part of me.

"So, what you're actually asking is for me to keep this a secret from your dad, who coincidentally scares the crap out of me?" I say, diverting back to the original subject matter.

"You're scared of my dad? Why?" He looks surprised.

"Because he dislikes me."

"He doesn't dislike you." He brushes me off.

"He thinks I'm a distraction."

"A distraction for whom?"

"You. And the rest of the guys, of course."

"Oh. Right. Well then, you're the perfect person to keep my secret 'cause you're scared of my dad, so you'll never give me up to him." He smirks as he starts walking toward the building.

"Hey, now, hang on there. Because your dad scares the crap out of me is the exact reason that this is gonna cost you."

Stopping, he turns back. With his head tilted to the side, he gives me an assessing look. "Interesting. Go on." He gestures his hand at me.

"Well, if you do get your godly arse hurt here today"—that comment earns me an eye roll—"then I'm out of a job because your dad would have me fired quicker than I could say stop."

He stares at me for a long moment, the tip of his tongue pressed up against his teeth.

He has a nice tongue. *Can someone have a nice tongue?*

I bet it kisses well. Among other things.

Now, I'm imagining me sucking on his tongue and then Carrick using his tongue on me and—

For God's sake, Andi. Sort yourself out.

I snap myself out of my dirty daydream.

"So, you're bribing me for your silence?"

I can't get a read on his tone. He sounds too even, and now, I'm starting to worry that I might have said the wrong thing. Sure, I was joking, and he usually gets my humor, but he might not be getting it this time.

"Sort of," I falter.

"Well, you either are, or you aren't. Which is it, Andressa?"

"Are..." I give a lame toothy grin.

He stares at me for the longest moment. Then, I see a flicker of amused admiration in his eyes. "Blackmail. I'm impressed." He grins as he puts his fist up and fist-bumps me.

I let out the breath I was holding.

"So, what's this gonna cost me then?" He starts moving backward toward the door, so he's still facing me.

"Hmm." Pressing my lips together, I tap my finger on them. "I don't know."

"Sex? I can be your sex slave for a week. Hell, you don't even have to blackmail me to get that. I'll do it for free."

I shake my head, fighting a grin. "You're a sex maniac."

"I'm not a maniac. I just love having sex. There's a difference."

"Sure there is."

"Oh, Jesus. Please don't tell me that you're one of those people who doesn't like having sex. Because if you don't, then you've been doing it with the wrong people, and that means we definitely have to do it."

"Of course I like having sex!" *Okay, I said that a little too loud.*

"Thank God."

"And you and I are definitely not doing it."

"Shame."

I roll my eyes. "Why are we talking about this again?"

"Because sex is the most interesting thing in the world, and I'm awesome at it."

He stops in front of me, staring down into my eyes. I feel his gaze sizzling into me. I'm suddenly struggling to find my breath and the ability to move.

Sexual energy is crackling between us. And I so want to act on it...find out if he is as good as he says he is.

But I can't.

"No sex, buddy." My voice comes out hoarse, so I clear it. "Just friends, remember?" I indicate between us.

"Ah, right. Of course. I forgot myself for a minute there." In reproof, he clicks his tongue against his teeth. "And we're not just friends. We're best friends, Amaro. Get it right."

"Sorry." I hold my hands up in mock surrender.

We start walking again.

"So, come on then. Put me out of my misery. What's my ransom?"

"I haven't decided yet. I think I'm gonna pocket this one and use it when I really need something."

"Well, make sure it's something you really, really need 'cause you'll only get away with bribing me once." On a wink, he pulls the door open and gestures me through.

We approach the ticket counter. I see the guy behind the counter looking at Carrick like he knows him, but he's just not sure where from.

I wonder how long it'll take Ticket Counter Guy to figure it out.

"What racing sessions do you have?" Carrick asks him.

"We do a quick circuit, which lasts for up to fifteen minutes," Ticket Counter Guy says in really good English. "Or you can hire for longer if you want."

Carrick looks at me. "What are you up for?"

"You choose. I don't mind."

"We'll hire for fifteen minutes. But we can add more later if we want?"

"Sure," Ticket Counter Guy says. "Just tell the marshal, and you can pay for the extra before you leave."

He prints off our tickets while Carrick and I argue over who's paying.

"Seriously, you're not paying, Andressa."

"Come on. You pay for everything. Even when we go out drinking, you're always paying for everyone's drinks."

"How much did you earn last year?"

I'm taken aback. "What's that got to do with anything?"

He leans in close to my ear. The feel of his body millimeters from mine sends me spiraling.

"You know how much I earned? Twenty million. I'm paying for the fucking tickets."

I lean back, meeting his eyes. "Okay," I placate.

I quickly look at Ticket Counter Guy, who's definitely trying to pretend he's not listening.

With a winner's smile, Carrick hands over his credit card to Ticket Counter Guy.

When we've paid, Ticket Counter Guy tells us we need to give our tickets to the karting marshal.

We're just about to head in when Ticket Counter Guy says, "You're…Carrick Ryan, right?"

I see the dismay flash through Carrick's eyes. It was silly to think Carrick could come here and not be recognized.

Carrick steps back to the counter. "Yeah…but I'm just here to have some fun with my friend. So, I'm not here, okay?"

"Okay," Ticket Counter Guy says. "But can I get your autograph?"

"Sure," Carrick says on a smile.

"Will you sign my cap?" Ticket Counter Guy pulls off the Formula 1 cap he's wearing.

Carrick nods, and Ticket Counter Guy hands it over along with a marker.

"You a racing fan?" Carrick asks while he signs his name.

"Huge fan. Me and my younger brother always watch on TV. You're our favorite. My brother's gonna be gutted that I met you, and he didn't."

"You ever been to the Prix?" Carrick asks.

"No." Ticket Counter Guy pulls a face of discomfort. "Tickets are too expensive for a guy who works on the counter at the karting ring."

I feel a little pull in my chest.

Carrick must feel it, too, because he says, "What's your name?"

"Sulaiman."

"Nice to meet you, Sulaiman." Carrick hands him the cap and marker back. "Write down your and your brother's names and your address for me, and I'll have two VIP tickets couriered to your house."

Sulaiman looks like he's just been punched in the face—in the best kind of way.

"Really?" he asks wide-eyed.

"Really." Carrick smiles.

I'm watching Carrick, intrigued, and I can see it in his eyes—how making other people happy makes him happy.

Now, I get it—why he has to pay for everything. It's not about showing how much money he has. It's about being able to make other people feel good with his money.

There's a big softy buried underneath all that alpha and sexual ego.

And it just pulls my heart straight in his direction. I'm currently having a hard time keeping a hold of it.

Sulaiman quickly scribbles his details down on a piece of paper and hands it to Carrick, who folds it up and puts it in his wallet.

"I'll have the tickets sent to you tomorrow," Carrick tells him.

"Thank you so much." Sulaiman reaches over, grabbing Carrick's hand and shaking it. "I can't tell you how much this means to us. My brother will be so happy when I tell him."

"Wait till I'm gone to call him though 'cause I'm not here, remember?" Carrick taps his nose.

Sulaiman does the same thing. "Got it."

"I'll see you and your brother after the race." Carrick starts to walk away, and I follow.

"Bye! And thanks again!" Sulaiman calls after us.

"That was a really nice thing you did," I say. Walking alongside Carrick, I bump his arm with my own.

Glancing at me, he shrugs. "If it means I get half an hour of peace with you without race fans turning up, then it's worth it."

"I don't think that's why you did it. I think you saw a guy who doesn't have much, and you wanted to make his day."

He stares ahead, as he speaks. "I was never dirt poor like that guy back there, but we didn't have a lot either. Everything we did have, my dad put into my racing, so I kinda know a little of what it's like to be skint."

I feel a swelling in my chest. I have to press the heel of my hand there to contain it.

I did know that about Carrick. He's not your typical comes-from-a-rich-family-into-the-rich-sport driver. He came from a modest background, and both he and his dad have worked hard to get him to where he is now.

"You're a big softy at heart, Carrick Ryan." I nudge him again this time with my shoulder.

He gives me a look of horror. "Fuck, don't go saying that in public. You'll kill my image."

"God, yeah, we wouldn't want that to happen." I let out a chuckle. "So, is this another secret I have to keep?"

"Hmm…I guess so." He glances at me, a smile in his eyes.

"I'm gonna lose count of all these secrets I have to keep for you," I tease.

"Well, if you play your cards right, you might get to be one of those secrets."

And there he is.

I roll my eyes, scoffing. "In your dreams, Ryan." I give him a little shove in the direction of the exit out to the track. "Now, get your arse out there, so I can beat it."

"Ha! That's definitely in *your* dreams, Amaro."

"We'll see." Lifting my chin, I give him a haughty look as I pass him by, heading to the marshal.

Once we've had our safety talk with the marshal and Carrick's signed an autograph for him, too, we're suited up in track overalls.

We've definitely come on at the right time as there's only the two of us here using the track. The karts are out waiting on the track for us.

I pull the band out of my hair, letting out my ponytail. I won't be able to get the helmet on with my hair up like that. It needs to be tied into a plait, which is how I always wear it when I'm in a garage or at the track.

I'm running my fingers through my hair, getting the tangles out, when I see Carrick watching me.

The heat in his eyes is discernable, but I play it off.

"You've never seen a girl do her hair before?" I say with a tilt of my lips.

"I've never seen you do your hair before. And I've never seen it down either. Looks nice."

"Thanks." My cheeks flush. "But it's not staying down." I start to quickly plait it. When I'm done, I fasten the band at the end.

Carrick is still watching me.

And the way he's looking at me is making me want things I really can't have.

I pull my fireproof balaclava on, covering my face. "You getting yours on? Or are you delaying 'cause you're worried I'm gonna beat you?"

He grins widely. "Prepare to get your arse kicked, Amaro."

I love winding him up about this. Seriously, there is no way I'm going to beat Carrick out here, but it's fun making him think that I think I can.

I'm not a bad racer, but I'm definitely no champion like him.

Carrick pulls his balaclava on, covering his gorgeous face, and then he brings his helmet down over his head, keeping his visor up. He puts his gloves on.

I pull my own helmet on and then my gloves.

"Ready?" He jerks his head in the direction of the karts.

"Yep."

We walk over to the karts, and an idea strikes me. Carrick never lets anyone pay for anything, and I'm guaranteed to lose. So, I'm thinking a bet is in order, and I know he won't be able to turn it down because he's too competitive.

"I think we should bet on this race."

He turns his face to me, so I can see his eyes through his still open visor.

"Oh, you do, do you?"

"Yep."

"All right. What are the terms?"

"Loser buys dinner."

He pauses for a minute. "Deal."

He puts his gloved hand out to me, and I shake it.

Smiling to myself, I snap my visor down and climb in my kart.

Carrick gets in his beside me.

The marshal stands at the side of the track, green flag in hand.

We're on for fifteen minutes. Looking at probably less than a minute a lap, it's going to be about fifteen laps.

He holds out three fingers, indicating his countdown.

Three…

Two…

I rev my engine.

One.

Flag goes down, and we're off, zooming and building speed down the track.

Carrick is ahead of me but not as far as he should be, and I know he's holding back for me.

I should take it as a nice thing, but I'm competitive by nature, and it just pisses me off. I don't need sympathy.

We're racing around, but Carrick isn't putting too much distance between us. He's either trying to wind me up or be kind.

Well, whatever it is, it's bugging the hell out of me.

My killer instinct kicks in, and I now have to win this race no matter what.

When I eventually see the marshal on the track, he's showing the white flag, telling us we're on our last lap, and I already know what I'm going to do.

I'm going to win, no matter what.

Carrick is still just ahead of me, and I know he's just waiting until the last corner to get through, and then he'll fly off and cross the finish line.

Yeah, not going to happen, buddy.

We approach the final corner.

I see my opportunity coming up. We're down at forty kilometers per hour to take the corner, so I take advantage. Instead of slowing further to take it like Carrick is, I keep speed and clip the back end of his kart, spinning him off the track and onto the dirt.

Ha!

Glancing back to check that he's okay, I see his kart on the dirt, and Carrick's head is turned my way. I don't have to see his face to know he's pissed.

Laughing to myself, I slam my foot on the pedal and zip over the finish line.

The checkered flag comes down, and I win.

Winner!

Grinning to myself, I drive my kart over to the pit. Stopping, I climb out and pull my helmet and balaclava off.

Seeing Carrick driving in toward me, I start dancing around, doing a little victory dance.

Carrick slams on the brakes, parking the kart behind mine.

He climbs out, yanking his helmet and balaclava off. He's scowling.

Oh, he's mad!

That only makes my smile wider, and keeps me dancing.

"I can't believe you just did that!" he exclaims.

"Did what?" I play dumb.

"Knocked me off the track! You fucking cheated!"

Stopping my winner's dance, I place my hands on my hips. "I did not cheat. I won."

"By cheating!" He throws his hands up.

"Oh, someone's a *bad* loser. Well, if you hadn't been doing the pity drive, you might have thought of the move yourself and won. You're just mad 'cause I got there first! A strategic move is not cheating, Carrick."

He growls, which only sets me off laughing.

"I beat the great Carrick Ryan, and he can't take it!" I sing.

He gives me an exasperated look, a hand tugging on his hair. "You didn't win because you fucking cheated!"

"Winner! Winner! Andi's the winner!" I chant. Lifting my hands in the air, I move my body around like I'm doing a cheer.

"Cheater!"

"Sore loser!"

I'm laughing so hard now that I have to bend over to catch my breath. I currently have tears in my eyes. I can't remember the last time I laughed this hard. But I do remember the last time I did laugh, and it was with him.

It's always with him.

I see his feet approaching, and as I lift my head, I find he's standing directly in front of me, his face all shades of serious.

I wipe the tears of mirth from my eyes with the backs of my hands, still chuckling. "Beat by one of your mechanics—and a female one at that. What's this gonna do for your reputation, Carrick? This could kill your career. You'll be ruined if this ever gets out."

His lips twitch. "Am I being blackmailed again?"

I tilt my head to the side, grinning. Lifting one shoulder, I say, "Maybe."

He shakes his head. I can tell he's desperately trying not to laugh, but his eyes are shining with it.

"Blackmail, cheating, and now blackmail again. Who are you? And what have you done with the Andressa I know?"

"Maybe you don't know me as well as you think you do." I wink, ticking his nose with my finger.

He catches my finger, holding it.

The instant my skin makes contact with his, it's like something supercharged has just conducted its way through my body.

I suddenly feel very alert and *very* aware of him.

The way his chest is lifting on each breath. The parting of his lips as he exhales. How tense his body is. How very close he is to me.

Everything is heightened. And the air thick all around us.

I meet his eyes, and my mouth dries instantly.

The laughter that was in them is gone and has been replaced with something else entirely.

Something heated.

It's a heat I feel deep inside of me.

His fingers slide over my hand, curling around it, gripping. "Andressa, you're—" His voice has changed. It's deeper, husky.

"The winner?" I cut him off, trying to inject sass into my voice. But it didn't work. I just sounded all breathy.

I need to bring us back to where we were, but I don't know how.

He's slowly pulling me in closer to him, closer to everything I want but can't have.

"Like no one I've ever met before."

Wow.

And fuck.

Fuckity fuck, fuck, fuck.

I'm pretty sure he's thinking about kissing me right now, and I really, really want him to.

God, I want to kiss him so bad.

My lips are readying themselves for the action.

But I can't. He's a driver. I can't get involved with him.

I step away, breaking the moment, and my hand slips from his.

I see disappointment flicker over his face, but I pretend not to see it.

Putting my helmet down on the car, my hand still burns from his touch. I clasp it into a fist to rid myself of the feel of him. I clear my throat. "So, you owe me dinner, Ryan."

Dinner. Shit. I was supposed to lose, so I could pay for it.

Could I be any dumber? I'm blaming my idiocy on the brain mush he is clearly able to reduce me to.

Turning back to face him with my feelings firmly locked away, I offer a light smile, but I can tell it's shaky. I just hope he can't.

He's still staring at me, the look in his eyes unreadable.

I hold my breath, waiting for him to speak.

Lifting his hand, he runs his fingers through his hair. Then, his lips tip up into a soft smile. "Not that you deserve dinner because you cheated...but technically, you did win. So, fine, I'm buying. What are you in the mood to eat?"

You. I just want you.

Resting my hand on my hip, I tilt my head to the side, clearing my mind of all my wanting-Carrick thoughts. "What am I in the mood for?" I purse my lips and then make my decision. "Local food."

He smiles. "Great choice. I know just the place to take you."

KUALA LUMPUR, MALAYSIA

WE DROVE FOR ABOUT FORTY MINUTES, and now, Carrick is parking on the street, near what looks to be a market.

Carrick brought us here as he knew the way, but I'm driving back to the hotel later, and I can't wait to get my hands on this car.

I climb out of the car, joining Carrick on the pavement. "So, where are we going?" I ask, hooking my fingers under the strap of my bag, holding it to me, as we start to walk into the market.

"There's this great little place just a bit farther up."

As we walk along, I'm looking at the stalls and storefronts, getting distracted by all the sights and smells—fresh food, clothes, jewelry. There are street artists painting portraits and some old men sitting at a table, playing a board game that looks similar to checkers. All around is traditional-sounding music, one song fading into another.

Then, I see this little kitschy stall lined with what looks to be Disney jewelry, and that's when I spot it.

"Oh my God, is that a Lightning McQueen necklace?" Stopping, I turn and walk over to the stall.

I'm a bit of a Lightning McQueen fan. Seriously, *Cars* is the best Disney movie ever. Give me that over Disney princesses any day.

As I approach closer, I see that it is definitely a Lightning McQueen necklace, and it might just be the coolest thing I've ever seen. It's a little McQueen pendant hanging from a silver chain. I'm guessing the chain probably isn't silver, and my neck will turn green after an hour of wearing it, but I don't care because I want it.

I curl my hand around the pendant, and I'm just about to ask the man how much it is when I feel Carrick's heat press up behind me.

"Why are you looking at that *Cars* necklace like it's a Tiffany's diamond?"

I tilt my face to his. "Because to me, it is. What might be one girls' junk is another girl's treasure."

His eyes are sparkling at me in the sunlight. "So, am I to take it that you're a *Cars* fan?"

"Um, yeah." I look at him, astonished that he even has to ask. I mean, who doesn't like that film? "Aren't you?"

A smile touches his eyes. "No."

"What? Why not?"

"Because I'm not five years old."

That earns him a jab in the ribs from my elbow.

I stare at him, curious. "You've never seen the film, have you?"

"No."

"How is that even possible?" I exclaim. My hand slipping from the necklace, I turn to face him.

"Because, again, I'm not five years old."

I give a disappointed shake of my head. "You're seriously missing out. And you call yourself a race car driver." Pausing, my hands find my hips. "Seriously, you have to watch this film. It's amazing. That's it." I make a decision. "We're watching it when you're free next."

He presses his lips together, and I can tell he's holding back a smile. "What are you going to do? Buy it and force me to watch it?"

"No, I already have it on DVD, dopey."

Something dawns on his face, and I realize my slip up.

"You have it with you, don't you?"

My cheeks explode with color, my eyes going to my feet. "Maybe," I mumble.

"You travel around the world and take a Disney DVD with you, don't you?"

He's dying to laugh. I can tell.

I'm just dying because he now knows how big of a dork I am.

"It's my security blanket," I say defensively.

His fingers find my chin, lifting my face to his. His face is alight with humor. "You know, normal people actually have a real blanket for security."

"Are you saying I'm not normal?" I try to give sass under his scrutiny.

"No. I'm saying you're unique."

"Unique bad or unique good?" I bite my lip.

His mouth kicks up at the corner, but a flare of something else is in his eyes, something a little more serious. "Oh, definitely good. You're…unprecedented, Andressa."

Oh. Wow.

A frisson of pure delight shivers through me.

"So, you want the necklace?"

"Mmhmm…"

He hasn't stopped looking at me, nor I, him. I'm dazzled, caught in his sweet spell.

He tears his eyes away from mine, and I instantly miss his stare on me. Then, I see him getting the necklace off the rack.

Before I can stop him, he's holding the necklace up and saying to the market vendor, "How much?"

The vendor says, "Fifty-five ringgit, but you can take it for fifty."

Carrick pulls his wallet out, and I see him get out way more than fifty ringgit.

He hands the money to the man. "Keep the change."

I don't know how much Carrick gave him, but the man's eyes light up at the money, and he quickly tucks it away into his money belt.

"Here." Carrick gestures for me to turn around.

So, I do, putting my back to him. "You didn't have to do this," I say softly.

"I wanted to."

He places the necklace around my neck. The pendant lays cool against my skin.

Fastening it, he lays his hands on my shoulders. "Now, you'll always have your security blanket with you."

I feel something deep and meaningful settle inside my heart.

I lay my hand over the pendant. "Thank you." I glance at him over my shoulder.

His eyes flicker to my lips. The blue in his eyes darken, and then he lifts his gaze back to mine, stepping away from me. "Come on. Let's go get that food."

We walk on a little farther until Carrick stops outside a small restaurant. It's so obscure that I would have walked past it.

"Here?" I point to the building.

"It doesn't look like much from the outside, but wait until you see the inside."

Carrick opens the door for me, and I step into a little Malaysian oasis. He wasn't kidding. I'm almost tempted to step back outside to check that I'm still in the real world. I feel like I've just stepped into Narnia.

The ceiling is high, and pretty red lanterns are hanging from it. The tables are dark wood, all laid with colorful place settings, differing in rich reds and greens and purples. The wooden chairs have cushioned backs, all equally as colorful as the place settings. The walls are gold-lined with beautiful paintings, and a drape is hanging around the back window, which surprisingly looks out onto a pretty garden complete with a water fountain.

"Mr. Ryan!" A small, Malaysian chap comes wandering over from the bar area with a big smile on his face. "Good to see you again. I was wondering when you would be coming in. And I see you've brought a friend. Hello," he says to me, smiling wide.

"Hello."

"Guntur, this is my friend Andressa Amaro. Andressa, Guntur Wan. He is the owner of this fine place," Carrick informs me.

"Beautiful place you have here," I say.

"Thank you," he says with a wave of his hand. "But the decor is nothing compared to the food." He gives me a wink, making me chuckle.

"He's not kidding," Carrick tells me as Guntur seats us. "Why do you think I haul arse over this way every time I'm in Kuala Lumpur?"

"Well, thank you for bringing me with you." I smile, meeting his eyes over the table.

"What can I get you to drink?" Guntur asks us.

"Sparkling water for me," I say.

"Same," Carrick tells him.

Guntur hands us each a menu. "We've added a couple of new dishes since you were last here," Guntur tells Carrick, patting his back in a friendly way. "I'll be back soon with your drinks."

"So, how did you find this place?" I ask Carrick. "It's not exactly on the tourist map."

"When I first started in Formula One and I was out here for my first race, I met Guntur through one of the sponsors. He's a relation of some sort. Guntur is a huge race fan. Anyway, he gave me his card for the restaurant, told me to come out. Said he served the best nasi lemak in the whole of Malaysia. I had no clue what nasi lemak was, but I was bored one night, so I took a drive and came out here. Had some nasi lemak plus a ton of other food, and now, I come back here to eat every time I'm in Kuala Lumpur. And Guntur is a great guy."

"Yeah, he seems nice." I rest my chin on my hand. "And what is nasi lemak?"

"It's their national dish. It's basically rice cooked in coconut milk and pandan leaf."

"Are you into cooking?" I ask, bemused, trying to imagine him in the kitchen.

"No, I'm reading it from the menu." He gives me a cheeky smile, eyes flickering down to the menu before him.

Laughing, I shake my head at him.

"So, what are we having?" Guntur has appeared back with our drinks.

I thank him as he places my water down in front of me, and I glance down at my menu. With no clue what to order, I look at Carrick for help.

"You want me to order for both of us?"

"Please." I smile.

I listen to Carrick rattle off what sounds like an awful lot of food while I take a sip of my water.

Guntur scribbles down the order and then disappears off into the kitchen.

"So, I can't believe I've never asked you this before, but whereabouts in Ireland did you grow up?"

"Houth. It's an old fishing village not far from Dublin."

"Does it have any beaches?"

"Nah." He laughs. "Off the harbor is a scrap of rocks you can just about stand on to get near the water. Nothing like what you have in Brazil."

"I didn't always have those beaches, remember? I was born in the UK."

"Yeah, of course," he says. "Whereabouts in England are you from?"

"London."

"And why did you move to Brazil?"

I take a sip of water, preparing myself for my response. "My dad died when I was ten."

"Jesus, Andressa. I didn't know that. I'm sorry."

"It's okay. You didn't kill him."

He stares at me for a moment, looking uncomfortable.

"Sorry. Poorly timed joke."

I wave it off, and his face relaxes. I just wanted the look of pity on his face gone. I can take it from anyone, but on him…it bothers me.

"Anyway, my mother didn't have any family in England, but she has a lot in Brazil. We were alone in England, so she took me back to Brazil to live."

"Must have been hard—losing your dad and moving halfway around the world."

"I managed." *Just barely.* "And I have loads of cousins and aunts and uncles, so it was nice to be around family."

"How did your dad die? If you don't mind me asking."

"In an accident."

"What kind of accident?"

"The worst kind." My voice is harsh, and I instantly feel bad, so I try to lighten the subject by changing it. "So, how did you end up becoming a Formula One driver?"

"My dad was a mechanic—"

"I didn't know that." I lean forward with interest.

"Yeah, I grew up around cars. My granddad—my dad's dad—was a mechanic, too, so I guess cars are in my blood. When I was seven, my dad took me and a few of my friends go-karting for my birthday, and from that moment on, I was hooked. I was karting on a regular basis, entering competitions. I loved it. Couldn't get enough. My dad quickly realized how serious I was about it, and of course, he saw how good I was, especially since I was winning all my races." He gives a cheeky smile.

"So, he started dedicating a lot of his time to my dream. With all the races I was entering, it was hard for him with work, so he ended up having to reduce his day hours and take on more nighttime off-the-book jobs to earn money.

"Then, when I was thirteen, my granddad passed away, and he left everything to Dad—his house and a good bit of money he'd saved over the years. Karting was good in Ireland, and the races were decent, but I wanted more. Dad saw that there were more opportunities with karting in England and the possibility to progress to Formula One. So, he sold Granddad's house and our house, and he moved us to England. He rented a place and took on jobs when he could. He used the money from Granddad and the house sales to keep us afloat.

"I entered into Intercontinental A when I was fourteen, which I think is now called KF-two. Then, the year after, I progressed up to Formula A. The next year up, I was up to Formula Super A. I moved up through F-three, F-two, and then to F-one by the time I was twenty."

"Wow. That's quite some story. Your dad did a lot for you to help get you where you are," I say, starting to see the reason for Owen's protectiveness over Carrick's career.

"Yeah, he did. He's great. The best dad a guy could ask for."

That brings a lump in my throat. "What about your mum?"

His eyes darken. "She's not around. Hasn't been for a long time."

"She left?"

"When I was two. Apparently, she wasn't mother material."

"Oh, Carrick...I'm sorry."

I can't imagine anyone leaving a child. My mum would never have left me, and my dad...no way. The only way he left me was in death. And to leave someone like Carrick...I can't imagine. He just shines so much.

Reaching over the table, I touch my hand to his, curling my fingers around it. "She missed out big, Carrick. Really big."

His eyes flicker to my hand, lingering there a moment, and then they lift to my face.

My heart starts to pump in my chest.

I slide my fingers away. Picking my drink up, I take a nervous sip.

"What's your favorite car?" he asks out of the blue, assumably to fill the awkwardness I just created with my little hand-holding moment.

"Oh, that's easy. Jaguar XK-one twenty."

It was the car my father drove, his pride and joy. He had it until the day he died. I haven't seen that car since. When my dad died, my mother got rid of his cars at auction and gave all the money to charity. I was angry for a long time about that.

"What about you?"

"Usually the one I'm driving. I'm fickle like that."

He grins, and I laugh.

"How did you know you wanted to be a mechanic?" he asks.

"Same as how you knew you wanted to be a driver. I grew up around cars. It was a natural progression. My mother probably wished I had done something else with my life though."

"Like what?"

"Anything but a mechanic. I think she secretly wanted me to be a model, like she was."

"Your mother was a model?"

"Mmhmm." I probably shouldn't have told him that. It wouldn't take a genius to link my mother to my father with the help of Google, not that I think Carrick is going to go Googling my mother or me.

"You know it's funny. The first time I saw you, I had you down for being a model."

I roll my eyes at him.

"So, is your mother anyone I would have heard of?"

"Probably not. She gave up modeling after she had me. She was incredibly beautiful though, still is."

"I can imagine."

"Here. I have a picture of her." I get my phone from my bag and hand it to him, showing him the screen saver picture I have of my mother and me. I took it just before I left Brazil.

"That's your mother? Fucking hell, you look like sisters. She's a definite MILF."

"Ew!" Reaching over the table, I grab my phone from his hand. "That's gross! You can't perv on my mother!"

He's laughing now. "Sorry. I'm not saying I would like to…erm, *you know* your mother, but I can imagine that some men would like to *you know* her—a lot."

"Jesus, Carrick. You're making this worse." I drop my head into my hands.

"Sorry." He chuckles.

I lift my head, shaking it at him. "Moving on. I've been meaning to ask you this for a while. Do you have any ritual things you do before a race?"

My dad did. He always had to wear black boxer shorts and socks. Before every race, he would also have a plain egg omelet for breakfast. I never did learn why.

"Yep."

I wait, but he doesn't expand.

"Well…, are you gonna tell me what it is?"

Arms on the table, he leans forward. "Okay." He lets out a breath. "I have to eat a bar of Galaxy chocolate before each race."

"Really?" I smile. "Why?"

Eyes on me, he rests back in his seat, keeping his hands on the table. "After we first moved to England, I don't know if it was the pressure or being in a different country or what, but I wasn't winning races. I was coming in fourth at best. I was panicking because Dad had given up so much by moving us to England, and I was getting frustrated because I knew I was capable of more.

"Anyway, on this particular day, I was hungry because I'd forgotten to eat, and my dad was all, 'You will lose this race on an empty stomach.' So, he went off to get me something to eat. Anyway, he came back, telling me there was only this shitty vending machine. Then, he held out a bar of Galaxy chocolate, and I was like, 'What the hell is that? I'm not eating that. It's women's chocolate. Men don't eat Galaxy. They eat Yorkie.' You remember the adverts?"

"I do." I laugh, loving the way he's telling the story.

He's so animated with his eyes all lit up.

"So, my dad got pissed off and said, 'Well, they haven't got any men's chocolate, so eat the bloody women's chocolate, and shut the hell up!'"

I snort out a laugh. "So, what did you do?"

"Sulked for about a minute, and then I ate the fucking bar of Galaxy, and it was the best chocolate I'd ever tasted—not that I admitted that to my dad at the time. Then, I got in my kart and won my first ever race in England."

He smiles fondly, and I can see the memory in his eyes.

"And since then, before every race, my dad buys me a bar of Galaxy from a vending machine, and I eat it. It's my one weird thing."

"But what if there isn't any Galaxy chocolate in a vending machine? Or worse, there isn't a vending machine?"

He leans forward, a sexy-arse smile on his face. "There's *always* a vending machine, Andressa, and there's *always* a bar of Galaxy in it."

"Ah." The power of being Carrick Ryan.

Guntur appears at our table with a huge tray in his hands, laden with food. He starts placing the plates in front of us. Then, another waiter puts down a green leaf before me.

"Banana leaf," Carrick tells me when he sees me looking at it. "It's instead of a plate."

"Oh, right. Cool."

After all the food is laid out, I stare at the rices, meats, vegetables, and other things I don't even know how to describe, and Guntur tells us to enjoy our meal.

Looking up, I say to Carrick, "So much for your healthy eating." I smile, so he knows I'm teasing.

"You see any overweight Malaysian people around here?"

I give a glance at the few people seated in here. "Nope."

"Well, there you go then." He grins.

"Okay, Jabba," I tease. "So, what should I try first?"

He gives me a look and then muses over the dishes. He picks up a rice dish. "Try this."

We have a great time over dinner, eating and talking. We chat about school, friends, and random stuff, like favorite music and books—just everything and anything.

We're there for hours, the time just disappearing. It's one of the best days I've ever had with someone.

When we're done, Carrick pays, again refusing to let me pay or even go half. And I don't bother arguing, saving myself the how-much-did-you-earn-last-year speech.

"Thanks for today, the karting and the food," I say as we walk back out into the early evening sunshine.

"Anytime."

We walk back through the market and to the car. When we reach it, Carrick tosses me the keys.

I grin like the cat that got the cream.

"Back to the hotel?" I check, climbing in the driver's side.

"Yeah, but take the long way."

I put my seat belt on and turn the engine. She purrs like a kitten. The stereo comes to life with the pumping sound of Philip George's "Wish You Were Mine."

"You ready for the ride of your life?" I tap my hand on the steering wheel as I turn my face to him, and I find he's already looking at me, his expression unreadable.

"Yeah, I'm ready."

Something in his tone makes my heart bump against my chest.

I slide the car in gear. Checking my mirrors, I pull onto the street. Pressing the pedal to the metal, I drive us out of there.

🇨🇳 SHANGHAI, CHINA

"SO, WHAT DID YOU THINK?"

Carrick and I are in the living room of his hotel suite, and we've just watch *Cars*. I finally talked him into it. I'm sprawled out on the sofa, feet up on the coffee table. Carrick's at the other end of the sofa, and there's a huge bowl of half-eaten ice cream between us. It was the best ice cream I've ever eaten. It reminded me of the mound of ice cream that Macaulay Culkin had in *Home Alone*.

Clearly, Carrick is on a hiatus from his health kick. But I'm giving him a pass tonight because it was race day, and he came in third. It's unusual for him. He's usually first or second. Rarely third. He said the car was understeering. Ben and I checked it, but we couldn't find anything wrong, so I don't know what happened out there.

But Carrick has understandably been in a shitty mood about it ever since. He's competitive, and he doesn't like losing.

When he said he wasn't up for going out, I said I'd stay and hang out with him while Petra and the guys went out.

I don't mind since we all leave for Bahrain tomorrow, but Carrick has to stay on for some press and sponsor things, and he has to film an advertisement. I won't see him for a few days until he joins us there, so I'm happy to spend this time with him before I leave.

We ordered a mix of food along with the ice cream from room service, and we've had a fun night.

But then, every night I spend with Carrick is fun. It's fair to say that we've grown closer recently. A lot closer. I see him most days, and if I don't see him, we text or call.

He's fast becoming the best friend I've ever had.

"It was okay," he muses.

"Just okay?" I give him a look of mock disgust.

He spent a good majority of the film laughing. I even saw him get misty-eyed at one point.

"Yeah, just okay."

"You lie." Sitting up, I remove my legs from the coffee table and curl them under me, facing his side. "You loved it. Admit it."

"I said, it was just okay." He frowns.

His mood is still off. I thought the film might help, but the edge is still there.

I need to make him laugh.

"Tell the truth. Say you loved *Cars*, and it was the best film you've ever seen, or you're gonna get it."

"I'm gonna get it?" That raises his brow.

"Mmhmm."

"And how exactly how am I gonna get it?"

I eye the bowl of ice cream and then grab it. Lifting the bowl up to chest level, I pull the dripping spoon from the ice cream, letting it drip back into the bowl. "Admit that *Cars* was the best film you've ever seen, or you're getting creamed." I give him a cocky look.

His brow lifts higher. Feet off the coffee table, he sits up, eyes alert, turning his body toward me. "That so, Amaro? You do realize that I can move really fast. I'll have the bowl out of your hands, and I'll be covering you in ice cream before you even get a chance to flick that spoon in my direction."

"That so?" I raise a brow. "That's a bold statement to make."

He gets up on his knees on the sofa, facing me. "Not bold. Fact."

"Are you challenging me, Ryan?"

He tilts his head to the side. "Yeah. Why? You chicken, Amaro?"

"Ha! Not likely. Challenge accepted."

Then, it all kind of happens pretty quickly. I scoop up some ice cream, lifting my hand to flick it at him. *Fuck, he can move quick.* He wasn't kidding. I just manage to get a small splatter of ice cream on his shirt before I find myself flat on my back and the bowl out of my hand, gone somewhere on the floor, with a smirking Carrick pinning my hands above my head, plucking the spoon from my fingers.

"What were you saying?" he says cockily from above me, holding the spoon tauntingly over my face.

"Aargh!" I squeal, closing my eyes, anticipating the ice cream drip.

"Do you give?" His voice is deep.

It causes a ripple in my lower belly.

I open my eyes, staring into his. "Never. I'd rather get covered in ice cream than submit."

Something flashes in his eyes at my last word choice.

"Just do your worst, and get it over with." Scrunching my eyes up, I ready myself for the ice cream covering.

Then, I feel it—something very large and very significant pressing against my thigh.

My breath catches, and my eyes open to meet his.

His face is much closer to mine than it was a moment ago.

And the look in his eyes now...it's hot.

Like the flick of a switch, I feel my whole body come alive against his.

His body on mine, and his hard-on pressed against my thigh. Knowing that just being this close to me does that to him does crazy insane things to me.

I bite my lip.

He draws a sharp breath. His chest contracts on the movement. His eyes darken with want.

Lowering the spoon to my mouth, he runs the base of it over my lips, coating them in ice cream. I suck in a breath at the cold contact.

Tossing the spoon to the floor, he lowers his head. Keeping his eyes on mine, he very slowly runs his tongue along my lips, licking the ice cream from them.

Sweet Jesus.

I'm frozen. Every muscle is locked tight in place. I couldn't move even if I wanted to.

And I really don't.

I really, really don't.

Since the moment I met Carrick, all I've thought about is what it would be like to kiss him, to taste him…and now, it looks like I'm about to find out.

Even though I really shouldn't be doing this because no good could ever come of it, I can't seem to find the will to stop.

But I should at least try.

"What are you doing?" I whisper. My words are weak and pointless.

He blinks those blues of his slowly, moistening his lips with his tongue.

God, he's beautiful.

When his eyes open back to mine, I see just how wired with desire they are, and it hits me straight between my legs.

"I'm winning," he whispers.

Then, he takes my mouth in the most sensual, delicious kiss I've ever experienced.

Every nerve ending in my body sparks to life. It's like I've been sleeping, my body lying dormant for these last twenty-four years, and now, he's awoken me with the single touch of his lips.

His tongue moves into my mouth, sliding along mine. I can taste the sweet ice cream on him.

He tastes like every single one of my dreams come true.

On a moan, my arms go around his neck, my fingers curling into the hair at the nape.

My action seems to set him off. On a growl, he knees my legs apart. Lying between them, he presses against me. Every hard inch of him is nestled up against my aching sex.

God, that feels amazing.

And I know I'm in the worst kind of trouble because I don't want him to stop, especially when he starts grinding himself against me.

The famous bass line from Fleetwood Mac's "The Chain" suddenly blasts loudly from my phone on the coffee table, jolting me from Carrick and from the moment I've let myself fall into.

Shit! What am I doing?

"Ignore it." He brushes his lips over mine again, and his fingers thread into my hair, bringing me back for more.

And God, do I want to keep kissing him.

But my brain has kicked into gear now, and it's saying I need to stop this.

Because nothing good could come of this continuing. Apart from a ruined friendship.

Carrick's a driver. And he's my friend.

I feel an uncomfortable twist in my gut.

Pressing my hands against his chest, I push him away. "Stop. We need to stop." I'm breathless.

"Stop?" He looks less than pleased at that idea.

I kind of am myself. But stopping is the right thing to do.

"Yes. Stop." I wriggle out from underneath him, sliding off the sofa. I get to my unsteady feet and start to back up. I need to put some distance between us. "That...it shouldn't have happened." I touch my fingers to my lips. I can still feel him there.

Carrick is sitting up now, staring at me in confusion and frustration. "It absolutely should have happened. And it needs to keep on happening." He gets to his feet.

"No. I can't do this with *you*." My voice is sharp. I don't mean it to be.

"You can't do this with *me*?" His face snaps into anger. "What the fuck is that supposed to mean?"

You know that moment when you know you're digging yourself into a hole, but you can't seem to stop the digging, no matter how hard you try?

Yep, I'm there right now.

"It means, you're *you*, and I'm me." I press a hand to my chest.

"I'm me?" He's starting to look beyond pissed off.

I'm getting confused, and I'm exasperated. Quite frankly, I'm also horny. "Yes! You're Carrick Ryan, man-whore supreme! You shag anything that moves, and I don't want to be one of those moving shags! And I work for you, and you're a driver, and I don't get involved with drivers. You know that!"

The silence hits like a dull thud in my head. I'm not fully aware of everything I just said, but I know it wasn't good. I'm getting that from the way he's looking at me like I'm a really bad taste in his mouth.

Sighing, I drag a hand through my hair. "Look...that came out all wrong—"

"No, I think it came out just right." His voice is tight, hard.

"I..." I don't know what to say. I let out a resigned sigh. "I should probably go."

"Yeah. You probably should." He's not looking at me now. He's turned away, facing the window.

Picking my phone and room key off the coffee table, I slip my feet into my flip-flops.

When I reach the door, I say to his back, "I'll see you later?"

REVVED

I wait a beat and get no answer. Yanking the door open, I let it slam shut on my way out.

How could I have let that happen?

We kissed, and now, we're mad at each other, and it's just stupid.

I'm sitting on my bed in my room—like I have been doing for the past two hours since I left Carrick—going through the emotions of anger and sadness and anger again. I'm at resignation now. And regret.

Big time regret.

I hate how we left things. I don't want to fight with Carrick.

He's the best thing in my life.

My mum always says you should never go to sleep on a fight. Honestly, I'm not looking at much sleep tonight if I don't sort this out with Carrick.

I don't want this to spoil what we've become.

A kiss really shouldn't spoil things.

And yes, kissing him has sparked that crush of mine to intense life, but I can control myself around him. Because I'd rather have some Carrick than no Carrick.

Decision made, I put my flip-flops back on, grab my phone and room key, and head for the elevator.

My stomach is a riot of nerves the whole ride up to his floor.

When the door pings open, I fill my gut with determination, and I march my way to his door.

Hand raised, I knock on his door and wait.

And wait.

No answer.

Is he not here?

I knock again, a little louder this time.

Still nothing.

I stand here for a moment, feeling deflated. I was all ready to talk this out with him, and he's not even bloody here.

I wonder, *Where is he?*

Maybe he went out and met up with Ben and the rest of them.

I'll just text him, ask him if we can talk. If I have to go out and meet him, that's fine. I just really need to talk to him.

I haul my deflated self back to the elevator and press the call button. Then, I quickly type out a text to Carrick, asking if I can see him, saying that we need to talk. I've just pressed Send on the text when the elevator pings its arrival.

As the door slides open, I lift my eyes from my phone to the sound of female giggling.

My heart stops dead.

Carrick. And he's not alone.

He has a very attractive, petite local girl pressed up against the wall of the elevator.

His mouth is on hers. His hand is up her dress.

The mouth and hands that were touching me only hours before.

Tears instantly burn my eyes, pain lodging itself firmly in my throat.

I stumble back a step, and my movement catches the girl's eye.

"Oops." She giggles, her voice heavily accented. "We have company." She taps his shoulder with her fingers.

Lifting his head from her, he turns to me. Glazed drunk eyes meet with mine.

For a split second, as his blues burn into mine, he looks shocked that quickly transforming to guilt, and then his eyes harden to black.

And I suddenly feel very cold.

"What the fuck are you doing here?"

I'm taken aback by his acidic response.

"I..." I blink, faltering.

He's never spoken to me this way before.

Then, I force spine into my back. "I came to see if we were okay. Clearly, you are." My tone is hard and brittle as I gesture a hand to him...*them*.

As if realizing it's still there, he removes his hand from under her dress, reminding me where it was.

I'm going to be sick. Actually sick.

I'm wondering if I can make it to a bin or anything that will hold vomit before I do it right here in front of him.

Stop, Andi. Deep breaths.
He's free to do this. And this is who Carrick is. What he does.
But he was with me...
And I pushed him away.

Well, he certainly had no problem with finding a replacement.

"Carr, who is this?" Her voice sounds uneasy. She's probably worried I'm his girlfriend or something.

I part my dry lips to speak.

But Carrick beats me to it. "She's nobody."

Nobody.

If he had hit me, it would have hurt less. I jerk back from the shock, pressing the heel of my hand to the blade of pain he just stuck in my chest.

Unaffected by the hurt he just inflicted on me, he steps out of the elevator, leading the girl out by the hand.

He gestures. "Elevator's all yours." His voice is monotone, almost like he's bored of having to actually talk to me.

I glance in the elevator, but all I can see is him in it with her. Him pressed up against her. Kissing her. His hand—

"I'll take the stairs."

"Whatever." He walks past me, leading her toward his suite.

Taking a lungful of air, I hold it in and force my feet to walk in the direction of the stairwell while I hear the disappearing sounds of her giggling as they go inside his suite.

I tightly wrap my arms over my chest, holding myself together, while my inside quietly cracks open.

I reach the door to the stairwell. Shoving it open with my shoulder, I fall through, and the breath I was holding in painfully whooshes out of me.

A sob hitches in my throat. I catch it, covering my mouth with my hand, and hold it in as I run down the stairs.

Shoving my key in my door, I fall into my room. Letting the door close behind me, I crumple up against it.

Removing my hand from my mouth, I press it to the pain in my stomach as the sob breaks free. Tears spilling from my eyes, I move my fingers to curl around the little car pendant hanging around my neck.

eight

SAKHIR, BAHRAIN

THE NEXT DAY, I left China without having to see Carrick.

Now, I've arrived in Bahrain with the guys and turned my phone on. I'm sitting on the bus to take us to the hotel, and I'm staring down at a text message from him.

I'm sorry.

He's sorry.

For what? For kissing me? Kissing her? For having sex with her? For being the world's biggest arsehole?

Aargh!

A sharp shot of anger pulses through me. I delete the message and throw my phone into my bag.

"You okay?"

I lift my eyes to see Uncle John standing by my seat.

"Mmhmm. I'm good. Just tired." I force a smile.

He takes the seat next to me. "I hear you. I think I'm getting too old for all this traveling."

"Never." I look at him, smiling. "You wouldn't know what to do if you stopped. You love it."

"Sure I do." He gives me a wink. "But I'm still getting old."

"Well, to me, you still look the same as you did when I was a girl." I curl my hand around his arm and rest my head against his shoulder.

"I'm glad you're here."

"Yeah, me, too."

"Like old times." He lets out a long breath. "You've been spending a lot of time with Carrick."

And there it is.

I lift my head and meet his eyes. "And?"

"And I want to make sure that you're okay."

He stares at me, and I feel like he can see right through me. He's always been able to know when something is going on with me.

"I'm fine. Carrick and I are just friends."

"I'm sure you think that. But does he?"

I think back to yesterday. "Yeah, he does."

Another long stare, and then he seems to settle on it. "I just worry about you, kiddo."

"I know you do, and I appreciate it, but everything's fine. I promise."

Except it's not.

He lets out a long breath. "Even though I see you every day, I feel like I've barely spent any time with you since you arrived."

"Yeah, I know what you mean. But I get it. We're all busy. You are more than most."

Uncle John is always working past the clock.

"Yeah, well, I want to spend some time with my girl. When we get to the hotel, you wanna have dinner with me? Or are you too tired?"

Smiling, I say, "I'm never too tired to have dinner with you."

I'm sleeping when the knocking on the door starts.

I had dinner with Uncle John and then came straight up to bed as I was shattered.

Petra isn't here. She was flying back to the UK for a week as there's some catering thing to be done back home, and then she's coming out. I can't wait until she gets here. I could do with some female company right now.

So, I'm alone in my hotel room with someone knocking on the door.

Stumbling out of bed, I flick on the light, blinding myself in the process. Glancing at the clock, I see that it's five a.m.

Approaching the door, I look through the peephole.

Carrick.

Shit. What's he doing here?

I thought he was still in China. I'm sure he had some press things to do before coming to Bahrain.

But he's here, meaning he couldn't have left much longer after I did.

On a deep breath, I open the door.

"Hey." His eyes flicker to my bare legs before lifting to my face.

I'm wearing pajama shorts and a T-shirt. And now I'm remembering that I also don't have a bra on.

Great.

I fold my arms over my chest. "What are you doing here? I thought you were still in China."

Staring at him, I notice his eyes look bloodshot and glazed. *Has he been drinking?*

"I came early. Private jet," he explains.

"Well, that's great, Carrick, but it's ridiculous o'clock in the morning, and I was sleeping."

"Sorry, I just…" He scrubs his hand over his face. "I wanted to talk to you."

I wanted to talk the other night, but you were too busy screwing some other woman to talk to me.

"Well, couldn't you have waited until a reasonable hour?"

I'm being a bitch because I'm hurt.

Hurt that he slept with someone. Hurt that he replaced me.

But most of all, I'm hurt because he thinks that I'm nobody.

"She's nobody."

Those words keep ringing in my ears. And they shred me to pieces every single time.

I thought I was something to him. I thought I was his friend.

Clearly not.

"No, I couldn't wait." His voice is as firm as his stare.

So, I give him a pissed off look back, and I let out an exaggerated sigh. "Well, what exactly is it that you want?"

He leans his shoulder against the doorframe, putting him closer to me, and I instantly smell the whiskey on him.

He has been drinking.

I don't know why, but that just pisses me off even more, fueling the hurt and ire in my belly. "You've been drinking?"

He gives me an awkward look. "A little. On the flight." He lets out a sigh. "Look, Andressa, I just—"

"How did you know what room I'm staying in?" I cut him off, the thought out of my mouth the second my brain thinks it.

Discomfort flickers through his eyes. Then, he straightens to his full height, his arms coming across his chest, confidence filling his gaze. "Do you really want the answer to that?"

I stand up straight, mirroring him. "Yeah, I really bloody do."

Putting his hands on the doorframe, he cockily leans forward. "Because I'm Carrick fucking Ryan, and I have a fuckload of money. Those two things can buy me pretty much anything I want, including the number of the hotel room that you're staying in."

Not me. You can't buy me, Carrick.

Aargh! I'm so ready to slam this door in his arrogant fucking face. This isn't him. Not the real him. Not the Carrick I've spent the past month getting to know.

This...I don't know who this version is, but he's a complete tosspot, and I really want to punch him in his rich pretty face.

I take a step forward, poking a finger in his chest, forcing him to drop his hands and move backwards. "What the hell is this? This isn't you! You don't say shit like that—especially not to me! And coming up here like you own the place, finding out my room number, waking me up at the butt crack of dawn—you have no right! You know some would call that illegal or maybe an invasion of privacy or fucking stalking!" I all but scream the last part.

He at least has the decency to look contrite. He retreats back a step at the force of my anger.

"Jesus." He shudders out a breath, dragging a hand through his hair. "This is not going how I wanted this to go."

"No? How did you think it was going to go with you turning up here out of the blue, drunk and acting like an arrogant prick?"

He steadily meets my eyes. "I might have been drinking, but I'm not drunk."

I drag a hand through my bed-tangled hair, withdrawing into my room. "Look, I'm tired, and I'm not in the mood to fight with you."

I start to shut the door, but he puts a hand against it, stopping me.

"Please, Andressa. Just wait..."

I let out a sigh, lifting my eyes to his. "What?"

"I texted you."

"I know."

I can see from his expression that he wasn't expecting that reply.

"Why didn't you text me back?" His words are soft. He sounds wounded.

Good, because so am I. Deeply fucking wounded.

"Because I didn't have anything to say."

He looks like I've just told him that his favorite car has been crushed to smithereens.

He moves back, looking like he's going to leave, but then he stops. "I didn't sleep with her."

The words are spoken so softly that I wonder for a moment if he's actually said them.

Oh.

The sense of relief I feel at hearing that is immense. And it's wrong because I shouldn't feel anything, especially not for him.

His eyes lift to mine. There's desperation in them, and I feel it deep inside, like an ache in my bones.

"Why are you telling me this?" My voice is cold, devoid of emotion.

"Because…I thought…I don't know what I thought." He shakes his head. "I just want you to know that I'm not the complete bastard you think I am."

Just half a bastard then.

"And I'm sorry. So very fucking sorry."

"You've nothing to be sorry for. You're a free agent. You can do whatever you want with whomever you want. It's none of my business. I'm nobody, remember?"

That hurts him. I see it flicker through his eyes.

Good. Now, he knows an iota of what I've been feeling since he said it to me.

Then, surprisingly, his pain turns to anger. And that pisses me right off.

"You don't think I did anything wrong? I kissed you, dry-humped you on that fucking sofa, and then a few hours later, you found me in an elevator with another woman, who I was readying to fuck."

I really don't need a recap of one of the worst nights I've had in a long time. *Is he trying to get a reaction out of me?* Because if he is, then he's going to get one—big time.

"But that's just a standard night for you, isn't it?" I bite, only just getting started with him.

It was a low blow, and that was exactly what I was aiming for.

What I wasn't planning on was how much the look of hurt on his face hurts me.

I step away from him, needing the distance. "Look, I'm tired and angry, and you've been drinking. We shouldn't be having this conversation right now. We're getting nowhere."

"Yeah...you're right." He lets out a defeated sigh. "Before I go...I just want you to know that I am sorry. Beyond sorry. You deserve better than the way I treated you. I was so fucking out of line. What I said...God, Andressa, you're not nothing. You're everything. Aside from my dad, you're the best person I know." Raking a hand through his hair, he drags his eyes back to mine. "And not that this is an excuse for my behavior, but I just don't...deal well with rejection."

Clearly.

"She didn't look like she was rejecting you from where I was standing."

"Jesus, Andressa. I meant you."

Looking away, I hide my pain and wrap my arms over my chest. "What do you want me to say, Carrick?"

He moves before me. Earnest eyes stare into mine. "Just tell me that I haven't fucked this up." His voice is close to a whisper, a desperate whisper. "I don't want to lose my friend. I don't want to lose *you*."

I swallow past my own bitterness as a hand of pain wraps around my heart and squeezes. "You haven't lost me. We just...screwed up, and we're working through it. We'll be fine."

And I ignore the little voice in my head asking me how the hell any of this can be fine when I clearly feel for him like I do.

🇪🇸 BARCELONA, SPAIN

I'M IN SPAIN, and it's late and hot. I'm still at the track, finishing up after today's practice sessions. I'm here on my own as I told the guys to head back to the hotel. They were dying to go out for a drink, and I was too tired to even consider it, so I told them I'd finish up.

Now, I'm finally done for the day and so ready for my bed that it isn't funny.

Things have been on the up with Carrick and me since China and Bahrain.

We tiptoed around one another while we were in Bahrain. Then, when we saw each other in Korea for that leg of the tour, after having a few days apart, we just fell back into our old ways. But even for the time we've spent together, we haven't spent any time alone. We've always been with the guys and Petra.

Whether that's a conscious move on his part or subconscious on mine, I'm not sure. I'm just glad that we're friends still.

But the image of him with that woman in China is still seared into my mind. I wish there were some way to expunge it from my brain.

"I need a favor."

My head whips up at the sound of Carrick's voice.

It's weird to be thinking of someone and have that person just appear like that.

"A favor?" I raise a brow at him, watching him walk toward me, as I wipe my grimy hands on my overalls. "And what are you still doing here?"

"Meeting with Dad and Pierce."

"Oh. So, this favor?"

"Hmm." He's looking at me with a sexy smile growing on his face.

"Well, what is it?" I'm suspicious because Carrick's favors usually involve me doing something that potentially puts my job at risk.

Stopping in front of me, he lifts his hand, and he sweeps his thumb over my cheek.

I part my lips on a breath as my skin ignites on a blaze of flames.

"Oil." He shows me his thumb.

"Oh." I rub my arm against my face. "So, this favor?" I step back, away from him and over to the workbench.

"I need a date. More specifically, I need you to be my date. I have to go to this sponsorship event tomorrow night. It's our biggest sponsor, so it's kind of a big deal."

"And you want me to go with you?"

"Yep."

"Why?"

"Because I don't want to go alone. And because you're awesome."

Laughing, I shake my head. "I meant, why me?"

"Because you'll make what is guaranteed to be a boring-as-fuck night a million times better."

His compliment flushes through me, all the way down to my toes.

"And I want to spend some time with you. Just me and you. As friends…" he adds at my expression. "I miss hanging out, just us."

I miss hanging out, just us, too.

"Okay." I smile.

His face lights up, and I like the way it makes me feel. I like making him happy.

"What time does it start?" I'm thinking of the practice sessions tomorrow—if I'll be able to slip away for an hour to get an outfit and have time to get ready after.

"It starts at seven thirty. And don't worry. I'll speak with John, let him know you're coming with me and get him to let you off early."

Yeah, I'm sure that'll go down well. "Let me talk to him."

"You sure?"

I give him a look. "I'm sure." I walk over to the basin to wash my hands. "So, what should I wear?"

"It's black tie, so a dress."

"Dress. Got it."

Shit. I have nothing to wear and no clue what to buy. I'm a jeans-and-T-shirt kind of girl. I'll have to ask Petra. I'm sure she'll come shopping with me. She loves shopping.

Carrick reaches into his back pocket and pulls out a credit card. "Take this."

Reaching for a paper towel, I dry my hands. "What is it?"

"What does it look like? It's a credit card, you dope." He chuckles.

"Your credit card?"

"Yeah."

"And why are you giving it to me?"

"So you can buy a dress." He shoves it into my hand.

"Erm, nope. No way am I taking your money."

I push the card back at him, but he holds his hands up, refusing to take it.

"Take it. You're doing me a favor by coming with me. You shouldn't have to drop a shitload of money on a dress that you're only buying to help me out."

"How do you know I don't own a dress already?"

He folds his arms. "Do you?"

I fold my arms, mirroring him. "No, but that's beside the point."

"It's the only point, so take the fucking card and buy a dress." He walks away before I can get another chance to give it back to him. "See you tomorrow." He throws a wink back at me.

The minute he's gone, panic mode sets in. *How in the hell am I going to buy a dress and make myself look pretty by tomorrow night?*

I've reached high-level dread, wondering why the hell I agreed to go to this event with Carrick by the time I get back to my room, and I'm surprised to find Petra here.

"I thought you were going out?"

"Changed my mind. Thought I'd have a night off and hang out here with you."

I drop down on my bed and turn onto my side, facing Petra. "I need some help."

"Okay." She takes her eyes from the TV to look at me. "Is this about Carrick?"

My head jerks back. "What do you mean?"

"Come on. I know there's been some weird tension thing going on between the two of you. You left China all weird, and you've been the same since."

"No, I haven't. And there's no tension between me and Carrick."

"Sure there isn't." She rolls her eyes.

I pretend not to have seen her, as I don't want to get into my Carrick problems with anyone. I know Petra, and I like her, but I don't know her well enough to trust her with my Carrick crap.

"Anyway, this is Carrick-related, kind of. He's asked me to go with him to this event tomorrow night—as friends," I add when I see her brow rising. "And I need a dress." I won't tell her that Carrick is paying for the dress because she'll think for sure that something is going on. "But I have no clue what kind of dress to get or where to get it from here in Barcelona, and I need your help because I'm crap at shopping."

She claps her hands together with glee. "Of course I'll help."

She glances at the clock, and I follow her gaze, seeing that it's seven thirty.

"Lucky for you, we're in one of the best cities for late-night shopping. The shops are open till nine." She gets up off the bed. "What's your budget? Because Passeig de Gràcia has the best designer shops, but they also have Zara and Mango."

"Well, I don't want to spend too much." I can feel Carrick's credit card burning a hole in my pocket. "But I want to look good."

"Hot on a budget. Got it. Come on, chick." She pats my leg as she passes by. "We've got some serious shopping to do and limited time to do it."

And that's how I find myself in the fitting room at Mango on Passeig de Gràcia.

Petra yells for me, "Have you got it on yet? You've been in there for ages!"

"Yes."

"And?"

I run my hand down the dress again, looking at myself. I just...I don't know. I think I look okay, but it's a little risqué for me. It's red satin, floor-length, strappy with a plunging neckline, so you can see definite cleavage. But that's not the risqué part. It's the split up the side. Granted, it's not skintight, but you can see definite leg when I walk, like up-to-the-thigh high.

"Jesus…your legs go on forever."

I flush at the reminder of Carrick's words to me that first day in the garage.

Would he like me in this dress? Would I care?

I think I already know the answer to that last question.

"Andi?" Petra calls, impatience in her voice. "If you don't come out in the next three seconds, then I'm coming in."

"Okay. I'm coming out." Taking a deep breath, I pull the curtain back and step out.

"Holy fuck," Petra says, getting to her feet.

"Is that a good holy fuck?"

"It's a very good holy fuck." She grins. "You look amazing, not that you look like shit normally, but you're always in those god-awful overalls or jeans and a T-shirt. All this time, you've been packing this under there." She waves a hand over me. "Carrick is gonna come in his pants when he sees you wearing this."

"Nice." I grimace at her choice of words. "Seriously, you think it's okay?" I turn to look at myself in the mirror. "It's not too…red?"

"Not at all. And with your coloring, you can carry it off, no problem."

"So, you think I should get it?"

"I definitely think you should buy it and maybe wear it every day." She smiles, coming to stand beside me, looking in the mirror. "God, I feel so like a bloody midget next to you." She pouts.

Petra's only five-five, which is a good height. I'm just so bloody tall.

"I think we should go minimal on the jewelry," she says. "Maybe just some earrings. Don't want to take the emphasis off the dress. Oh, shoes. You definitely need some heels. Maybe black or nude. We'll have to scout some out."

Heels? "Er, Petra, I'm not used to heels."

"We'll go low." She pats my arm. "Three, maybe four inches."

Three or maybe four inches? "I was thinking more like one inch. Seriously, I won't be able to wear them. I'll fall over and make an arse of myself. And I'll look like a giant. Can't I just wear flats?"

She looks at me like I just asked for coffee on my cereal. "No, you can't bloody wear flats! It'd be an insult to this gorgeous dress. I'll teach you how to walk in them. And you won't look too tall. You'll look like a freaking supermodel. Now, go get changed." She ushers me back into the fitting room with a pat to my behind. "We haven't got much time left, and we need to get you those heels."

🇪🇸 BARCELONA, SPAIN

I'M STANDING OUTSIDE THE HOTEL'S BEAUTY SALON, wondering what the hell I'm doing here. This isn't me. I don't do this girlie stuff. Sure, I go to the hair salon for a trim when my hair needs it. But getting my nails done? Hell, no. It's too embarrassing.

I glance down at the text I got from Petra this morning. She was already up and out before I woke up as she had to get an early start on breakfast for some meeting that Pierce and the rest of the management team were having.

> *Hotel salon. 4 p.m. I made you a nail appointment. Be there. See you back at the room afterward, so I can do your hair and makeup.*

I look at my hands. They're all dry, and the skin is rough. Oil stains are around my cuticles, and my nails have been bitten down. *Ugh.* The nail technician is going to take one look at my hands and run screaming.

"Can I help?" says a heavily accented voice.

It's then I realize the door to the salon is open, and a woman is standing there, looking at me.

I must look like a crazy person, just standing out here staring at the place.

"Oh, um, yes, I have an appointment...to get my nails done." I hide my hands behind my back. "My friend made it for me."

"Oh, you are Andi?" She smiles at me.

"Yes," I answer tentatively.

"Wonderful! Come in." She steps back, waving me in. "I'm Martina."

She presses her hand to her chest. When I see how nice her nails are, I cringe again at my own bitten mess.

"I have you booked in with Alma. She'll be out in a few minutes. Sit down."

I'm ushered into a chair.

"Would you like a drink?"

"Coffee would be great. Thanks."

Martina disappears through the salon, leaving me to panic about being here. The salon is a hub of activity with women getting their hair done. They all look stylish and glamorous, and I'm none of those things.

I'm actually considering bolting when Martina appears with my coffee.

"Here you are."

She hands it over, and I take it from her.

"Thank you."

I've just taken a sip of my coffee when a well-groomed dark-haired woman in her thirties steps around the counter.

"Andi." She greets me with a smile. "Would you like to follow me through? I'll bring your coffee." She takes it from my hands.

Nervously, I follow her down a corridor and into a room.

"Take a seat. So, what are we doing today?"

"My nails…they're kind of a mess."

"Okay. Can I see?"

I realize that I'm sitting on my hands again. "Sorry." I give a nervous laugh. Then, I pull my hands up and rest them on the table in front of me.

She doesn't seem appalled, which is a good thing. Either that, or she's really good at masking her disgust.

"I'm a mechanic," I explain.

She nods.

"And I bite my nails," I carry on awkwardly. "But I have somewhere special to be tonight, and I need them to look nice…if possible."

"Don't you worry. I'll have your nails looking amazing in no time."

One hour and thirty minutes later, I walk out of the salon, feeling like a new woman. Well, a new hand woman, that is.

They feel so soft, and my nails are painted blood red, a darker shade than my dress, which Alma said would complement it. She did something called a paraffin wax on my hands to help soften the skin. I've never heard of it before, but I want to have one done every day. So relaxing. While I was waiting for the paraffin wax to work its magic, Alma gave me a pedicure, so my toes now match my fingers.

I'm a girl almost ready to go. Just the rest of me to sort out now.

Letting myself into our hotel room, I drop my bag on my bed and flash my nails at Petra.

"Very nice. Right, get yourself in the shower and wash your hair, and I'll fix it up for you and put your face on."

"Not a lot of makeup though." It's not really me.

"I'll keep it light. You don't need a lot."

"What about my hair?"

She stares at me for a long moment. "With that dress, I'd normally say up, but you never have your hair down, so I think you should wear it long with loose waves."

"You're the boss," I say with a wave of my hand. Grabbing my toothbrush, I drop some paste on it and start scrubbing my teeth. "Are you going out tonight?" I call from the bathroom.

"Yeah, gonna go out for a beer later with the boys," she calls back.

I spit and rinse. Shutting the bathroom door, I hop in the shower.

Half an hour later, I'm shaved to within an inch of my life. Legs, bikini, and underarms are all baby smooth. I dry off and apply my body lotion. Then, I pull on some shorts and a tank.

I come out of the bathroom with a towel on my head. "I'm all yours."

I pick my phone up, and I sit down at our makeshift dressing table, which is actually a desk with a mirror propped against it, and I check my messages.

There's one from Carrick.

How did the shopping go?

I got a dress and shoes. ☺

Glad to hear it. I'll pick you up at 7:30 p.m,

See you then. x

I hit Send before I realize that I put a kiss at the end. *Why did I do that?* Oh God, what if he gets the wrong idea and thinks—

Oh, whatever, I really need to stop worrying and just enjoy myself.

"Ready?" Petra stands behind me with a hairdryer in one hand and a makeup bag in the other.

"Ready." I smile back.

"What do you think?"

"Petra…I love it." I smile back at my reflection, touching a hand to my hair.

She has done an amazing job. My hair is in loose waves down my back, and my makeup is neutral and pretty.

"Are you professionally trained?" I ask her.

"No, but my mum is a stylist. You pick things up."

My mother's a model, and the only thing I picked up was her good genes.

"Well, thank you, Petra's mum. Actually, what time is it?" I glance at my phone. "Shit! It's twenty past seven. Carrick will be here in ten minutes."

Grabbing the dress and my new underwear set, I go into the bathroom.

Yes, I bought new underwear. Petra talked me into it. She said I needed it to go with the dress. It's red and pretty, tasteful and not slutty—not that anyone but me will be seeing it.

Ripping the tags from the bra and knickers, I quickly put them on. Then, I slip into the dress, pulling the zipper up as far as I can.

I come out of the bathroom. "Petra, can you zip me up the rest of the way?"

I move my hair over my shoulder, out of the way, while Petra zips me up, and I put on the earrings I bought.

"Done."

"Thanks." I grab my perfume and spritz myself with it.

"Shoes." She hands them over.

I slip my feet into them, taking a moment to steady my balance. We went for three-inch heels—I talked her down from four—but I still feel like a giant.

"Do I look too tall?"

"You look stunning." Taking me by the shoulders, she turns me to the mirror.

Wow. Is that me? I look good—no, not good. I look hot. I look like my mother when she was my age.

I smile at Petra in the mirror. "Thanks for your help. You have no idea how much I appreciate it." My eyes catch on the necklace that Carrick bought me.

No matter how much I love it, I can't turn up at a fancy party wearing a Lightning McQueen necklace. I don't want to embarrass Carrick. Unclipping it, I carefully place it in my vanity bag for safekeeping.

There's a knock at the door. I glance back at it, butterflies swooping full-force into my stomach.

"You want me to get it, or you?" Petra asks.

"You. Me."

"Any decision on that?"

I take a deep breath. "I'll get it." I walk the short distance across our room to the door, my hands trembling a little. I'm surprised at how nervous I am. I feel like it's a first date.

Not a date, Andi. Just two friends going out together.

Hand curled around the handle, I pull it open.

eleven

🇪🇸 BARCELONA, SPAIN

CARRICK. *Holy shit. He looks...amazing. Gorgeous.* He's wearing a tux. Jesus, my ovaries have just started doing cartwheels, and I'm pretty sure that I've just ruined my new undies.

"Fuck..." he breathes. "You look..." He slowly shakes his head. "Actually, there aren't any words to describe how you look right now."

Okay...

"So, is that a good fuck or a bad fuck?" I fidget nervously, smoothing a hand down my dress.

"Every fuck is a good fuck, Andressa—at least with me it is."

His eyes do that lazy perusal of me that has me hot in all the right places. When they meet back with mine, they are...blazing hot.

"It's a really, *really* good fuck. Put it this way, every man in the room—actually, every man in the world is gonna wish they were me tonight."

"Really?" I blush.

He steps closer, his fingers skimming my jaw. "Really. You look stunning, Andressa. Absolutely stunning."

My blush deepens at his compliment. And my jaw is still tingling from where he just touched me.

"You ready to go? I have a car waiting downstairs."

"Uh, yeah, I just need my clutch."

As I turn, I find Petra behind me, clutch in hand.

"Thanks." I smile, taking it from her.

"Hi, Carrick." There's a grin in her voice.

I give her a look before turning back to him.

"Petra," he says.

"I'll see you later," I say to her, stepping out into the hallway.

"Have fun, kids. Don't do anything I wouldn't."

I lift a hand, waving to her, and Carrick and I start to walk down the hall.

"And if you can't keep it in, then keep it covered!" she calls.

I nearly die with embarrassment. I swing a murderous look at her, but all I get back is laughter.

Carrick chuckles.

We reach the elevator and wait in silence for it to arrive.

When the door opens, Carrick lets me go in first. Stepping in, he presses the button for the ground floor and stands beside me.

"You're not wearing your necklace," he comments.

My eyes swing to him as my hand touches the empty space. "I took it off. I thought I should at least pretend to be a grown-up tonight. And...I didn't want to embarrass you by wearing it."

He looks at me like I've just lost my mind. There's something deep and dark in his eyes. "I bought you the damn thing. And the *last* thing you could ever do is embarrass me."

I nervously swallow down. "I can put it back on if you want. It's just up in my room."

"No, it's fine." He stares ahead. "Just don't ever take it off for that reason. I always want you to be who you are. Don't ever try to be someone you're not. I happen to really fucking like who you are."

We arrive at the ground floor, and I'm glad. After that comment, I was pretty sure a vacuum came in and sucked all the air out of the elevator, leaving me gasping for breath.

Carrick guides me through the lobby with a hand on my back. We step out into the warm evening air, and a car is waiting for us. The driver opens the car door as we approach. I climb in first, and Carrick gets in beside me.

It's not until we're in traffic that I remember I still have his credit card.

"Oh, here's your card back." Getting it from my clutch, I hand it to him. "And thank you for the dress," I add.

His eyes skim down my body, and I have to stop from squirming under his perusal.

"It was worth every penny."

I blush again. I really need to stop with that.

We arrive at the event. Carrick offers me his hand to help me out of the car, which I'm grateful for. It's an awful lot easier to get in this car than out of it in this dress and shoes.

"Thanks," I murmur as he closes the door behind us.

Then, he does something that surprises me. He takes hold of my hand like it's the most natural thing in the world for him to do.

Maybe it is. He does spend a lot of time with women. He's probably done it without realizing.

So, I don't question it, or what the tingling sensation in my body means either.

I feel him rub his thumb over my hand, and then he lifts it, looking at it.

"I had a manicure," I explain, knowing why he's staring at my hand with interest.

He smiles softly. "Looks pretty."

And I'm mush on the floor. Just a big pile of girlie goo.

Once we're inside, I glance around, taking in my surroundings.

The venue itself screams fancy. And it's filled wall-to-wall with beautiful people wearing beautiful clothes, women with jewelry dripping off of them like ice. Everyone exudes wealth.

This is the glamorous side of Formula 1 that I don't usually see, and I feel a little out of my depth.

Carrick grabs us a couple of glasses of champagne from a passing waiter.

"Let the crazy begin." He chinks his glass with mine.

And crazy is right because that is the only quiet moment we have together—or I should say him. The moment people see he's arrived, they're on him like bees on honey.

It's interesting to watch how he is with these people—charming with the females, of course, but he's guarded, not the relaxed guy I spend my time with. He's more serious, focused, like he feels he has something to prove. Maybe he does.

All I know is I'm glad he's not *this* Carrick with me, that he feels he can be himself with me.

I've been working my way through some serious glasses of champagne, which keep magically appearing in my hand. After making as much small talk with strangers that I can manage, I excuse myself to the restroom.

When I come back to the party, Carrick is talking with an attractive blonde. He's wearing that gorgeous flirty smile of his. And he looks very interested in whatever it is she is saying.

A flash of jealousy hits me. Hard.

Annoyed with myself for feeling that way, I decide to leave Carrick to his conversation, and I head to the bar.

I want to order beer, but all the women here are drinking wine or champagne or fancy-looking cocktails. I don't want to stick out like a sore thumb with a bottle of Bud in hand, so when the bartender asks for my drink order, I ask for champagne. Might as well continue on as I've been going.

"If you wanted a drink, you should have come and told me. I would have gotten you one."

I jolt at Carrick's voice beside me.

I slide a glance at him. "You looked busy. I didn't want to interrupt." Shit, that came out sounding a lot like jealousy. And I really didn't mean it to. *Did I?*

A grin edges his lips. "I wasn't busy. And you're always a welcome interruption. You know that."

The bartender puts my drink on the bar. Carrick hands him his credit card before I get a chance to pay.

"Jameson on the rocks, please, mate."

I frown at him. In response to my frown, I get, "Andressa, I don't take a woman out and expect her to get her own drinks."

"That's what you would do on a date. This isn't a date," I remind him.

The bartender puts a whiskey down in front of Carrick.

He picks it up, holding the glass near his lips. "Maybe not, but I'm still buying your drinks. End of."

"Neanderthal."

He snorts.

Did I mention he was drinking whiskey at the time?

"Shit, it's gone up my nose!" He winces, cupping his nose with his hand.

The sight of him, all handsome in his tux with whiskey dripping down his chin, is one I'll always remember.

Laughing, I grab a napkin from the bar and pass it to him.

"Thanks." He dries off and then shakes his head, trying to clear it. "Fuck, that felt weird."

He grins that boyish grin of his at me, and it punches me in the chest, leaving me feeling momentarily breathless.

"Anyway, where were we?"

"I called you a Neanderthal, and you snorted whiskey up your nose."

"Thanks for the thorough recap." His blue, blue eyes sparkle at me under the lights of the bar. "I've been called things before but never a caveman."

Putting my glass down on the granite, I rest my elbow on it. Chin in my hand, I stare up at him. "What do you usually get called?"

"Do you mean before or after sex?"

My face immediately flushes. I'm not a prude—I work with rowdy, oversexed men all day long—but Carrick just talks so openly about sex in a one-on-one way that I've never known before.

It always sounds so intimate when he talks about it.

Or maybe it sounds intimate because the sex he talks about, I want him to be having with me.

"You're blushing." His fingertips touch my cheek. "Have I embarrassed you?"

"Nope." Moving my head back, I pick my glass up and take a gulp of champagne. Then, I straighten up, resting my side against the bar. "Before sex?"

"Sex god. Stud. Fuck-me-baby-use-that-big-cock-of-yours-on-me-show-me-the-stories-about-you-are-true."

Okay, I'm definitely blushing now, and there's no hiding it.

"I get the point," I say, lifting a hand to cut him off, to which he chuckles. "And what do you get called after sex?"

He looks away from me to stare at the sea of people before us. His expression turns...changing to something I don't understand.

"Bastard. Arsehole. Selfish-arrogant-prick-who'll-one-day-be-a-washed-up-race-car-driver-who-no-one-cares-to-remember."

I feel the air shift, the temperature in the room dropping a few hundred degrees, and I realize that he means it. He really believes what he just said.

This beautiful talented man thinks he'll end up alone.

I stare at him, stunned. *How is it even possible he thinks that?*

Carrick's eyes are now currently trained on his drink, like he thinks all the answers he seeks are in there, and he just looks so goddamn lonely that I want to wrap my arms around him.

But I can't.

So, I attempt to make him feel better in the only way I can right now—humor.

I put my glass down. "Well, that's bullshit because I'll remember you."

His eyes lift from his whiskey. "Oh, yeah?"

"Yeah. I won't be able to forget you because we'll have been married and divorced twice, and you'll still be in my life because we'll have kids whom you pay a hefty child support for. And I'll feel sorry for you because, by that point, you'll have aged really badly, after getting kind of ugly and fat, so I'll give you a sympathy shag every now and then."

"You paint quite the picture."

"It's a talent." I shrug.

"So, married...twice?"

"Yep, you bought me the second time as I'd burned through all the millions you gave me from our first divorce." I lift my glass, taking a sip of champagne.

"And how did I get you the first time?"

"Sex. I was young and naive." I grin, expecting him to smile back, but he's not.

There's something in his stare that has my heart beating faster, my breath disappearing, and my eyes looking away— while I try to find air.

I focus my eyes where his just were, on the people milling around and chatting, some out on the dance floor.

Anywhere but on the man beside me.

The man who is becoming increasingly dangerous to me with each passing second.

Carrick leans in, so his arm is pressed against mine, close to my chest. It feels like he's actually burning my skin through his clothes.

"I'm sorry about people monopolizing my time tonight."

I flash him a smile. "It's okay. I get it. You're the star attraction, and I'm your arm candy."

"You do make for good arm candy, especially in that dress."

"I know, right? I'm totally rocking the classy look." Okay, the fizz is really starting to go to my head.

"More than you realize."

Something dark and unexplained is in his tone that makes my pulse ratchet up.

Taking a sip of his drink, he nods in the direction of the dance floor. "Do you want to dance?"

"Um…I don't know. I'm not really a dancer." *And in these shoes, I'll probably be lethal.*

"Lucky for you, I'm an awesome dancer. I'll dance for the both of us."

Shaking my head, I laugh. "God, you're so—"

"Good-looking? Hot?"

"I was going to say cocky."

"Endearing, isn't it?"

He grins, and then he takes my almost empty champagne glass from my hand and puts it down on the bar. Grabbing my hand, he starts to lead me off, only just giving me a chance to grab my clutch off the bar top.

Usher's "Caught Up" starts to pump through the speakers as we walk to the dance floor. I watch as we pass by people, how they look at him…like he's a glowing light and they are the moths drawn to him.

Carrick's presence just commands attention. Take away the racing, the fame, and I think he would still be the same.

Confidence and virility just breathe from him as naturally as the air from his lungs.

I also see the looks I'm receiving from women, looks I've been receiving all night. Luckily for me, those looks of distaste and jealousy just bounce right off me. Being an only female in the working world of men toughens a girl right up.

What I am actually feeling from the envious looks is a tremendous buzz. They want him, and he's with me. Well, for tonight anyway.

Carrick stops us in the middle of the dance floor and turns to face me.

I feel awkward. I'm not really sure what to do, where to put my hands. I'm also holding my clutch, which makes it even more difficult.

Should I put it on the floor? It's just so pretty and new. I don't want it to get ruined.

Deciding to keep my clutch in hand, I rest my wrists awkwardly over his shoulders.

Carrick chuckles.

Taking my clutch from my hand, he shoves it in his jacket pocket. Then, he takes my hands. Lifting one, he places it on his shoulder. Keeping hold of the other, he wraps his fingers around it. Then, sliding his free hand around my waist, his fingers press gently into my back, pulling me closer.

I'm trying not to tense, but his nearness and touch are driving me crazy. Neurons are firing like bullets to my nerve endings, igniting fires that shouldn't be lighting for him.

"Relax," he says low into my ear.

That only sets off more shivers in me, heading southward.

"Have you never danced with a man before?"

"Um…" I bite my lip. "Sure I have. But not like this." *Not with a man like you, a man who can switch my body on with a single look…a single touch.*

He raises a brow. "Not like this?"

"Yeah, you know, the proper kind of dancing. When I dance with a man, I'm usually drunk, and I'm, um…" *Shit, how do I finish that sentence?* That I'm on the pull, dancing with the guy I'm planning on taking home to have sex with—on the rare occasions when that does happen?

His hand tightens around mine, and I watch as his mouth forms the words hanging in my mind, "When you're on the pull."

Heat engulfs my face, so I turn away. "Something like that."

He leans in, so his lips are next to my ear, grazing it, as he speaks, "Just so you know, the dancing I want to do with you most fucking definitely isn't proper."

Holy fucking what?

My eyes flash back to his, but his blues give nothing away.

Before I get a chance to speak, he says, "How many boyfriends have you had?"

My head jerks back in surprise. "Um, what?"

"I asked how many boyfriends you've had."

"And why exactly are you asking that?"

"Curious."

"You know what that did?"

"Yeah, it killed the cat—and satisfaction brought it back, so I'll take my chances. How many boyfriends, Andressa?"

Smiling at his quip, I loosen up and decide to answer. "A few. Nothing serious."

"A few? I thought you'd have them lining up."

I give him a look. "Shockingly, no. Not all men want to date a grease monkey."

"Grease monkey?" He barks out a laugh. "Jesus, you're far from that. And you're wrong about men not wanting a hot-as-fuck woman who works under the hood. Trust me. There's nothing sexier."

Hot-as-fuck woman...

"When was your last relationship?"

His question momentarily throws me. I'm still stuck in my hot-as-fuck daze.

But his persistent intrusion into my personal life brings a frown to my face. "Jesus, Carrick, what is this? Question time?"

"It's called getting to know you."

"You already know me."

"I don't know everything."

"Do you need to know everything?"

His eyes darken...deepening like an endless chasm, which I could easily fall into.

"About you? Yes."

My heart skips a good ten beats before restarting back up.

Swallowing, I try to catch the breath he just stole. "Well, there are better things to learn about me than my dating history," I mumble.

"I'm fully aware of that, but just humor me."

"Fine..." I huff. "My last boyfriend was, um..." *Marcelo, but can that really be classified as a relationship?* We only dated for two months, and I was on the road with the team for a good portion of that. "About two years ago," I finish with.

"You haven't been with a guy in two years?"

I can't tell if he's shocked or appalled. Maybe both. It makes me feel uneasy and embarrassed.

"No. I said I haven't been in a relationship in two years, not that I haven't *been* with anyone."

That's actually been...shit. Okay, it's not far off from two years—about eighteen months. *What the hell have I been doing?* No wonder I'm as hot for him as I am. I've been depriving my body of sex for way too long.

"I've been busy." I sound defensive, but I can't help it. "And there's not a lot of time for dating when you work in racing, if you haven't noticed." Not that it stops him, but then he doesn't exactly date.

"What was his name?"

"Whose?"

"The guy you dated two years ago."

"Marcelo."

"Sounds like a ponce."

Laughter escapes me, shaking my shoulders. "He was all right. What about you?"

"Me? I've never had a boyfriend, especially not one with a poncy fucking name like Marcelo," he deadpans.

I playfully swat his shoulder. "You know what I meant. Girlfriend. Spill."

"One."

I feel a sharp stab of jealousy. If he'd said ten, I'd have felt better. But one girl means that she had his heart. Maybe she broke it, and that's why he's the player he is today.

I focus my stare over his shoulder, like something's caught my attention, so he can't see what I know is readable in my eyes. "How long were you together?"

"A day."

"A day?" I say, aghast. I look back to him, my eyes wide with shock. All trace of my jealousy is gone.

"Yeah…" He lets out a wistful sigh, which punches me straight in the chest. "Her name was Payton Ahearn. Totally loved her, and she dumped me for fucking Tommy O'Connor, all because he got her a necklace. I never did get over it. She ruined me for all other women."

My face creases in confusion.

"I was six." He grins.

"You're an idiot." I giggle. I actually fucking giggle. *What the hell is wrong with me?*

Aside from the fact that I'm turning into a total girl, I'd say it's relief. I'm relieved because no one has held his heart yet.

Why, Andi? Because you want it, him, for yourself?

"I am an idiot." The seriousness in his voice moves through me, bringing my attention back to him.

His eyes hold mine, and something unknown in them captivates me. But I want to know. And it's how badly I want to know that is scaring the hell out of me right now.

Usher ends, and Rihanna begins singing "Diamonds."

"I'm sorry about China," he says the words so softly.

My eyes dip, right along with my heart. The grip my fingers had on his dinner jacket loosens. "I know." I sigh lightly. "You've already said. And I already told you, you didn't do anything wrong."

His fingers find my chin, lifting my face to his. "Yes, I did. I proved to you that I'm everything you think I am. You stopped our kiss because you think I'm a player, that I use women."

"You do use women, and you are a player. But that's not why I stopped kissing you."

His brows pull together as his hand moves back to my waist. "So, why?"

"Because I don't get involved with drivers."

"You say that a lot."

"I say it because it's true."

"And why exactly don't you get involved with drivers?"

"Aside from the fact that I work for them...for *you*." I flash him a serious stare before looking away. "I have my reasons."

"Ones you're not going to tell me?"

My eyes come back to his, giving him my answer.

"And what if I wasn't a driver? Would you have sex with me then?"

My body jolts at his words, and he feels it. And he definitely likes my response. I can tell from the smile touching the edge of his lips.

"Jesus, you're so bloody...forward."

"You don't get anywhere in life by going backward."

Does he have an answer for everything?

"Exactly how did we go from me not getting involved with drivers to you and I having sex?"

"We haven't gotten to the sex yet. Trust me. When we do, you'll know."

"Yet?"

"Yes. Now, answer the question."

How to answer? It's hard to focus with him so close—his scent filling my head, his hands touching me and clouding my judgment.

"You're my friend, Carrick…" I let my voice drift, my words linger.

"That's not an answer. And the reason you won't answer is because you're afraid."

Afraid doesn't even cut it. I'm terrified. Terrified of what this all means. Of what's going to happen. Because if he makes a move, I know for certain that I won't be able to stop him…because I don't want to.

"Shall I answer for you?" His voice is low, decadent.

Licking my dry lips, I nod.

He moves in, his mouth so very close to mine. His breath blows over my lips, drying the moisture I just gave them, and his stare is doing all kinds of extraordinary things to me.

"Your answer is yes, you would. You're afraid to say it out loud because you know, once you do, it makes it real—this thing between us—and then you won't be able to stop it from happening. What, deep down inside, you know is inevitable."

Is he a mind reader?

He tilts his head back a touch, so his eyes are level with mine. "How did I do?"

My eyes drift to his mouth. His full perfect lips. *God, I want to taste them again.*

Focus, Andi.

I force my eyes away, and with a shrug of the shoulder, I say, "You did…meh."

Meh? Jesus, what the hell was that?

I'm dying right now.

Fucking dying.

I close my eyes on a long blink. When I open them, I see a smile has kicked up the corners of his mouth while his eyes continue to fuck the hell out of me.

"Meh?" Low laughter rumbles in his chest. "Jesus, Andressa. Well, deny it all you want, but you know it's true. You want me to fuck you."

"And you want to fuck me," I fire back.

"Sure I do. I'm not the one denying it here." He lifts his hand from my waist to cup my cheek, his thumb touching dangerously close to my lips. "So, what do you say?"

"To what?"

"Fucking."

"I'd say you're seriously overconfident about it."

He throws his head back on a deep laugh. It makes me glow inside.

A smile is still touching his eyes when he says, "You say that now. It'll be a different story afterward."

"Won't I be calling you a bastard afterward?" I refer to our earlier conversation.

"Probably. But do you care about that right now?"

Do I?

I shake my head before even realizing what I'm doing.

I see lust burst to life in his eyes, and I feel it in every part of me.

We're still dancing, but I don't feel so awkward anymore. Now, I just feel turned on like I never have before. I feel connected to him. So very connected. Attuned to his body.

My skin is burning hot like a furnace. My hands are itching to touch him in places I really shouldn't.

His fingers slide into my hair, and it feels like heaven. He moves closer to me, leaving hardly any space between us.

"I love your hair down."

There's a low groan to his voice that makes my belly quiver, in turn making me want to pull him in the rest of the way. Bring him in to the point where I don't know where he begins and I end.

He twists strands of my hair around his fingers. "From the moment I saw you in the garage, bent over my car with your hair tied up, I haven't been able to get the image out of my mind of me unraveling it and getting my hands all tangled up in it while I fuck you—hard."

Sweet Jesus.

"Carrick..." My fingers curl into the lapel of his jacket.

What am I going to say? Stop talking to me this way?

I'm not sure if I can because I don't think I want him to stop—ever.

"I...this isn't a good idea." My voice is breathy. I don't sound like me at all.

"The best ones usually aren't. Now, tell me to kiss you."

"I..." *Say no. No good can come of this.* "No." But my voice trembles, betraying me. *Stupid voice.*

"Stop fighting this...*me*...and just say it, Andressa." His words are whispered, coaxing, and his mouth is so close to mine, a hairbreadth between us.

My lips are aching for his. The memory of our kiss in China explodes in my brain, kicking all my hormones to life.

But he's my friend. And he's a driver.

Do I really want to go there with him?

Yes, I really do. I'm tired of fighting my feelings for him.

I want him to kiss me. Actually, I want him to fuck me—for hours.

Rationality has left me. Gone. Buggered off. And I couldn't give a shit right now.

If I lose my job, so be it. All I care about is having Carrick kiss me, touch me, and make me feel amazing, so

I'll forget all the reasons why I shouldn't be doing this with him.

Which, I know he'll be more than capable of the instant I let him.

"Carrick…"

"Say it."

"Kiss me."

I feel his chest jump on a breath. His fingers tighten in my hair. I close my eyes with anticipation.

His lips ever so gently touch the corner of mine, pressing a soft kiss there.

My heart is pounding.

I feel the tip of his tongue as it touches my lips, gently running across the seam, tasting me. My lips part, a soft moan escaping.

We're both breathing heavily. His warm breath mixes with my own, the smooth scent of whiskey and his rich aftershave teasing my senses.

I open my eyes to find his blues burning into mine, so intense that his stare breaks me down until all that's left is need.

Pure need.

It ripples through me. I'm now his for whatever he wants to do with me.

Everyone and everything around us disappears. All I can see is him.

All I know is how badly I want him.

I've never needed to be kissed by anyone as desperately as I need to be kissed by him now.

I slip my hand around the back of his neck. "I want you," I whisper softly.

Something hot and intense flashes through his eyes. Then, his lips slam down on mine. His hand fists my hair, and his fingers grip my waist, holding me to him, as he devours my mouth in the most intense kiss I've ever experienced.

All of the built-up tension between us, from the moment I met him to our kiss in China and every moment since, is exploding right here, right now.

His tongue slides along mine, a groan vibrating through his chest, and I feel it between my legs.

The rough of his growing stubble is erotically scratching against my skin. His hand finds my bum, and he holds it firm as he presses his hips into mine.

Holy God.

He's hard.

Really hard.

And I have to have him. Now.

Nothing but having Carrick inside me matters right now. The world could end, and I wouldn't give a shit as long as I got to have sex with him first.

Honestly, it's taking everything in me not to unzip his trousers right now and examine just exactly what I'm going to be getting.

We need to be in a room alone in the next few minutes, or I might actually die.

Carrick must be thinking the exact same thing because he breaks away from me, panting heavily, eyes blazing into mine. His gruff, sexy-as-hell voice asks, "You wanna get out of here?"

A smile teases my lips as my head tilts to the side. "Is that a trick question?"

He grins the sexiest grin I've ever seen, and before my knickers can excuse themselves from the party, he grabs my hand and practically drags me out of there and in the direction of his waiting car.

Twelve

🏁 BARCELONA, SPAIN

THE DRIVE BACK TO THE HOTEL is fraught with tension—well, on my part anyway. I'm restless and arguing with myself in my head about what a bad idea this is versus what an awesome idea it is.

With Jason Derulo's "The Other Side" playing in the car, the bad-idea theory is starting to win out.

If Carrick was keeping me busy right now and actually had his hands or mouth on me, then I wouldn't be thinking about anything else, except for him, but that's not currently the case.

Surprisingly, the only part of me that Carrick is touching is my hand, which is held firmly in his, and not in a sexy-fingers-linked way. No, he's holding my hand like my mum used to when I was a little kid.

Add to that, our hands are resting on the leather seat—in the very notable gap between us—which he put there, might I add, and I'm left feeling like I'm on one of those awkward first dates. You know, the blind-date kind where the guy's not really into you, but he feels like he has to hold your hand out of obligation while he counts down the minutes until the date is over.

Yeah, I'm kind of there right now.

I'm actually starting to wonder if this is *the* Carrick Ryan—famed womanizer—sitting beside me, or some testosterone-missing clone put in his place. He's not behaving like the same guy I was just kissing at the party.

By the time the car pulls up outside our hotel, I'm about sixty percent sure that I'll back out of having sex with him.

But…I just keep getting flashes of him kissing me, and I can still taste him on my tongue and smell his aftershave on my skin. It keeps swaying me back to keeping my mouth shut and to just go with the flow.

We climb out of the car. Carrick places his hand on my lower back, guiding me inside the hotel. Okay, here's something. It might be the smallest of touches, but it feels like the most intimate.

And I'm right back to the awesome.

When we reach the elevators, he guides me into a waiting one. Once safely inside, he presses the button for his floor.

I watch as the door slides shut, and my heart starts to race at the knowledge that we're finally going to be alone.

This is it. He's going to ravish me the second those doors slide closed, shutting the rest of the world out.

Only…they're shut now. The lift's ascending, and he hasn't made a move, not a frigging move.

Okay, what the hell is going on?

I saw him in China…with that woman. The thought of it makes me want to vomit. But his hands were everywhere. Everywhere! He was all over her like white on rice, but with me, nothing. Not a bloody thing!

He definitely fancies me. That I do know. So, why?

Maybe he just thought she was hotter than me. Maybe *she* got him hotter than I do.

Oh God. Now, I definitely do feel sick.

Should I do something? Make a move? Does he want me to be more sexually forward? Maybe that's what gets his motor revving. I just always got the impression that Carrick is all about being in charge, alpha to the max, but maybe I'm wrong.

I glance across at him, trying to get a read on him, and see that his hands are flexing restlessly at his sides. As my eyes slide from east to west, I catch sight of a definite bulge straining against his zipper.

Okay, so he's still hard for me. Then, why? I just don't get it.

Oh God. Maybe he's changed his mind. He might be hard because he's a sex maniac, but he might have realized that this isn't a good idea with us being friends and me working for him, and he doesn't know how to tell me.

Mortification starts to lick my skin.

Okay, I have to say something before my head explodes.

"Carrick…" My voice carries loud in the quiet confines of the elevator. "Look, if you've changed your mind about this—you and me—it's fine." Well, it's not fine. I'll probably die of humiliation and never be able to look him in the face again. *But what else can I say? Please shag me out of pity?* Not likely. "I mean, it's probably not a good idea for us to sleep togeth—"

The rest of my words are yanked from my mouth as I'm wrenched up hard against his body. Then, I'm spun around, none too gently, and pinned against the wall.

Grabbing my hand, he presses it against his straining zipper. "Does this feel like I've changed my mind?"

My breathing hitches, and my heart starts to pound against my ribs. "N-no," I stammer.

My fingers curl around his cock on instinct.

A hiss escapes him, his eyes closing, as he rests his forehead against mine. "So, why the fuck would you ask me that?"

"Because, in China, when I saw you with that woman in the elevator, you seemed…more into her." I cringe on the last part. Ugh, I hate how vulnerable I sound and that he's seeing how much that night affected me.

"Jesus…Andressa." Moving his head back, he takes my face in his hands, his eyes burning mine. "You think because I'm not nailing you in this elevator right now that I don't want you?"

"I don't know. It's stupid. Just forget I said anything."

I try to move away, but he's not letting me go anywhere.

His eyes turn dark and serious. "You couldn't be more wrong. I want you so fucking badly that I can't see straight. I haven't been able to since the moment I laid eyes on you. That's the fucking problem. You think I wanted her more than I do you? I didn't want her at all. I wanted you *then* and every day before and every day since. All I want is *you*. I was holding back just now—and trust me, it's been taking every ounce of strength I have to do so—because you deserve better than me feeling you up in an elevator." He runs his thumb over my lower lip, his eyes darkening further.

"You're worth so much more." He replaces his thumb with his lips, giving me the softest of kisses, sucking gently on my lower lip, making my body go lax. "But if I'd known for one second that it would make you think this way, then I'd have done whatever you wanted me to." Another butterfly kiss. "I'd have fucked you in here." And another. "I'll fuck you wherever you want me to." One more. "And then, I'll take you to my bed and fuck you all night long."

Sweet baby Jesus. What the hell am I supposed to say to that?

The elevator comes to a stop on his floor, the door opening.

"So, what's it gonna be? Are we starting in here or in my bed?"

I stare at him. So many thoughts and emotions are running through my mind, but I don't know which to grab a hold of first.

So, I run with the only thing I know for certain right now.

I don't want to be an elevator hook-up.

"Take me to your room."

Slipping his hand into mine, he leads me out of there. The short walk down the hall to his room is a killer. My heart is pounding like a jackhammer with each step I take.

This is it. I'm going to have sex with Carrick.

Holy shit! This is so not a good idea. But damn if it isn't going to feel good.

He slots his key card in the door, and he pushes it open. Then, I'm unceremoniously yanked in and shoved up against the wall.

He kicks the door shut with his foot. "The time for holding back is over," he growls. "I'm gonna fuck you good and hard." Then, his mouth descends on mine, leading me into the wettest, dirtiest, hottest kiss I've ever had.

My fingers curl into the hair at the back of his neck, a low moan escaping me.

Carrick's hand finds its way to my leg via the nicely placed split in my dress. His fingers slide up my inner thigh, causing me to gasp.

My skin is burning up. My breasts are swollen. And I know I'm more than ready for him.

I just need him to keep touching me, kissing me. I don't ever want him to stop. I've never been this needy…this desperate for a man before.

Kissing him like I'm starved for him, I fumble to unbutton his dinner jacket. Popping the last one open, I slide my hands up his hard chest, pushing the jacket off his shoulders. His hands leave me for what feels like the longest second as he frees his arms from its confines, throwing his jacket to the floor. Then, his hands are back on me. The same hand is back inside my dress, but this time, his hand is on my arse, grabbing and kneading. His other hand is fisting my hair while he presses teasing hot kisses down my neck. And when I feel the erotic flick of his hot tongue against my skin, I almost come undone.

"No matter how sexy you look in it, the dress needs to go," he says gruffly.

I expect him to undress me here, but he doesn't. He takes me by the hand and leads me through the darkened suite, into the bedroom.

Leaving me by the end of the bed, he turns the lamp on, illuminating us.

Turning back to me, he smiles. It makes my stomach flip. He just looks so beautiful. My fingers are itching to be back on him. Well, all of me is itching to be back on him actually.

But he isn't moving. He's just standing there, staring at me.

Does he want me to go to him?

"What?" I whisper, my chest suddenly feeling tight. I can't ever remember anyone looking at me like this before. Like I'm the ultimate prize.

"Nothing." He blinks slowly, shaking his head. "You're just...so fucking beautiful."

Smooth talker. "Oh, you're good." I smirk.

He grins, tilting his head to the side. "And I'm about to get a whole lot better."

With promise and mischief sparking in those blues of his, he advances toward me, making my body tremble with need.

"Turn around." The quiet command in his voice has me practically melting at his feet.

Brushing my hair aside, he kisses my shoulder—his teeth grazing, making me squirm—as his hands smooth down my sides. Gripping me at the waist, he presses his erection against my bum. Leaning back, I rest my head on his shoulder as his hands slide up my stomach, coming up to cup my breasts through my dress.

My nipples are embarrassingly hard, and I groan when his thumbs press against them through the fabric.

"I need to see you." Urgent words brush my ear, causing me to shiver.

Skilled fingers find the zipper on my dress. He slides it down, the sound loudly erotic in the silence of the bedroom.

When he reaches the bottom, his hands come back up, and he slips his fingers under the straps of my dress and pushes them off my shoulders.

My breathing is so loud that it must sound like I have a microphone taped to my lips.

The dress slips down my body, Carrick's hands following its descent. When the fabric is pooling at my feet, he whispers, "Andressa…"

I look back over my shoulder at him, biting my lip. The look in his eyes is nearly enough to bring me to my knees.

Slowly, I turn to him. I watch his eyes widen as they travel down the length of me.

"Fuck…" he breathes hoarsely, his eyes meeting mine.

I thought his look was intense before, but it had nothing on this. The air is knocked from my lungs.

"Red is now officially my new favorite color." Reaching out, his fingertip traces the edge of my bra. "I'm the luckiest bastard on the planet. God, Andressa, I have never seen anything like you before in my life."

His words leave a mark on my insides.

To pull us back to where we are, I lean in and press a hot kiss to his lips. "Well, you'd better make the most of me then."

Something I can't discern flashes through his eyes, but it's gone as quickly as it came.

His fingers slide up into my hair. "Oh, I plan on doing a lot to you."

"Likewise. Now, strip. It's my turn to see you."

A knowing grin brings up his lips. He takes a step back from me, giving me ample view. He removes his bow tie and his fingers go to the buttons on his shirt as he toes his shoes off.

I move to step out of my heels when his gruff voice says, "Keep the heels on."

A definite throb starts between my legs.

Carrick pulls off his shirt with the confidence that only a man with a face like his can, and mother of God…I've hit the jackpot.

Never in my life have I seen a man who has a body like his.

Trousers hang low on his slim hips. My eyes devour the inches upon inches of smooth golden skin covering one, two, three, four, five…yep, a rippling six-pack, and sweet mother of Jesus, thank you! He has the V! I feel like I should take a photo just so I can look at it later when I'm alone.

He starts to unzip his trousers, cockiness still in his stance. But then, if I looked like him, I'd be the cockiest bastard on the planet.

The sound of his zipper lowering is agonizingly slow. I bite my lip with anticipation.

He drops his trousers.

And my mouth falls open.

Holy…cock.

It's big and thick and straining upward like a prayer. I feel like I should get down on my knees and beg for mercy.

"Like what you see?"

Biting my lip again, I lift my gaze. He's wearing the sexiest grin I've ever seen in my life. And the throbbing between my thighs intensifies to epic proportions.

I tilt my head to the side. "Does it work as good as it looks?"

The grin reaches his eyes, kicking up his brow. "Better."

The next thing I know, I'm in his arms, and he's kissing me deep and hard, his tongue sliding against mine. His hands grab my behind, and he lifts me. I wrap my legs around his waist.

I don't feel as tall as I am when I'm with Carrick. He's so male, so fucking confident in everything he does, that he makes me feel feminine.

But scariest of all is how vulnerable he makes me feel.

Somehow, we end up on the bed with me on my back and Carrick firmly situated between my legs.

Our kiss becomes harder, bordering aggressive. I put that down to the sexual tension that's been building between us for weeks.

His hand pulls the cup of my bra down, his thumb brushing over my sensitive nipple. I gasp, my hips jerking against him with need.

Seeming to enjoy my reaction, he breaks from our kiss, leaving me breathless, as he kisses his way down to the breast he just exposed.

When his lips close around my nipple, I all but orgasm.

"You like that?" he asks hoarse.

My response comes out somewhere between a moan and a whimper.

Then, he's getting to his feet.

I blink up at him standing there in all his godlike glory.

His hand wraps around my ankle, lifting my leg. Fingers sliding along my skin, he slips my shoe off and drops it to the floor. He presses a soft kiss to my instep, and my belly quivers. He removes my other shoe, tossing it over his shoulder.

Leaning over me, he hooks his fingers into my knickers and stares deep into my eyes. "Are you ready for me, Andressa?"

"Yes," falls from my lips in a breathy whisper.

As he pulls my knickers down, I lift my hips to give him purchase.

Not bothering to wait for him, I remove my bra, throwing it to the floor behind me.

I know the instant he sees my bare breasts for the first time because his eyes flash hot, like someone just struck a match behind them. Then, he lets out a rough-sounding growl, and that's when things get a little crazy. He's back on me, pinning me to the bed and kissing the hell out of me, while his hand cups my breast, pinching my nipple with just the right pressure. His other hand slips between us.

I almost come out of my skin at the first touch of his fingers on me.

"Fuck…" he groans. "You're soaked."

I should feel embarrassed, but I'm not. All I feel with him is…everything. Everything I shouldn't.

"I kinda want you…a lot," I admit in a whisper.

Lustful eyes meet mine. "I kinda want you, too. You have no idea just how fucking badly."

Lifting my head, I press a kiss to his lips as my hand reaches down and wraps around his bare cock, something I've wanted to do for a while now. He's scorching hot to the touch.

A groan escapes him.

"By the feel of it, I'd say you want me really, really bad," I murmur huskily against his mouth

I feel his responding grin. "And I'm gonna really, really take you." He pushes a finger inside me, driving up until he's touching his knuckle.

My legs shamelessly fall open on a whimper, and he starts to fuck me with his finger, his thumb rubbing over my clit.

"God, yes," I moan as my body begins to coil and tighten, starting the climb toward the amazing orgasm I know he's soon going to give me.

"You're so fucking sexy. That's it, babe. God, I'm going to fuck the hell out of your tight body all night long," he says rough.

I have no doubt about that. Carrick Ryan might be fast on the tracks, but I'm betting he takes his sweet time in the sack.

Pushing my fingers into his hair, I grip the strands as his mouth descends back to my nipple, sucking hard.

A jolt rushes through my body, going straight to my sex. "Yes!"

"Are you close, Andressa?"

"Yes, oh God, yes. Don't stop..." I beg.

Then, his fingers are gone, and I'm left cold.

"Que porra é essa?" I cry out. Yes, that came out in Portuguese. I do that sometimes when I'm surprised or pissed off.

"What did you just say?" There's a low growl to his voice that shivers right through me.

"I said, 'What the fuck?' When I said, 'Don't stop,' in English, did you somehow hear *that* in a foreign language?" I let out a huff of annoyance.

He rumbles out a deep laugh. "Andressa, I stopped because the first time you come, I'm going to be inside you. I want to feel your orgasm, not see it."

First time? There's going to be more than one?

"And you can speak your Brazilian filth to me while I fuck you as well."

My mouth drops open. He's such a...Neanderthal! But God...so hot.

Carrick reaches to the nightstand and gets a condom from the drawer. I try not to think of how many of the condoms from that pack have already been used on other women.

He has the condom on in record time, and he is back on me, pinning my body with his with my hands above my head. Without another word, he thrusts inside me.

I gasp at the fullness of him, my body tensing around him.

He stills, his whole body rigid, and his eyes close tight, almost like he's in pain. "Jesus...you're so fucking tight."

His eyes open, and the look in them makes my breath catch and my heart pound.

"How long has it really been?" He knows my little I-said-I-haven't-been-in-a-relationship-in-two-years-not-that-I-haven't-been-with-anyone speech at the party was bullshit.

I close my eyes. "A while…but not long enough to seal me back up to virgin status. Maybe you're just really big." I push a smile onto my lips as I lift my legs and slide them around his back.

I feel his responding chuckle vibrate through me. "Not arguing with you there, babe. But tell me, how long? I want to know." He brushes his lips over mine, making me quiver with need.

I open my eyes to his, a blush creeping on my cheeks. I'm not used to talking about past conquests with present guys, especially not with one who is currently inside me. "Eighteen months or so."

"How is that even possible?" He shakes his head, disbelieving. "Not that I'm complaining."

I shrug, looking away. "Honestly, I don't know. There just hasn't been anyone I wanted to sleep with, I guess."

That brings a cocky grin to his face, "Yet here I am." He nudges his hips against mine, pushing his cock in further.

Holding back a moan, I playfully swat his arm. "Are we gonna talk about my sexual history all night? Or are you actually going to fuck me?"

Bringing his face down to mine again, he kisses me, nipping my lower lip with his teeth. He licks the sting away. "Oh, I'm definitely going to fuck you." He pulls out and slams back in hard but then stills again.

Releasing my hands, he traps my head between his forearms, his fingers threading into my hair. He stares down at me, and something in his expression changes. I get the sudden feeling of falling.

"Andressa, this…with you, is so much better than I ever imagined it could be."

My breath catches, leaving me feeling off balance. I close my eyes.

"Just...fuck me, Carrick...please."

"Open your eyes."

The moment I do, he pulls out of me and then, drives back inside, all the while holding my stare. "Is this what you want?"

"Yes," I moan.

His grip on my hair tightens as he starts to fuck me, slamming in and out, my body pinned to the bed by his.

"More...harder," I beg.

Dipping his head, he kisses me with all the desperation I know I'm feeling as he pounds in and out of me, giving me exactly what I want.

Then, he's kneeling up and taking hold of my leg, moving it around to the other side of his body. Tilting my hips, he starts up again, this time with slower thrusts. His fingers find me, and he starts to tease my clit.

"Carrick..." I moan.

"That's it, babe." His voice is raw and raspy as his tempo increases, moving in and out of me with confident hard thrusts.

Then, without warning, I'm coming, crying out his name. It's like a mirror of explosions, all ricocheting off one another, never-ending, creating the most amazing orgasm I've ever had.

"Jesus..."

I blink open my eyes at the tone in Carrick's voice. His eyes are on me and filled with what I think is awe.

"What?" I whisper shyly. *Was I too loud?* I've been known to be quite vocal at times.

"Nothing." He shakes his head, blinking rapidly. "You just...I've never...felt anything like that before."

I suddenly have this feeling like someone is standing on my chest.

I place my hand over the ache.

Leaning in, he kisses me again, deeply, his tongue tangling with mine.

The next thing I know, he's breaking away from my lips, and I'm moving, being lifted up. Carrick sits back on his haunches, bringing me with him to sit in his lap, with my back against his chest and my legs on either side of his.

And he does all of that while keeping his cock inside me. The man is a goddamn magician.

"Ride me," he groans in my ear as his hands slide up to cup my breasts. He starts to tease my nipples, gently tugging on them.

My head falls back, desire flooding me. Gripping his arms for support, I rise up on my knees, feeling his cock easily glide out of me, and then I slam back down on him.

"Fuck. Yeah, just like that," he growls, his grip on my breasts increasing.

Feeling empowered at how I'm making him feel, I start to ride him like I'm a goddamn porn star. Okay, maybe porn star is pushing it, but I'm doing a damn fine job, if I do say so myself, and Carrick seems like he's enjoying it from the words of heated praise he keeps groaning in my ear.

His hand slips between my legs, his fingers touching my clit again, but I'm still overly sensitive from my epic orgasm only minutes ago.

I press my hand to his, stopping him. "Carrick, no, I can't again—"

"Hush," he admonishes. "You can, and you will. I want to feel you come again."

He sounds so fucking hot when he's being dominant that I don't even argue. I just remove my hand from his and let him work his magic.

And wouldn't you know it? In record time, I'm right back there, climbing the precipice to heaven.

"Carrick…" I whimper. I need to press my legs together to somehow relieve the pressure yet part them and never have him stop.

Without warning, I'm lifted off him and flipped onto my back. Then, Carrick's head is between my legs, and his mouth is on me.

"Oh my God!" I cry out, my hands gripping his head.

He pushes his tongue where his cock was only moments ago. Then, he's sucking on my clit and wrenching my second orgasm of the night from me in seconds, leaving me yelling his name and my body dropping lax into the bed.

He climbs up my body, hands on the bed, and he hovers over me.

I stare up at him in wonderment.

His lips are glistening with me, his eyes dark, the skin on his face taut. He looks like a man holding on to the edge of control, which is fast slipping away. He runs his tongue over his lower lip, tasting me. It's the most erotic thing I've ever seen.

I raise my hips to his, letting him know what I want—him back inside me. Honestly, I never want him to leave.

Gripping my hip, he pushes that amazing cock of his in, shoving right up to the hilt. His hand moves from my hip to cup my behind, angling me up, so he can slide deeper.

I watch him with fascination as he fucks me, revealing in how truly beautiful he is, even more so as he reaches that moment where all sense is gone, and the only thing that matters now is reaching orgasm. Pure animalistic fucking.

"Fuck! Andressa…" he says, drawing out my name, his body shuddering. The veins in his neck are straining, his eyes closing as if it's all too much, while he rides out his orgasm inside me.

When he's finished, his head drops to my shoulder, panting. We're both sticky with sweat, desperately trying to catch our breaths.

Oh my God, I just had sex with Carrick! Hot, sweaty sex…and it was amazing!

Lifting his head from my shoulder, he cradles my face in his hands and kisses me. "I'm just gonna go clean up," he murmurs.

I give a gentle nod, and then he's slipping out of me, leaving me feeling oddly empty.

I watch as he walks to the bathroom, loving the sight of his tight arse, and I'm surprised to see that Carrick has a tattoo on his back. A really large tattoo of what looks to be a fallen angel.

Maybe that's what he is—my fallen angel.

No! Stop thinking like that. Carrick isn't your anything, and he never will be.

Once the bathroom door has closed, I cover my face with my hands and let out a muted squeal.

Holy shit! I just had amazing sex with Carrick, like porn star sex—only better!

Okay, deep breaths…calm. He'll be back in a minute.

I hear water running in the bathroom. Moving my hands from my face, I stare up at the ceiling, forcing my breaths to even out.

The adrenaline is starting to fade. I retrace those words in my head again.

I had sex with Carrick.

Oh God. I slept with a driver. The very one I work for.

I had sex with my friend.

All of my promises to myself, and I break them in the most epic way.

What's going to happen now?

The bathroom door opens, revealing Carrick, before my panic can properly set in.

I sit up. Bringing my knees to my chest, I wrap my arms around them.

Carrick's gaze is soft on me.

I feel that softness deep inside of me, like a gentle caress, and it scares the shit out of me.

I see that he has a washcloth in his hand.

"I thought you might want to clean up," he explains, walking over to the bed.

"Thanks."

I reach for the cloth, but instead of giving it to me, he gently parts my legs with one hand and presses the cloth to me with the other.

Bloody hell. No wonder he has so many women wanting to stay with him if he cares for them like this—aside from the obvious hotness that is Carrick and the amazing sex and orgasms he gives, of course.

All of the guys I've slept with have rolled over and gone to sleep the second they were done, leaving me to fend for myself.

I watch his face while he cleans me. The way his long lashes brush his cheekbones each time he blinks. The multitude of blue hues, which all blend together to make his stunning eye color. He's perfect.

Carrick suddenly looks up, catching me staring, making my cheeks stain. Holding my gaze, he leans in and presses a soft kiss to my lips.

My heart actually skips a beat. *Stupid heart.*

He tosses the cloth onto the dresser and climbs on the bed beside me. He cages me in with his long legs, his arms coming around me, and he presses a kiss to my shoulder.

I feel kind of awkward now. I mean, he's being really sweet and everything, but I'm not sure what I should do. Of course I've had one-night stands before but never with someone who's my friend…someone I work for, whom I have to see again in a few hours' time.

Should I leave?

Yes, I probably should go. Carrick doesn't do repeats, and I shouldn't have done this in the first place, no matter how amazing it was. And he has a race tomorrow. He needs his rest.

Resting my chin on my shoulder, I look at him. "I should go. Let you get some sleep. You have a race tomorrow."

His brow furrows. "No, stay." He swallows a breath. "I really want you to stay."

I bite my lip, scared by how much I do want to stay with him. I really shouldn't…but I don't seem to have it in me to fight my wants versus what's right in this moment. "Okay." I smile gently.

Warmth fills his eyes.

I move so he can pull the covers back. I climb inside. He gets in next to me, lying down and facing me. He brushes my hair back from my forehead.

It feels intimate.

I know, with everything we just did, and I say him brushing hair from my face feels intimate, but it just somehow does, so much more than the hot sex.

"I didn't know you had a tattoo," I say, trying to change the direction of my thoughts.

"Yeah."

"When did you get it done?"

"A week after I signed with Formula One. It was my present to myself."

"Youngest ever driver to sign. I'd have thought you'd have bought a house or something extravagant like that."

"Buying a house was the last thing on my mind back then." He smiles.

"Yeah, I guess partying and women were at the forefront." *They still are.*

The smile drops from his face, and he looks away. "Something like that. Anyway, I wasn't the youngest driver. I was the same age as William Wolfe when he signed with Formula One."

Hearing Carrick say my father's name jolts me, reminding me why I shouldn't be here in his bed. My heart starts to pound.

"Hey, you okay?" His fingers touch my cheek.

"Fine." I force a smile, trying to calm my racing heart. "Can I have a look at your tattoo?" I need him to stop touching me, stop looking at me the way he is. It's too much.

"Sure." Carrick rolls onto his stomach, so I straddle his back, sitting on him.

The tattoo is of a fallen angel. A man is bowing down, head lowered, his wings shielding his body. There's script right above it, spanning the length of his shoulder blades.

PAIN IS TEMPORARY. VICTORY IS FOREVER.

It's beautiful.

I trace my finger over it. "It's beautiful, Carrick." *Just like you.*

He lifts his head from the pillow and looks back at me, chuckling. "Never tell a man that his tattoo is beautiful, babe. Tell him it's badass but never beautiful."

"Sorry." I laugh. "It's totally badass." I put on a gruff voice, trying to sound dude-like. "It's the most *badass-ist* tattoo I've ever seen."

"*Badass-ist?*" He raises a brow.

"It's a word." I grin. "Well, in my world it is anyway."

"You're crazy." He laughs, making me smile. Reaching back, he wraps a hand around my wrist and tugs me forward. I fall off his body to the mattress, lying beside him. Lifting up, he pulls me to him and maneuvers me beneath his body. He frames my face in his hands. "But I really, really like Andressa Amaro's crazy world—a lot."

My heart and head collide, causing panic to ripple through me, but it's all swallowed up by his kiss. And the exact moment his tongue slides against mine, everything disappears, except for him.

He kisses me for what seems like forever. Gentle and tender. And I don't ever want him to stop.

When he finally does stop, lifting his face from mine, he gives me such a look of want that my heart actually aches.

I can't fall for him. I can't.

"I should get some sleep if I want to win tomorrow," he says on a stifled yawn.

"Of course." My voice trembles. If he notices, he doesn't say anything.

He reaches over and turns the light off. Then, he pulls me to him. Tucking me into his side, he tangles his legs up with mine. He presses a kiss to my forehead. "Night, babe," he murmurs, his voice already sounding sleepy.

"Night," I whisper, my eyes still wide open.

Thirteen

BARCELONA, SPAIN

I AWAKE WITH A START. It's still dark out, but the sun is starting to rise. And there's a warm solid body wrapped around me.

Carrick.

I'm in his bed.

And we had sex.

Amazing hot sex.

Images flash through my mind of the night before, making me tingle in all the right places. But what also comes with those images and tingles, now that the champagne and sex-crazed hormones have worn off, is a mixture of regret and concern.

I slept with Carrick.

A driver.

I broke my cardinal rule.

Shit. Shit. Shit.

I can't believe I did that. Well, I can believe it…but you know what I mean.

And worst of all, I'm feeling things I shouldn't be. Like how amazing his body feels wrapped around mine and the desire to never leave.

Wanting more. Wanting him. Again and again.

Oh God.

I can't think this way. Not that Carrick would ever want to be with me long-term. He's a wham-bam-thank-you-ma'am kind of guy. But this is about me, what I'm feeling for him. That's the problem. I can't be crushing on him.

And right now, here in his arms, I'm way too comfortable. It's time for me to go.

Carefully, I slide my leg out from between his. Holding my breath, I wait to make sure that I haven't woken him. When I'm sure he's still asleep, I lift his arm and slide out of bed like I'm some kind of ninja.

Staring down at him in the dark, I resist the urge to brush back the hair falling across his forehead.

He's beautiful.

And I really need to get the hell out of here.

I step away from the bed, and being as quiet as humanly possible, I tiptoe around, picking up my discarded clothing.

Taking them with me, I go into the living room and dress quietly and quickly.

Remembering that my clutch is still in Carrick's jacket pocket, I retrieve it from where we left it in the entryway last night in my haste to get it off him.

Memories of last night flood my mind. Carrick kissing me in this very spot, touching me…how much I wanted him. My body starts to ache to go back to him, to curl myself around him and never let go.

It would be so easy to take this dress back off, go in there, slide back into his arms, and wait to see what would happen when he wakes up.

But I can't.

So, I hang his jacket up on the hook. And with my heels and clutch in hand, I quietly let myself out of his suite.

I go to the elevator. The hotel is dead. I check the time on my phone—6:03 a.m.

When the elevator arrives, I get in the empty space and press the button to my floor.

Padding barefoot down the hall to my room—thankfully not seeing a soul—I slot the key card in the door, trying to be as quiet as possible, so not to wake Petra. But the sound of the lock clicking open sounds really loud in the quiet.

Closing the door softly behind me, I move through the room, placing my shoes on the floor in the entryway. I put my clutch and key card down on the dresser.

"Seeing as though you're coming home at the crack of dawn, I'll take it that you had a good night?"

"Jesus!" I nearly jump out of my skin at the sound of Petra's voice. "You frightened the shit out of me!" My heart is pounding like a bitch.

Laughing, she clicks the lamp on, temporarily blinding us both, and then she rolls over in bed to face me. "So, you shagged Carrick then?" She has the smuggest grin on her face.

Sitting down on the edge of my bed, I dig my toes into the carpet, and lift my shoulders, giving nothing away.

"Uh-uh. No way, missy. Spill. I need something to brighten my morning. I had a shit time last night."

"Why? What happened?" I lift my head, concern furrowing my brow, knowing she went out with the boys last night.

"Oh, nothing major." She waves it off. "It was just crap without you there, and Robbie was being a twat, like usual."

I get a little glow, on the knowledge that she thinks her night would have been better with me there. "You know Robbie fancies you, right?" I grin.

"What? Robbie? No, he doesn't...does he?" She meets my smiling eyes.

"Of course he does. It's totally obvious from the way he looks at you all the time, all moon-eyed."

She gives a little humph. "So, why does he act like a twat around me then?"

"Because...he's a man." I give a helpless shrug. I have zero clue as to why men are the way they are.

"Speaking of men and their weird ways—nice diversion tactic with Robbie, by the way—Carrick. Spill. I want deets."

On a sigh, I say, "Yes, I had sex with him."

"I knew you wouldn't be able to resist him! Was he awesome? I've heard he fucks like a porn star."

God, he absolutely does. But I don't say that. I just stare down at my nicely painted fingernails.

"Oh my God. Was he bad?" She sounds aghast. Her hand is clamped over her mouth, eyes wide.

"No," I hasten to say. "He was…great. Amazing." *Like nothing I've ever known before.* "I just…I think I made a mistake by sleeping with him."

"Why?" She gets out of bed and comes to sit by me. "Was he an arse afterward?"

"No, not at all. He was really sweet in fact, but I just…" I let out a sigh and rub my face.

"Are you worried that you'll lose your job?"

My eyes widen with the shock of her words, worry hitting me full throttle. "Well, I wasn't, but I am now. Do you think I'll lose my job because I slept with him?"

"No," she quickly says. "Amy only lost her job because it ended up in the news, and it was so close to all the Rich and Charlotte shit going down. There's no way you'll lose your job. John wouldn't let it happen."

"Yeah, I guess." I sigh.

"So, what's worrying you then? I mean, how did you guys leave it?"

"Um…well, we didn't exactly leave it. Afterward, he asked me to stay, and we fell asleep. Then, I woke up, and Carrick was sleeping, so…I just kinda…left."

"Oh my God! You snuck out!" She cackles. "Well, that makes a change. A woman sneaking out on Carrick. It's usually him doing the running."

I slide a glance to her. "You think he'll be mad?"

"Nah, he's...Carrick," she says his name as though it's an explanation. "But...he asked you to stay over after you guys had sex?" The tone of her voice has changed to surprise and curiosity.

"Mmhmm." I start to chew on my thumbnail.

Petra swats at my hand, stopping me.

I give her a look, and then I let out another sigh. "I said I'd leave, so he could get some sleep, but he said he wanted me to stay, so I agreed."

"Wow..."

"What?"

"Well, from what I've heard, Carrick doesn't ask girls to sleep over. He usually pushes them out the door the second after he's come."

"Nice," I mutter.

But he wasn't that way with me. If anything, he was sweet.

"Do you think he *likes* you?"

I shoot her a look.

Do I?

Even if he did, it doesn't change anything.

"Nah, not like that. I mean, sure he wanted to shag me, but beyond that, we're just friends. He was probably just being nice because I work for him."

"He wasn't nice to Amy or Charlotte."

"Yeah, but they didn't work on his team. I keep his car running. Maybe he thought I might cut his brakes if he were a bastard to me." I grin, but I don't really feel it inside. Honestly, I don't know what I feel. Just talking to Petra about this has me all rattled and confused.

Petra chuckles. "I doubt that's why. I don't know. He is different with you. I've seen the way he looks at you. He might really like you, Andi."

"No." I vehemently shake my head. "Carrick's not into me in that way. He just wanted to shag me."

She stares at me for a minute with a light in her eyes, and then it dims. "Yeah, you're probably right. Just me and my romantic notions about taming bad boys. I'm getting carried away. I do love a good love story. But you're right. Carrick's not the relationship kind."

I know it's true. I all but forced her thoughts in that direction. So, why does hearing her say it bother me so much?

"So, you don't think he'll be pissed that I snuck out then?"

"Nah, he'll be fine. Guys don't get upset by that sort of stuff. It's us women who freak out if we wake up and the guy isn't there. We're more emotional about sex than they are—well, maybe barring you."

"Hey!" I playfully push her, making her laugh. "What's that supposed to mean?"

"I just mean, you're the one who snuck out on Carrick. All the women he's slept with generally hang in there until the very end, clinging on to the hope that he might offer them a little more."

"Yeah, well, I'm not like those women. I know who Carrick is and what last night was about. Anyway, I don't get involved with drivers." I get up from the bed, and retrieve my phone from my clutch. "I'm gonna hit the shower and then head into the track."

"Cool. Well, I'm going back to sleep while you have a shower. Wake me up when you're done, so I can jump in. Gotta go in and prep the food to feed the rich and obnoxious." She gets up from my bed and climbs back in hers.

I get my necklace from my vanity bag, and take it with me into the bathroom. I shut the door and turn the light on.

I set the shower to hot. Pulling the toilet seat down, I sit on it and stare down at the necklace in my hand.

I might know what last night was, and I might have been the one who left Carrick's room, but I'm not feeling as easy about it as I just made out to Petra.

It's affected me. In fact, I've never felt so affected by anything…or by someone in my whole life.

Closing my eyes, all I can see is him. I can still smell him on my skin, still feel his touch.

I just wish…
What? What do I want?
Carrick?

I almost laugh out loud at myself.

I've been wishing for too many things since Carrick came into my life. That he wasn't a driver. That I could have him.

This needs to stop.

Taking a deep breath, I steel myself and swipe the screen on my phone, bringing it to life.

Using Google, I type *William Wolfe accident* into the search engine.

Images of my father's crash flood my screen.

I feel a pain stab so sharp through my heart that it makes me gasp. But I need to look at these pictures. I need a reminder as to why I can't have Carrick. He lives a dangerous life, and I can't go through losing someone I love again.

I can't risk it.

I need to put a stop to these feelings I have growing inside of me for Carrick.

I can't fall for him. Because nothing good could ever come of it.

Even still, I fasten the necklace back around my neck and climb in the shower.

After I've showered and dressed, leaving Petra as she's getting ready, I duck out of the hotel, fearing bumping into Carrick. So, I skip breakfast there, and on my way into the track, I opt to grab a toasted bagel from a deli near the hotel.

I'm just not ready to face him yet. It's going to be awkward, and I don't know how to handle it, so for now…I'm not handling. I'm avoiding.

And quite successfully so far. I've been hiding out in the garage all morning. Carrick doesn't usually come down until right before race time, so I'm safe. I don't even dare to go to the restroom in case I see him out there.

I'm being stupid. I know I can't avoid him forever, but I just need this time to get my head straight before I face him.

I'm under his car, doing a few last checks, when I hear his voice.

My whole body freezes. And the belly of his car disappears from my view as images from last night flood my vision, making my body crackle to life.

I can hear him and Uncle John talking about the problem the car was having during yesterday's practice. It was oversteering. That was the first thing I fixed when I got in this morning.

"It's all sorted." Uncle John's voice draws closer.

That means Carrick's coming over, too. *Shit.*

"Andi fixed it. She's been here, working on it, since early this morning," Uncle John says.

"Has she now?"

There's something in Carrick's tone that I can't decipher, but his beautiful Irish brogue touches me in all the right places, making me shiver.

Touching me just like his hands did last night. His hands on me…him inside me…

Oh God. Focus, Andi. No Carrick sex thoughts.

Knowing I'm going to have to acknowledge the men standing near my legs, especially the one who saw me naked last night, I plaster on a neutral face and push myself out from under the car.

Shit.

He looks…gorgeous. Unfairly hot.

Why does he have to be so damn good-looking?

It makes things so much harder. It's not that Carrick being ugly would make it any easier because he'd still be him, and that's what I like best of all—the Carrick underneath all the pretty.

Oh, Jesus. Stop it. Stop it now.

The next thing you know, I'll be breaking into song about the blue, blue of his eyes.

Which are currently sparkling down at me. There's an unreadable expression on his face. His dirty-blond hair is all messed up, like he hasn't touched it since he left the bed—the one he shared with me.

And now, I can't stop thinking about Carrick and me in bed.

Him naked. All of that smooth golden skin. His six-pack. His huge co—

"Good morning," he says, bringing me back to my senses. His brow is lifted, and there's an unmistakable gleam in his eyes.

He knows where my mind just was.

I blush immediately. Covering up, I mutter out, "Good morning," and get to my feet.

I need to sort myself out and quick. Otherwise, Uncle John will figure me out straight away. The way I'm currently acting, I might as well have the fact that I had sex with Carrick last night written all over my face in permanent marker.

I can do this. I can be a grown-up and act like nothing has changed because really it hasn't. I just know what Carrick looks like naked. That's all.

Oh God.

"Your car's all ready." I force my eyes up to his, but I feel a jolt the instant our eyes meet. Taking a quick breath, I swallow down. "You'll have no problems. It'll handle perfectly now."

"John, you got a minute?" That's Ben calling.

"Sure. I'll catch up with you before the race." Uncle John pats Carrick on the shoulder. He goes over to Ben, who is on the other side of the garage, leaving Carrick and me alone.

I watch Uncle John go. When I bring my eyes back to Carrick's, he's still staring at me but more intensely now.

That causes my heart to ratchet up and a swarm of butterflies to invade, mercilessly attacking my insides. I'm starting to feel hot, and I have a strong urge to run away.

"So, yeah…I'd better, um…"

I start backing away, but Carrick follows me.

"Andressa"—his voice is lowered—"can we talk?"

What I should say, as a mature adult is, *Yes, of course we can talk.*

Sadly, I'm not feeling that mature right now, which is why I act like a complete child. I mutter out, "Uh…I can't right now. I need to, um…wash my hands."

I lift my dirty hands up as proof, and then before he can say another word, I hotfoot it out of there like my arse is on fire.

My heart is practically beating out of my chest by the time I make it to the restroom.

I stand at the sink, my hands trembling.

Jesus, what the hell is wrong with me? Why can't I just talk to him?

Because you're scared of what he's going to say.

He'll say what needs to be said—that last night was a one-night stand. It's what I need to say. Because that's all it was.

Even if I wasn't who I am and I could be with him, this is Carrick. He doesn't have girlfriends. He has one-night stands.

I rub at the weird sensation in my chest, which has left me feeling a little breathless, and in turn, I smear more dirt onto my overalls.

I sigh at myself in the mirror.

I need to act my age and talk to him. I'm a grown-ass woman. I can have a conversation with the man I had sex with last night.

I just need to get the inevitable over with, so Carrick and I can get back to normal. Whatever our normal is.

Deciding that I'll talk to him the next time I see him, I pump out some soap into my hands with a renewed sense of purpose. I run the hot water tap and scrub my hands clean. I've just grabbed some paper towels when my phone pings a text in my pocket.

I dry my hands, dump the paper towels in the bin, and get my phone from the pocket of my overalls.

Carrick.

My heart starts to beat faster.

I don't know what the fuck that just was, but we need to talk —now. Driver's room. Two minutes.

My fingers tremble as I type out my reply.

Okay.

I look at myself in the mirror again, trying to build my courage. I give myself a pep talk. "You can do this. It'll be easy. Carrick is a player. He's well versed in one-night stands. You're both grown-ups. You can do this."

Taking a deep breath, I leave the restroom and head straight for Carrick's room.

I take another deep breath before knocking on his door.

"Come in." His gruff voice comes from the other side.

Hands trembling, I step inside before closing the door behind me.

Carrick is leaning up against the window, arms folded, eyes giving nothing away.

"Hi," I say, my voice sounding tiny.

"What the hell is going on, Andressa?"

"What do you mean?"

"I mean"—he unfurls his arms, straightening up—"that, first, I wake up to an empty bed. Then, I come down to the garage because we need to talk about last night, and you act like I've got a deadly fucking disease and run for the hills."

"I wasn't running. I had to—"

"Wash your hands. Yeah, you said." His fingers rub at his forehead, his eyes flashing impatience. "Don't bullshit me. I know when I'm being avoided."

"I'm not avoiding you." *Liar. Liar.*

He gives me a look and then a sigh. He links his hands behind his neck, tipping his head, as his eyes go to the ceiling.

I watch the muscles in his arms flex and tense, and I get a flash of him above me last night—his arms tensing beside my head as he moved inside me. It leaves me with this unfamiliar feeling in my chest.

"I thought we had a good time last night." His voice is softer, gentler, as his eyes come back to mine, his arms dropping to his sides.

I suddenly feel exposed. I wrap my arms around myself, staring past him and out the window at the city skyline beyond. "We did have a good time…"

"But?"

"But…" I exhale. "That was last night, and…well, this is today."

"What does that mean?"

"It means…I don't know, Carrick." Dropping my arms, I shrug helplessly. "I guess it means that we move on from last night and go back to where we were."

Something resembling incredulity flickers in his gaze. "You're blowing me off."

"I'm not blowing you off. I just…we slept together, and it was amazing, but…that was last night, and this is today."

"So you keep saying."

He's not making this easy, and I don't understand why. I thought he would want this. In all honesty, I thought he'd say this before I did.

I run my hand over my plait, tugging on it. "What do you want me to say?"

"Say what you mean."

"You need me to spell it out?"

"Yeah, I really do."

"Why are you being this way?"

He shrugs, and it pisses me off.

"Fine. Last night was a one-time thing, never to be repeated." It comes out sounding harsher than I mean it to. I see something that looks an awful lot like hurt flash through his eyes, and it makes me feel like a bitch. "We both had something we needed to get out of our systems, and we did that last night. Anyway, it's not like you're interested in having a relationship with anyone, and I don't get involved with drivers."

God, I wish I could. I really, really wish I could have you.

He's looking at me like he doesn't even know me. Right now, I have to agree with him. I don't recognize myself either. I'm not the girl who says these types of things.

His eyes go to the ceiling again, and he blows out a breath. "So, what happens now?"

"I don't understand what you mean."

His eyes come back to mine, his brow furrowed. "What is there not to understand? What the fuck happens now?" He enunciates the words.

I can tell he's getting angry.

It makes me squirm uncomfortably. "Well…I guess we go back to being friends."

He lets out an incredulous laugh. "You're friend-zoning me?"

I frown, displeased. "We were always friends first, Carrick."

He gives a hollow-sounding laugh. "I can't believe I'm being given the let's-be-friends speech."

"That's not what's happening here."

"No?" He gives me a direct hard stare. Then, looking away, he places his hands on the back of the chair in front of him, gripping it, and his eyes go to the floor.

It feels like forever before he looks back up at me. And when he does, I wish he hadn't because he looks cold. The warmth in his eyes that I've grown so used to is gone, and it's been replaced by something stony.

"And what if I said I don't want to be your friend?"

A sharp blow hits me, dead in the center of my chest, leaving me gasping for air.

The thought of not being friends with him…it's inconceivable. He's become too important to me in such a short space of time for me to lose him.

"Carrick…"

"Answer the fucking question." His voice is firm and resolute.

I don't know what to say. My throat feels tight. I nervously wring my hands in front of me.

I'm trying to clutch at words, but I'm getting nothing.

All I have stuck in my head is the total dismay of never being able to be close to him again…to talk to him.

I never even factored that into the equation.

Swallowing past my fear, I part my dry lips. "Then…I'd respect your wishes." *And I would spend the rest of my life missing you.*

"Of course you would." He sounds bitter.

I'm so confused as to what's going on here.

"God, Carrick, are you being this difficult because you didn't get in first to say that last night was a one-night stand? Have I bruised your ego or something? Because if that's the case, then I'll gladly step outside and come back in, so we can start all over again. Then, you could give me the one-night-stand speech." I'd do just about anything to get back to where we were.

"Yeah, that's what this is about—my bruised fucking ego," he snaps.

"I just…I don't understand you!" The anger bursts from me. I'm practically tearing my hair out here. "You sleep with women all the time. Why are you making such a big deal out of this?"

Something in his expression changes, and that's when I see his eyes close down, shutting me out. "I'm not. Whatever, Andressa. We're done here." Turning, he walks away from me and over to the window.

"Done?" Panic slaps me in the face. "Carrick, I can't lose my job over this." The words are out before I can stop them, and I know it's the wrong thing to say, but it's too late now.

I don't even know why that was the first thing out of my mouth, why I interpreted his words that way, because what I'm more afraid of is losing him from my life. That takes precedence over anything.

He turns back to me, his expression hardened. And I feel sick to my stomach.

"Wow…" A bitter laugh escapes him. "I didn't realize you thought that low of me."

"I don't. I just…I mean—" I trip over my words, trying to correct my error.

He lifts his hand, stopping me. "You still have your job. Contrary to popular belief, I do actually have some fucking integrity." He turns away from me, giving me his back. "Shut the door on your way out."

"Carrick..." I take a step toward him. "I wasn't trying to be a bitch. It's just you know...Amy and Charlotte—they both lost their jobs because they slept with you." *Why can't I stop talking?* I know I'm making it worse, but the words just keep spilling.

I see his back stiffen. Slowly turning to me, the look on his face hits me like a blast of liquid nitrogen turning me to ice.

The way he's looking at me...it's like he actually hates me.

I feel winded.

His jaw is clenched so tightly that it looks like it might shatter. "Get the fuck out, Andressa. *Now.*" The low warning in his voice is worse than any words he could have yelled at me.

Biting my lip to stop from crying, I turn to the door. Curling my trembling hand around the handle, I yank it open. Slipping out into the hall, I shut the door behind me and fall against the wall beside it.

My body is shaking, my heart racing.

Oh God. I think I just made a huge mistake.

My stomach bottoms out. I clutch a hand to it as a sob rises in my throat, but I catch it in time, covering my mouth with my hand. But I can't stop the tears from falling. I swipe at them with the back of my hand.

I can't believe I said those things to him. I need to fix this, but I know, there's no way he'll listen to me at the moment. He's too angry, and I'd probably end up saying even more dumb stuff.

Blinking rapidly and taking calming breaths, I shove my emotions down under a steel trap door for me to deal with later.

I'll let Carrick calm down, and then I'll talk to him after the race. It'll be fine. We'll be fine.

Right now, I have a job to do, and I can be a better friend to him by making sure his car is running perfectly for the race. That's what's important right now.

Taking a deep breath, I square my shoulders and make my way back downstairs to the garage.

When it comes to race time, Carrick comes down to the garage, but he doesn't look my way, and I don't try to talk to him. Now is not the time, not before his race.

He exits the garage and heads to the track to talk to the press.

When his interviews are done, a gaggle of stunning models and grid girls are fawning all over him, and he's lapping up the attention. They're all beautiful girls wearing next-to-nothing hot pants and T-shirts with advertisements splashed across their ample chests.

Seeing him with those girls stings. One particularly beautiful blonde girl sidles in close to him, claiming his space from the others. She presses her body against his side and puts her hand on his chest, getting his undivided attention.

I feel a flash of jealousy so strong that it shocks me to the core.

It takes me a while to realize that my hands are actually flexing restlessly at my sides.

I try to breathe through the hurt, to look away from them, but I can't. I can't take my eyes from the scene unfolding before me.

He's flirting with her, placing his hand on her shoulder and twisting her hair around his finger, while she talks to him.

I close my eyes on a long blink. When I open them, Carrick is staring straight at me.

The look he gives me is empty, almost as if he's seeing straight through me. It's like I no longer exist to him.

It hurts, more than I could have ever anticipated. My heart feels like it's actually being crushed.

Then, dismissing me with his eyes, he stares down at the girl, giving her that flirty grin of his, as she speaks to him. Brushing her hair aside, he leans in and says something in her ear.

I can only imagine what he's saying—actually, I take that back. I don't want to imagine.

She gives him a coy smile, and the hand that was on his chest slides lower.

My stomach knots painfully. I press a hand to it, trying to hold myself together.

And when I catch the movement of his hand going down to cup her behind, I know I've seen enough.

Tearing my eyes from the scene, I mumble to Uncle John that I'm heading to the restroom, and then I all but run there, holding my breath and the tears that want to spill.

Locking myself in a stall, I put the lid down and sit on the toilet, and I let the stupid tears run down my cheeks.

I know I'm being ridiculous. This is how it has to be.

It hurts to see him with other women, and that's normal, of course. I just...I didn't expect to see him with another woman so soon.

Then again, this is Carrick Ryan I'm talking about. He doesn't stay down for long.

And this is good. Seeing him with her, how he was all over her—it's the reminder I needed of who he is.

A player.

A driver.

Not the man for me.

But still, I sit in there, hiding out in that toilet stall until I feel sure that I won't burst out into tears if I go out there and see Carrick pawing another woman.

By the time I get back to the garage, the race has already started. I didn't realize I'd been gone so long.

"Where the hell have you been?" Ben hisses, coming up next to me.

"I'm sorry. I was feeling a bit unwell." I press my hand to my stomach, feigning sickness. It's not a total lie. I was feeling sick after seeing Carrick mauling that girl.

Ben eyes my face for a moment. "You do look a bit peaky. Do you need to go back to the hotel?"

"No, I'm fine now." I force a smile, and then I turn my attention to the screen to watch the race.

Carrick finishes fourth.

It's a disappointing finish and surprising, seeing as though he qualified first yesterday. It's just not like him to finish off-podium. It never happens.

And for a sickening moment, I wonder if I'm to blame. Maybe our fight before his race affected his concentration.

Thinking that, I start to hate myself even more for what I said to him.

When Carrick pulls into the garage, I'm determined to talk to him, but he climbs out of his car without a word or look to anyone. He walks straight out of there, heading upstairs to the driver's room.

I'm just about to follow him when I see Owen going up after him.

Then, I'm pulled back into work, and I don't see Carrick again for the rest of the day.

Later, when I arrive back to the hotel, after having to prep the car for shipping, the first thing I do before going to my room to clean up is go straight to his room. We need to sort this mess out and get our friendship back on track because I can't lose him. He's become too important for me to lose.

When I arrive at his room, I find his door open, and a housekeeper is inside.

"Carrick Ryan?" I say to the woman. "The man who was staying here?" I explain at her blank expression.

"He checked out, ma'am," she tells me in broken English.

He left.

My heart sinks, and it's in this moment that I realize that maybe Carrick and I aren't fixable. Maybe last night was the last time I'll ever be close to him again.

As I walk away from the room, this sickly hollow feeling sinks down on me, crushing me to pieces. And I hate myself just a little bit more.

fourteen

MONTE CARLO, MONACO

I HAVEN'T SEEN CARRICK in close to two weeks. When he left Barcelona, he headed straight back home to the UK.

I only know this because, later that night over dinner, I finally broke down and asked Uncle John about what happened to Carrick after the race. He told me that Carrick was in a foul mood because he'd come in fourth and that he caught an early flight home.

The next day after Carrick left, I flew out with the rest of the team to Monte Carlo, and it's where I've been ever since.

Monte Carlo is a hard place for me to be. From the moment I signed with Rybell, I haven't been looking forward to coming here. Monte Carlo is where my life changed forever fourteen years ago.

Circuit de Monaco is the track where my father had his accident.

The place where he died.

Uncle John keeps asking if I'm okay. Before we flew here, he even said to me that I could miss this race. He said I could change my ticket and go back to the UK. It was sweet of him, but I know if I had done that, it would have raised questions, and I don't like questions. And if I'm to have my career in Formula 1, then I can't avoid this place forever. Best to get it over and done with.

So here I am.

It has gotten easier the longer I've been here, but racing day will probably be a different story.

The first time I went to the track, I came alone, and it was...painful.

Especially afterward, when I went to see the statue commemorating my father in Casino Square.

I stood there for a long time, just staring at it, wondering what my life would have been like if my father had never died.

It's not that I haven't had a great life because I have. My mother made the best of what we had left without him, but I've felt his loss for the last fourteen years, like a gaping hole in my heart.

And it only fueled to remind me why Carrick could never be the man for me.

I know my mother is worried about me being here. She's been calling twice a day, every day, checking to make sure I'm okay.

I know it's hard for her, me being here. It drags up bad memories.

I've made sure to keep myself busy. When I'm not working, I've been doing touristy stuff and going out with the guys at night, having fun.

Today is Thursday, and racing weekend starts tomorrow. Carrick arrived today, not that I've seen him. I just heard he was getting in today, and it's evening now, so he should be here.

I don't know where things stand between us.

I haven't heard from him, not that I've tried to get in touch with him either. I did almost crack and text him to apologize a few days after he'd gone back to the UK. I was feeling emotional from being here, and I missed talking to him. I typed the whole text out, but then I chickened out before sending it, and I erased it.

I know the time when I have to face him is fast approaching, and I'm dreading it.

I'm worried that he'll ignore me because I know that will hurt more than anything.

Hence, why I'm out in a bar with the team, drinking up some Dutch courage in case I do see Carrick tonight.

We're in a bar called Pattaya, which overlooks the harbor. It's really pretty here. We're sitting outside, and I'm sipping on a glass of local beer, chatting with Ben. Petra's not arrived in Monaco yet. Her brother's wife went into early labor yesterday, six weeks early, so she delayed her flight. She wanted to stay and make sure everything was okay with the baby. Fortunately, it was, and now, Petra is the proud auntie of a baby boy yet to be named.

She could only get on an evening flight in, so she'll be arriving later on. I can't wait until she gets here. Even though the guys are great, to be honest, I'm missing her company.

"Carrick just texted, asking where we are," Ben informs me. His eyes are down on his phone as he types out a text, presumably back to Carrick.

"He's here?" My voice comes out sounding a little strangled. I cover it with a cough.

"Yeah, he's coming to meet us." He puts his phone down on the table.

Panic slides a hand around my throat and squeezes tight. I take a few calming sips of my beer.

I can do this. It's going to be fine.

Needing a moment, I excuse myself to the restroom. When I get back, Carrick still hasn't arrived.

My nerves are on edge. I can't sit still in my chair. I feel like I'm about to come out of my skin, and my head is rotating every few minutes, looking for a sign of him. I just need to see him, so I know how things stand between us.

It's been a long while since Ben texted him back, and I'm starting to think that maybe Carrick's not coming after all. But then I hear Robbie start catcalling, and the rest of them join in, so I know Carrick has arrived.

My stomach and head fill with butterflies, making me feel a little dizzy.

Be breezy, Andi. Breezy…

Trying to act nonchalant, I cast a glance back over my shoulder to Carrick.

And I feel like I've just been smacked in the face with a brick.

He's walking toward us with a girl attached to his arm. A really pretty and tall—probably about my height—model-looking girl with long brown hair.

Those butterflies I was feeling turn to dust, and I'm just left empty.

I can't believe that he's picked up some random and brought her with him.

Of course he has. This is Carrick.

Deep breaths. It doesn't matter.

It's none of my business what he does and who he does it with. All I care about is getting my friendship with him back on track.

Right?

Pressing my lips together, I turn back to the table. I grab my phone off it and stare down at it, like I'm reading something really interesting.

"Hey," Carrick says from behind me.

Not hearing his voice, that Irish twang of his, for nearly two weeks has it shivering through me.

I clamp down the feeling, pushing it away.

Assuming he's talking to the whole table and not directly to me, I don't turn around, but I do mutter a vague-sounding, "Hello."

Some of the guys get up to greet him, doing that manly handshake thing, Ben being one of them.

"I'll get you a drink," Ben says.

"Nah. Don't worry. I'll get them. What are you drinking?"

"Beer," Ben tells him.

"Get me a cosmo, will you, baby?" the girl says.

Baby?

She has a really nice English accent, sweet and posh. Not like my fucked-up English mixed with Brazilian accent.

"Sure thing, babe."

Babe?

The memory of being in bed with Carrick, his body wrapped around mine, his sleepy voice murmuring in my ear, "Night, babe," slams into me painfully.

Their terms of endearment seem awfully forward for two people who just met.

Or maybe they didn't just meet.

The thought makes my empty feeling quickly turn to a sick feeling. A really sick feeling.

"Let me get you a chair," Ben says.

I'm assuming he's speaking to the girl.

He drags over a chair, putting it next to me.

Thanks, Ben.

Out of the corner of my eye, I see her sit in the chair with the grace of a gazelle. She's wearing a short skirt, which rides up, revealing more of her long tanned legs.

I look down at my own legs, thanking my mother for passing on her good genes to me and thanking my good sense for at least wearing jean shorts to show them off—not that it's a competition in any way. And in no way do I look anywhere near as nice as she does. She's dressed up for a night out, completing that short skirt with heels and a halter top. All notably designer compared to my high street jean shorts, flip-flops, and red T-shirt, which has the word *Geek* emblazoned across the chest.

God, I am a geek.

Actually, the only things I have going for me right now are my legs and my hair. I'm wearing it down, and it looks pretty.

Since when did I start caring how I look or comparing myself to other women?

Since Carrick.

"What's everyone else drinking?" Carrick asks.

A multitude of drink orders are shouted at him, mostly beer.

"I'll give you a hand at the bar," Ben offers, laughing.

I feel a hand—*his* hand—on my shoulder, and I freeze.

"What about you?" Carrick asks, his voice low.

Tipping my head back, I glance up at him, making sure to keep my expression blank. "What about me?"

Something flickers through his eyes, but it's gone before I can get a read on what it was.

"Drink—can I get you one?"

"No. I'm good. Thanks." I point at my beer on the table.

He stares at me for a beat. "All right then." He gives me a sharp nod and walks away.

Without control, my eyes follow him inside the bar.

Berating myself for staring, I do a quick glance of the table to make sure no one saw me watching him. Then, I relax in my seat. Well, relax as best as I can with Carrick and his girl here.

I can feel the presence of her sitting beside me like a thorn in my side.

I know I'm flat-out ignoring her, and my mother didn't raise me to treat other women this way.

She always says, "As women, if we can't respect one another, then how can we expect men to respect us?"

Treat someone how you want to be treated, Andi.

Being in the modeling industry, my mother encountered a lot of bitchy women, and it taught her not to be the same, and that's what she taught me.

But right now, I am acting like one of those bitchy women, and I don't like myself for it.

So, even though talking to Carrick's girl is the last thing I feel like doing, I force the politeness in me, push my phone into my pocket, and turn to her.

Seeing how pretty she is up close makes me feel even worse.

Suck it up, Andi. She hasn't done anything to you, and she doesn't deserve for you to be a bitch to her. Your issue is with Carrick, not her.

"Hi," I say, smiling.

Turning her head, she gives me a blank look. "Er, hello." Then, she turns away and gets her phone out of her bag.

Okay...that was a little odd. Maybe she's just shy.

I scramble around my head for something else to say. "So, are you on holiday in Monaco or just here for the race?"

She pulls her eyes from her phone to look at me again. She gives me a stare that can only be described as stupid—as in, she thinks I'm stupid. "Um, both."

Ignoring the stupid stare, I smile again and say, "Cool. So, when did you get in?"

She sighs loudly, giving me the impression that I'm annoying her. "This afternoon with Carr."

She came in from the UK with Carrick?

I feel like I've just had a defibrillator to the chest. I actually jolt in my seat, and my breath whooshes out of me, right along with these words, "You came with Carrick? From the UK? On the plane? Together?" I know I sound a little odd, but I don't care.

"Didn't I just say that?" She gives me a sharp look. "Of course I came with Carr. I am his girlfriend. And he practically begged me to come, couldn't bear to be away from me. So, I said, 'What the hell?' I have a few days off work, so why not?" She lifts her hand and starts to examine her nails.

His girlfriend? I feel like I've just been punched in the face.

How long has she been his girlfriend? I didn't know Carrick did girlfriends. Was she his girlfriend when he had sex with me?

Something strange, solid, and cold settles in my stomach.

I pick up my beer and take large gulps just for the need to do something aside from vomit or maybe scream.

I've just finished swallowing when I hear the rattling sound of disgust come from my neighbor.

"Ugh, I don't know how you can drink that stuff."

I drag my eyes to hers. I see that she's staring at my beer like I just drank rat poison.

"Beer?"

"Yes, it's so…disgusting. Just having it near me makes me want to be sick." She wrinkles up her nose.

And I have the sudden urge to punch it.

So much for me respecting other women.

I've just lowered my glass to the table, when she says, "So, who are you anyway? I mean, why are you here? Are you someone's girlfriend or something?" She wafts a hand at my friends around the table.

"No!" I let out a little laugh, shaking my head. "I work for Rybell." I can tell from her expression that she has no clue what that means, so I clarify, "I work for Carrick."

That gets her attention because I see her gaze sharpen, and she starts to appraise me in a whole new light. I'm pretty sure, in this moment, if she didn't before, she now sees me as competition for Carrick's attention, and that makes her instantly dislike me.

I feel like telling her not to worry. I'm definitely not competition for her. Carrick is barely talking to me, let alone anything else.

I can see she's about to question me further, but Carrick and Ben return with the drinks, halting all conversation.

"Sienna, here's yours." Ben hands her a fancy-looking cocktail.

Sienna—so that's the girlfriend's name.

"Thank you," she says in a sickly sweet voice.

After handing everyone's drinks out, Carrick pulls up a chair beside Sienna and takes a sip of his beer. Seeing that he's drinking beer tugs a smile onto my lips, knowing just how much his girlfriend hates it.

Girlfriend. The word keeps crushing my insides to dust.

As I move my eyes away from him, I see Sienna is staring at me.

She knows I was looking at him.

Feeling uncomfortable, I say the first thing that pops into my head, "So, what do you do for a living, Sienna?"

She gives me a confused look. "I'm in The Diamond Babes."

The Diamond Babes?

"I'm sorry. I don't know what that is." I give an awkward smile.

I hear a covered laugh, and I'm pretty sure it comes from Carrick, but it's hard to be sure as I can only see the back of his head because he's faced away, talking to Robbie.

Sienna makes a sound of total disgust, her face screwing up. "You don't know who we are? How is that even possible?"

I'm kind of feeling stupid right now, like I should know who these Diamond Babes are.

"The Diamond Babes are a girl band from the UK," Ben kindly informs me. "They're quite popular."

"We're not 'quite' popular." She air quotes.

I really hate air quotes.

"We're the biggest girl band in the UK," she corrects him very loudly.

"Right…" Ben utters before sipping on his drink.

I give an awkward smile. "I'm sorry I didn't know who you—the band are. I only recently moved back to the UK. I've lived in Brazil for the last fourteen years. And I'm not very up on your kind of music."

"*My* kind of music?" She lifts a perfectly plucked brow. "I'm assuming you mean the good kind."

"Yeah, something like that," I mutter before picking up my beer and taking a drink.

I hear another catch of laughter, and from the tell of Carrick's shaking shoulders, I definitely know it's coming from him. Sienna seems oblivious to the fact. And I know it's wrong, but I like that I can still make him smile even if it was through a dig at his girlfriend.

But then, I just feel mean. So, I say, "I'll have to check your music out. I'm sure it's great." When I actually mean, I'd rather poke my eyes out with needles than listen to your music.

The compliment works, and her face relaxes. "You said you work for Carrick. What exactly is it that you do? Are you, like, his maid or something?"

Maid? Do we live in the nineteenth century?

Ben splutters out a laugh from beside me. I have to hold back a shock of laughter myself.

I expect Carrick to laugh, too, but surprisingly, he doesn't.

"No, I bloody well am not his maid!" I exclaim, injecting humor into my voice.

Carrick turns his face in my direction, and he catches my eye. He's looking at me liked he used to—like I'm his friend, like I matter—and it hurts like a mother because I know he no longer feels that way.

Ignoring the ache in my chest, I force my eyes back to Sienna. "I'm a mechanic," I tell her.

"You're a mechanic?" She screws her face up with what can only be described as total disgust.

Seriously, you'd think I'd just told her I was a serial killer. That, or I wipe Carrick's arse for a living.

"But isn't that a man's job?"

"Depends on who you're asking."

"Hmm...well, yes, I suppose...looking at you now, I can see that you are well suited to men's work." Her eyes give me the up and down. "You have the right build and a very"—she waves a hand at me—"masculine vibe about you."

Masculine vibe? The right build? What the fuck? I'm the same size as her!

Seriously, who is this chick?

I couldn't care less if she is in the UK's biggest pop band. She's mean. She might be pretty on the outside, but she's plain ugly on the inside, and I'm getting that from just spending less than ten minutes with her.

I've met mean girls before, but she is a bitch through and through. I have never met someone so confrontational in all my life.

My body tenses, my hands balling into fists, and I'm just about to open my mouth and let the pop princess know exactly what I think of her when Ben slings his arm around my shoulder, pulling me close to him.

"Take it easy," he whispers in my ear.

I flicker a glance at him, and he gives me a calming smile.

"She's not worth it."

"Yeah…" I exhale. "You're right."

Loosening his hold but keeping his arm around me, he leans forward and says loudly, "Actually, Sienna, Andi is our best mechanic. She's better than all of us put together. She's the most talented mechanic I've ever worked with. Honestly, I don't know what the team would do without her."

I know he's just saying it to be kind and to stick up for me, but irrespective of why, it works because I feel a hundred times better than I did a moment ago. And I kind of love Ben in this moment,

Grinning up into his face, I say, "Are you drunk? Because it's not like you to give me a compliment."

His eyes smile at me. "I give you compliments all the time. You just never listen."

"Aw." I grin at him, and then I lean in and whisper, "You're a good friend, Ben."

He shrugs, and then he says quietly, "I can't have our best mechanic getting sacked because she knocked out Carrick's latest squeeze."

Laughing softly, I pat his arm, which is still around me.

Ben lifts his arm from my shoulders, and I turn to the table to get my drink, but I freeze at the sight of Carrick's angry eyes on me. His jaw is set so tight that it looks like it might shatter.

Then, without warning, the anger in his eyes flames into something else entirely, setting my body on fire. I have to press my thighs together to contain the sudden ache, and I can feel my body quickly stirring to life as memories of our one night together flicker through my mind.

Coming back to my senses, knowing there's a table full of people here, I break our stare. Then, I catch sight of Sienna's eyes swinging between Carrick and me, and I know that she saw the look that just transpired between us.

Her brows pull together, like she's working something out.

And then I see it settle on her face. She knows Carrick and I have slept together.

Fuck.

Something really uncomfortable stirs in my stomach.

She twists in her seat to face me. "So, your name is Andi?" she says, her tone biting.

"Yes..." I answer carefully.

"Andi..." she says in a bitchy singsong voice. "Andi, who has a man's job and a man's name. Maybe you should just go the whole hog and have a sex change, not that there's much to change!"

She belts out a laugh like it's the funniest thing she's ever heard. She glances around the table, expecting the others to be laughing with her. But what she's failing to realize is that these are my friends, not hers. And no one is laughing.

"Sienna," Carrick snaps out her name in warning.

"What? It was just a joke! Can't you people take a joke?" She lets out an awkward laugh.

God, I'm so fucking done here that it's not even funny.

"Sure it was a joke." Pushing my chair out, I get my jacket off the back and pull it on. "Just like your face. But the thing is, Sienna, yes, I could trade my vagina for a cock, but sadly for you, you can't fix ugly." Throwing a quick glance around the table, ignoring Carrick's eyes and Sienna's open mouth, I say, "I'll catch you all tomorrow." Then, I turn on my heel and start walking away.

I hear Carrick calling my name, but I just ignore him, moving my legs as fast as they'll go.

"Jesus, Andressa. Just wait up, will you?" He finally catches up with me. He tugs on my arm, pulling me to a stop.

"What?" I shake my arm free of his hand. My skin is left burning where he just touched me.

"Are you okay?"

"I'm fine."

I turn away and start walking again.

"Jesus, just...wait!"

Sighing, I turn back, putting my hands on my hips. "What do you want, Carrick?"

"I just..." His eyes go to the ground. He looks unsure for a moment. Then, he lifts his eyes back to mine, his confidence back. "Where are you going?"

"To the hotel."

Then, wouldn't you know? Little miss pop princess comes marching up in her pretty heels. "Carrick!" she cracks his name out like a whip. "Where the hell do you think you're going?"

He turns his head to her and gives her such a stare that I even shudder. Seriously, his look could take down a bear. I'm not surprised when she shrinks back because I probably would at the level of anger emanating from him.

"I'm making sure Andressa is okay." His voice is like granite. "So, go back to the bar, sit the fuck down, and try not to offend any more of my friends before I get back."

Friend? Oh, so now I'm his friend.

"Ugh! Whatever!" She throws up her hands, swivels on her heel, and sashays back in the direction of the bar.

The moment she's gone, I turn and start walking.

Goal—get away from Carrick.

Plan—catch a cab and go to bed.

And possibly cry.

Carrick falls in step beside me.

"What do you think you're doing?" I flash an angry look his way.

"Coming with you."

"Well, I'm going back to the hotel and then straight to bed, and you're most definitely not invited."

He lets out a throaty chuckle, and I have to fight hard to keep the smile from my lips.

"Habits" by Tove Lo and Hippie Sabotage starts to hum from the speakers of one of the bars we pass.

I love this song. The lyrics. Just sometimes…I wish I could numb the pain.

Out of nowhere, I suddenly feel exhausted and sad. Really sad.

Wrapping my arms around myself, I say in a quiet voice, "Go back to the bar, Carrick. I'll be fine on my own."

"Andressa, I know you think I'm a total bastard, but there's no way I'm letting you walk around late at night on your own. Anything could happen to you."

"Like you'd care." I regret it the moment I say it.

He grabs my arm. Pulling me to a stop, he stands in front of me, way too close. I can practically taste his aftershave on my tongue and feel the warmth of his breath on my face.

His hand is still on my arm, and it's burning me from the outside in, right down to my core.

I need him to stop touching me…and never stop touching me.

I'm so confused, and it hurts like a physical pain.

"Of course I'd care," he says low. "You're—" He cuts off. Rubbing his forehead with the heel of his free hand, he takes a step back.

He drops his hand from my arm, and I'm more than relieved for the space.

"You're my friend, Andressa." He sounds resigned.

I just don't know to what he's resigned.

I laugh, and it's a hollow sound. "We're hardly friends right now."

His face tightens, and I see his jaw start to work angrily.

Not wanting another fight, I step around him and start walking again.

A moment later, he's back beside me, keeping pace, but he says nothing more, and silence ensues.

"How have you been?" he finally asks in a soft voice.

I keep my eyes fixed ahead. "Good. You?"

"Same."

We lapse back into that horrible silence. It's heartbreaking being in such an uncomfortable silence with him. From the moment I met Carrick, finding something to talk about was never an issue for us.

Just everything else it seems.

I hear a noise behind us. Glancing over my shoulder, hoping it's not the pop princess, I see a man. It's the same man, I now remember, who was lingering outside the bar we were in. I also remember seeing him hovering nearby when Carrick first caught up with me. I just didn't register it in my anger.

I only noticed him before because he's such a big guy, and now, in the darkness of the harbor, he looks even bigger and a little menacing. He's walking way too close to us for my liking.

"Carrick…" I hiss. "I know this might sound a little crazy, but I think we're being followed." I jerk my head back in the direction of the huge dude.

Carrick looks back and chuckles. "Don't worry. He's my security. Dad assigned me a guard while I'm here. You know, it being Monte Carlo, race crazy, and with me being—"

"You." I smile.

"Yeah." He laughs again. "And with the press attention being a little more intense because of Sienna—" He cuts off.

The lightness that I was just feeling is obliterated.

He lets out a sigh. "I'm sorry about the way she spoke to you."

"It's not your fault." I shrug. *She's a stark raving bitch all on her own.*

"Yeah, but she's here with me. And she had no right speaking to you the way she did. It won't happen again."

I don't care how she spoke to me. I just care that she's here with you. I hate that she's here with you.

Of course, I don't say that. I just shrug again and say, "It doesn't matter."

"When it comes to you, *everything* matters."

His words knock the air from my lungs.

I want to know what that means. And I don't.

God, I'm so screwed up.

Dipping my chin, I stare down at my moving feet. "How long have you known her?"

"Not long."

At least he didn't know her before he slept with me. Still, I don't know whether to feel better or worse at that fact.

"I met her after I got back to the UK."

When you left Barcelona and me behind. "Right."

"I didn't invite her here."

"Mmhmm."

"She just kind of invited herself, and Dad was there when she said something about coming. He thought the press she would bring would be positive—you know, with me actually being with just one woman for once."

He laughs, and it's an uncomfortable sound. I really don't like it or any of what he's telling me.

"And…I guess I just went along with it."

I stare at him blankly. "Why are you telling me this?"

He blows out a breath, pushing his hands into his jean pockets. "I don't know." He lifts his shoulders, looking helpless.

We've reached the main road now, and luck is on my side because I see a cab with its light on approaching. I put my hand out to flag it down.

The cab pulls up, and I reach for the door handle, but I pause.

For the past two weeks, I've wanted to apologize to Carrick for what I said to him, and this might be the only chance I have.

My heart starts to beat in my chest, my fingers trembling, as I turn back to him. "Carrick…what I said in Barcelona about my job and Amy and Charlotte, I shouldn't have said it. It was a shitty thing to say."

"You didn't say anything that wasn't true."

"Well, still…I am sorry." I let out a light sigh. "The worst thing is, I don't know why I said it because that wasn't what was at the forefront of my mind at that moment." *Not losing you was.*

Gripping the handle, I stop myself from saying any more. No matter what, I don't think anything I can say will get us back to where we were before that night.

"Anyway, thanks for walking me. I guess I'll see you tomorrow." I climb in the cab, closing the door behind me, leaving Carrick where he is standing on the street.

fifteen

▰ MONTE CARLO, MONACO

BECAUSE I'VE BEEN AVOIDING CARRICK and his pop princess, I didn't go out on Friday night even though Petra had begged me to. I stood fast and stayed at the hotel with room service and Jason Bourne for company. I was in the mood for a kick-arse movie.

As it turns out, it was a good job I hadn't gone out because Carrick and the pop princess were there. Petra has taken a real dislike to Sienna purely because of the way she'd treated me. But Petra did say Sienna had been fine with her—a bit snooty, but nothing how she had been with me.

Seems like her ultimate bitch is reserved solely for me. Or maybe she heeded what Carrick had said to her.

Petra did tell me that Carrick had barely spoken to Sienna all night, preferring to drink with the boys. She also said he'd pulled her aside and asked where I was. She said he'd looked disappointed when she told him that I wasn't coming out. She made some white lie up for me, saying I was just feeling a little unwell, so he wouldn't think I hadn't gone out because of him.

See? This is why I love this girl.

I didn't see Carrick much yesterday. I kept busy with work, and I didn't see him until it was time to come down for qualifying. I did wish him luck as I handed him his helmet. But that was the extent of our contact.

I hate the way things are between us. I just don't know how to get them back, so I've decided to give up trying.

I figure it's for the best anyway.

I'm just counting the minutes until this weekend is over, so I can get away from them both.

But, mostly, I'm counting down the minutes until this day is over.

It's race day, the day I've been dreading since I arrived here.

Petra and I did go out last night. She wasn't taking no for an answer two nights in a row, and as it turned out, Carrick was at some sponsorship thing. The drivers always have loads of them that they have to attend throughout the racing season.

So, Petra and I went out for a few drinks with the boys, and then we broke off on our own to go have some girlie fun.

And we definitely had a lot of fun, judging by the stonking headache, dry mouth, and aching body I've just woken up to.

"Ugh," I groan, rolling over, feeling like there's a pneumatic drill going off in my head. I blink open my eyes that seem to have lost all moisture, and immediately, I close them again, squinting at the sliver of light coming in from the blinds.

I hear a similar deathly sound coming from Petra's bed.

"Fuck," she moans. "I'm dying. Actually dying."

"Same here. And I'm blaming you," I grumble. "It's race day. I've got a tongue like sandpaper, and I can't currently see straight."

"We'll get some coffee down you, and you'll be fine."

I turn my head on the pillow and give her a look. *God, that hurts.* "I'll need a gallon of coffee to sort this out." I point to my head.

"Greasy fry up and coffee, and you'll be golden."

"Ugh, don't talk about fried food right now!" I cover my mouth with my hand, feeling sick. "I'm never going out drinking with you again," I utter between my fingers.

"Hey, don't blame me. It was your idea to drink Sambuca."

"Was it?" I give her a look of surprise.

"Yep."

Images of last night start to come back to me—us doing shots, singing karaoke, dancing on tables.

Ah, fuck.

"Oh God…" I sigh. "Did I make an arse of myself last night?"

"A little bit of an arse." She chuckles. "But so did I, so you're not alone, and it wasn't like anyone we knew was there. But you had a good time, and it took your mind off of you-know-who and the pop princess."

"Yeah, I guess," I mumble.

"Look, Andi." She rolls onto her side, facing me. "I know you said that what happened with Carrick was a one-time thing…but I just wonder if you said that because you know what he's like, not because it's what you wanted. Because it's bothering you an awful lot, him being here with her."

"It's hardly bothering me at all."

"You hid behind a tree yesterday, so you wouldn't have to talk to them."

"You saw that?" I cringe.

"Yeah, I saw that."

I let out a sigh. "It's just…sure I like him, and I know we could never be together. Yet knowing all that, it still—"

"Hurts to see him with another woman."

"Yeah," I exhale, rubbing at my dry eyes.

"Why could you and him never be together?"

"Because he's a man-whore."

She chuckles. "I don't know. I think, with the way it went down with you two and from what you told me how Carrick behaved…maybe he did want more with you."

"I doubt it. Irrespective of that, I don't get involved with drivers anyway." I roll onto my back, staring up at the ceiling.

"Why?"

"I just don't."

She blows out a breath. "You can tell me, you know. You can trust me. I won't tell anyone. I know you might think I'm a gossip, but I can keep things private that truly matter."

I stare at her and suddenly find myself in a rare moment of honesty. "I lost someone I loved to Formula One. He died in an accident on the track."

"I'm sorry, Andi."

"It was a long time ago." I shrug like it doesn't matter, but it's all that matters.

"Is that why you work for Formula One? To somehow still be close to this person?"

Petra is more perceptive than I give her credit for.

"Partly. I studied engineering at university because I wanted to learn how to build better engines. People are always going to race, but I want to be able to help make a car be as safe as it can be before they take it out on the track. Also, I work here because I love it. Cars are all I've ever known. I grew up with my head under the hood of a car." I chuckle, a hint of sadness in it. "Yeah, I guess being here, doing this, does make me feel close to my dad."

I realize my slip up immediately, and I freeze cold.

"It was your dad who died?"

I flash a panicked glance at her, suddenly feeling like I can't breathe.

"It's okay, Andi," she reassures in a soothing voice. "I won't say anything to anyone. I just—why do you keep it a secret?"

I let out a long sigh, and then I turn to her. "I keep it a secret because my dad is—was…William Wolfe."

"Oh." She looks taken aback. "Oh. Fuck. Andi...why didn't you tell me? But wait—" She shakes her head like she's clearing it. "Didn't he...your dad...didn't he...*die*...here in Monaco?"

"Yes." I lie back, staring at the ceiling. I can feel tears pooling in my eyes, so I suck in a breath, keeping them at bay.

"Jesus...Andi. Why the fuck didn't you tell me? I can't imagine what you've been going through being here, especially with today being race day, and having to deal with all the Carrick and Sienna crap."

"I just didn't want people to know and think that Uncle John gave me the job because of who my dad is, so I kept it to myself."

"Hmm...I guess I can understand that."

I look across at her again. "Petra, here, only my Uncle John knows that William is my dad, and I want it to stay that way."

"You can trust me. Anything you tell me stays here." Pressing her lips together, she does the lock-and-throw-away-the-key action over her mouth

"I appreciate it." I smile softly at her.

"Gotta say, you make a whole lot more sense to me now—with the whole not-dating-drivers thing."

I let out a sigh. "When you see your dad die on the track and then watch your mother go through the pain of losing him..." I turn my head and look at her. "I don't want that for myself."

"But you do like Carrick...right?"

"Sure, I like him. But nothing can ever come of it."

"I understand, considering what happened with your dad...but Carrick isn't your dad, Andi."

My eyes meet hers. "But he is. Besides the whoring around—well, my dad was a bit of a one before he met my mum—Carrick is everything he was. And that's what everyone says about Carrick. He's the next Wolfe.

Everything about Carrick—from the early rise to Formula One to his recklessness and easy attitude to the way he drives…there's a hell of a lot about Carrick that's similar to my dad."

"But it doesn't mean that he's destined for the same fate."

I cringe at her choice of words.

"Jesus…sorry. That didn't come out right."

"No, it's okay. I'm usually fine with this stuff. I mean, it's been fourteen years. But today is just a weird day for me, is all. I'm more sensitive than usual."

There's a slight silence.

Then, she says, "Carrick will be fine today. You know that, right?"

I close my eyes, blowing out a breath. "Yeah."

"Look, just playing devil's advocate here, but it clearly worries you when Carrick races, and you like the guy, so whether you're with him or not, you're still going to worry, right?"

I open my eyes and look at her. "Yeah, but there's a difference between worrying over a friend than over a boyfriend—or worse, someone you love."

She stares at me for a long moment. I can see her wheels turning behind her eyes.

Lying on her back, she puts her hands behind her head. "Do you think the pop princess will be at the track today?"

"It's race day, so I would expect her to be there."

Sienna hasn't been at the track at all since she arrived in Monaco, which has been perfect for me because I've been able to hide there.

"She's such a bitch," Petra mutters.

A smile touches my lips, and I turn on my side to face her. "You know you don't have to dislike her just because I do."

She frowns, clearly displeased by what I said. "I dislike her because she was a bitch to you—and she makes crappy music."

I laugh at the expression on her face. "Well, I appreciate your support."

I fall onto my back. Lifting my hands to my face, I look at them. They're all rough and dry. I screw my face up.

I bet Sienna's hands are beautiful and soft.

Ugh. I really need to stop comparing myself to her.

Letting my thoughts escape me though, I say, "I wonder why he's with her. I mean, I get that Sienna's beautiful, but she's so bloody mean."

Petra lets out a laugh. "He's not *with* her, Andi. He's just shagging her. Sorry." She grimaces at my anguished face. "But come on, you must see it."

"See what?"

She sits up in bed, wrapping her arms around her knees, and I turn back onto my side, propping myself up on my elbow.

"Aside from the longing looks Carrick gives you when he thinks no one is looking, have you actually taken a good look at Sienna?"

"He doesn't give me longing looks." I stick my tongue out at her. "And unfortunately, yes, I have seen her."

"And you don't see it?"

"See what?" I'm getting frustrated now.

"How alike you both look."

"I do not look like her! God! Thanks a lot!" I huff.

Sure, Sienna is beautiful, but she's so ugly on the inside that it mars her exterior and in no way do I resemble someone like her.

Petra lets out a sound of frustration, shaking her head. "I don't mean that you're like the mega bitch. I just mean that you look incredibly similar."

"Come on, Petra. I'm not exactly standout-looking. I have brown hair, brown eyes, and olive skin."

She rolls her eyes. "Sure, you're not standout-looking with your mile long legs, supermodel body, and stunning face. Granted, I hate that bitch Sienna, but she is beautiful, like you. She has exactly the same attributes as you."

"As do a million other girls."

"Yeah, sure, because, of course, all women look like supermodels." She stretches out her legs, indicating the shortness of them in comparison to mine, causing me to laugh.

"Just think about it. Carrick went back to the UK, seriously pissed off with you because you blew him off, and when he comes back, he brings your look-alike with him. Coincidence? Me thinks not." She taps her finger to her head.

"Maybe he just has a type," I challenge.

"The only type Carrick has is pretty with a vagina that's open for business. But now, I'm starting to think that maybe now he has just one type—Andi Amaro."

"And I think you might still be drunk." I show her the middle finger.

Letting out a loud laugh, she sticks her tongue out. "Deny it all you want, but deep down you know I have a point." Swinging her legs over the edge of the bed, she gets to her feet. "Right, I'm hitting the shower."

I watch her disappear into the bathroom. Then, I pull the cover over my head, trying not to think about the last thing she just said, but unfortunately, those words are swimming around like little sharks gnawing away at my brain.

Three hours later, after a mountain of croissants and coffee, I'm still feeling like crap.

Even though my mood was already rubbish due to the hangover, a phone call with my mother before breakfast left me feeling emotional. Today might not be the exact date of when my dad died, but this particular race has always been a difficult one for us.

So, I was already feeling crappy when I had to bear witness to Carrick and the pop princess kissing outside the hotel as I was leaving with Petra.

It hurt badly, seeing him with her, like someone punched in through my chest and was squeezing the life out of my heart. I know it was only harder to see because my head is in a weird place today.

But his body language did look kind of off. He seemed uncomfortable to be kissing her in public. His hands were on her arms, not around her, and he didn't look to be pulling her closer, more like he was trying to push her away. It's not that I was examining them or anything or that I've spent all morning breaking it down into microscopic details in my head.

Anyway, what do I know? I'm probably just seeing what I need to see at the moment.

He must really like Sienna for her to be here, irrespective of what he said about just going along with it for the publicity. Carrick's not one to do anything he doesn't want to.

The next morning after the bar incident, Ben did tell me that when Carrick had gotten back to the bar, he and Sienna had had a massive row. Apparently, he'd reamed her out for the way she'd spoken to me. Ben said she'd tried to downplay it, said Carrick was making a big deal out of nothing. Then, Carrick had told her if she couldn't behave herself that she could just fuck off back home. Ben said she'd started crying, right there in front of them all, saying she was sorry and that she would apologize to me—which I'm still waiting for. Ben said it was just really uncomfortable, and that Carrick and Sienna had left soon after.

Probably to go have make-up sex.

Ugh! I have to stop having these torturous thoughts. I'm going to drive myself insane if I don't.

"Penny for your thoughts?" Petra's voice comes from behind me.

I swivel on my stool to see her holding a steaming mug in her hand.

"I brought you coffee."

That brings a smile to my face. "Have I told you how awesome you are?"

"I am awesome," she agrees. "And because of how awesome I am, I thought you could do with some cheering up after this morning. You know…" She pulls out a huge chocolate muffin from behind her back.

"Ah, I take it back. You're not awesome. You're spectacular." Reaching over, I take the coffee and muffin from her. I put the coffee down on the desk but keep hold of the muffin.

"Also, I thought I should let you know that the pop princess is here," she tells me in a quiet voice.

Even though, I knew it was likely that Sienna would be here with it being race day, I was praying to the gods that she might not turn up. I'm not up to seeing any more public displays of affection today.

Grumbling to myself, I take a huge bite out of the muffin.

Ah, chocolate spongy goodness. Nothing beats it.

"Where is she?" I ask through my mouthful of muffin.

"Up in hospitality, and surprise, surprise, she's being a bitch. She talked to me like I was a piece of crap because I put semi-skimmed milk in her tea instead of skimmed milk. I mean, the horror of it!" she says with dramatic flair.

I laugh.

"I should have spit in it, the cow."

REVVED

Nodding, I take another bite of muffin. "This is so good," I mumble. "You want some?" I offer it to her.

"No, thanks. You need it more than I do. Just don't come upstairs if you don't want to run into her, okay? I can't see her coming down here."

"God, yeah, she wouldn't want to be around us lowly mechanics." I slap a hand over my mouth as I spray crumbs from it, some hitting Petra. "Oh God! Sorry!" I snort a laugh through my hand, trying to keep the muffin in.

"You're seriously gross." Petra chuckles, brushing crumbs from her top. "You've got chocolate on your cheek as well, you tramp."

I rub at my cheek with my arm. "Gone?" I angle my cheek to her.

She gives it a quick look. "Yep, you're good. Just make sure you look in a mirror when you're finished with it, yeah?"

I give her a thumbs-up as I take another bite.

"So, we going out tonight?" she asks, resting her back against the desk.

"Er…I don't know. Probably not. I'm still recovering from last night."

"You say that now, but when Carrick wins today, you're gonna want to celebrate." Her face drops when she realizes what she's said.

I lift my hand, stopping her from apologizing, and I give her a reassuring smile. "You're right. I probably could do with going out. And it will be good to celebrate when Carrick wins."

"Attagirl. Well, I best get back upstairs. I'll catch you later."

Turning back to my desk, I put the half-eaten muffin down and take a sip of coffee, clearing the sponge from my mouth.

"Hey, don't I get a coffee?" That's Robbie calling to Petra.

"Sorry, only one pair of hands, and they were full." She gives me a wink, walking backward.

"You heard of these things called trays?"

"You heard of these things called legs? Use them if you want something. You know where I am." With a bounce in her step, she turns and jogs up the stairs.

"What do you have that I don't? Aside from the obvious," Robbie says, letting his gaze drift to his crotch.

God, he's acting like a total dickhead today. Normally, I can put up with his weirdness, but today, I just really don't feel like tolerating him.

"I don't know, Robbie. Maybe this thing called a personality." I turn away, but something in me isn't done. I feel all fired up, and I guess all the stress and sadness inside of me just wants to come out on him.

I spin my stool back around. "You know, if you want to shag Petra so bad, then why don't you stop acting like such a twat all the time and be nice for a change? She might actually be interested in you if you did."

His face reddens. I've embarrassed him.

The thing about embarrassing a man in front of other men is that they come out fighting, and they fight dirty.

"You mean like you did with Carrick? Don't think we all don't know that you've been polishing his dick. And now, he's fucked you off for something far better, and you're all bitter and twisted up about it."

I feel my throat close up, and my eyes start to sting.

Don't cry. Don't you dare bloody cry, Andi Amaro.

And, really, what can I say to that? He's right-ish.

"What the fuck is going on?"

My eyes swing to the sound of Carrick's hard voice. He's standing at the bottom of the stairwell, and he looks mad—no, scrap that. He looks livid.

At first, I think he's talking to me, but then I see his eyes are trained on Robbie.

"Nothing," Robbie stammers. "We were just—"

REVVED

"Don't bullshit me. I heard what you fucking said. Saying shit like that will get you in big trouble." Storming over to the pinboard, Carrick snatches a piece of paper from it, not even removing the pin, which drops to the floor.

I'm stock-still my seat. He hasn't even looked at me yet.

I'm wondering if it's my turn next, but then he starts to walk away, and I let out the breath I was holding.

That's quickly sucked back in when Carrick stops at the bottom of the stairs and turns around. He strides over to Robbie with angry determination.

I'm frozen in shock, not sure what to do. Neither are any of the guys. And I'm guessing Robbie thinks the same. We're unsure of what's going to happen.

When Carrick stops inches from Robbie's face, fists clenched at his sides, I actually wince, fearing that he's going to hit Robbie.

Robbie stumbles back a step.

"You're an annoying little prick, Robbie, and I'm sick of your shit. Pack your crap, and get the fuck out. You're fired."

"Wh-what?" Robbie chokes out.

Carrick takes another menacing step forward, leaving no space between them. "Are you deaf as well as stupid? I said, you're fired, so get the fuck out!" Then, he turns on his heel and storms out of the garage.

There's a moment of horrified silence.

My wide eyes swing to Robbie, who's just standing there, looking shocked to hell.

Then, my body springs into action. Jumping from my seat, I sprint across the garage, heading for the stairs. I start quickly climbing them.

"Carrick!" I call out to his back as he nears the top step.

He stops and slowly turns to me.

I take a few more steps up, closing the gap between us. "Please reconsider firing Robbie. He might be a twat at times, but really, that was my fault. Honestly, I started it. I wound him up about something that's none of my business. I was a bitch, and he was just biting back. If anyone should be fired, it's me."

He stares at me for a long moment, his expression tight, brows knitted together.

Then, I see his face relax, something warm passing through his eyes.

He shakes his head. "Robbie berates you in front of everyone. Then, you come running after me to plead his case, and you offer up your own job instead of his?"

I walk up a step. "I never claimed to be bright." I tip my lips up into a half smile.

A hint of a smile touches his eyes, and then he turns serious again. "He ever talks to you like that again, and he's gone."

I blow out a breath. "He won't. Thank you."

Our eyes catch and hold, and the air between us suddenly becomes thick and electric.

I see it explode in his eyes at exactly the same time it does in mine—memories of Barcelona. Me in his arms…him inside me.

He takes some steps down, bringing him closer to me. He holds my stare the whole time. My stomach is flipping like an acrobat.

He stops a step away from me.

My heart starts to beat out of my chest.

"I miss you." His voice is so low, so filled with meaning, that it grabs a tight hold of me.

I part my lips on a breath to speak—

"Carr!"

I blanch at the sound of Sienna's voice.

Carrick's eyes lift to the ceiling, and he lets out a sound of annoyance.

The moment is broken.

I take a step down away from him. "I should let you go. And I need to get back and let Robbie know that he still has a job."

Carrick stares at me for the longest second and then gives a sharp nod. He turns, taking the stairs up two at a time.

"There you are," Sienna's voice says. "I was getting lonely without you."

I stop listening and jog down the rest of the stairs, my heart racing the whole time.

"I miss you."

When I get back to the garage, Robbie is still there, still looking shell-shocked. A few pairs of eyes lift to me, Robbie's included.

I walk over to him. "You're good. You still have your job."

He blows out a relieved breath. "Shit…thanks, Andi." He drags a hand through his hair. "Look…I'm real sorry about what I said."

"Don't worry about it." I wave him off. "I'm sorry, too. I shouldn't have said what I did about Petra." I'm going to owe her an apology, too.

"Well, whatever. You saved my arse, so first drink is on me tonight, okay?" He holds his fist out to me.

"Okay," I say, giving him a fist bump.

The race is fraught with tension for me, especially when Carrick blows a tire and comes into the pit. The guys quickly get it changed and have him back out on the track.

But after that, I can't take my eyes from the screens. My heart is in my mouth for the rest of the race.

Petra gets a little time off from the kitchen and comes down to watch the race with me. I should take a break, I even need the restroom, but I'm too afraid to move in case anything happens.

Then, I start to feel sick, wishing that I had told Carrick that I miss him, too. Wishing that we were okay, back to how we used to be before Barcelona. Then, all of these terrible scenarios begin to play out in my mind, and in each one of those scenarios, I lose him permanently.

I suddenly feel hot, and the room spins.

"Hey, you okay?" Petra touches my arm.

I turn my face to her.

One look at me, and she's saying, "Come on. Let's get you out of here." Then, she's leading me out of the garage with her arm threaded through mine.

Instead of taking me to the restroom, she takes me up to Carrick's private room. Oddly, being surrounded by his stuff, I start to feel a little better.

She sits me down and gets me a drink of water.

"Thanks." I curl my fingers around the plastic cup and take a sip of the chilled water. "I don't know what happened. I just felt a bit weird."

I don't go into the fact that memories of my father's crash were bleeding into a vision of Carrick dying in exactly the same way.

There's a knock at the door, and it pushes open, revealing Uncle John.

His eyes go to Petra and then back to me. "I saw you dipping out. You okay?"

"Yeah. I'm good." I smile to reassure him.

His eyes flick to Petra again. I know he's cautious to say anything in front of her.

"Petra knows...about my dad, Uncle John. I told her this morning."

"Good." He nods. "About time someone else around here knew." He gives me a smile. "I can't stay though. I have to get back. I just wanted to check and make sure you were okay."

"Thanks, Uncle John."

I stop him just as he's opened the door. "How's Carrick doing out there?"

He turns back to me. "Real good." He smiles big. "He's still leading."

That brings a smile to my lips.

I stay with Petra in Carrick's room for a few more minutes until I feel like myself again, and then we go back down to watch the rest of the race.

It's still tense for me. But at least I don't freak out again.

Carrick finishes first.

The relief I feel at seeing him pull into the garage is immense. And the knowledge that he won here in Monaco and how great that will feel for him turns my relief into elation.

When he pulls off his helmet and fireproof balaclava, he climbs out of his car, and his hair is all stuck to his head. He has the biggest smile on his face. He just looks so goddamn beautiful that it makes my heart swell.

He meets my eyes across the garage, grinning at me.

Congratulations, I mouth to him through the crowd of our team as they all jump on him, cheering and celebrating.

But his eyes never leave mine, and when he starts to make his way over to me, pushing past the guys, my heart starts to beat faster, butterflies swarming into my stomach.

Then, I hear an almighty screeching sound, and my head jerks around to see Sienna running across the garage. She launches herself at Carrick, jumping up, and she wraps her long legs around his waist. Her arms around his neck, she plants a full-on kiss on his mouth.

Unable to watch, I look away. Blinking through the sting in my eyes, I quietly make my way out of the garage.

sixteen

MONTE CARLO, MONACO

"YOU'RE HAVING A GOOD TIME?" Petra asks, a sway in her stance.

She's standing before me, drink in hand, looking a little drunk. Well, we all are. We're in a La Rascasse, a bar that is situated on the famous bend on the Formula 1 track, the bend in which Carrick cornered like the pro he is and brought home the trophy.

We're all out celebrating the win. Minus Carrick. He had to attend a prearranged sponsorship party. His dad and Uncle John are there, too. So is Sienna.

But I'm not thinking of either of them tonight. I'm out having a good time with my friends.

I was relieved when I found out that Carrick wouldn't be here as I didn't want to be forced to spend time around him and the pop princess. Now that I'm out and having fun, I'm finding that I'm missing him. It seems weird to be celebrating his win without him here.

"I'm having a good time." I smile at Petra.

Then, Ben comes over, stumbling a little, and slings his arms around the both of us. "You girls okay for drinks?"

"I'm good." I show him my half-full glass. I've been going steady tonight, pacing myself, as I know it's going to be a long night, and I'm already feeling a little tipsy.

"I'll have another, and so will Andi," Petra informs Ben.

Ben shoots a look at me in question. Out of the corner of my eye, I can see Petra with her you-will-have-another-drink face on.

"Okay. Looks like I'm having another drink."

I down the one in my hand, wincing at the burn. I'm on double vodkas and lemonade—hence, the pacing, but I guess that's out the window now.

Petra gives a little cheer, clapping her hands, as I put my empty glass down on the nearby table.

I follow them both over to the bar.

"So, what are we having?" Ben asks.

"Shots!" Petra yells out.

I flash a look at Ben, who grins and shrugs his shoulders.

"Looks like we're having shots," I mutter.

Not that it matters what I say as Petra is already leaning over the bar, and she has grabbed the attention of the barman, placing her drink order.

I honestly don't know how she does it. It's heaving with people in here tonight, but every time she goes to the bar, she gets served straight away. I always have to stand there like a plant, waiting for ages to be served.

I'm going to have to find out her barman-whispering secret.

"So, how are you doing?" Ben knocks his shoulder with mine.

"In general or tonight?" I give a grin.

"Both."

"I'm great."

His eyes linger on my face for a little too long, like he's trying to get a read on me. And he must see something there because he says, "Are you sure?"

"Sure, I'm sure." I let out a nervous laugh.

"Just…with what happened with Robbie this morning, what he said about you and Carrick."

I freeze. Then, I kick-start myself back to life. "It doesn't matter." I give a halfhearted shrug. "It's all sorted now."

Ben gives a slight nod of his head. "It was good of you to sort it out with Carrick, so Robbie could keep his job."

I shrug again, averting my eyes. "It wasn't fair for Robbie to lose his job over something so stupid."

"Yeah, you're right, but not everyone would have had the balls to go after Carrick and talk him around like you did. It was cool of you, Andi. You're a good person."

A wide smile spreads across my face. "I really need to spend more time around Drunk Ben. I always get the best compliments from him when I do."

Chuckling, he shakes his head, and then his eyes turn serious. "He was right though, wasn't he?"

"Who?" I give a confused look.

"Robbie."

The smile slips from my face. I'm pretty sure my color drains away, too.

"Not in how he said it," Ben clarifies. "But there is something going on between you and Carrick."

Was.

"Look, you don't have to say anything," he continues.

Good, I think. Because the thought of talking about this right now is escaping me. I'm still dealing with the shock that Ben is actually saying these things.

"I just want you to know that I think Carrick is a mug for letting you slip through his fingers. And if you need a mate to talk to…well, I'm your man." He pats my arm with his hand.

But because I'm me, I don't want Ben to think badly of Carrick as he hasn't actually done what Ben thinks he has. Carrick didn't let me slip through his fingers. What we did, having sex and wrecking our friendship in the process, is on both of us, and now, we're in some weird place where he's moved on, but I can't seem to even though I know I have to.

And well, that one is all on me.

"Thanks." I clear my clogged throat. "But it's not like you think."

"No?" He frowns. "So, if I tell you that Carrick just walked through the door with Sienna in tow, it wouldn't be a problem for you?"

Holding my breath, I press my lips together in some form of a weird smile and shake my head. "No. It won't be a problem at all."

"Good, because he just walked in with Sienna."

Fuck.

Twisting my head, I look over my shoulder, and through the crowd of people, I see Carrick. It's impossible not to see him. He stands out wherever he goes.

He looks stunning in his tux, top button of his shirt undone, his bow tie lost somewhere along the way. Strands of his hair, in that little to no effort style of his, tease his forehead. His blue eyes dance under the lights as he stops to chat with some racing fans.

My heart sets off, doing a little thumpity-thump beat in my chest.

And I really need to get a grip because I'm starting to sound like a love-struck teenager. I'm actually making myself feel nauseous with my moon-eyed thoughts.

"You're definitely okay?" Ben's voice comes in my ear. "Because we can make a break for it before they get over here, if you want?"

Turning to look at him, I smile at his quip. "I'm good. But thanks for being awesome."

He gives me a wink, followed by a smile.

I know he can see through my bullshit, and I appreciate that he doesn't call me on it.

My mask is beginning to slip, and I really need to get it set back in place before Carrick sees it, too.

"Here you go." Petra hands me what looks like a Jägerbomb and then gives one to Ben.

"This a Jägerbomb?" I ask.

"Yep. And you've got one more to drink after this, so get supping, girl."

Okay...

To be quite honest, I'm ready for this drink now. I need the alcohol courage to get me through the next however long of the Sienna show.

"On the count of three..." Petra starts.

I tip the glass to my lips before the countdown even begins, and I down the whole thing.

"Fuck!" I blow out a breath of fire, slamming the glass down on the bar.

Petra is staring at me with what can only be described as total admiration.

"Attagirl!" Lifting a hand, she high-fives me. "Come on, Benny Boy, we got some catching up to do."

They both down their Jägers. A string of curses come from them as they blow out fiery breaths. I laugh at them, feeling a little lighter already.

I've just downed my second shot when I sense Carrick behind me. He doesn't have to say anything nowadays for me to know he's there. I can just *feel* his presence, like he's actually touching me.

Thankfully, after the Jägers, the room is starting to look an awful lot prettier. So, I think I can contend with him and the pop princess.

Then, I do feel him. His hand gently presses against my waist. My body freezes and then explodes back to life. Memories of his hands on my naked skin in that hotel room in Barcelona flood my mind.

"Hey." His deep voice comes in my ear, causing a shiver to hurtle through me.

Turning, I look at him, loving the feel of his hand, and it stays on me, sliding around my back, eliciting more shivers to run deep inside of places where I really shouldn't be feeling shivers.

His blues glitter at me, and I feel a flutter in my chest. He just looks so beautiful.

I really hate that.

"Hey." I smile.

I glance around for Sienna, but she's nowhere to be seen. Maybe she got carried off by the natives—wishful thinking on my part.

"Congratulations on the win, by the way. You were amazing. Really, really brilliant. The way you greased that corner on the last lap—amazing!" I'm grinning like a lunatic now and waving my hands about like a conductor. I need to get a grip.

This is what too much alcohol does. It turns me into an even bigger idiot than I already am.

"Thanks." He smiles, and it reaches all the way to his eyes. Then, he dips his head to mine. "I missed you earlier. I wanted to celebrate with my best—" He pauses for a beat as though thinking over his words. Then, he says, "Mechanic. One minute, you were there, and then you were gone. Where did you go to?"

I ran off because I couldn't bear to watch her all over you.

And that thought is like a douse of water over my fire.

I can feel my smile fading, so I force it back, brightening it up. "Sorry about that. I had an errand to run." *Liar. Liar.*

"Right." He nods, not moving his eyes from mine, and I'm starting to feel a little more than exposed, like he can see right through my bullshit, just like Ben could before. "Maybe we can have a drink tonight to celebrate?"

"Sure." I smile widely again.

Then, I watch as his eyes do that thing they do where they run down me, taking me in, stripping me bare. He hasn't done that since Barcelona. It makes me feel weak and needy for what I can't have.

He brings his mouth to my ear. "You look beautiful tonight." His words whisper over my skin, making my head feel light.

"Where's Sienna?" It's like a reflex, but it's definitely the kick I need back to the here and now.

Something akin to annoyance flickers through his eyes. He drops his hand from me, taking a step back. "Restroom."

"Carrick, you want a drink?" That's Ben.

He lifts his chin in Ben's direction. Then, his eyes follow, and I feel like I can finally breathe for the first time since he arrived.

"Beer would be great. Thanks, mate."

Realizing that I'm facing Carrick with my back to Ben and Petra, I turn around to face them, standing beside Carrick.

Petra's eyes are on me the moment I turn. I can see the concern in them, so I give her a reassuring smile.

"I didn't know you were coming tonight. I thought you were stuck at that boring party," Petra says to Carrick.

"Yeah, I was, and it was worse than boring, so I snuck out to come and hang with you guys."

"Of course you did. We're way more interesting than a bunch of stuck-up rich people. No offense." She grins when she realizes what she said.

Carrick's rich, but he's far from boring.

He's the most interesting person I've ever met.

Oh God, I'm at it again.

"None taken. And you're right. The people here are a hell of a lot more interesting."

The depth of his voice lifts my eyes to his to find him staring straight at me.

My mouth dries.

"So, how did you know where we were?" I ask, moistening my lips with my tongue.

Something flashes through his eyes. It looks a lot like lust, but because I'm in denial right now, I'm going to pretend it wasn't.

"Ben told me earlier where you were going to be."

"Oh, did he?" I slide a look at Ben, but he's facing away, trying to get served at the bar.

"Andressa." Carrick's hand touches my lower back, pulling my attention back to him. His eyes look deep and serious. "Can we talk? There's something—"

"God, I thought I was never gonna get back to you! It's packed in here. Why are we here again? The party we were at was way nicer."

Sienna's annoying voice rings in my ears like an alarm bell.

I step away from Carrick, causing his hand to fall away, leaving a distinct chill where he just was.

"Get me a drink, will you, Carr? I'm gonna need a large one if I'm forced to stay here for the rest of the night." She lets out a dramatic sigh.

Annoyance flickers through me. You'd think he'd brought her to a dive with the way she's acting. This place is really nice—hence, the reason why it's so full of people.

Biting my tongue from telling her to piss off back to where she came, I turn to look at her.

She looks really nice in a knee-length black lacy dress, which looks like it cost more than my entire wardrobe. And granted, there's a little bit too much lace, revealing a lot of her assets, but she can carry it off.

She looks a lot prettier than I do right now. I hate that.

But I can handle it. I'm a strong woman who treats other women with respect.

Pushing my dislike for her aside, I force myself to be polite and smile at her. "Hello, Sienna."

She gives me a blank stare at the sound of my voice. "Oh, good. *You're* here." Then, she rolls her eyes.

Okay...seems Carrick's little talk with her clearly had no effect.

God, I would love to punch her in her face—just once—but of course, I won't.

So, sucking it up, I give a tight smile. "I am. And now I'm going. Restroom break. Nice seeing you as always."

I'm going for the kill-her-with kindness theory. It'd be awesome if it actually worked. That was a joke—kind of.

I walk over to Petra, who is currently scowling at Sienna.

"Restroom," I say with a jerk of my head.

"Let's go." She takes hold of my hand. "Back soon, Benny Boy." She pats his shoulder as we pass.

By the time we make it to the restroom, I am actually in need of going.

When I'm finished, I come out of the stall. Petra is at the sink, applying her lipstick in the mirror above it. I can see her eyeing me carefully as I wash my hands, but she doesn't say anything.

I appraise my outfit in the mirror. I'm actually wearing a skirt tonight. Cute little floaty black number that I got when I went shopping with Petra the other day. I've teamed it with a pretty sparkly strappy black top and some low silver heels. My hair is down in loose waves.

I look nice. Well, not as nice as the pop princess, but whatever.

I blow out a breath.

"You okay?" Petra asks.

"I'm great." I flash her a smile, and then I get my gloss from my clutch and start applying it to my lips.

I've been faking smiles and saying, "I'm great," a lot lately.

"I didn't know Carrick and the mega bitch were coming tonight." She grimaces.

That's brings me around to face her. "It's not your fault they're here. And I didn't know they were coming either. But it's not a big deal." I lift my shoulders in a way that says I don't care—when we both know I really do. "I'm fine about it." I turn back to the mirror to finish applying my gloss. "I'm over the whole Carrick-and-Sienna thing anyway." I press my lips together, making a smacking sound. Then, I fasten my tube of gloss up and drop it in my clutch.

"Sure you are." She gives me a disbelieving look. "This is me you're talking to, Andi, not Ben. You don't have to bullshit me. If you don't want to spend the night around Carrick and the mega bitch, then we can go somewhere else, no problem. Today has been a tough day for you, and I'm not having the good mood we've got you in ruined by that talentless, humongous pain in the arse."

I snort out a laugh at her candid description of Sienna.

Yesterday, I did succumb, out of morbid curiosity, and listened to one of the most recent songs by The Diamond Babes. Not my thing, but I can see why they're popular. The main singer is really talented. That being said, Sienna is definitely only there to make up the pretty numbers. Petra insisted on playing me some of their live stuff—you know, just to torture me. It's fair to say that Sienna can't sing a note, and that's not me being a bitch. She really can't.

"Okay..." I concede on a breath. "But I am fine to stay, I promise. I need to get over my stupid crush or whatever it is that I have going on for Carrick, and the way for that to happen is for me to be around him and her."

She stares at me for a long moment, her head tilted to the side.

"What?" I shift, uncomfortable.

"It's not just a crush, is it?"

"What?" I give a nervous laugh. "Of course it is. What else would it be?"

"Love? If not love, then it's definitely well on its way to being that."

"I am not in love with Carrick!" I scoff.

Am I?

No...definitely not.

Her hands go to her hips. "Andi, I might not have known you for a long time, but I'm good at reading people, and you might not even realize it yourself, but you're in love with him."

I laugh loudly because I really don't know what else to do.

I'm not in love with Carrick. Definitely not.

I pick up my clutch, tucking it under my arm, as I'm gearing to leave the restroom and put a quick stop to this conversation.

"If Carrick wasn't a driver, would you be with him?"

I'm jolted back to that moment in Barcelona, dancing with Carrick at the party, when he asked me pretty much the same question, only in a different context.

Sighing, I lean my hip against the sink. "Maybe."

She mirrors me. "I think it's a definite yes."

"Are you a psychic nowadays?" I smile so not to come off as bitchy.

But she doesn't say anything.

A somber sigh escapes me. "Okay, fine. Yes, maybe I would risk being with Carrick if he were just a normal guy. But he's not a normal guy. He puts his life at risk every time he climbs in that car and pulls onto those tracks. And that's not something I can live with. But really, all of this is a moot point because Carrick *is* a driver, and he's not exactly into me in that way. Sure, he wanted to shag me, and I think he probably would again, given the chance, if he weren't with Sienna, but he is, and he definitely doesn't want a relationship with me."

"Oh my God!" She throws her hands up in the air. "Andi, I adore you. I do. But you are *the* most deluded person I have ever met."

"Thanks!"

"Seriously, if you went out there and told Carrick to dump the mega bitch and be with you, he would in a heartbeat. A fucking heartbeat. How do you not see that?"

Turning to the mirror, I curl my fingers around the edge of the sink as I try to control my emotions. I look up at her in the mirror.

"Because if he did care about me, then he wouldn't be here with Sienna. That's not what you do when you care about someone. And it's definitely not how you show someone that you care." I bite off the last word.

"You blew him off, Andi! And Carrick is a man who isn't used to being blown off. You seriously injured his pride, and this is his way of retaliating. I'm not saying it's right, but it's obvious that's why he brought her here. He's out there with Sienna, trying to show you that he doesn't care when it's as clear as glass that he does."

Is that true? Is that why Carrick brought Sienna here?

No. And to think it would only be pure vanity on my part. I'm not that important to him.

"I don't think so, and even if he did bring her here for that reason, it doesn't matter because—"

"He's a driver, and you can't be with him! I got the memo on that one. I just…" She lets out a wistful sigh. "You guys would be amazing together. I just wish you could see that." Turning to pick her clutch from the counter, she finishes with, "I just wish things were different for you, is all. You deserve to be happy."

I wish for that, too.

"As do you." I put my arm around her, giving her a half hug.

"You know what you need to do? Shake it off, like Taylor Swift is always telling us to do. Shake off all the Carrick-and-Sienna crap. It'll make you feel a million times better."

I let out a laugh as Petra grabs my hands and starts to shake them around. Then, she's wiggling her body, and I'm laughing and joining in with her.

"Did it work?"

"Actually, it did." I grin at her.

"Cool. Well, let's get our hot arses back out there and take a lay of the land. You can forget all about Carrick. And I'm thinking I need to pull me some fine Frenchman tonight and get laid French-style."

"Is there a French way of getting laid?"

"Dunno." She shrugs. "But they invented awesome kissing, so I'm betting they fuck just as well, if not better."

Laughing, I thread my arm through hers and let her lead me back out into the bar.

Seventeen

▬ MONTE CARLO, MONACO

"DRINK?" Petra says into my ear the moment we're back in the thick of the crowd.

I nod in response.

We head back to where we left Ben and Carrick. My heart starts to pick up pace as we approach, and I'm a little more than relieved to find them gone.

"I wonder where Ben is," Petra says.

"He'll be with the guys." I squish myself into a small gap at the bar to try to get my drink order in.

Petra stands on her tiptoes, looking around. "Ah, yeah, there he is. He's outside in the seating area with the rest of them."

Turning my head, I follow her finger in the direction it's pointing. I can see the guys, some seated around a small table, some standing.

Sadly, Sienna is there, sitting with her back to us, talking with one of the pit guys. Carrick is standing, facing our way, talking to Ben.

Almost like he hears me think his name, his eyes flicker straight in my direction, so I quickly look away, turning back to face the bar, hoping to get the bartender's attention.

"Why don't you go over to them?" I say to Petra over my shoulder. "There's no point in both of us waiting here. It could be ages. I'll come over with the drinks in a few. You can go chat with Robbie," I say teasingly.

I told Petra what I'd said to Robbie and all about our fight. She was fine with it, and I was glad because the last thing I would ever want to do is upset her.

"Maybe I will." She sticks her tongue out at me. "I might even pass up my plans for a French shag if Robbie acts like a normal person for once."

I let out a laugh, shaking my head. "Go on." I give her a playful shove.

Watching as she weaves her way through the crowd, I turn back to the bar, sighing at the sight of both the barmen down at the other end of the bar.

The DJ must have just turned up the music, and Calvin Harris's "I Need Your Love" starts to pump through the speakers.

It's impossible not to dance to this song, so I find myself moving to the beat, singing along with the words.

I feel a body press against my side. Turning my head, I find Leandro Silva standing next to me.

Holy shit!

Leandro Silva drives for one of the best teams in Formula 1. He's brilliant, and he was considered number one for a long time—until Carrick came along and knocked him off his spot, that is. It's rumored that they have a mutual dislike for one another.

I've admired Leandro's driving for a long time. He's one of my favorite drivers, and it helps that he's Brazilian, not that I'm biased or anything. I've wanted to meet him for forever. Of course, I've seen him at the track, but I've never gotten up the nerve to go over and introduce myself.

I wonder what he's doing here.

"Hello." He gives me a panty-dropping smile, a sexy dimple appearing in his cheek.

Oh God.

Did I mention that Leandro is really good-looking? Like *really* good-looking. Not better than Carrick. Just different. To Carrick's dirty-blond hair, Leandro's is black. To Carrick's blues, Leandro's eyes are as dark as night. And to Carrick's golden skin, Leandro's is olive.

Okay, I'm guessing you get the picture.

"Hi." I try to smile, but it comes off as more of a grin, and it feels awkward on my face. And that's probably because I'm staring at him like a starstruck idiot.

It's just...I've watched this guy race on the TV since I was sixteen! He's a hero back home in Brazil.

"You're Andi Amaro, right?"

He knows my name!

Hang on...he knows my name?

"How do you know my name?" It comes out sounding a little shorter than I intended, so I give a curious tilt of my head to play it off.

He lets out a deep chuckle. "You're famous. Did you not know?"

"No." I screw my face up. "Famous for what exactly?"

He angles his body toward mine. We're suddenly awfully close for two people who have just met. So close that I can see the hint of chocolate brown that centers his eyes, and I can smell his musky aftershave. But then to be fair, there isn't exactly a lot of spare room here at the bar.

"There aren't many female mechanics in Formula One—and definitely none as beautiful as you."

My cheeks redden.

What? I'm a girl, and Leandro Silva just called me beautiful. He's a brilliant driver and a hot older guy—well, when I say older, I mean, he's thirty—so, of course, I'm going to be flattered.

"Sorry, I forgot myself. I expect you to know who I am, but you might not. I'm Leandro Silva." He holds his hand out to shake mine.

"Of course I know who you are," I reply, my face flushing, as I slip my hand into his.

His hand is warm and rough. And I feel a spark of something. But nothing like what I feel when Carrick touches me.

Removing my hand from his, I turn back to the bar.

"So, I hear that you are a fellow Brazilian. Well, half-Brazilian. The other half is English, correct?"

I look at him, a smile tugging on my lips. "You know way too much about me."

He shrugs, a grin touching his eyes. "When I find someone interesting, I make it my business to find out everything I can."

Is he flirting with me?

It's no secret that Leandro likes his women. He's a serial dater, but the women are always models and actresses. Definitely not female mechanics.

And I don't know why—maybe it's the Jägerbombs or my feelings over Carrick and Sienna, the jealousy eating away at me—but I find myself leaning in and saying with a flirtatious tilt to my mouth, "And you find me interesting?"

A definite heat enters his eyes. "Very. I've wanted to meet you for quite some time now."

I don't know why, but I flicker a glance across to Carrick. And when I see that he's not even looking but talking to Ben, it pisses me off, which in turn fuels me even more to flirt.

I look back to Leandro, giving him my undivided attention. "I've wanted to meet you for quite some time, too. I really admire your driving. I've seen all of your races."

Okay, that was lame. I really shouldn't be allowed to talk to men.

But surprisingly, it seems to work on him, as he leans in even closer.

"You're a fan?"

"Mmhmm."

"So, why are you working for Ryan when you clearly should be working for me?"

Resting my arm on the bar, I give a one-shoulder shrug, tipping up the corner of my lips. "Because he offered me a job, and you didn't."

"How stupid of me."

"I know, right?" I bite down on my lip.

Lifting a hand, he sweeps my hair from my shoulder and brings his mouth close to my ear. "I might be being forward here, but I was wondering if you'd like to get out of here and come to a party with me."

I tilt my head back, looking him in the eyes. "Is *party* code for your hotel room?" I raise a brow.

He lets out a throaty deep laugh. It makes me smile. "No, it's actually code for party. But if you want to go to my hotel room, I would have no problem with that."

Whoa! Okay. This is moving way too fast, and I'm getting in a little over my head.

I definitely should not be allowed to flirt with men—especially when I'm only doing so to piss someone else off, and it's clearly not even working.

God, I'm so stupid.

Stepping back a little to put some space between us, I say, "I think we need to put the brakes on this a bit. I need to know a man for longer than five minutes before I even think about sleeping with him."

A couple of hours, minimum.

Okay, don't say that.

I turn my body back toward to the bar, leaning into it. "And anyway, I don't get involved with drivers." I rest my chin on my hand and grin up at him.

He chuckles. "Yeah, so I've heard."

That straightens me up. "You've heard? From whom?"

"Ryan." He tilts his head in the direction of where Carrick is. "I asked him about you, and after he not so politely told me that you were off-limits, he informed me that you don't date drivers anyway, so I'd be wasting my time."

I shoot a look at Carrick. And this time, I find that he's staring right at me, and he looks pissed.

Good, because I'm feeling majorly pissed off myself. *Who the hell does he think he is warning Leandro away from me?*

"I can't believe he did that," I fume.

"To be fair to Ryan, if you worked for me, I would have done the same thing. I would definitely want to keep you all to myself."

Something fires up inside of me.

Decision made.

I focus my eyes on Leandro. "Just to be clear, I'm not going to sleep with you, but if the offer to get out of here and go to that party is still on, then I'd really like to take you up on it."

"Are you coming with me just to piss Ryan off?"

"Partly," I confess. "Is that a problem?"

"Nope. No problem at all." He grins, his eyes crinkling at the corners.

"Cool. Well, just give me a minute to let my friend know I'm leaving, and I'll be back."

As I weave through the crowd toward Petra, I'm bubbling with anger.

Who the hell does Carrick think he is? He warned Leandro off me! He had no right!

I can't believe he cockblocked me!

He can sleep with whomever he wants—annoying fucking pop-tarts—but I'm not allowed.

Screw that. Bastard.

Well, not that I'm actually going to have sex with Leandro, but Carrick doesn't know that. Yes, I know it's childish, but I'm not feeling very mature right now, and my primary goal is to piss Carrick off.

"Hey." I tap Petra on the shoulder, pulling her attention from Mike, one of Nico's pit guys.

So much for talking to Robbie, who is currently sitting in a chair, with a scowl on his face while he nurses a pint of beer.

"Hey, where's my drink?" she complains to my empty hands.

"Oh, sorry. I forgot," I say, distracted. "But guess who I just met at the bar?"

"Matt Damon?"

"No. Why? Is he here?" I swivel my head on my neck. It's not unusual to see celebrities out and about while the Prix is happening.

"No!" She laughs. "It's just a dream of mine to meet Matt Damon in a bar. Or should I call it a sexual fantasy?"

"Okay, TMI. Anyway, it was *Leandro Silva*." I put a dramatic effect to his name.

"Leandro's here?" Her head starts to swivel on her neck just like mine did moments ago. I see when she spots him because her eyes spark. "God, he's so fucking hot," she says with a weird moaning sound to her voice, which freaks me out a little.

Shaking it off, I say, "Yep, and he just invited me to go to a party with him."

Her eyes widen. "Seriously? You're going, right? Please tell me you're going!"

With a mind of their own, my eyes search out Carrick. He's not looking at me, but I can tell that he's listening to our conversation in the way that his chin is tilted in our direction.

"I told him yes…" Taking hold of Petra's elbow, I steer her away from prying ears. "But now, I'm not so sure," I whisper.

In all honesty, my anger and confidence has started to wilt now that I'm here telling Petra with Carrick only a few feet away.

"What?" She looks aghast. "Why not?" Then, she flickers a glance in Carrick's direction and looks straight back to me.

I'm rewarded with a disapproving look.

"I just think…maybe it would be a mistake to leave with Leandro," I quietly tell her.

"How? It's not like you're going to have sex with the guy. You're just going to a party with him."

"But I'm not going for the right reason," I whisper. "I only said yes after Leandro told me that Carrick had warned him off me."

"What" Her mouth pops open, forming an O. "You're shitting me?"

I see a few of the guys heads turn at her yelling, one being Carrick's.

"Pet…" I chastise, my eyes briefly meeting with Carrick's curious ones.

"Shit. Sorry." She puts her hand over her mouth and talks through her fingers. "He seriously did that?" she whispers.

"Yeah, he seriously did that, and it pissed me off. And then I found myself saying yes to going to this party with Leandro, but I'm going for the wrong reason."

She takes her hand from her mouth and rests it on my shoulder. "Andi, if you were going to revenge shag Leandro—which I would totally recommend if you weren't *you*—God, I would tell you to revenge shag that hot Brazilian until you couldn't walk. But because you are you and I know you'd torture yourself for about a year after doing so, then I say no to any shagging. But I do say a big fat yes to going to this party with him."

"But what if he tries to kiss me?"

"Then, snog his face off!"

I give her something between a disapproving and humorous look.

"Okay," she says placatingly. "Let's say he does try to kiss you and you don't want him to, then you push him off and say no thanks. Seriously, honey, you're overthinking this. Just go have fun with the hot older man."

I bite my lip, hesitating.

"Look, do you want me to come with you? Act as a buffer?"

"Would you?" I brighten up. I'm such a chicken.

"Of course. A change of scenery would be good right now, and I'm sure Leandro has some hot friends at this party."

I notice that something in her tone is off. "Petra, is everything okay?"

"Yeah, everything is fine." She smiles, and it's as forced as mine have been all night.

I give her an unconvinced look. "You sure?"

She flicks a quick glance in Robbie's direction. Then, she looks back at me, plastering a bright smile on her face. "Sure, I'm sure."

She's so not okay, but I'm not going to press it with her. She'll tell me when she's ready to.

"Thanks." I wrap my arm around her shoulder, giving her a squeeze. "You know that you're the best female friend I've ever had, right?"

"I'm the only female friend you've ever had."

"True."

I give her a cheeky grin, and she laughs.

Reaching past Ben, she grabs her clutch off the table. "Right, boys, we're loving and leaving you. See you all tomorrow."

"Where are you going?" That's Carrick, and he's not looking at Petra. He's looking at me.

I open my mouth, but nothing except for air comes out.

Thankfully, Petra notices my struggle and answers for me, "Leandro Silva just invited Andi to a party, so we're going there."

His eyes widen, anger sparking to life in them.

Feeling uncomfortable, I avert my eyes to the floor. I don't even dare to look at Sienna right now.

"Sacking us off for a rival team?" Ben dramatically slaps a hand to his chest. "That hurts."

"Sorry, Benny Boy, you know I love you, but no way can a girl turn down a night partying with Leandro Silva." Petra flashes him a smile.

Tugging me by the hand, she leads me off into the crowd, heading back to the bar where Leandro awaits.

We've made it halfway when I feel a hand curl around my arm, pulling me to a stop.

Carrick.

I lose my hold on Petra. She casts a glance over her shoulder.

Seeing that Carrick is behind me, she nods her head in the direction of the bar. "I'll go introduce myself to Leandro. See you in a few."

I give her an uneasy smile, and then I watch as she goes.

Heart pounding, I turn to face Carrick. "What do you want?" My words come out short.

Hurt flickers across his countenance, but that doesn't stop him from saying what he's here to say, "Are you really leaving with Silva?"

"To go to a party, yes."

"He's bad news, Andressa."

"He seems okay to me." I fold my arms over my chest.

"He's a player. He uses women for sex and then discards them like trash."

"So do you."

Sighing, he shakes his head. "But we're not talking about me. I just…" He pinches the bridge of his nose with his thumb and forefinger.

Dropping his hand, he stares at me, and I can't tell if it's pity or sadness that's in his eyes right now.

"I just don't want to see you get hurt. Silva is only using you to get at me, to try to psych me out for the next race because I beat him today. It's how he works."

Okay, so it was pity.

He thinks I can only get a man when one is trying to psych him out for his next race.

Mother-effing bastard.

"Wow!" I let out an incredulous laugh. "So, you're telling me that he's just using me to get at you? Do you have any idea how bloody arrogant that sounds? You know what, Carrick? Fuck you!"

I spin on my heel, more than ready to get away from him, but he grabs my wrist, stopping my flight.

"Just fucking wait," he growls.

"No. Now, get your hands off me."

Instead of doing as I ask, he tugs me to him so that my body is flush with his. His other hand goes to my back, fingers pressing into my skin, holding me in place. The feel of his hard body against mine is painfully familiar. And an ache starts to throb deep inside of me.

My heart is beating out of my chest, and my palms are starting to sweat. Because more than anything, I want to feel his skin pressed up against mine. Every naked inch of him. I want to lick and kiss and taste every single part of him.

"I don't want you to go with him." His voice is low, raw.

And it exposes me.

"Yeah, well, I didn't want you to bring Sienna here, but we don't always get what we want." The words are out before I can stop them.

I watch his face blank as his chin jerks back.

Mortification and regret shower down over me like a bad storm.

I shouldn't have said that. I just basically told him how I feel in a roundabout way.

Fuck. Fuck. Fuck.

I definitely need to get away from him—*now*.

As if my prayer is answered, I see a furious Sienna stomping toward us. And to be fair, she's right to be angry.

Carrick is currently pressed up against me after he left her to try to stop me from leaving with Leandro.

I'd be angry, too.

Actually, I am angry. I'm bloody furious.

He's here with Sienna. He shouldn't be behaving this way with me. It's definitely a case of him having his cake and wanting to eat it.

Well, there'll be no eating of this cake tonight. Or ever again.

I'm done.

"Speaking of your girlfriend, she's coming over, and she doesn't look happy."

He doesn't say anything. He's just staring at me like he hasn't even heard what I said.

"Did you hear me, Carrick? Sienna is coming over, so let me go."

But he doesn't let go. He just continues to stare into my eyes, and my resolve is starting to break.

"Carrick, *please*, you need to let me go." My words come out in a pleading whisper.

Suddenly, his hands drop away from me like I just shocked him. His eyes are bright with a panic I don't understand.

Without another word, I'm out of there, pushing my way through the crowd to the bar.

"All right?" Petra asks me, eyeing me carefully the instant I get to her and Leandro.

"Perfect." I force a smile, trying to ignore the adrenaline soaring through my veins.

Then, I turn to Leandro and say, "Ready to go?"

"More than ready." He smiles.

Resting his hand on the small of my back, he guides me out of the bar.

And I don't look back once.

eighteen

▬ MONTE CARLO, MONACO

"OH MY GOD! I couldn't believe it when that guy got up on the bar and started to strip!" Petra laughs as we stumble out of the taxi.

"That was crazy!" I laugh. "But he definitely had the body to strip."

"Right?" Petra grins at me, flashing her eyes.

It's two a.m., and we're just getting back from the party that Leandro took us to.

When we arrived there, we met up with Leandro's mechanics. They were all great guys. Petra and I had such a good time. And Leandro was awesome. I had such a laugh with him. The guy is hilarious. He kept telling me jokes and cracking me up. And you know, I didn't once think about how hard today had been for me. Or about Carrick. And contrary to what Carrick had said, Leandro didn't hit on me once. He was a true gentleman.

He did however give me his number and asked me to call him.

I might, but just as friends, and nothing more. He's hot and fun, but it just wouldn't be a good idea.

It was just nice to be out having fun and not think about my Carrick woes.

But now, I'm back at the hotel, knowing Carrick's here somewhere with Sienna, probably in bed.

Ugh. God.

So, yeah, I'm back to torturing myself by thinking about him again.

Will this ever end? I just wish I could scrub my feelings for him away, so I'd be free of feeling this way.

I think I just need some distance, and I'm hoping I'll get that in Canada. Sure, Carrick will be there, but he'll be busy training. I'll have time to get my head straight.

Petra and I stumble in through the deserted lobby, giving a cheeky wave to the night desk manager when he greets us.

I let out a big yawn, more than ready to fall into my bed and pull a pillow over my head, when Petra comes to a sudden standstill.

"Andi..." she murmurs low.

"Hmm?"

"Carrick's over there in the bar."

I raise my eyes to find him sitting at the hotel bar, a glass of amber liquid in his hand, held midair. His eyes are fixed firmly on me. His hair is all ruffled up, like he's been driving his hand through it all night. He's still in his tux. Well, the jacket is gone, and his shirtsleeves are rolled up, but he still looks as handsome as ever. But what is holding my attention is his expression. He looks lost and angry and relieved all at the same time. It's one hell of a combination.

Blood whooshes to my ears with the sudden pounding of my heart, and I find myself instantly feeling sober.

"Go talk to him," Petra urges.

"Why?"

She gives me a look. "Because he's clearly waiting on you."

My forehead creases in confusion. I don't see what's so clear about that.

"I highly doubt it," I mutter.

"Jesus, Andi, you're the dumbest, smartest person I've ever met. Just go talk to him." She gives me a little shove in his direction. "I'll see you upstairs." Leaving me, she heads for the elevator.

I take a deep breath. Then, on unsteady legs, I walk toward Carrick.

His eyes stay trained on me the whole time, making me feel exposed and vulnerable, so I wrap my arms around my chest in attempt to shield myself from him.

As I get closer, I hear the soft sound of the Arctic Monkeys' "Do I Wanna Know?" playing. Coming to a stop at the end of the bar, a few feet from where Carrick is sitting, I see the music is coming from his phone, which is on the bar in front of him, next to a half-empty bottle of Jameson.

The bar is empty aside from us, and the bar itself looks to be closed, yet Carrick is sitting here, drinking.

I guess you can do whatever you want when you're Carrick Ryan.

"Hi," I say softly.

He silences the music on his phone. "Hi." He lets out a long breath. "So, did you have a good night?" His tone is harsh and off, and it instantly gets my back up.

In turn, it makes me answer a little too enthusiastically, "I did. It was brilliant. I had a lot of fun."

I see a muscle twitch in his jaw. Bringing the glass to his lips, he takes a long drink.

I know my response annoyed him, and instead of making me feel better, it just makes me feel crappy.

"Did you just get back?" I ask, leaning against the bar. I put my clutch on it. Laying my arms on the cool marble, I clasp my hands together.

"No," he answers tightly. "I got back a few hours ago."

"What are you doing down here on your own? Can't you sleep?"

"Something like that." He drains his glass and immediately fills it back up.

Stilling, I tilt my head to the side, studying him carefully.

Carrick likes to drink as much as the next person, but I've never seen him drink like this before. He's downing Jameson like it's water.

It's obvious that he's angry about something, and I'm getting it loud and clear that, that something is me. He's pissed off about me leaving with Leandro earlier.

I should feel angry with him for acting this way because he has no right to be mad, but I'm not. I'm just saddened by it.

I hate that we're still here, still fighting. I just want us to be okay.

"Carrick…are you okay?" I make sure to keep my voice soft, gentle.

"I'm just fucking peachy."

Okay…

I run a hand through my hair and take a calming breath. "Look, I know you're angry with me, and I'm guessing it's because I went to that party with Leandro."

Fiery eyes meet mine. I notice how bloodshot they are, how tired he looks.

"I don't know, Andressa. Is that what this is about? Is there something I should be pissed off about? Please do tell me. Because I'm just fucking dying to hear all about your brilliant night with Silva."

Aargh!

Anger explodes in me to catatonic levels. He's been spoiling for a fight from the moment I got here. Well, now, he's going to get one.

"What the hell is wrong with you? You're throwing a tantrum because I went to a party with one of your racing rivals! Is that it?"

"I'm not throwing a tantrum. I'm pissed off because I warned—" He cuts off.

"You what?" I take a step around the bar toward him. "Warned Leandro off me. Yeah, I know. He told me."

He flashes me a furious look. "Silva's a fucking prick who needs to learn to keep his mouth shut."

"*'Silva's a fucking prick.'* God! Do you hear yourself? You sound like a child! The only prick around here is you! Warning him off me. What are we? In school? You had no right to do that!"

He swivels his stool around to face me, his feet hitting the floor. His eyes are wide and livid. "I had every right! Just the same right I had when I asked you not to go to that fucking party with him, but you still went! Were you doing it to piss me off? Because if you were, then it fucking worked!" he roars that last part at me.

It takes me back a step, and I falter for a moment. Then, my gloves go straight back on. "I went because I can! I'm free to do as I please! I don't have to answer to you! I'm not yours!"

I barely get the chance to register what's happening before he rushes me. Gripping me by the back of my head, fingers tangled in my hair, he slams his lips down on mine, hard.

There's only a millisecond of hesitation before I kiss him back. A moan of pleasure works its way up my throat as our tongues touch then tangle together. I can taste the whiskey on him, feel the absolute desperation of his kiss, and it sends me spiraling, switching on a light inside of me that I'm not sure I can turn off. Or if I even want to.

But I have to because he's with someone else.

God, what am I doing? This isn't who I am. I don't do things like this.

I shove him away, using all my might. Stumbling backward, breathing heavily, I press the back of my hand to my lips. I can still feel him there.

"I can't believe you just did that," I whisper, hating myself for letting it happen...for how much I wanted it—him.

"It needed doing. You needed to be kissed by me as much as I needed to kiss you. Still fucking do." The predatory look in his eyes ignites and enrages me.

"I'm not sure your girlfriend would agree," I bite back.

"She's not my girlfriend."

"No? Well, that's not what she tells anyone who'll listen, and she's here, sleeping in your bed, so I'd say she's as close to being your girlfriend as it gets!"

He squeezes his eyes shut, his jaw clenched with obvious annoyance. "I'll say this one more fucking time. She is not my girlfriend." His eyes flick open, and he pins me with his stare. "Never was, and whatever the fuck she was before, she isn't anymore because I ended it."

Oh.

That takes me back a step. "You ended it? Why?"

Sighing, he looks to the floor. When he looks back up, I meet his eyes and see the blatant unease in them.

"Because of you."

My heart putters to a stop.

"Me?"

"Yes...you." The way he's looking at me, the softness in his eyes, is touching me like a warm caress.

"Sienna was a mistake that had gone on for long enough, and I realized that tonight in La Rascasse...when you said what you said about her being here."

Fucking oh!

I know where he's going to go with this, so I try to distract him away from what he's going to say because I can't go there with him right now.

"Is Sienna okay?"

He raises a brow. He knows I couldn't give two shits whether she's okay or not. But still he answers, "I'm sure she's fine. It's not like she actually gives a shit about me. All Sienna wanted me for was what I represent, what I could give her—visibility outside of the UK. She's more upset at losing that than me."

How can he even think that? How could anyone have Carrick and recover from losing him? It's not possible.

I know I couldn't—hence, the reason I find myself in the position I'm in.

I take a step back to him. "Are you okay?"

His eyes lift, holding mine. "No. But not for the reason you're thinking."

"And what reason am I thinking?" My voice is jumpy, all over the place. Just like my mind.

"That I'm down here, drowning my sorrows over Sienna. But you're wrong. I couldn't give a shit about her. I was just using her as much as she was using me." He drives a hand through his hair, disharmony pulling down his gaze. "I stayed down here because I needed to see you. I needed to know that you came back, that you didn't go with him to his…hotel."

He looks like he's in pain, and I feel it like it's my own.

"You know I wouldn't do that," I say softly.

His eyes lift, searing into mine. "Just the thought of him even touching you…" His hand goes to the back of his head, pulling on his hair.

"Nothing happened, Carrick. We partied. He gave me his number and asked me to call him, but that's it."

His brows pull together, uneasiness lining his face. "And…are you going to call him?"

"No."

"Why not?"

I take another small step toward him. It's like I'm being pulled to him on an invisible thread. "Because I don't want him."

The agony disappears from his eyes as a heat enters them. "Who do you want, Andressa?"

You.

Panic swallows up my words. "Carrick…I…"

The air between us is too thick, too much, and I can't breathe properly. I'm so confused. I know what's right, what I should say, but I can't seem to find the will to do what's right.

All I can see is him.

He clouds my vision, like steam on a mirror, and no matter how much I clear it away, he still comes back.

Reaching out, he wraps his hand around my wrist, pulling me to him, and I let him.

He presses his forehead to mine, cupping my cheeks in his palms, and I feel a sense of peace that I haven't felt since Barcelona.

"Right before you left the bar with Silva, what you said about not wanting Sienna here, I knew right then that I'd fucked up." He strokes my cheek with his thumb. "You were just so unaffected in Barcelona. When you stood there and told me that it was just a one-time thing, I believed you, and it hurt like a bitch. I wanted you to think that I didn't care, too. So, I let her come here because I wanted you to think I was past it, past you…but I'm not."

I don't know why, but instead of making me feel better, that angers me.

"So, you brought another woman here to make me think that you don't care about me when you do. That's some fucked-up logic, Carrick."

I pull away from his hold, but he grabs me before I can get anywhere. Yanking me against him, he holds me with my back pressed to his chest, an arm banded around my waist, the other pressed over my breasts. My heart is banging against my rib cage.

"I never claimed to be a fucking genius," he hisses, his lips at my ear. "Do you know how hard it's been for me to be around you and not be able to touch you in the way I want? It's been driving me crazy."

"So, you fuck Sienna to make yourself feel better. Nice."

"I'm sorry. I screwed up, and I'm sorry. You rejected me, and I…reacted badly."

He rests his forehead against the back of my head. I can feel his breath blowing through my hair onto my neck, driving me crazy.

"Do you know what I thought of every time I fucked her?"

"No! And I don't want to know!" I gasp, hot tears instantly hitting my eyes.

I try to struggle free but to no avail. His hold on me is too strong.

"You. I thought of you every single time. I imagined that she was you. And yeah, I know how screwed up that is, but it doesn't make it any less true. I can't get you out of my head. And do you know what the worst thing is?"

There's something in his tone, something so solemn that makes me turn my face to his, finding his expression just as grave. It makes my heart twist.

"It's that you don't even want to be in here." He taps a finger to his head. "The one girl that I want, and she doesn't want me."

I feel crushed.

"Carrick, I do want you. I just can't—"

The rest of my words are swallowed up by his kiss.

"Don't…" he rumbles against my lips. "I don't want to hear the can't right now. I just want to hear the want." He slides his fingers into my hair, tilting my head back so that I'm looking directly in his eyes. "Just tell me that you want me."

I do want him.

My body is vibrating with the need I feel for him.

The need I always feel for him.

The need I'm constantly trying to bury.

But I can't bury it tonight.

Closing my eyes, I let out a breath. "I want you."

His lips come down hard on mine, his hand fisting my hair. I turn in his arms, pressing my breasts against his chest, wrapping my arms around his neck, as he devours me with the most intense kiss I've ever had.

"I need to be inside you," he says, panting against my mouth.

My eyes open to find his on mine, and they are filled with a raw possessiveness, casting a sexual spell over me. And I let it take me over.

"Yes."

The word is barely out before I'm moving, being pulled through the bar. Pushing through a door, he tugs me inside, and I find myself in a deserted stairwell.

Everything happens pretty quickly after that.

Carrick's mouth crashes down onto mine as he pushes me up against the door. His hands are everywhere, like he can't touch enough of me. And my hands are pretty much the same.

I'm just absolute desperation.

My body is craving the feel and taste of him, remembering how amazing it feels to have him inside me.

Then, my skirt is being pushed up over my hips, and my knickers are torn off with one snap of the elastic. Carrick plunges his finger deep inside me. A whimper of pleasure falls from my lips as my head falls back against the door.

I'm lost, drowning in sensation.

"Always so wet for me," he growls.

Meeting his eyes, I grab his cock through his trousers. "Always so hard for me."

He pushes himself into my hand. "From the moment I saw you."

Desire rockets through me.

Leaning in, he sucks my lower lip into his mouth, his finger slowly moving in and out of me. "Tell me to fuck you, Andressa."

I'm so desperate for him that my body is shaking, yearning to have him inside. I don't care that I'm in the stairwell at the hotel. I don't care that anyone could come in and catch us. I don't care that I shouldn't be doing this.

I don't care about anything but having him inside me, making me feel only the way he can. Like no one ever has before.

I nip his lower lip with my teeth, loving the feel of his body's response to it. "Fuck me, Carrick."

His eyes flame wild with need. Slipping his finger out of me, he places it in his mouth and sucks me from it, making me feel dizzy with lust.

Holding my eyes, he gets a condom from his pocket. He unzips his trousers, shoving them down over his hips, just enough so that his cock springs free. He rips open the condom with his teeth and deftly rolls it on.

Not once does he look away from my eyes.

Then, his hands go under my thighs, lifting me. He spreads my legs and thrusts up inside me.

"Ah," I moan, my eyes closing on the feel of him.

My head thuds back against the door as he starts to fuck me, each thrust becoming harder and more insistent than the next.

Moving his lips up my neck to my mouth, he desperately kisses me. "Fuck. I've missed this…*you*, so much," he pants, his breath mixing with my own.

I've missed you, too.

"God, Carrick…I…"

My mind and body are spinning out of control, his pelvis and cock hitting all the right places.

"Come for me. I need to feel you tighten around my cock. Give this to me."

His hand moves between us, and he rubs my clit with his fingers. Then, I'm blowing apart in his arms, coming hard and fast.

"Fuck…Andressa," he groans, pressing his forehead to mine, holding my stare.

I feel his cock start to jerk inside me, his body tensing. And I watch with fascination, bordering obsession, as the waves of desire wash through his beautiful eyes. The moment is so intense that I feel like I'm falling.

I'm falling.

And then I'm wishing I could stay here forever. Stay in this moment with him and never leave. Closet it…*him*…keep him.

I want him. Not just for one day. I want him for all the days.

Then, reality comes crashing down on me, hitting me with the force of a tsunami, and I realize what I'm doing.

Wishing for things I can't have.

The crash back to earth leaves me feeling breathless, like my chest is cracking under the pressure.

Carrick presses a soft kiss to my lips, jolting my attention back to him.

"Stay with me." His lips move in soft, tender kisses over my cheek toward my ear, his hand curling around the back of my neck. "I'll get us a room."

"Where? Next to the one you have with Sienna." It's a shitty thing to say, and I instantly regret it.

Pulling back, he gives me a harsh look, and it makes me feel even worse than I already do.

I can barely meet his eyes. "I can't stay with you." I can feel the fear growing in me like a monster, readying to come out of the closet.

I let myself be selfish with Carrick, taking what I wanted with no thought for him or the consequences. I shouldn't have. It was wrong of me. I know I can't have him, yet I had sex with him again.

I'm leading him on. I'm not the type of person who does this. I don't get involved with someone who I can't give myself to even if just for a short time.

And I can't give Carrick any of my time. I'm not the right person for him.

I don't want to hurt him—that's the last thing I would ever want—but I don't know what else to do.

God, I hate how weak I am when it comes to him.

And knowing all of this, knowing how much I've screwed up with him, makes my panic climb to the highest level, and the worst thing about me when I panic is the person I become, the person I'm not.

"Don't do this, Andressa…"

He tries to cup my cheek, bring my face back to his, but I do what I do best when I don't know how to deal, especially with Carrick. I push him away—literally.

He moves back, slipping out of me, and I immensely feel his loss. Almost like he's taking a part of me with him as he goes.

He yanks up his trousers, fastening them. His movements are rough with suppressed anger.

Ashamed, I move away, pushing my skirt down over my hips, smoothing it out. Bending, I pick up my ruined knickers from off the floor, closing my hand around them.

"I can't believe you're doing this again," he says it so low, so harsh, that I freeze.

I lift my eyes to his, and I hate what I see there. "I'm not doing anything."

Denial—it's my best friend and my worst enemy.

"Just fucking don't." He stops me with his hand, his lip curling in disdain. "You're doing exactly what you did in Barcelona, except I'm awake to see it this time."

Shame lowers my eyes. "I'm…sorry. I just…" I hesitate, stuck on the words that are tearing me to pieces. The words that are going to hurt him. "I'm so sorry…" I whisper. "But…I can't do this…with you."

"Can't do what exactly?" he snaps angrily.

I lift my eyes to his. I owe him that at least. "I can't…" I pull in a strengthening breath. "I can't give you any more than what just happened."

He lets out a short bark of harsh laughter, but I can see the hurt in his eyes, and it's shredding me to pieces.

"Fucking unbelievable!"

Out of nowhere, a shot of anger bursts through me. "What is it that you want from me?" I cry.

Fury flashes through his eyes. He takes an angry step toward me, backing me up. "Isn't that already clear? I want you!" Lowering his eyes, he lets out a ragged breath. "I just want…you."

So many thoughts and feelings hit me at once—fear, exaltation, panic, want, confusion, need.

But the overriding, dominating feeling, as it always is when it comes to Carrick, is fear. Deep-rooted dark fear.

And as always, with my fear comes panic, and panic is in my driving seat.

"I'm sorry…" My lips tremble. "I can't be with you. You're just…too big a risk for me to take."

The look on his face. I never want to see that look on another human being for as long as I live.

He lets out a solemn, bitter laugh. "You know, I really wish I knew what that meant."

His eyes meet with mine, and the anguish I see in them crushes me to pieces.

"From the moment I met you, Andressa, I thought you were strong, maybe the strongest person I'd ever met, and I admired that about you." He lets out a staggered breath. "But I've come to realize something." He leans in to me, his face close to mine.

I suck in a breath at the absolute blackness in his eyes, feeling it closing in all around me.

"You're not strong. You're a fucking coward. And I'm done."

Moving me aside, he yanks the door open, and he's gone, leaving me with only the resounding bang of the door as it echoes in the stairwell and deep inside my mind.

You're a fucking coward.

Coward.

He's right. I am.

I fall back against the wall, feeling like I've been shot.

The pain is unbearable. It feels like my heart is actually breaking, shattering into unforgiving icy shards inside of my chest.

Ironic, I guess, how I've always been so afraid of Carrick, of wanting him, afraid of the way I feel about him, and staying away for the fear of getting my heart broken.

But as it turns out, I've broken it all on my own.

And I have a feeling there's no fixing it now.

nineteen

SPIELBERG, AUSTRIA

WHEN CARRICK SAID HE WAS DONE, he meant it.

Andressa Amaro no longer exists to him. If she's in a room, he leaves it.

She's invisible to him.

Andi, his mechanic...well, she just barely exists.

At the track, he barks orders at her when he has to and ignores her the rest of the time.

I'm pretty sure it's obvious to everyone, but they're saying nothing, and I appreciate it. I'm guessing that's due to Petra putting a gag order on them. Uncle John did notice Carrick being shitty to me the other day, and I got the raised eyebrow, which means his questioning will come sometime soon. I'm not looking forward to when it does.

I know people will draw their own conclusions as to why Carrick hates me. They'll probably have the right conclusions. But for now, I just choose to live in my state of denial that everything is okay when it couldn't be further from it.

In the first week while we were in Canada, Carrick was barely around, but when he was...it was horrific.

The first time I saw him after that night in Monaco, he looked at me like he hated me. It was painful. Actually, that's putting it mildly. It was excruciating.

I have no one to blame but myself, but that doesn't make it hurt any less.

I miss him with a physical ache. He was the best friend I ever had. That's gone now, and I don't know how to deal.

But I do know, feeling as badly as I do at the moment, how much worse it would have been if I had taken that step forward with Carrick and then lost him in the future.

I know I made the right decision—for him and me.

So, for now, I'm just living in a perpetual state of agony, waiting for things to get better.

Only…they don't seem to be getting better.

If anything, it's gotten worse—well, for me anyway. This past week in Austria, Carrick's gone from being angry with me to nothing.

It was like the flip of a switch.

So, instead of being mad with me all the time, he just seems indifferent, like he no longer cares enough to be angry.

Now, when he's forced to acknowledge me, I don't get hate stares. I get apathetic looks.

And they're heartbreaking.

At least when he was angry with me, I knew it was because a part of him still cared, and I had that to hold on to. Even though I don't deserve anything, I had that, and I clung to it to get me by.

But now, that's gone, and I'm just left empty, waiting for the hurt to subside.

I can't tell you how many times the words have been on the tip of my tongue, standing there before Uncle John, wanting to hand in my notice. But the cruel, sadistic side of me won't let me because I can't bear to leave Carrick.

Yes, I know how screwed up that is, but it is what it is, and I'm stuck with it until either Carrick fires me or I have a nervous breakdown, the latter looking quite likely at the moment.

If neither of those things happen, then, I'm doomed to ride the misery train I've created until the season is over in five months, and I'm forced to leave him behind, unless I decided to torture myself further and come back for the next season.

I'm sad, pathetic, and weak. I do know that. I just can't seem to change who I am or the way I feel at the moment.

I know Petra is getting frustrated with me over the Carrick-and-me thing—or the lack thereof, as the case may be. She doesn't understand why I won't be with him. She's still being the same awesome friend, supporting me, but I can see it in her eyes that she doesn't get it. For her, it's simple—you care about someone, then you're with that person.

I know she tried to understand me and my situation, but she can't fully grasp the reality of what I feel unless she's lived through what I have. So, with her, I now put on the full act that I'm okay with everything, that I'm past everything. And I leave my tears for those moments alone when I'm in the shower, and it's all just gotten a little too much for me to contend with.

When I got back to my room that night after Carrick and I had sex, Petra was awake, waiting on me. I took one look at her and burst into tears. After she let me cry on her shoulder, she said she thought that I should tell him, about everything—my dad, how I feel, and why I won't be with him.

But I can't. Because if I do, I know he'll talk me around. And it'd be great for a while…but it'd only be a matter of time before something happened out on the track while I watched him race. That would set me off. I'd freak out and only end up hurting him worse than I have now. I know, in the long run, I'm not strong enough to stay.

I am a coward. Just like he said.

That is one of the reasons I'm where I am right now. Well, only a small part of the reason, the main being that I can't miss the chance to be close to him again—and when I say *him*, I mean, my dad.

I heard about a vintage car show here, hosted by some rich guy, and my dad's car will be at the show with a bunch of other vintage racing cars and cars of dead celebrities.

It worked well as an excuse to get me out of going to a dinner tonight. Uncle John asked me to attend as his plus-one, but I know Carrick is going also. He wouldn't want me there, and I'm trying to make things as easy as possible on him.

I wonder who Carrick's plus-one will be.

There's been no more Sienna. I did see she'd sold her story to one of the dailies about her heartbreak over Carrick dumping her. But since her—or I should say, me—I haven't heard of him being with anyone else. Doesn't mean he hasn't. From past experience, I know that nothing keeps Carrick down for long.

So, here I am, wandering through the big glass doors of the showing. I hand my ticket to the woman at the entryway. She gives me a pamphlet that details the layout of the show, and I make my way inside.

As I walk through the main door, I see the room is already buzzing with people. A waiter in a suit, standing by the door, hands me a complimentary glass of bubbly, which I take gratefully. A bit of liquid courage.

I know it sounds a bit crazy for me to be so nervous about seeing a car, but this car represents and holds most of my best memories with my dad. So the thought of seeing it leaves me feeling a little shaky.

I haven't seen his car since my mum sold it at the charity auction, right before we left England to move to Brazil. I was so angry with her at the time. The others, I could let go of, but this one, this was *our* car. In this car, he took her out on their first date, he drove them away from the church after they'd gotten married, he took me to my first day of school. He always took me out in that car every chance he could, just for a drive.

He loved that car. He'd bought it as a wreck and restored it. That car was an extension of him, our family, everything that he represented.

REVVED

It took me a long time to realize why my mum had gotten rid of it. Having it would have been a constant reminder of everything she had lost.

And after meeting Carrick and having him in my life, even for a small portion, I understand it even more.

I look down at the pamphlet, looking for my dad's car. I want to see the others, but I need to see his first.

It's in the center showing. Looks to be one of the main attractions here.

I fold the pamphlet and put it in my bag. Then, I down the bubbly. I give my empty glass back to the waiter, thanking him. I take a deep breath and make my way to my dad's car.

I glance at other cars as I pass, noting which ones I'm going to come back and pay more attention to, but my focus is on the black Jaguar XK120 M Roadster that I can see on the podium up ahead.

My heart starts to beat faster with each step I take.

It hasn't changed. It looks exactly the same, and it's as pristine as ever. The wheel trims are still painted bright red to match the red interior lining and red leather seats.

It looks like it hasn't been touched since the day it left my family.

As I move near it, I press my hand to my beating heart.

There's a placard in front of the podium, asking people not to touch the car. Then, another one is beside it, detailing the car's history with my father's name right at the top. It briefly talks about how he restored the car and how he had it up until his death in 2001. Then, it was bought at an auction and has remained in this collection ever since.

I take a step closer to the car. I can smell the fresh wax coming from the paintwork. I quickly glance around to see if anyone is watching, and then I gently touch my fingers to the car. The memory of the last time I was in it with him comes back to me like it was only yesterday.

"Come on, Dad. Drive faster!" I said over the sound of the breeze whipping through my hair. *"You're driving like an old-aged pensioner!"*

"I'm doing seventy." He laughed.

"Like I said, driving like a pensioner. How can the world's number one racing driver go this slow? Seriously, how do you win your races again?" I was winding him up to get my own way. I knew just how to play him to get what I wanted. He was so easy, my dad.

He slid me a glance and grinned.

I loved his smile. There was just something about it that always told me just how much he loved me.

"Fine." He gave a little huff. *"Just don't tell your mother I was speeding again with you in the car because she'll have my arse—head,"* he quickly corrected. *"She'll have my head if she finds out."*

I giggled at his slip up. *"My lips are sealed."*

I did the lock-and-key action and pretended to toss the key out of the car, making him chuckle.

"Seriously, I just don't get why Mum hates you driving fast, why she worries so much. It's your job, for God's sake."

"And that's why she doesn't like it."

I gave him a funny look.

He cast me a look and smiled. *"She worries because she loves me."*

"I don't worry."

He gave a soft laugh before looking back to the road. *"It's different for your mother. One day, when you're a grown woman and you have a man of your own—preferably when I'm senile, blind, and deaf—then you'll understand."*

"Ugh! God, Dad!" I squealed, shoving him in the arm, causing him to laugh loudly. *"I'm never going to have a boyfriend,"* I told him huffily, folding my arms over my chest. *"Boys are idiots."*

He looked at me again, tension in his brow. *"That kid Patrick still giving you a hard time?"*

Ugh, Patrick Webber, the bane of my existence. Seriously, the guy wound me up all the time. Constantly going on about how tall I was, calling me lanky and saying I was like a boy just because I was *into cars. Honestly, one of these days, I was going to punch him right in his perfect nose.*

"Nothing I can't handle." I shrugged.

"Well, if it gets to be too much to handle, you tell me, and I'll sort him, okay?" My dad chucked my chin with his finger.

I smiled back at him. "Okay, Daddy."

He looked back to the road.

"Dad?"

"Hmm?"

"I just...I want you to know that I don't worry like Mum does when you drive 'cause I know you're the best driver in the whole world. Not because I don't love you."

He stared at me for a long moment. Then, he reached over and put his arm around my shoulder, pulling me to him. He kissed the top of my head. "I know, kiddo. I love you, too. And you're right. I am the best driver in the world." I could hear the grin in his voice. "So, are we taking this baby up to maximum speed or what?" he said, releasing me as he turned onto a stretch of clear country lane.

"Maximum speed!" I yelled, laughing, putting my arms up in the air like I was on a roller coaster.

He let out a rumble of laughter, his foot pressing down on the accelerator. "Scream if you wanna go faster, Andi."

"You know you're not supposed to actually touch the cars."

I'm jolted out of my memory at the sound of Carrick's voice. My hand recoiling from the car, I swing around to him.

As I stare into his face, my heart thumping wildly. I see concern cross Carrick's brow, and I realize that my cheeks are wet with tears.

Turning my face away, I quickly brush them gone with my hands.

"Hey, are you okay?" His voice is soft, caring. He takes a step toward me, his hand reaching out, but then he stops before he touches me, as if catching himself.

"I'm fine." I force a bright smile onto my face.

"You don't look fine."

"Well am I. I'm great." I lift my voice. I know it sounds unnatural, but I don't know what else to do.

Because I won't explain to him why I was just crying while standing before William Wolfe's car.

I see his eyes flicker to my dad's car, and then they come back to me. I can see his mind working.

Don't connect the dots. Don't connect the dots.

"I thought you were at that dinner tonight?" I quickly go for a change of subject.

He stares at me for a long moment. Thankfully, he decides to let it go. "I was supposed to go, but then I heard about this showing today, so I ducked out. Sent my dad on his own."

He was going with his dad. The relief I feel at that is immensely scary.

"Was he angry?"

He shrugs, a smile teasing his lips. "A bit, but I've ditched him to come to a car show, not to go out partying, so he can't be too mad."

He gives a cheeky grin that makes my erratic heart swell in my chest.

And that makes me take a step back.

"Well, I'm sorry. I didn't know you were coming. If I had, I wouldn't have come." I don't know how true that is. I would have come because I had to see my father's car. I would have just come when I knew he wouldn't be here.

"Wow," he says with an incredulous tone in his voice and a hurt look on his face. "I know we're in a weird place right now, but you hate me that much?"

My eyes widen with shock. "No. I don't hate you. Of course not. And 'weird place' is putting it mildly, Carrick. You can hardly bear to be in the same room as me. When I said I wouldn't have come, I meant, for your sake. I know it's bad enough that you have to see me at work."

"Jesus…Andressa." He rubs his forehead with his fingers and then takes a step toward me. "That's not…I just…fuck." His eyes blink in earnest at me. "I'm really fucking sorry for the way I've behaved lately. The way I've treated you…I've been a complete bastard."

I wrap my arms around myself in protection. "You have nothing to be sorry about. It's me who should be sorry."

He shakes his head. "I think we've both been at fault in one way or another lately. I just…I don't deal well with rejection." He shoves a hand through his hair, looking awkward. "When I'm rejected, I act like a total prick."

"I know. You've told me that before. In China, remember?"

"Yeah, and I acted like a prick then, too. No wonder you don't want me."

My face drops. "Carrick…I…"

"Sorry. Just pretend I didn't say that and sound like the biggest fucking loser on the planet. Actually, can we just forget everything and start from the beginning?"

"Start from the beginning?" My brows pull together.

"Yeah. It could be like we just met for the first time. Forget everything that has happened and start fresh."

"Oh." I don't want to forget a moment of anything with him. Even the bad stuff. "Why?" I ask quietly.

He takes another step closer. The space between us is marginal now. I can smell his aftershave…*feel* him. My body starts to ache with need.

"Because I've come to realize that I'd rather have you in my life…than not at all." He blows out a breath, giving me hopeful eyes. "So, what do you say?"

Even though it stings that he just wants to erase our past like it doesn't matter, I know I have no right to feel that way. And I can't turn down the chance to have him in my life again.

I hold my hand out. "Hi, I'm Andi Amaro."

He glances down at my hand, a smile touching his eyes. When he takes hold of my hand, I feel those familiar sparks I always feel whenever he touches me, but this time, I feel an ache so deep that it burns into my bones.

Somehow, I manage to hold myself together.

"Carrick Ryan," he says. "It's nice to meet you, Andi."

"Actually, call me Andressa." I smile. "This guy I knew, the best guy ever, always insisted on calling me by my full name."

Lightness flickers in his gaze. "Sounds like a smart guy."

"He is."

"Okay, Andressa it is."

Slipping his hand from mine, he turns to my dad's car. Taking it in for the first time, he lets out a low whistle. "Wow, William Wolfe's car. I've heard about it, but I've never seen it in the flesh. Fucking stunning. Does it still run? Do you know?"

"I don't think so." I sadly shake my head. "They generally take the engines out of these classics to keep them pristine."

"Shame. Car like this should be driven."

"I know, right? It's such a waste for it to just sit around, not being used. He would have hated that."

Carrick looks back at me, questioning.

And I realize my slip up. *Shit.*

"I mean, I'm guessing he would have because no racing driver would want to see his car sitting around, not being used, right?" I'm fidgeting, so I fold my arms over my chest.

"Right." He looks back to the car, staring at it. "This is your favorite type of car, too, right? The Jaguar XK120 M Roadster."

He remembered.

"Yes," I say slowly.

"Hmm," he says.

Hmm. What does that mean?

He's staring at the car still, and I'm starting to feel a little jittery. Worried that maybe he's beginning to tie things together.

So, I decide it's time to make my exit, and really, I should leave him to it. I don't want to push this too far, ruin this even ground we've just found.

Stepping back, I say, "So…I'm gonna go look around. It was great bumping into you…and you know, sorting things out." I offer a smile. "I guess I'll see you later."

"Andressa," he calls me back.

My body tightens and yearns to reach for him.

As I turn, he's already moving toward me. "Do you…" He pauses, rubbing a hand over his hair. He looks nervous, which is odd because Carrick never gets nervous. "Would you mind if I come look around with you?"

I hold my breath as my heart leaps into my throat.

I know I said I didn't want to push things with him, but him asking to be around me right now is a whole different ball game.

"Of course not." I press my lips into a sincere smile, ignoring the bumpity-bump in my heart at the sight of his face relaxing into that amazing smile of his.

✚ BEDFORDSHIRE, ENGLAND

I'M IN MY APARTMENT, finally home. We're back for the British Grand Prix, which starts in a few weeks. We arrived in England yesterday afternoon, and I now have five days off work before I'm back at Rybell.

I plan on sleeping for four of those five days. All of the traveling and late nights spent working and partying have caught up with me.

I saw Carrick the night before we all left to come home. I was in the hotel bar on my own. Petra had already left, and Carrick was coming back in the hotel. He saw me, came over, and sat down to join me, and we had a drink together in the bar. I had to stop myself from remembering the last time we were together in a hotel bar.

It wasn't an easy memory to erase.

But that's what I've been trying to do, just like he asked. And we're doing okay.

Do I still have feelings for him?

Yes.

Do I still want to rip his clothes off his body each time I see him?

Absolutely.

But that gets us nowhere. So I'm focusing on the fact that we're talking, and I'm happy to have him in my life again even if there is a sense of awkwardness between us.

At times, it's almost like we're treading water, figuring out how to be around one another again.

And it's like he knows I've been thinking about him because my phone lights up with his name.

"Hi," I answer.

"Hey." His Irish lilt bleeds down the line, making my belly flip. "How are you doing?"

"I'm good. You?"

"Yeah, good. Look, I was wondering if you're free this afternoon. I've just…I've got something I want to show you."

"Sounds ominous. But, yeah, sure, I'm free."

"Really?"

"Why do you sound so surprised?" I laugh.

"I don't know. I thought you might be busy or something."

"The only thing I'm busy with right now is a bar of chocolate."

"Which chocolate?"

"Galaxy, of course." I smile.

He makes a moaning sound, and it practically has my toes curling.

"Do you want a moment alone with my bar of chocolate? I can put it on the phone if you want. I have FaceTime."

He barks out a laugh. "Nah, I'm good."

"So, what is this thing you want to show me anyway?"

"You'll see."

"Aw, come on! You can't leave me hanging. Just tell me."

"You won't be hanging long. I'll be there to pick you up in half an hour."

"Then, you'll tell me when you see me."

"No." He laughs. "Thirty minutes, Amaro. Be ready to go."

I glance down at the state of my unshowered-still-in-my-pajamas self. "Actually, can you make it forty? I need to get dressed."

"Please don't tell me you're naked right now."

"No!" I blush.

"Thank fuck. I'd have had to drive faster if you were."

"Oi!" I chastise playfully, liking that we seem to be getting over the awkwardness and getting back to us.

"Forty minutes and not a second later."

And then, he's gone, and I'm leaping from the sofa, making a dash for the shower.

I'm dressed in skinny jeans and a T-shirt, hair down and almost dry, rubbing balm onto my lips when I hear a car horn beep.

Going over to my window, I open it up and see a hot-as-sin red Lamborghini parked in front of my building.

Carrick pokes his head out of the window, grinning up at me.

"Two minutes." I signal to him.

Running around my apartment, I get my jacket, bag, and phone. I grab the bar of chocolate I bought yesterday while thinking of Carrick and shove it in my bag.

I let myself out of my apartment, lock up, and run down the stairs, exiting my building.

"Sweet ride." I whistle as I walk around his car, getting a good look at her.

She's an Aventador LP 700-4 Pirelli Edition with a matte black roof and engine hood, so you can see the mechanics beneath. A thin red stripe runs along the black roof, linking her to the Pirelli brand. She's brand-new, and there aren't many of her around.

"How long have you had her?" I ask, sliding into the rich leather seat.

"Not long."

I know they were announced at the start of the year, forecasting delivery for the summer, but I wouldn't be surprised if he'd gotten the first one. He's Carrick Ryan.

Having him driving around in a brand-new car is every manufacturer's dream, irrespective of the level of brand.

"She's beautiful." I run my hand over the dash.

"Yeah, she is."

The tone in his voice turns my head to him. He's looking at me. No, he's *staring* at me.

I swallow nervously and then start rambling, "Six-point-five liter V-twelve engine, delivering six-ninety horsepower, with ISR transmission, pushrod suspension, and permanent all-wheel drive, right? I bet she handles like a dream."

He's smiling at me, his eyes all lit up. "She does."

"She hits one hundred in two-point-nine seconds, right? Maxing out at three hundred and fifty kilometers per hour?"

"Mmhmm."

"You had her up to top speed yet?"

"No, I haven't had time to get her out on the track yet."

"Cool. Well, I'd love to be there when you do." Then, I quickly worry that maybe I've overstepped my boundaries with him. "You know, if I'm around or whatever."

"We can take her out this week if you want?"

"Really?" I beam at him.

"Really."

"Yay!" I clap my hands together, and he laughs at me.

"How can you be such a girl yet be so fucking cool with your car knowledge?"

"I'm just awesome. What can I say?" I shrug, grinning.

He's staring at me again, and I'm starting to get hot.

"I brought you something," I announce a little too loudly, jolting us back to the now. I reach into my bag and pull out a brand-new bar of Galaxy Cookie Crumble.

"Fuck, has that got—"

"Cookie in it? Yep. You haven't had it before?"

"No, and I'm wondering how the fuck not." His eyes are all lit up like a little kid. "Have I told you lately how amazing you are?"

"Not lately," I say, handing it over.

He rips it open and breaks some off, putting it into his mouth. Then, he starts making that moaning sound again, and I'm squirming in my seat.

Maybe bringing him the chocolate wasn't the best idea. I'm currently jealous of a bar of Galaxy chocolate.

"Fuck…that's good. You want some?" he offers me through a chocolaty mouthful.

"No, I'm good. Thanks. I wouldn't want to deprive you of any."

"Sorry." He grins. "It's just me and Galaxy have this thing. It's pretty serious."

"Clearly." I give him a teasing smile and love the smile I get in return.

"Come on then," he says, putting down the chocolate into the center console. "Let's get moving."

Putting the car in drive and stepping down on the gas, he roars down the street.

✜ BUCKINGHAMSHIRE, ENGLAND

Thirty minutes after leaving my place, we're in a quiet village called Radclive, and Carrick is turning off the country road and onto a small drive in front of a set of metal gates.

Pressing a button on the steering wheel, the gates open, and then we're driving up a curved long driveway. At the end of the driveway is a large Edwardian-style house surrounded by what I can only imagine is acres of land.

"Wow," I say, looking through the windscreen. "Is this yours?"

"Yeah. This is home."

He pulls up front and climbs out of the car, so I follow suit.

I'm a little nervous that he's brought me to his house, wondering why I'm here.

"I'll show you the house in a few, but what I brought you here to see is in the garage."

I walk with Carrick toward a massive outbuilding, which is located on the side of the house. He pulls a tiny remote from his jacket pocket and opens one of the garage doors.

We go inside, and I find myself in a purpose-built garage—or I should call it a showroom.

I'm astounded at the number of cars he has in here. There must be thirty, minimum, with plenty of space for more. They're mostly classic cars with a few modern ones.

"Wow, Carrick. This is amazing. I knew you collected, but…wow…" This place is like my dream come true.

"Thanks. I've got pretty much every car I've ever wanted, barring a few. But the one I wanted to show you is just down here at the end. It just arrived this morning."

I walk behind him, my eyes trailing over each car we pass—a classic Mini Cooper, a Dodge Viper…

"Here it is."

I turn to the sound of his voice, dragging my eyes off the yellow 1960 Lamborghini Miura, and—

Oh my God.

My heart slams against my ribcage. "Is that…" I take a step closer, my hands trembling.

"William Wolfe's car? Yeah."

I swing around to look at him. "You bought it?"

I can't believe he did that. Why did he do that?

A stupid hopeful part of me wishes it were because of me, that he somehow realized this car is important to me.

"I didn't steal it. Don't worry." He grins, pushing his hands into his pockets. "It was bugging me—what you said about it sitting there, not being used, and how Wolfe would have wanted it to be driven. So, I got in touch with the owner, and I told him I wanted it."

"And he just said yes?"

"Not right away. It took some persuading."

"How much persuading?"

"A lot—plus, a five-year VIP pass to the Prix."

"Wow. Expensive persuading."

"Drop in the ocean." He shrugs, walking around to the front of the car.

Sometimes, I forget how much money he has at his disposal.

I walk closer to the car, the tips of my fingers trembling to touch it. "Can I?"

"Sure."

Reaching out, I open the door. Then, taking a deep breath, I slide into the driver's seat.

I'm trying not to act weird, but it's hard.

This is a bittersweet moment for me.

Closing my eyes, I place my hands on the steering wheel, curling my fingers around it.

I feel the car move. Opening my eyes, I see Carrick getting in the passenger seat beside me.

"Are you happy I bought it?"

Beyond happy.

Tears are beating at the backs of my eyes. I fight them away.

Pulling my lips up into a smile, I say, "Of course, I'm happy for you, and happy that this car isn't going to be sitting around like an ornament anymore."

He's staring at me, almost like he's weighing something. "Good, because I need your help to get it up and running. If you want to, that is?"

Do I want to? Is the sky blue?

"Really?" I feel suddenly breathless.

"Yeah. But it's gonna be a big job. Total refit as she's empty. If you're up for it?"

"I'm up for it." I smile so big that it nearly splits my face.

Carrick returns my smile. "I'll pay you the going rate, of course."

Huh?

I stare at him like he's lost his mind. "I don't want you to pay me."

"Andressa, this is a big job. I'm not letting you do the work for free."

"I don't think you understand."

He really doesn't, and part of me wishes he did in this moment. God, I would sell my soul to be able to get this car back on the road. And with Carrick driving it, I'd give everything.

But I play it down. "Working on a car like this is fun for me, like what a day out at the spa is for other girls."

He shakes his head, laughing. "Andressa, you are like no girl I've ever known."

I tilt my head to the side, scrunching my eyes up. "Good thing or bad thing?"

"The best thing." His voice is deep with meaning.

My eyes catch his and hold. The air crackles between us, and I suddenly feel *everything*.

Blood beats in my ears, my pulse quickening.

Memories of him and me together…him inside me…are flashing through my mind, making me hot, making me needy.

Carrick looks away, breaking the moment. He clears his throat.

I need to say something to put us back where we were. I can't spoil things with him again, not when I've just gotten him back.

"So, no more talk of money. I'm doing this because I want to."

He turns his eyes to me. "If that's what you want."

"It is." I smile lightly, curling my hands back around the wheel, as I exhale. "So, when do we start?"

"Now, if you want?" He opens his door and gets out of the car. "You can help me draw up a list of what we'll need. I'll order it, and then we'll go from there."

Climbing out of the car, I say, "Let's get started."

twenty-one

✛ BUCKINGHAMSHIRE, ENGLAND

I'VE BEEN WORKING ON MY DAD'S CAR with Carrick nonstop for the past four days. I've hardly been home.

It's been amazing, doing this with Carrick, restoring my dad's car back to life.

Even though it's been amazing, it's been tough, too, and not just because I'm working on my dad's car. Even though that has been emotional for me, I've kept those feelings buried. I'm just praying that I won't burst into tears when I hear the engine running for the first time.

It's also been tough to be around Carrick. I'm like a pot waiting to boil over. My hands are permanently itching to touch him, and the sexual tension building inside me is at the point that I'm sure I'm about to spontaneously combust from it.

But it's not just the sexual tension that's driving me insane.

It's how I feel about him. That's tearing me up the most.

Being with Carrick so intensely these last few days has brought everything to the forefront, everything I've been fighting to hide.

My feelings for him have grown. They're more insistent and bigger, harder to ignore.

It was a little easier to pretend that I didn't want him, that I wasn't totally crazy about him, when we were traveling with the team or when he was angry at me or when we were dancing around each other, trying to build a bridge back to a friendship.

But this, being around him all the time in close proximity…it's getting to the point of being unbearable.

And instead of being relieved that we're almost coming to the end of working on my dad's car—well, Carrick's car—so that I can put that distance between us, I'm finding that I want to etch it out longer, so I can be around him—hence, the reason it's taken me two and a half hours to fit the wiper motor.

Two and a half bloody hours to do a job that should have taken me one hour maximum.

I just…I don't want this time to end. I want to be around him all the time.

I want him. I just wish I knew a way I could have him.

But all my wanting is fruitless. Carrick is past all of that now. He's past me. I can tell…feel it in the way he is toward me. It shows in his body language. There are no more accidental touches. He keeps himself at a friendly distance from me.

Aside from that little moment in the car the other day, he has shown no indication of feeling the way he used to about me.

He's affable, and we have our usual banter, but that feeling I always got from him, the one that told me he saw me through different eyes, is now gone.

I know he just sees me as a friend. I know that was what I wanted when I was telling myself that I needed him to stop wanting me, so I could stop wanting him. But now that he has, I hate it. It hurts like a bitch.

And now all I want is for him to see me the way he used to. Look at me the way he used to. I want him to want me like he did before…like I now want him. And it hurts beyond belief that he no longer does.

"How's it coming?" Carrick's voice comes from behind me.

It jolts me, stopping my thoughts and my humming along to the song playing on the radio.

I give another turn, tightening up the final screw. "Yeah, all done."

Turning, I see him holding two coffees in his hands. I give him a smile of appreciation.

I put the screwdriver back in the toolbox and wipe my dirty hands on a rag. After tossing it on the workbench, I take the coffee from him. "Thanks."

He leans back against the workbench. "So...we're nearly done."

My lips turn down at the corners, so I take a sip of my coffee, covering it. "Yeah, nearly done. Just need the starter motor, and we'll be finished."

"It'll be delivered tomorrow. I know you're back at work then...so I can fit it, if you want?"

"Oh, yeah? Okay, sure." I try to hide my disappointment with a smile.

Carrick's watching me. Dropping his gaze, he takes a sip of his coffee. Holding the cup against his chest, he says, "Will you come by tomorrow after you're finished with work? I was going to wait to start her up. I thought we could take her out together."

That brightens me up. "Sure. I'll try to get out early, and I'll come straight here."

"Cool." He smiles at me and takes another sip of his coffee.

The air feels strained between us, and I'm not really sure why. Maybe I am causing it because I'm feeling sad at the thought of my time here with him coming to an end.

I've just taken another sip of coffee when David Guetta's "Dangerous" starts to play out of the speakers.

This song was playing in the garage the first time I met Carrick.

I feel a sudden energy in the room. Like pure electricity.

I lift my eyes to Carrick and find he's already staring at me. There's something deep and intense in his eyes, and it's making my stomach flip and my knees weaken.

"This song…it was playing the first time we met." His voice is low with meaning.

And it's like he just read my mind.

I can't believe he remembers.

"You…remember?" My words come out in a breathy whisper.

"I remember everything."

Drawing a breath, I lower my eyes.

I feel like I'm being blasted with every single feeling I have for him. The feelings I've had since the moment I turned my head and saw him standing there in the garage at Rybell. The feelings that have kept on growing ever since.

Growing and changing into something so big that I can no longer see past them.

All I can see now is him.

I lift my eyes, and I'm met with Carrick's. The look there nearly brings me to my knees.

I start to tremble, right down to my bones.

Wordlessly, he puts his coffee down and slowly walks toward me, not moving his eyes from mine.

I'm paralyzed. And even if I weren't, I wouldn't move. I need him close to me right now more than I need air.

Taking the cup from my hand, he places it on the side. Then, lifting a hand, he brushes a stray hair from my face.

I suck in a breath. My body triggers to life under his touch.

"What are you doing?" My voice trembles.

"Taking what I want…what's mine."

He cups my face with his hand, running the tip of his thumb over my lower lip, sending a shiver hurtling through me.

"I can't do this anymore, Andressa. I thought I could handle just being your friend, but I can't. I'm tired of pretending, pretending that I don't feel what I feel for you. I want you, and it's not going away. And I know you feel the same. I can see it in your eyes…feel it in your body."

He runs his hand down the curve of my waist. "I'm sick of ignoring the inevitable."

He presses a gentle kiss to the corner of my lips, and I gasp.

"You're mine. You've been mine from the moment I saw you. And I'm definitely yours. So, I'm here, telling you that I want you today and every day after. I'm so beyond fucking crazy about you that I'm going insane from not being with you. So, whatever it is that's stopping you from being with me, like we both know you want, then just fight it, babe, because I can't be without you a moment longer."

"I..." My mind is whirling, my mouth dry. My body and heart are screaming for him, but my logic is trying to fight this.

But his words are penetrating my already crumbling wall. The way I feel about him is never going to go away, no matter how hard I fight it.

Then, it just suddenly seems so easy.

I have to try this with him. If I don't, I'll regret it for the rest of my life.

Staring into his eyes, I press my palm to his chest. I love the way his eyes close on the feel of me touching him. The beat of his heart so hard against my hand.

"I do want you," I whisper.

He opens his eyes and I see something deep move within them. "You want to fuck me? Or you want to be with me? Because I can't do one without the other. I can't keep fucking you and then losing you, Andressa. I need you. All of you."

"I need you, too. I don't want to keep running anymore." It's only then that I realize that I'm crying.

With emotion, Carrick watches the tear as it rolls down my cheek. He sweeps it away with his thumb.

I can feel his body trembling beneath my hand.

And it's in this moment that I understand just how deeply he feels for me, and I want him to know that I feel the same.

"I'm crazy about you," I whisper. "I want to be with you…all of you…if you'll have me?"

My words have some effect on him.

The next thing I know, he's kissing me and telling me, "God, you're all I fucking want. All I've ever wanted."

I fall into his kiss, pressing my body to his, wrapping my arms around his neck. He holds me tight, devouring my mouth, like he never wants to let me go.

And I don't ever want to let him go, but there are things I need to tell him…my fears, why I am the way I am. I need to tell him about my dad, so he knows fully what he's getting into with me.

"Carrick, wait…" I pant over his lips. "Before we do this, there are some things I need to tell you—"

"No," he growls against my mouth, halting my words. "No more talking. We can talk later, but right now, I just need to be inside you. That can't wait."

Like I'm going to argue with that.

"Okay," I whisper. "Okay."

Then, we're kissing each other, hard and desperate, like two people starved.

I guess we have been starved of each other.

Carrick starts pulling at my clothes, unzipping the rest of my overalls with just barely there impatience. Shoving them down my legs, I toe my shoes off and kick the overalls off, leaving me in jean shorts and my tank top.

I tear at Carrick's clothes with the same ferocity, pulling his overalls off. He kicks his shoes off and then yanks the overalls off his legs with an impatience that makes me smile.

My hands go to his jeans. At the exact same time, his hands go to my shorts, unbuttoning them, and then they're gone, whipped down my legs. All the time, we're both desperately kissing one another—mouths, cheeks, necks, shoulders, anywhere we can.

Then, he lifts me, turning with me, and puts me down on the workbench. He pulls my tank over my head. Cupping my breast over my bra, he brushes his thumbs over my already hard nipples, and I gasp.

"You're wet for me, Andressa?"

Biting my lip, I stare into his eyes. "Yes."

Reaching behind me, he unclasps my bra. Removing it, he tosses it to the floor. Cupping my breasts in his hands, squeezing, he dips his head, taking a nipple in his mouth.

"Yes." My head falls back on a desperate, urgent whimper.

My hands go to his head, holding him to me, as he starts to lick and suck my nipple, gently kneading the other breast with his hand.

Then, he's kissing his way up my chest, back to my mouth. He grabs a handful of my hair and starts to kiss me hard. There's an almost angry urge to the way he's taking my mouth.

And it's a huge turn-on, knowing how desperate he is for me.

After biting my lower lip, he licks the sting away. Hands grabbing my behind, fingers digging into my skin, he yanks me up against him, his erection pressing into me, making me even more desperate for him.

"I need to fuck you now, and it's gonna be a hard ride, babe, because I've gone way too long without you. But right after, I'm gonna take you up to my bed, and then I'll take my time with you. That okay?"

Um…like I'm going to say no.

Sliding a hand between us, I grab hold of his cock through his boxers, giving him a firm squeeze. "Fuck me now. I want you—hard."

His eyes ignite like a match has just been struck behind them. He yanks off his T-shirt. Then, hooking his fingers into the waistband of his boxers, he pushes them down over his hips, letting them drop to the floor.

My eyes greedily go to his cock. I bite my lip in anticipation.

"Keep looking at me like that, and this'll be over in seconds."

Grinning, I lift my eyes to his face. "I don't care how long we have. I just care that you're inside me, preferably in the next three seconds."

He whips my knickers off. Then, he's back between my legs, his cock pressed up against my wetness.

"Jesus, you feel so fucking good," he growls, taking my mouth again.

The kiss starts out tender, but we're both so desperate to have one another that it's soon back to bruising.

My fingers are digging in his bum cheeks, trying to bring him impossibly closer. Carrick has one hand on my breast, the other making its way down south. His thumb presses on my clit as he pushes his finger inside me, and he pinches my nipple with his other hand.

A charge so strong fires through me that I think I might come right then.

"God! I need you inside me!" I cry out.

Features taut with need, he draws his finger out of me. Then, I see something flicker over his face that looks a lot like dawning. "Fuck!" he bites out.

"I'd quite like to."

He looks at me, and I grin.

Touching a hand to my face, he says, "I haven't got a condom in here. They're in my wallet, which is in the house, on the kitchen counter."

Oh.

He stares at me for a beat. "Do you...want me to go get it?"

I know what he's asking. And what I do know is that I don't want him to leave right now. Not even for a second.

We could go to his house together and get a condom, but I don't want to wait. I want him inside me now.

Maybe I'm being reckless, but I don't care.

"Do you want to go get it?" I ask softly.

Something possessive enters his gaze. Holding my stare, he shakes his head. "I just want to be inside you."

"I'm on the pill," I say softly.

He slides a hand up into my hair. Pulling the tie out, he slips his fingers into my hair. "I'm clean, babe. I've been checked, and there's been no one but you since the last time we had sex."

I flush hot at the reminder of him taking me up against that door in the hotel stairwell.

"Me either. There's been no one but you."

Taking my hand, he presses it against his chest. "Babe, all that stuff in the past, the mistakes I made—"

"Don't..." My eyes lower from his, my mind going to things I don't want to think of.

He takes my face in his hands, forcing my eyes to his. "It was always you. From the moment I saw you, it was you, Andressa."

"Take me," I whisper. "Make me yours."

Moving a hand from my face, he takes his cock in hand and rubs it against my entrance.

My body starts to beg for him, my hips undulating.

He slowly starts to push in, and I gasp from the hot bare feel of him and from the dark and possessive look in his eyes.

I watch, rapt, as his face tightens, his jaw clenching, while he pushes all the way inside me.

"Andressa...Jesus, you feel phenomenal." His hips press against mine, and he takes my face in his hands again. "You're mine, babe, and you're always going to be."

"Yes," I breathe.

He kisses me passionately, deeply.

I hook my legs around his hips, digging my fingernails into his tight behind, urging him to move, and he obliges.

Carrick fucks me there on his workbench, hard and desperate. Clinging to one another, devouring each other's bodies, we take what we need.

And it's not long before I'm coming, blowing apart.

"Fuck…" he groans before biting down hard on my shoulder. "Fuck, babe, I'm coming."

I feel his cock start to jerk inside me as he comes, coating my insides with his release.

Wow. Hot sex in a garage with Carrick.

We definitely have to do that again—and soon.

His head is on my shoulder, his breathing heavy. I run my hands up his back and into his hair.

He lifts his head, and I see the flicker of unease in his eyes.

I know what he's thinking. He's worried that I'm going to leave again. It makes me hate myself for doing that to him those times before.

Gripping his strands, I bring his head to mine, and I kiss him hard, desperate. I pour everything I feel for him into it this kiss, holding on to him like my life depends on it. Because in a way, it does.

"I'm yours, Carrick," I whisper against his lips. "I'm yours, and I'm staying, if you want me to."

Tilting his head back, he stares at me. "You're not going anywhere because I'm nowhere near done with you, and I don't think I ever will be."

His words rock me to the core.

Hands on my behind, he lifts me off the workbench and starts moving across the garage, his cock still safely nestled inside me.

"Where are you taking me?"

"Shower and then bed, so I can fuck you again. And this time, I'm going to savor you, take my time."

Wow. Okay. I'm down with that.

It's only then I realize what that means. To get to his bed, we have to go outside.

Oh my God, he's taking me outside, and I'm naked, and so is he, and his semi-erect cock is still inside me!

"Carrick! No! We can't go out there. We're naked!"

"So?" He grins. "I live miles from anyone. We're all alone, babe. Don't worry." He presses a sweet kiss to my lips.

Then, pushing the door open, he steps out into the warm afternoon air, and I feel the light breeze touch my skin.

Squealing, I wrap my arms around his neck, burying my face into it. "I can't believe you're doing this!"

He rumbles out a laugh. "Believe it, and get used to it. Because I'm gonna be fucking you a lot, anytime the need takes my fancy, no matter where we are."

He slaps my arse, causing me to gasp. So, I nip the skin on his neck with my teeth, earning me a deep chuckle, which vibrates right though me.

He crosses the grass and steps onto the path up to the door, which takes us into the kitchen.

The moment we're inside, I breathe a sigh of relief.

Moving through the house, he takes us upstairs.

I've been inside Carrick's house plenty of times this past week, but I haven't been upstairs yet.

He walks along the landing and through an open door. In his bedroom, I get a quick glance before he takes us into his en suite, and I see a nice big bed centering a very masculine room.

He opens the door to his shower. Turning it on, a spray of cold hits me, causing me to squeal.

Getting me away from the cold water, he turns, pressing my back against the cool tiles. "It'll be hot in a second."

Then, he takes my mouth, kissing me, and I'm suddenly already feeling very hot.

I feel his cock start to harden inside me.

"Again?" I blink back at him.

"Always."

Then, he's moving, taking me against the wall of his shower, fucking me hard, and it's amazing and intense.

He takes me to the edge and comes over with me.

"What are you doing to me?" he pants, his eyes staring into mine with wonderment.

I touch his face with my hand. "Exactly what you're doing to me," I whisper.

He presses his forehead to mine, and closing his eyes, he lets out a groan. "I was supposed to take my time with you when I got you up here. You're turning me into an animal."

I let out a soft laugh. "I like that you're an animal with me. And there's plenty of time to go slow."

He opens his eyes. "Yeah, there is. All the time in the world." He kisses me and then lowers me to my feet, finally letting me go.

Stepping under the spray, he leads me under with him, and we shower together.

I wash Carrick's body. And he washes mine. Then, he watches me as I wash my hair using his shampoo. He's just standing there, leaning against the tiles, his body glistening with droplets of water, as I rinse the shampoo from my hair.

"What?" I smile shyly, wringing my hair out.

"Nothing. I'm just glad you're here…that we're here."

That brings a smile to my lips. "Yeah, me, too."

Turning the shower off, Carrick takes my hand and leads me from the cubicle. Handing me a towel he gets from the shelf, he gets one for himself, wrapping it around his waist. After squeezing the water from my hair with the towel, I wrap it around my body

I stare at him for a moment. Damp golden skin, wet hair—God, he's gorgeous. And he's all mine.

"What?" He grins.

"Just admiring your hot body." I smirk.

"Admire all you want." He drops his towel and then yanks mine from my body.

He picks me up, causing me to squeal. I've noticed that he likes to carry me around a lot, and I have absolutely no issues with that.

He pulls back the duvet on his bed and deposits me on the firm mattress. He climbs in beside me. Pulling me to him—entwining his legs with mine, his arm around my waist—he presses his face into my neck and kisses me there.

"Stay tonight?" His lips brush over my skin.

I tip my head back, so I can look into his face. "Like you could get me to leave." I smile.

That makes him smile, and he snuggles in closer. "I'll feed you soon. I just want to lie here and hold you for a bit."

"That works for me because I want to be held by you."

We lay in content silence, my fingers stroking over his back in a pattern of our names, and it's not long after when I hear Carrick's breathing start to even out.

He must be worn out from all the sex.

Then, feeling the most peaceful I have in a long time, I let my eyes drift shut.

When I awake, it's dark out, a low light in the room. As I turn my head, I find Carrick already awake, head on the pillow beside me, watching me.

"Hey." I smile, stretching my arms up. "How long have you been awake?"

"A while."

"You should have woken me up."

"You were tired."

It's then I notice the unease in his eyes. "Carrick...is everything all right?" There's a slight tremor to my voice.

"Everything's fine." He tucks my hair behind my ear. "You're still here, and everything's good."

You're still here.

Still.

He thought I was going to leave. Even after what I said in the garage, he still thought I was going to leave.

And I have nobody to blame but myself for him thinking that. What he needs from me right now is reassurance, and I'm going to give him it.

Turning my body to his, I rest my hand against his chest. "You thought I'd wake up and leave?"

He gives a light shrug of his shoulders, but I see it flicker through his eyes.

"I'm not leaving. And I'm sorry for every stupid thing that I did in the past—pushing you away after we had sex, running out on you, all of it." Leaning in, I softly kiss his mouth. "I'm here, and I'm not going anywhere."

He pulls me close, hooking my leg over his hip, pressing his forehead to mine. "I'm being fucking stupid. I know. I just didn't want to wake up and you be gone. Then, I was scared that you were going to wake up and realize that you made a mistake and leave."

"You're not being stupid. I've given you every reason to think this way, and I'm sorry. I can't change the past. But I can promise that I'll talk to you, explain everything I'm feeling, why I behave like I do."

"You mean freak out?"

I let out a small sad laugh. "Yeah, freak out."

Moving back, I lay my head on his pillow, so I can look at him.

"There's something I need to tell you—about me."

"Okay." He gives me a wary look.

"It's nothing bad about us." Now that I'm about to say it, it feels like I'm making a big deal out of it. "It's not crucial to anything. It's just something that I haven't told you, and you should know. I mean, I haven't told anyone here—well, apart from Petra. She knows and Uncle John knows, but he's always knew because—"

His hand touches my arm. "Andressa, it's okay. You can tell me."

Deep breath. One. Two. Three.

"My dad is William Wolfe."

I expect him to look surprised, but he doesn't.

Staring steadily back at me, he nods his head once. "Yeah, I know."

"You know?" Air whooshes into my lungs as my brows pull together in consternation. "How do you know?"

His cheeks redden a bit, and he bites his lip. If I wasn't so perturbed right now, I'd bite his lip, too, because he looks so goddamn sexy.

He blows out a breath before speaking, "When I saw you there at that car show, looking at his car, and you were crying, I just knew right then that there was something, and it was bugging the fuck out of me afterward. I knew the car was important to you. I just didn't know why—and that's why I bought it."

My chest tightens with so many emotions. Taking his hand, I kiss it. His face warms with his feelings for me. Cupping my cheek, he presses a kiss to my lips.

Keeping his hand on my face, he strokes my skin with his thumb. "I had to get that car, no matter what, so I called up the owner, and I got him to sell it to me. After the deal was done, I got off the phone with him, and I started researching the car, finding more about it, like what I was going to need to get it up and running again. There was no way that car was going to sit pretty in my garage—not after what you said to me. And honestly, it was a good reason to have you with me, to be able to spend time with you again.

"While I was researching the car, I stumbled on this picture of your dad with the car. He was standing in front of it with his wife…and that was when I knew. I remembered your mum from the photo you showed me in Kuala Lumpur. Sure, she looked younger, but it was like looking at you. I looked up your dad's Wiki page, and it was all there. Spouse, Katia Amaro-Wolfe. Child, Andressa Wolfe. It didn't take a genius to work out that you're his daughter, babe. I should have realized before because of John. I knew he'd worked for William and that they were good friends. I just…" Carrick rubs his face with his hand. "I don't understand why you didn't tell me. Why keep it a secret?"

I let out a sigh. "Because I didn't want people thinking that Uncle John gave me the job because of who my dad was, because Uncle John was my dad's best friend."

"No one would've thought that."

I give him a look. "They would have so thought that. I'm a moderately attractive young female mechanic—"

"Moderately attractive?" He raises a brow. "I'm more inclined to say you're the most beautiful woman I've ever seen in my life. I couldn't believe my eyes when I saw you that first time, bent over my car with your long legs and sexy arse stuck up in the air." He squeezes my bum with his hand. "Jesus, I almost came in my pants. Hottest fucking thing ever, babe."

Laughing, I lightly slap my hand to his chest. "If everyone knew who my dad was, they'd have thought that was the only reason I was there. I just wanted to prove myself before people knew I was his daughter."

"You've proven yourself more than enough times. You're brilliant at your job." He slides his hand down over my bum and along my thigh. "You do realize, now that I have you, I'm never letting you go, right? From my garage or my bed. You have to stay forever."

Forever.

I ignore the little ripple of fear in my chest. "Works for me." I smile. Running my fingers down to his abs, I start to trace them, loving the feel of him shuddering beneath my touch.

"It's because of your dad, what happened to him…that's why you didn't want to be with me?"

That jolts me back. Emotions flood me, stilling my hand.

"I didn't…I still don't want to go through losing someone that I care about again."

"You won't lose me, Andressa." He tips my chin up with his fingers, so I'm looking him in the eyes. "I'm not going anywhere."

"You can't promise that." There's a broken edge to my voice.

"No, I guess no one can. But things are different now, safer than they used to be when you lost your dad."

Carrick drives at speeds close to three hundred and seventy-five kilometers an hour. There's nothing safe about that.

"I just…the way I feel about you, Carrick…it terrifies me. That's why I tried to stay away for as long as I did. When I think about losing you…the panic consumes me, and I know it doesn't make sense, but it's the fear of losing you that makes me run."

"No more running, babe."

He presses the sweetest kiss to my forehead. It brings tears to my eyes.

"You terrify me, too." His lips brush over my skin. "I've never felt this close to anyone in my life. The way I feel about you…it's beyond anything I've ever known. But we can do this because we're meant to be together."

And as he wraps his arms around me, holding me tight, I try to ignore that tiny debilitating voice nagging away in the very recess of my mind that's telling me that it's only a matter of time before the fear takes hold again.

Twenty-Two

✢ BUCKINGHAMSHIRE, ENGLAND

I WAKE UP TO THE FEEL OF CARRICK. His body on mine, his mouth pressing soft, sweet kisses to my lips.

I moan my acquiescence, my lips parting, and he deepens the kiss, sliding his tongue into my mouth, bringing me to life in an instant.

My body feels deliciously sore in the only way it can be after having copious amounts of sex, but even still, I'm ready for more with him.

Last night, Carrick ordered us dinner in. We had pizza, which we ate in the living room. We also started to watch a movie, but I couldn't tell you a thing about it because I only saw the first ten or so minutes of it. We went at it again on his sofa, which ended up with me bent over the coffee table while he took me from behind.

After we caught our breath and cleaned up, Carrick suggested going to bed, which I was ready for—tired from all the sex. We made it to the staircase before we were going at it again. Clearly, I wasn't that tired.

He took me right there on the staircase. I didn't know you could have sex like that on the stairs, but apparently, you can.

I'm pretty sure I have carpet burns on my arse, knees, and elbows. Like I care though.

We're doing it like horny teenagers, and I love it. Sex with Carrick is like nothing I've ever known before.

He likes to screw me in lots of different positions. I try not to think about how he's so experienced in having sex in so many different ways.

Instead, I focus on his sexual appetite for me and how insatiable it is. And how I'm the same for him.

We can't get enough of one another. I've never been like this for a guy before.

But then Carrick's not exactly your average guy.

His kiss starts to slow, letting me up for air, and I blink open my eyes.

"Is this my wake-up call? Because I could seriously get used to this every morning." Stretching my arms up, I wrap them around his neck.

"Well, get used to it because I intend on waking you up every day like this." Another kiss. "You just looked so fucking sexy. I couldn't help myself." His hand slides down my side to my thigh.

"What time is it?" I ask, seeing the dawn light, knowing I have to be at work.

"Early. Now, shush, and let me kiss you again."

Obliging, I offer my mouth up to him, which he gladly takes.

It's not long before things are getting hot and heavy. Carrick begins kissing his way down my body. Pressing lingering kisses to my belly, he starts to lick a path downward.

Pushing my legs apart, he lies between them and puts his mouth on me.

"Oh!" My hips jerk at the feel of his tongue on me, my fingers curling into the bedsheet.

"God, you taste so good," he growls against me, the vibration of his voice hits all the right spots.

He pushes his tongue inside me, and I can't help but move in rhythm against his face.

My head presses back into the pillow, as he runs his tongue up to my clit. He starts licking with gusto, sliding a finger inside me and then another, fucking me with them.

"Yes," I moan. "God, Carrick, yes...right there." My toes curl into the bed, the muscles in my legs tightening, as

I feel it moving through my body. Then the coil snaps. And I'm screaming out his name, my back bowing up off the bed.

When it's over, I fall back, lax, into the mattress as he climbs up my body, taking my mouth in a kiss. The taste of me on him turns me on even more.

He's readying to put himself inside me, and I want that, but first…

Pushing him off me, I roll him onto his back and climb on top of him.

"You riding me, cowgirl?" He grins, slapping my arse.

His eyes are so full of heat and desire that I feel it ripple through me, right to my sex.

I bite my lip. "Maybe, but first…" I let my words trail off as I move down his body, readying to take him in my mouth.

I can't believe this is the first time I'm going to taste him. I've wanted to for so long. But he's always so in control in the bedroom, so I've just let him take the lead.

But now is my turn.

Kneeling between his legs, I take his cock in my hand. Curling my fingers around it, I move the shaft up and down. He hisses such a sexy sound that I feel it deep inside.

Licking my lips, I move my head down and slide his cock between my lips.

"Ah, fuck…" he groans, his hand grabbing hold of my hair. "That feels so good. Jesus, your lips around my cock…you have no idea how many times I've imagined this. Even better than I thought it would be."

Wanting to keep on pleasing him, I flatten my tongue, taking him further into my mouth, until he's pushing the back of my throat.

"God, fuck. Yeah, just like that, Andressa."

I start sucking him harder, sliding my mouth up and down his cock, taking him far back each time. I love the hot dirty praise spilling from his lips, the way his hand is pulling on my hair, as he fucks my mouth.

"Babe, fuck...ah, you need to stop, or I'm gonna come." He tugs on my hair, lifting my head from him.

"That was kinda the point." I pout.

"Another time. Right now, I want to fuck you."

He starts to move, to take over, but I stop him with a hand on his chest.

"No. Stay there. Right like you are." I slide my legs over his hips, so I'm straddling him, his cock pressed up against me.

He growls. "Always so fucking wet for me. You have no idea how much that turns me on."

Desire hurtles through me.

Lifting up on my knees, I take his cock in my hand and place him at my entrance. I slowly slide down on his length. I suck in a breath at the feel of him filling me. And his resounding groan tells me he feels as good as I do right now.

I start moving up and down, riding him. His hands quickly find my hips, fingers biting in my skin

Knowing I won't have long before he takes over, I ride him hard. My hands are on his stomach, but I can't get the grip I need for traction.

He offers his hands to me. Taking them, I link my fingers with his.

It's not long before he's sitting up, pressing his chest to mine.

I drop his hands and grip his shoulders. His hands on my behind, he takes control, lifting me up and down his cock, increasing pace.

"So good," I moan.

"That's it, babe. I need you to come for me."

The friction is almost too much to bear. My body goes into overdrive, and in no time, I'm shattering around him.

My eyes are locked on his as I come, unable to look away. I never want to look away from him ever again. And that feeling I've had of falling before hits me, but it's harder this time, bleeding into my veins, making me dizzy…

I love him.
I'm in love with him.
Oh God.

Before I can even process my thoughts, I'm moving backward.

Carrick is on top, his body pinning mine. His elbows are pressed against my upper arms, keeping them in place, as he frames my face with his hands.

He's moving in and out with sure hard thrusts, and I lift my legs, wrapping them around him, urging him in harder.

His features are tight. His eyes are dark with urgency and need. The way he's looking at me is somehow more intense than ever before, and it stops my breath.

"Andressa…" he groans my name like a prayer. "Fuck, babe…"

Then, almost as if it's too much for him, he closes his eyes. He brings his mouth to mine, breaking the connection between us, allowing me to breathe.

His body tenses, shuddering, as I feel his cock jerking inside me, filling me with his warmth.

We lie there for a moment, pressing soft tender kisses wherever we can reach skin.

Then, he rolls off me, taking me with him, so my head is on his chest, his arm around me.

"That was…" He sounds in awe and lost, and I'm right there with him.

"Out of this world." I tilt my head, so I can look at him.

"Don't go to work today." He touches my lower lip with his finger, tracing it. "Stay with me."

"I want to…but I don't want to let Uncle John down."

"You're not letting him down. You're pulling a sickie, like ninety percent of the population do. Technically, in a roundabout way, you work for me, and I'm saying it's more than okay for you to play hooky."

"That's because you'll benefit from me playing hooky."

"True." He presses his lips together, brow raised, a cute look on his face. "But I'll make sure that you benefit too."

I laugh, considering it.

"And the part for your dad's car is being delivered this morning. We can fit it and then take her out together."

And he's got me. I was eighty percent sure I was going to stay just from the feel of his hot body under my hands, but if I can be here to finish my dad's car…

"You know how to get me."

"Sure I do. If I didn't, you wouldn't be naked and in my bed right now."

I lift a brow.

"Granted, it took me a while," he adds. "But we got here in the end."

"We sure did." I smile, giving him a kiss. As I pull back, I remember that my phone is in the garage. I left it there yesterday. And if I'm calling in sick, then I'm going to need it.

"Ugh, I left my phone in the garage. I need it to call Uncle John and let him know I won't be in today."

"Use mine."

"Oh, yeah!" I laugh, but I abruptly stop when I see the less than happy look on his face. "What's wrong?"

"You don't want John knowing we're together?"

"I never said that. But if I call from your phone, he's gonna know in an instant that I'm not playing hooky because I'm sick but because I'm too busy in bed with you. And I'd rather my Uncle John not know those intimate details of my life."

"But you are gonna tell him that we're together?"

"If that's what you want."

"I do."

"Are you telling your dad and Pierce?"

He gives me a stupid look. "Of course. I'll be telling anyone who'll fucking listen that we're together. That I'm with the hottest girl in the world."

I roll my eyes at his cheesy line, but I'm secretly loving it.

"You don't think it'll be weird at work?"

"Babe, I'm pretty sure that everyone at work knows that we've at least slept together. The way we've been with each other these last few weeks, they know." Moving out from under me, he gets out of bed. Going over to his chest of drawers, he pulls out a pair of dark gray drawstring pajama bottoms and puts them on. "My dad even asked me about it the other day. Asked what was going on with you and me."

Lying on my side, I prop myself up on my elbow. "What did you tell him?"

"That I was pissed off because you wouldn't fuck me." He grins.

"You never said that!" I gasp.

"What else was I going to say?" He comes and sits on the bed. "That I was fucking cut up because you didn't want me? I don't go that deep with my dad, babe."

My eyes lower, my lips turning down at the corners.

"Hey." He chucks my chin with his fingers.

I look back up at him.

"Don't feel bad. That shit is all in the past. We're here now, and we're good." He tucks my hair behind my ear.

"No, we're better than good. We're great." I slide my hand around his neck. Bringing his lips down to mine, I kiss him.

"You want me to get your phone?" he says in between kisses.

"Would you?" I blink, looking into his eyes.

"I'd do just about anything for you." He winks and then gets up from the bed. "Back in a few."

I watch his hot arse leave the bedroom. Needing the bathroom, I climb out of bed and use the toilet.

After I've finished, my stomach is rumbling, and I'm dying for coffee, so I decide to meet Carrick downstairs.

I grab his Rybell T-shirt and boxer shorts that I wore last night when we had pizza because all my clothes are still scattered around his garage. I hope he retrieves them when he gets my phone.

I make my way downstairs and into the kitchen. I've just got the coffee brewing and bread in the toaster when Carrick appears with my phone, my clothes, and a box in his hands.

"Delivery guy turned up while I was outside. Starter motor's here." He puts the box down on the counter along with my clothes, and he hands me my phone.

"He was early," I comment.

"Yeah. Aw, you're making coffee and toast. You're the best girlfriend ever." He presses a kiss to my cheek as he passes by me.

I freeze at the term, surprised to hear him calling me his girlfriend. Then, I relax, letting it seep into me.

I am his girlfriend. And he's my boyfriend.

And I sound like I'm still in high school.

"You want jam, Nutella, or peanut butter on your toast?" he asks me from the fridge.

"Um…Nutella."

"Good choice." He comes over with a jar of Nutella, putting it on the counter in front of me.

"I should call Uncle John and let him know I'm not coming in."

"Call him. I'll finish breakfast."

Taking my phone, I walk out into the hall. I see a few texts from my mum, Petra, and Ben, and I have a missed call from Uncle John.

Swiping the screen, I call him back.

"I called you yesterday. I was hoping to have dinner with you last night." Uncle John's voice comes down the line.

"Sorry. I was out with a friend." I choose not to elaborate. I can't tell him now, not with me pulling a sickie. "That's kind of why I'm calling. I think I ate something last night that disagreed with me, and I feel ill. Stomachache." I actually press my hand to my belly, like he can see me.

"Are you okay? Do you need me to come around, take care of you?"

"No." My voice goes unnaturally high, so I rein it back in. "No, I'll be fine. I just need to sleep it off, I think. I'll be fine by tomorrow."

"Well, no rush. Just come in when you feel up to it."

"Okay. Thanks, Uncle John."

"I'll call you later, check how you're doing. Feel better soon, kiddo."

Saying good-bye, I hang up with him. Then, I reply to my mum's text. If I don't, she'll start freaking out.

Then, I go back into the kitchen.

Carrick's already poured the coffee and made my toast, all set out for me on the breakfast bar. He's munching on his own toast, reading something on his phone.

He lowers it when he sees me. "Okay?" he checks.

"Yeah, fine." I sit up on the stool. "I feel crappy lying to him, but if it means I get to spend the day with you, then it's worth it."

That earns me a heart-stopping smile.

After we've finished breakfast, I load the plates and cups into the dishwasher, seeing as though Carrick made breakfast.

We take a shower together, which ends up being longer than it should, as I end up bent over, hands pressed to the tiles, with Carrick taking me from behind.

We finally make it down to the garage where I put on my overalls over another one of Carrick's clean T-shirts and boxer shorts. As my clothes are grubby, I've put them in his machine to wash, so at least I'll have some clean clothes to go home in.

Carrick seems to quite like me in his clothes. Honestly, I like wearing them. I like smelling of him.

We have the starter motor fitted in less than an hour. Quick easy job with the both of us. But I let Carrick do most of the fitting. I'm quite happy to sit back and watch his delicious arse bent over the car.

"Seriously, I feel like a piece of meat with the way you're ogling me from back there." His voice comes from under the hood of the car.

"Welcome to my world. And seriously, you're complaining? I thought you liked being adored by women."

He lifts his head, looking back at me. "I do." Moving out from under the car, he comes over to me, sliding his dirty hands around the waist of my overalls. "But only by one woman." He kisses the tip of my nose.

"Nice save."

"I thought so." He grins.

"How's it looking?" I nod at the car.

"All done." He smiles.

I feel a little tremor inside my chest.

"You ready to try her out? See if all our hard work's been worth it?"

My eyes come back to his handsome face. "I think it's been worth it even if she doesn't run." I smile, referring to him and me, the time we've spent doing it, bringing us together.

"Definitely worth it." He rubs his nose over mine and then softly kisses me once.

Stepping back, he pulls the car key from his overalls and gives it to me. "Come on. Start her up, babe."

I follow him to the car. Opening the driver's door, I climb in.

He puts the hood down with a gentle clunk and gets in the passenger seat beside me.

I look at the key in my hand for a moment and then push it into the ignition. I glance at Carrick, and he gives me an encouraging look.

After a deep breath, I turn the key. She chugs a little as I feel the mechanics all trying to rub together, adjusting to each other.

Releasing the ignition, I wait a few seconds, then, I turn her again, and this time, she comes to life.

I beam at Carrick. "She's working! I can't believe she's working!"

"I can. You can fix anything you put your mind to."

But not me. I can't fix the broken in me.

I bite my lip, feeling myself waver.

"Are you getting emotional on me?" he asks.

"A bit." A tear slips from my eye. I wipe it away.

"Well, I might make this either better or worse." He reaches into the glove box and pulls out some papers. He holds them out for me to take.

"What are these?" I ask, taking them from him.

"If my girl doesn't know what a logbook looks like, then I'm gonna be worried."

I hear the hint of nerves in his voice as my eyes start scanning the papers.

Fuck...

"Carrick...I...you..."

"She's yours."

"No," I gasp. "Carrick...it's too much...you can't..."

"I can, and I have." He turns in his seat. Reaching over, he takes my face in his hands. "I bought her for you. She belongs to you. It's what your dad would have wanted."

I close my eyes on a blink, and tears roll down my cheeks. My throat is thick with emotion.

"I love it, what you've done…but it's just so much money. I can't take that kind of money from you."

"It's nonnegotiable. The paperwork's done. It's legal and binding. The only way you're getting rid of this car is if you sell her, and I don't think you'll do that." He gives me a winning look.

I should be mad at him for doing this…spending so much money on me. But how can I be angry with such a beautiful man who has done such a beautiful thing for me?

"Carrick…I…" *Love you.* "I'm beyond crazy about you." Then, I kiss him, with everything I have.

When we finally break apart, breathing heavily, he rests his forehead against mine. "I really want you right now, but I think it'd be kind of creepy if I fucked you in your dad's car."

"Not kind of creepy. It'd be totally creepy."

He chuckles. "Well, let's take her out for a drive, see how she opens up. Then, we're coming back here, and I'm spending the rest of the day inside you, fucking you in every room in my house and quite possibly the garden."

Grinning at him, I say, "Sounds perfect."

twenty-three

BUDAPEST, HUNGARY

IT'S FAIR TO SAY that Carrick and I have grown incredibly close these last few weeks. We've reached a level of intimacy that I never thought I would be able to have with a man.

We're together a lot, only apart when I'm working or he's training.

Carrick did want me to forego sharing a room with Petra and just stay with him, but I felt I should maintain some form of independence from him. He wasn't happy about it, but I was firm.

Staying in his room with him would almost be like living together, and I don't want to rush things. Although my stuff might be in my and Petra's room, I still sleep in Carrick's bed every night. It's a hard task, staying away from him, so having my clothes and belongings in another room is the only way to make it feel like we are actually going slow.

Everyone knows that we're together. Carrick was insistent about that. He told his dad and Pierce, and I told Uncle John, who wasn't as surprised as I'd thought he would be. Of course I told Petra, and she just flipped out with excitement. I got an, "About fucking time," from Ben.

Apparently, the sexual tension between Carrick and me has been killing everyone.

Carrick won the British Grand Prix. It was a great moment for him. Winning at home is always a huge thing.

And he also won in Germany, too.

I was proud of him. But at the British Grand Prix, that was the moment I realized how hard being with Carrick is going to be for me. Watching him race on that screen, I had a full-blown panic attack.

It came out of nowhere. Fortunately, I had sense enough to get myself to the restroom before anyone could see it.

I didn't tell Carrick about it. He was too happy with his win, and I didn't want to bring him down, so I haven't said anything. It happened in Germany, too.

And now, we're in Budapest, and the race is a few days away. To say I'm anxious is putting it mildly.

I just need to find a way to deal with this. If I'm with him, he's always going to race. I'm always going to have to watch. I have to learn to deal.

"I look okay?" I ask Carrick.

We're in my room. He's laid out on my bed, looking handsome in dark jeans and a shirt, watching TV while I dress.

Petra's out having dinner with the guys. Carrick and I are going to have dinner with his dad.

It was Owen's idea.

I'm nervous. I know Owen doesn't like me.

"You look beautiful." Carrick gets up from the bed and comes over to me. Wrapping his arms around my waist from behind, he stares back at me in the mirror. "You always look beautiful."

I'm wearing a cute little sleeveless knee-length floral dress with these gold sandals that I got when I went shopping with Petra. She's such a big help with buying girlie clothes for me.

Biting my lip, I glance back at him. "I just want to make a good impression. I want him to like me."

"He does like you." He chuckles. I feel his chest rumble against my back.

I raise a brow at him.

"He does," he maintains. "He thinks you're a good influence on me."

"He thinks I distract you."

"You do distract me. You're a bad...bad distraction, Andressa." He runs his tongue up my neck to my ear. He nips my earlobe with his teeth, making me shiver.

"I'm bad, huh?"

"Mmhmm...you're really, really bad."

He slides his hand up my stomach. Cupping my breast, he brushes his thumb over my already hard nipple. The feeling shoots straight to my sex.

"And I'd show you exactly how bad if we didn't have to go to dinner right now."

Turning in his arms, I tip my lips up at one corner. "We could cancel and stay here. I'll let you punish me for being bad." Lifting my arms, I press my wrists together, giving him an innocent look.

That gets his attention. I see lust flicker to life in his eyes and feel it press up against my hip.

"Fuck. Now, I'm hard." He glances at his watch and groans. "We're already late, and I can't fuck you quick." Cupping my chin in his hand, he gives me a hard kiss, slipping his tongue into my mouth, making me groan. "When we get back, I'm tying you to my bed, and I'm gonna show you exactly how bad *I* can be."

Releasing me, he backs away with the hottest look on his face ever, making my insides tremble.

"Now, let's get this fucking dinner over with, so we can come back, and I can fuck the hell out of you."

Feeling hot between the thighs, I decide to wind him up because I'm not getting my own way. "Oh, and just so you know, I'm not wearing any knickers." I give him a saucy look as I pass him, grabbing my clutch off the dresser.

I was going to save that nugget of information for later, but I just couldn't help myself.

"Please tell me you're kidding." His chest presses up against my back, bringing me to a stop, as his hand lifts my dress, finding me bare and ready for him. "Jesus, you're not kidding." He groans, dropping his forehead to my shoulder.

"Just think how much easier it'll be to access me later." I flash my eyes back at him as he lifts his head.

"God...this is gonna be a long-ass dinner, knowing you're sitting next to me, bare. Don't be surprised if I drag you off to the restroom and fuck you right there."

My eyes widen. "You wouldn't. Not while we're out with your dad."

"Wouldn't I?" He raises his brow. Then, he slaps my arse as he moves away. Opening the door, he says, "After you."

We're meeting Owen at Costes. It's Carrick's favorite restaurant here in Budapest. And as we're staying at the Four Seasons, it's only a short walk away, so Carrick and I go on foot.

We arrive at the restaurant first.

We're seated and ordering our drinks when Owen arrives. "I'm not late, am I?"

"No, you're fine," Carrick replies.

"Andi, lovely to see you."

Owen leans over the table to kiss my cheek, so I rise up to meet him.

He takes the seat opposite me. Picking his menu up, he gives his drink order to the waitress.

"So, how's your day been?" Owen asks Carrick.

"Good. I trained this morning. Then, I took Andressa for a drive over Chain Bridge, and we went to see a few landmarks."

"Oh? Where?"

"Saint Stephen's Basilica, and we also visited Shoes on the Danube Bank," I answer.

"Oh, yes, I've been to the Danube Bank. Hauntingly touching, I found."

"Yes, it was."

The waitress comes back with our drinks.

I pick up my menu and start looking at the food choices. "What do you recommend?" I ask Carrick.

"Veal. That's what I usually have."

"But…isn't veal baby cows?" My brows draw together.

"Yep."

"Jesus, I'm not eating baby cows!" I screw up my face in disgust. "I'll have the steak instead."

Carrick sputters out a laugh. "You won't eat baby cows, but you'll eat adult cows? Where's the logic, babe?"

"They're babies!" I gesticulate. "It's just wrong!"

"But it's okay to eat the mammy cows?"

Fuck. He's got me there.

"Fine. I'll have the crayfish."

"But what if that's a baby crayfish?"

Bastard.

Carrick's eyes are filled with mirth. Even Owen is choking back a laugh.

I narrow my eyes at Carrick, and then my gaze goes back to the menu, quickly scanning. "I'll have the spinach ravioli." I slap my menu shut, jutting out my lip.

"Aw, babe, I'm just teasing. Have the steak."

"No, I'm oddly off it now."

"Don't sulk." He tugs on my pouting lips with his thumb and finger.

As if I could stay mad at him.

"I'm not sulking. Promise." I smile easily. "I'm good with the ravioli."

He smiles back at me with such warmth that I feel it coat my skin like the sun is shining on me. He hangs his arm around the back of my chair.

As I turn my face forward, I see Owen watching us with obvious interest.

It makes me wonder if Carrick is always this affectionate with women in front of his dad. Owen doesn't seem surprised by it, so maybe Carrick is.

Then, I have the thought of whether he was like this with Sienna, and I suddenly feel ill.

I'm glad when my glass of wine appears in front of me. I take a deep gulp.

"Are you ready to order?" the waitress asks.

Carrick slides me a grin. "Yeah, we are."

We place our orders and settle back into a comfortable conversation.

Owen asks me about my family, but I artfully dodge any conversation about my dad with Carrick's help. Then, Owen asks me about my time in stock car racing. He seems genuinely interested.

And I'm feeling relaxed. Maybe that was the point. Relax the prey and then swoop in for the kill when it's least expected.

"I'm just gonna go to the restroom," Carrick says to me, a wicked gleam in his eye.

If he thinks I'm leaving this table to join him, he's got another thing coming.

Not that I'm adverse to public restroom sex with Carrick. I'm just adverse to it while we're out to dinner with his dad.

"Okay." I give him a sweet smile. "Don't be long."

He playfully narrows his eyes, and then he surprises me by taking my chin in his hand and kissing me softly on the lips.

"Back in a few."

I watch him go, the feel of his kiss still lingering on my lips. Then, I turn back to the table.

Owen is watching me. And something in his expression has changed. He looks harder now. And it leaves a sinking feeling in my stomach.

"He likes you. A lot."

"I'm glad. I like him a lot, too." I smile, but it feels forced.

Owen sits forward, elbows on the table. "Did you know that Carrick's mother left when he was only a young'un?"

"Yes, he told me."

He seems surprised at that.

"Well, because of her leaving, he doesn't trust people easily. He doesn't let them close. Especially women. Hence, the way he's lived his life, jumping from one woman to the next. Until you. For some reason, you're different. He trusts you. He's let you in. And I'd be glad for that—relieved, to be honest—because all I want for him is for him to be settled with a good woman. And you are lovely, Andi. You're not like your average girl. You're smart and beautiful, but…"

And there it is. The *but* that I knew was coming.

"I see it in you, what was in my ex-wife. You have the exact same look in your eyes that she always had—the look of flight. Hers was because she thought there was more out of life to be had than she would get with Carrick and me. She was always looking for bigger and better things, running toward what she thought that was. But you…" He shakes his head, his eyes assessing me. "You look to me more like you're running from something rather than toward it."

I feel winded. He can see right through me, and in this moment, I feel the most vulnerable than I ever have.

"Owen—"

He lifts a hand stopping me. "I reckon I know what you're gonna say, and you don't need to. All I'm asking of you is, if you don't think you can make it for the long haul with Carrick, then leave him now. Break his heart while he can still recover from it and not years down the line when it's too late, and he'll never recover."

I feel like he just punched me in the chest. I'm fighting for air.

And what do I say?

That he's right. That I know each time watching Carrick race, my fear is growing exponentially. That one day soon, it's going to explode and take control of me, and I'll run from him.

That I wake up each morning, looking at Carrick's face, knowing how weak I am. Knowing that, one day, I'll hurt him, and I won't be able to stop myself from doing it.

That I know I'm not good enough for Carrick, and I never will be.

"Everything okay?" Carrick's standing by the table.

I quickly clear all emotion from my face and throw on a smile before looking up at him. I think quickly on the spot. "Of course. Your dad was just telling me some funny stories about when you were a kid."

"Oh God," Carrick groans, dropping into his seat. "What did you tell her, so I can quickly repair the damage you've done?"

"Nothing bad, son." Owen glances at me. "Nothing for you to worry about anyway."

I pick up my glass of wine and chug it back.

The rest of dinner passes by in a blur for me. I make sure to join in the conversation and laugh in all the right places, but all I have buzzing around my mind are Owen's words.

We've just finished dessert, and I'm more than ready to leave.

"Are you staying for coffee?" Owen asks. "Or an after dinner brandy?"

"I'm okay," I answer.

"Carrick?" Owen says.

I look at him when he doesn't respond to his dad straight away. He's staring at me, and I can see it in his eyes. He knows I'm not a hundred percent myself.

"You tired?" he asks me.

"A little. But you go ahead and have a drink. I don't mind."

He looks at me for a few seconds longer. He seems to be weighing something up in those beautiful blues of his. He pulls them from me to his dad. "No, I'm fine. Thanks, Da."

I love it when he does that, drops the D and calls his dad Da. It's so sweet.

"I reckon we'll head back to the hotel now." Carrick calls the waitress over for the bill.

"I'll get this one, son." His dad puts his hand out as Carrick reaches for his wallet.

"Okay. Cheers, Da."

Owen is the only person I've seen Carrick let pay for anything. Must be a father-son thing.

Once the bill is settled, I get up from my seat. Carrick helps me into my coat.

"You coming back to the hotel with us?" Carrick asks Owen as we leave the restaurant.

"No, I have somewhere to be." He nods in the direction of a waiting town car. "But I'll see you tomorrow."

"Okay."

"Was lovely spending time with you outside of work, Andi." Owen kisses my cheek.

"You, too." My smile is tight.

As we start walking, Carrick puts his arm around my shoulders, and I put mine around his back. His free hand takes hold of my hand, sliding his fingers through mine, holding it against his hip.

"I'm sure my dad's got a hook-up in every country we go to—that, or he has a gambling problem." He chuckles to himself.

"What makes you say that?"

"Ah, for at least one of the nights we're in each country, he just always disappears off to 'somewhere to be' with no further explanation."

"Has there been anyone serious since…your mum?"

"There was no one when I was a kid, none that I knew of. Then, there were a few girlfriends when I got a bit older, but his focus has always been on my racing career."

"He loves you a lot."

"Yeah, he does. Sometimes too much. I think he's that way because he feels he has to make up for my mother leaving."

"You can't blame him for that."

"I know."

"My mum's the same," I tell him. "Since my dad…she's a bit overprotective at times."

"How's she coping with you being away, traveling the world?"

"She's slowly getting better about it." I laugh lightly.

"How about you dating me—a driver? How does she feel about that?"

He's never really asked about my mum's opinion about him before. I'm guessing seeing his dad tonight has sparked that.

"She's happy, if I'm happy."

Honestly, she hasn't said much when I tell her things about Carrick and me. I think a lot of that has to do with his reputation. And a part of what he does for a living, too.

"And are you?"

I smile wide. "Very."

He leans in and kisses me. "Me, too. Like I've never been before."

Taking a hold of his hand that's over my shoulder, I lift it to my lips, pressing a kiss to it. I snuggle into his side.

As we walk on, I hear the soft sound of Ed Sheeran's "Thinking Out Loud" start to play from the speakers outside a restaurant just across the street where people are sitting out front, dining in the beautiful evening.

"I love this song," I murmur.

Bringing me to a stop, Carrick says, "Dance with me?"

I glance around. "Uh, here?"

"Yeah, here. I want to dance with my girl under the stars." He gestures to the bright night sky.

Then, he twirls me in his arms, so I'm facing him. Moving his arm from my shoulder to my waist, his free hand takes my hand.

"You want to dance right here in the street, next to a litter bin?" I toss a glance in the bin's direction.

He slides a glance at it, a grin sliding onto his face. "You can't deny the romance of what a bin can bring to a situation."

"Oh, yeah, all that dirty litter…so sexy." I start laughing, loving the feel of his own laughter against me.

"Shut up, and dance with me. You're killing the moment."

"Okay," I acquiesce, letting him move us to the music. But I'm feeling self-conscious and a little silly. I cast a glance at the restaurant across the way. "People are staring," I whisper.

"So, let them stare. I don't care because I'm not looking at them. I'm only looking at you."

That brings my eyes to his. He's looking at me like he always does—with such intensity that I feel it deep inside my heart, curling around the place where he's already deeply embedded.

"What if someone recognizes you?" I ask just to try to keep myself grounded and not lose myself in him completely.

But then he goes and says, "Then, they'll see me dancing with my girl, whom I'm crazy about." He stops dancing, his eyes serious. "And I am, babe, completely fucking head over heels crazy about you."

Any sense of grounding I had floats up to the stars along with my heart. Leaning in, I rest my forehead against his, closing my eyes against the depth of emotions I'm feeling. "I'm crazy about you, too."

And I stay there dancing with him on that street in Budapest until the song fades, knowing that the time I have with him is quickly running out and not knowing how to stop it from happening.

twenty-four

MARINA BAY, SINGAPORE

I PRESS MY FINGERTIPS to the cool glass as I stare out of the window, looking out at the illuminated Marina Bay Street Circuit that Carrick will be racing on tomorrow.

It's late. Carrick's in bed sleeping, and I'm scared.

My fears have been growing exponentially with each race. For the days running up to each one, I struggle to sleep. My mind is all over the place. And I feel like I don't get a break from the worry because the races come around so quick.

I'm exhausted, drained, and so very confused.

And here, in Singapore, I'm feeling the worst I ever have. I'm really struggling, and I don't know if it's because tomorrow's race is at night—nine p.m., in fact. It's not that Singapore has a bad track. It's just darkness, even though illuminated, hinders visibility.

With the thought of Carrick climbing into his car and going out on the track tomorrow night…I feel sick to my stomach.

Carrick knows that, since we got together, I worry about the races. He knows I'm worried about this one. He just doesn't know the extent.

He doesn't know about the panic attacks.

And I don't want to talk to him in detail about them or my fears because there's nothing he can do or say to make me feel better. The only way I would feel better was if he weren't racing, and that's never going to happen.

One, because he can't stop. Racing is who he is. And two, I would never ask that of him and not just because I know what his answer would be.

Racing is what makes Carrick. It's in the air he breathes, the blood that runs through his veins.

And even though I know all of this, I know this is who he is, it doesn't abate my fears.

It's bleeding into everything I do. I'm beyond meticulous with checking his car, so much more than I used to be. Where I was vigorous with the safety checks on his car before, now, I'm obsessive. I'm checking everything three or four times. So painstakingly thorough about it that Ben is starting to notice.

Every time Carrick pulls out onto the track, I don't breathe until he's come back in safely.

Is this how my mum felt all the time when my dad was racing?

All those years with him, sick with the worry that one race could be his last.

Until it finally was.

I rest my forehead against the cool glass, trying to still my racing thoughts.

"What are you doing, babe?"

The sound of Carrick's rough sleepy voice catches me off guard, freezing my muscles in place.

Forcing myself to relax, I turn to him. "I couldn't sleep."

He closes the distance between us. Sliding his warm hands up my arms, he cups my shoulders. "You're worried about tomorrow's race?"

"A little." *So much I can barely breathe.* I can't look into his face, fearing that he'll see the truth in my eyes.

Taking my face in his hands, he tilts my head back, making me look at him. "It's gonna be fine." He drives the point with a solid stare. "I've driven this circuit tons of times. *I'm* gonna be fine." He presses his reassuring soft lips to mine.

I feel a swell of tears. Swallowing them back, I wrap my arms around his neck, holding him.

"I'm sorry I woke you," I murmur against his mouth.

He pulls back. "You didn't. The cold empty space in bed where you should be was what woke me. I don't like reaching out and you not being there."

"I'm sorry. Go back to bed. You need your rest for tomorrow. I'll be there in a few minutes."

"No, what I need is you." His hands slide down my back. Lifting my slip with rough fingers, his palms cup my bare bottom as he takes my mouth again, firmer this time.

I know what he wants. I want it, too. I always want him. More so lately with a desperation, fearing that each time I do have him might be the last.

Carrick's body presses mine against the glass. As the kiss deepens, I feel his erection against my stomach, sending lightning bolts of desire shooting through me.

Breaking from my mouth, he pulls my slip off my body. Pressing me back up against the glass, it's cold and unforgiving against my skin. He brushes his thumb over my nipple, making me gasp into his mouth.

After kissing his way down my jaw, my neck, and my chest, he presses a kiss to each breast before lowering to his knees. Staring up at me in the dark, he slides his hand under my thigh. Lifting it, he places it on his shoulder. Parting me with his fingers, he presses his mouth to me.

My fingers sink into his hair on a gasp as his hot tongue laps at me. I look down at him, his head between my legs pleasuring me, my hips rocking against his mouth.

I love him. So much it hurts. And I can't tell him. Because if I do, it makes it real, and if I lose him…

It's all becoming too much to bear.

I close my eyes against the fear and love and confusion, and I focus on the way he's making me feel right now. The escape to heaven he's offering me.

Then, his tongue touches me in just the right way, and I shatter around his mouth.

Wordlessly, he gets to his feet. My fingers pull on the drawstring on his pajama pants. I push them down his hips, letting them drop to the floor.

He steps out of them, kicking them aside. Lifting my leg, he hooks it over his hip. Then, dipping his hips slightly, he thrusts up inside me.

"Carrick..." I moan, my hands gripping his upper arms as my head falls back against the glass.

Eyes on me, he kisses me, almost desperately, tangling his tongue with mine, as he takes me there, up against the glass where anyone could see us.

The sex is intense and deep...so very deep. We don't speak. In the dark surrounding us, the only sound is our ragged breaths.

I'm shaking by the time I reach my second orgasm, my body tightening firmly around his.

Then, my name is growling from his lips as he pumps into me, filling me with all he has.

He rests his forehead to mine, panting, his breath touching and mixing with my own. "There isn't a single moment in my future where I don't see you in it." His words are whispered, his fingers threading into my hair.

I'm choked by emotion, unable to speak.

And if I could speak, what would I say? Don't bank your life with me. Yes, I want that, too, but I don't see it like you do. I fight for it daily, but ultimately, I don't know if I'm strong enough to stay.

I can't.

So, like the coward I am, I say nothing and conceal my weakness. Wrapping my arms around his neck, I bury my face into him.

Lifting my legs, Carrick brings them around his waist, and he carries me back to bed.

REVVED

Gently laying me down on the mattress, still inside me, he rests his head on my chest, and that's where he stays for the rest of the night.

twenty-five

🇸🇬 MARINA BAY, SINGAPORE

"I SHOULD BE DOWN THERE, doing last-minute checks."

"Babe, relax, Ben and Robbie have got it. The car's fine. She's more than ready. You're more use to me here." He wraps his arms around my waist from behind. Chin resting on my shoulder, he stares out the window in front of us. "I like having you here with me before a race. You're my new pre-race ritual."

That should make me feel warm and safe, but it doesn't. Nothing can penetrate the wall of fear that's built up inside me.

I've been riding on nerves all day, nerves that I've been fighting to conceal from Carrick. I don't want to put his focus off. I don't want him worrying about me. I want him focused on his race.

I haven't been able to eat all day. I hardly slept last night. After Carrick carried me to bed, I just lay there, watching him, as he slept on me. As I ran my fingers through his hair, my body was stiff from the weight of him, but I couldn't move because I didn't want to. I was scared that it could be my last night with him, and I needed him as close to me as possible. I needed to hold him.

I'm so scared that this race is going to take him from me.

I know I'm being irrational. But I can't help it. It feels beyond my control now.

I wish I were different. Wish that I were stronger for him.

When did things get so bad for me?

The moment I fell in love with him.

My fear just keeps escalating, growing like a monster. And I just keep having the insistent urge to tell him to not go out there. To stay here with me forever. To never leave.

Each race has just gotten worse than the one before, and I wonder when it's going to reach its peak and if that peak will be manageable. Right now, it's barely feeling tolerable.

I feel like I'm on the edge of a cliff, staring down at the rocky bottom, with no choice but to fall.

"Babe...talk to me."

My mind jolts back to him. "About?" I try to keep my voice even, light.

"About why your body is locked up tight even though I'm wrapped around you."

I turn my head, looking at him. "I'm just a little nervous...about the race."

"I've told you, there's nothing to be nervous about. You've seen me race a hundred times before."

"Not exactly a hundred times. And you weren't the most important person in my life then." The words fall from my lips. It was the wrong thing to say but the right thing to say for so many differing reasons.

His eyes fill with warmth and everything he feels for me, which I know is a lot. I just don't know exactly how much.

Carrick hasn't said that he loves me.

Even though I want him to love me, a part of me—the cowardly part—doesn't want him to. If he did, it would make everything so much harder.

"You know that goes both ways, right? You're at the top of my list...not that it's a long list. Well, actually, there's only you and my dad on it."

He grins, turning me in his arms to face him. I brush my thumb over the curve of his smile, and he bites down playfully on it.

"I like that you worry about me, but you do remember who I am, right? Carrick Ryan, best driver in the world. I've got this racing shit down pat, babe. I'm going to do this race, and then we'll celebrate my win in bed where I'm going to fuck you six ways from Sunday."

I force a smile. "Only six ways?"

"There's my girl." He brushes his lips over mine. "God, I fucking adore you, Andressa."

And I love you, Carrick.

There's a knock at the door before I can reply.

"Time." Ben's head pops around the door.

"Coming." Carrick gives me another kiss.

I can taste his pre-ritual race Galaxy chocolate on his tongue, and for some reason, it chokes tears in my throat, bringing that desperation rising in me again.

Curling my fingers into his racing overalls, I press harder to his mouth, needing more from him.

Giving me what I want, his arms come around me, crushing me to his body. He kisses me almost like it's the first and last time he ever will.

Please come back to me.

Breaking off, panting, his eyes alight with desire. He presses his lips to my forehead, humming the words over my skin, "Fucking adore you, babe."

Sliding his hand into mine, he grabs his helmet off the side, and we leave his room together, following Ben downstairs to the garage.

Carrick pulls his balaclava and helmet on. He winks at me before pulling the visor down. Then, he climbs in the cockpit. Ben straps him in. The steering wheel is fitted.

He's ready to go.

Come back.

His head turns to me just before it's time for him to pull out for the tire warm-up. He taps two fingers to his helmet, and then he pulls out of the garage and onto the tracks.

And I step back to watch him on the screens.

I'm driving myself insane. I can't talk to anyone. A few times, Petra and Ben have tried to make conversation with me about the race, but my stare always stays fixed on the screens, my mouth mumbling back one-word responses.

My eyes are dry and sore because I'm so afraid to blink in case I miss something.

I can't miss a thing.

Carrick's been driving well…really well. But he hasn't come in for a tire change yet, and that's starting to bother me. He's going to need a change soon. He's been riding the car hard.

He's on a straight at the moment, fast approaching a corner. A backmarker is in front of him, and I know Carrick is getting frustrated, wanting to pass. I can see it in the aggressive movement of his car. I don't need to be on the control desk to know that he's cursing the other driver to hell. I can hear Owen's voice from here, telling him to take it easy.

I flick a worried glance in Owen's direction, but my eyes go straight back to the screens, scanning for the circuit marshal with his blue flag to tell the backmarker to let Carrick pass.

I see the flag come up. *Thank God.*

They're almost on the corner when the flag comes up, and I expect the backmarker to slow down, pull back, to let Carrick pass.

But he's not slowing.

Did he not see the flag?

Then, I see it happen in the split second before it does.

The other driver, in his arrogance, doesn't slow enough for the turn. His back wheels spin out just as Carrick is cutting past to outbreak him. The backmarker's rear-end tails out, straight into the path of Carrick's car. It hits the front, sending Carrick's car spinning out across the track and slamming into a wall.

No!

The scream gets caught in my throat.

I want to run, go to him, but I'm frozen in place. My eyes are wide with fear, my hands covering my mouth, as I desperately search the screens for a sign that he's moving in the cockpit. I can see the debris of his car littering the track, and the marshal is scrambling the wall to get to him.

There's silence all around. Apart from Owen. I can hear his frantic voice, checking for Carrick, asking him to respond that he's okay.

My heart is beating so hard that it's painful.

Please be okay, baby. Please.

Then, I see Carrick's hand move. Yanking off the steering wheel, he throws it out of the car.

He's okay. Thank God he's okay.

There's a collective exhalation of relief.

I'm relieved. Beyond relieved. But still, I can't breathe.

Why can't I breathe?

Because he could have died. That crash could have killed him. One wrong hit—that's all it takes, and he's dead.

Just like my dad.

"Thank God he's okay. I was worried there for a second." Petra is beside me, exhaling her relief, her arm around my waist.

I didn't even know she was here.

"Hey, you okay?" she asks me.

I blankly stare back at her. I try to move my lips, but nothing's working as it should. All I can do is nod my mute head.

He could have died. He was lucky this time.

But what about next time?

I move my eyes back to the screen. Carrick's out of the car now, walking back to the pits. He looks angry. He'll be mad and frustrated at coming out of the race.

He's okay. He's coming back.

But still, I can't breathe.

Why can't I breathe?

Because he could be dead right now. Just like your dad. He could have died in that car.

My head starts to spin. My vision blurring. My heart pounding. Blood roaring in my ears. The tips of my fingers tingling.

Panic slides her ugly hands around my throat and squeezes.

I have to get out of here. I can't do this.

Stumbling away from Petra, I mumble something incoherent. I hear her call after me, but I can't stop.

I break out of the garage and into the empty hallway, gasping for air.

I can't breathe.

I see a water fountain and stumble toward it. Running the cold water, I put my mouth to it, wetting my dry lips. Breaths still burning my throat, my chest heaving, I lean my weighted body against the fountain, and I place my wrist under the running water—a trick I read about to help try to calm a racing pulse in the midst of a panic attack.

It takes for what feels like forever for me to maintain some form of control. For the blackness to clear from my vision.

But I'm still not right. My mind is still restless with fear. I'm still agitated.

All I can think and see are the what-ifs.

What if his car had hit the wall at the wrong angle? Instead of walking, he would have been carried out of there.

What if the gas tank had ruptured on impact? What if the car had caught fire? He wouldn't have even had the chance to be carried out of there because he would be…

Jesus. My vision blurs again. I rub roughly at my eyes.

I can't do this anymore.

I can't keep feeling like this. I can't go there again. I can't lose someone I love in that way.

And Carrick deserves better than me. Better than I can give him.

Any normal girlfriend would have been running toward him, needing to feel him and touch him to know that he's okay.

Not like me—running away, hiding out in the hallway, having a panic attack—because it's all too much to deal with.

He deserves so much more. I'm not strong enough to be with him. I'm broken.

His dad was right. I should leave him now while the damage is minimal. I should have left him weeks ago. I should never have let it get this far.

I was just fooling myself, thinking I could do this.

Because I can't.

As I turn from the fountain, I see Carrick's vending machine filled with his chocolate. It sets off an intense crushing pain in my heart.

"Andressa?"

Closing my eyes on the sound of Carrick's voice, I take a deep breath before opening them and turning to face him.

He looks confused. Pissed off. But scared. It's there in his eyes, a tiny flicker of fear and uncertainty.

"What are you doing out here? I was looking for you."

"Are you okay?" I ask, my voice shaking.

"I'm fine." He brushes my words off with impatience. "What I'm not fine about is getting back from the track and you not being there."

"I-I'm sorry." My lips tremble.

"What's going on, babe? Are you okay?" He takes a step toward me.

Instead of staying put or moving toward him, I take a step back. And he understands instantly. I see it clearly in the show of dismay that passes over his face.

"Andressa…what's going on?" His voice wavers.

"I-I just…I don't think I can do this anymore." The words leave me in a breathless rush.

"You can't do…*what* anymore?" His words are carefully spoken. Almost like he's afraid to say them for fear of what will come.

I take a deep breath. "This." I gesture a helpless hand between us.

"Babe, if this is about the accident…it was just a bump."

"It wasn't just a fucking bump!" The words rip from my throat. "You could have died out there!"

"Bullshit. It was minor. I've had worse. I'm here, Andressa, and I'm fine."

He tries to placate me with his hands and words as he attempts to move closer to me, but I ward him off, moving further away.

He doesn't like that. It's clearly written all over his face in lines of deep frustration. But I can't absorb anything of him. All I'm attuned to are my own fears right now.

It's almost like it's not really me standing here, thinking and saying these things. It's like I've stepped out of my body, handed it over to someone else, and I'm staring back at myself in abstract horror, unable to stop myself from destroying the best thing I've ever had. Because all that matters right now is stopping the fear and panic, willing to do anything to make the noise in my head stop, make the debilitating and crushing panic stop, even if that means wrecking everything.

Him. Me. Us.

Tears start running down my face. "You're fine now, but what about the next time? One wrong hit. That's all it takes, and then you're gone—forever. I thought I could do this...but I can't. I'm sorry." My head is shaking, and I'm stepping backward, farther away from him.

In this moment, I just need to get away. I can't see past the fear. I'm blinded by it. And right now, I will do anything to stop feeling this way.

Turning mid-stride, I start walking away. But he grabs my arm from behind, pulling me back to him.

There's fire and ire and hurt in his eyes. "That's it?" he growls. "You say you can't do this anymore, and then you just fucking walk away?"

My mind is reeling. I feel trapped, cornered like a wild animal. And like a wild animal, I'll do what's necessary to get away even if it means hurting the one person who doesn't deserve to be hurt by me.

"Yes, that's exactly how it is! I told you that I can't do this anymore! I tried, and it's not working. Now, let me go." I tug at my arm, but his hold is too strong, and it's like he doesn't even feel me.

"I can't fucking believe this...all this time together...I..." He pauses, taking a ragged, painful-sounding breath. Then, his eyes meet mine, holding me with such a power I can't even begin to explain. "Jesus...Andressa, is this really happening? Are you really...leaving me?"

Deep breath...

"Yes. I am."

The look on his face...I never want to see that look on anyone's face ever again. I think I'm actually witnessing heartbreak in this moment, and I hate myself for it. Abhorrently hate myself.

He drops my arm like I've just scolded him.

"I'm sorry..." My voice breaks, tears running over my lips into my mouth. My eyes lower with shame and the pain of my own heart breaking. I turn and start walking away again.

"Andressa! You can't just leave like this! You can't leave me!" The panic in his voice is palpable.

It slices over my skin like the razor blades of pain I deserve, burrowing deep inside, splintering into my bones, crucifying me.

I keep my lips pressed together. If I part them, I'm afraid I'll weaken and turn back to him and take it all back. So, I continue walking away from the only man I've ever loved.

"You're leaving because you're afraid, but I'm not your dad, Andressa! Do you hear me? I'm not him. I'm not gonna die on those fucking tracks!"

Stopping at the mention of my father, I turn back to Carrick. "You don't know that!" I cry out. "I believed with all my heart that my dad wouldn't die out there! I was so fucking sure of it! I thought because he was the greatest driver in the world that it somehow made him invincible! Immune to death. That he would never die. And I was fucking wrong!" I scream, my chest heaving with emotion. "One wrong move in that car, that's all it takes, and then you're gone—forever." My voice is cold, hard, detached. I don't even recognize myself right now. "I fell victim to my certainty once, and it tore me apart. I won't do it again."

I think it's in this moment that he truly realizes that this is actually happening.

His hard mask slips into place, armoring himself against me. "You go, and we're done for good. You walk out that door. I won't chase you." His voice is rough with emotion but serious, deadly serious.

A tremor of fear runs through me, seeping into my consciousness. A tiny part of the real me is screaming that I'm making the biggest mistake of my life.

No. I have to do this. It's the right thing for the both of us.

I take a deep breath. Wrapping my arms around myself, I fix my eyes on his. "That's the point...I don't want you to chase me."

I turn away but not before seeing the debilitating pain filling his eyes. It shreds me with each step I take away from him.

"Andressa...just fucking wait...please! I-I...love you!"

I freeze. My breath leaving me in a painful rush, like I've just been punched in the chest, as his words ricochet through me. My body jolting, knees buckling, I have to fight to take in air to stay on my feet.

I hear him move toward me, his low voice nearing. "*Please*. I love you. That has to count for something. Just...don't go."

"I love you, too," I whisper the words so quiet that he won't hear. But I needed to say it to him just once.

I breathe through the agony, and tears start to spill down my cheeks again. I pull in a strengthening breath. Then, I start walking, and I don't stop until I'm out the door and out of his life.

twenty-six

TWO MONTHS LATER

🇧🇷 SAO PAULO, BRAZIL

REGRET…it slows down time in the worst possible way. Like a silent killer, it slides its hand around your throat and chokes the life out of you.

Even though I know leaving Carrick was the right thing to do, it hasn't stopped the regret from creeping in.

When I ran, I was in a haze, trapped in a fog of panic and fear.

But once the fog lifted, it hit me with the force of a freight train. It was like the settling after the storm, coming out to see the wreckage.

I'd left him. I'd actually left him. There was no going back.

I would never again be able to talk to him, see him, be close to him…touch him ever again.

I lost it for a few days there. I couldn't pull myself out of bed. I couldn't stop crying. I was a mess.

I still am in a lot of ways.

I know it sounds crazy…that I sound crazy. At times, I think I might actually be readying to board the batshit crazy train. But that night in Singapore, the build up to it, I was so afraid, so consumed by everything I was feeling that I couldn't see past it.

And now I'm seeing past it, and I miss him with a physical ache. It's not abating. If anything, it's getting stronger.

Not much has changed about the way I felt about Carrick racing. I still worry every time he climbs into the car. I still watch on the television from the confines of my home, worrying for him the whole time. The only difference here is, I feel a sense of detachment from it. Not physically being there lessens the crazy in me I guess.

When I left him that night in Singapore, from the track, I went straight to the hotel. I quickly packed my stuff and got a cab to the airport. I had to fly to Istanbul on a connecting flight to Brazil, taking the better part of a day.

Uncle John and Petra had called me while I was on the plane. I'd had voice mails and texts from both of them. While I was in Istanbul, waiting on my flight to Brazil, I texted them both, telling them I was fine and that I would call when I could. I also texted my mum to tell her I was coming home. I just couldn't deal with talking to anyone at that point.

It took me forever to get home to Brazil, and I was exhausted and drained by the time I landed in São Paulo. My mum was waiting at the airport for me.

I was so relieved to see her standing there. I fell into her arms in the heap of mess that I was. She didn't ask anything. She just held me and stroked my hair, soothing me.

I haven't really talked to Mum—or with anyone for that matter—about what happened. All she knows is that I broke things off with Carrick, and I left the team.

I have spoken to Petra and Uncle John. I called them my first day back in Brazil after I'd cried a river to my mum. I didn't expand on anything that had happened. I just told them that I couldn't be with Carrick anymore. That it wasn't working for me. I think they both knew the real reason, but they didn't question me on it, which I was grateful for.

I apologized profusely to Uncle John for just leaving him in the lurch like that.

He told me to stop being daft, and then he asked when I was coming back.

I told him that I wouldn't be returning.

He won't have it though. He won't fill my job. He's hired a temporary mechanic, some guy called Pete, to cover my work until I do come back.

But how can I?

Carrick said if I left he wouldn't chase me. He meant that.

There's been nothing. No calls or texts. Not that I expected there to be. But I guess…I don't know. I don't know what I expected.

But it's right this way. Clean break.

You think it'd make things easier. It doesn't. It makes them harder somehow.

Not being with Carrick, I feel like I've lost a limb. Nothing could ever have prepared me for how badly I feel at not being with him.

I thought living with the fear over his races was bad. It was child's play compared to how I feel now.

So, why don't I go back? Why don't I call him up and tell him I'm sorry and beg him to take me back?

Because nothing's changed. I'm still me. I'm still not good enough for him. I walked away from him, and I hurt him.

And he's moved on now anyway.

Not with anyone else—well, not that I know of. But after I left, I couldn't help myself from looking for news of him.

In the beginning, there wasn't much. News on how his poles had been slipping back. I felt the blame for that immensely. And there was a photo of him taken a few weeks after we'd broken up. He didn't look good. He was pictured leaving a sponsor dinner with his dad. He was dressed in jeans and a shirt, unshaven. He looked tired.

It hurt me that he looked bad, that he was clearly hurting, but a dark part of me was relieved to know that he wasn't over me.

But then a few weeks ago, I saw news that his poles were picking up and that he'd taken first place in both his American and Mexican races.

I was happy for that.

Then, yesterday, I saw a picture of him here in Brazil. He's in São Paulo for the penultimate leg of the tour. He was at some event, surrounded by models, and it knocked me off-kilter.

He looked better. He looked like Carrick. He was smiling. He was happy.

It felt like a punch in the gut, seeing that picture, knowing that he's over me now. I know it's hurt that I deserve, but that doesn't make me feel any less shitty.

I knew it was coming, I just didn't know how hard it would be to know he was over me. And I guess just knowing that he's here, only an hour's drive away from me, is making things hurt more.

Even more so right now because I'm on my way into São Paulo to have dinner with Uncle John, Petra, and Ben. I'm driving in. I borrowed my mum's car to save me from having to take the train. Mum was invited tonight, but she already had plans. So, we're going to have dinner another night with Uncle John before he leaves.

I'm meeting them at a restaurant called Pizzaria Speranza. It's a great place with amazing pizza. I'm trying not to think about how much Carrick would love it there.

I'm so looking forward to seeing the three of them. It'll be nice to see them, catch up. I've talked to them on the phone, but it's not the same. I miss them.

It's funny how I got so attached so soon—well, I mean, with Petra and Ben. I was already attached to my Uncle John. I guess it's from being on the road together. You spend way more time together than you normally would.

I've resolved myself not to ask how Carrick is. I've refrained from mentioning him when I speak to them on the phone. But there has been the odd occasion when his name has come up with Petra. Especially in the beginning after I left, she would tell me how much he was missing me.

It was hard to hear. And it made it even harder to stay away.

But I'm poison to Carrick. He doesn't need me in his life. He's better off without me, and I think he's realized that now.

I park in front of the restaurant. They're already here, seated outside. So, the moment I'm there, they're on me.

Petra is the first to reach me, and she hugs the life out of me. "Bloody hell! I've missed you!"

"Missed you, too, Pet," I say, feeling a rush of emotion.

Holding me back by the shoulders, she stares into my face. "Not saying that you look like shit, but you look tired, and you've definitely lost weight, and there wasn't much there to lose. You doing okay?"

"I'm doing fine." I brush her off with a smile.

I'm not fine. She knows that. I know that. And she's right. I have lost weight. When I'm down, I'm one of those people who loses their appetite.

"Good to see you, Andi." Ben moves in to give me a hug. "It's just not the same around the garage without you."

"Aw, Ben, I'm really feeling the love right now." I laugh against him, but honestly, I'm fighting tears.

The moment Ben releases me, Uncle John's lifting me off my feet into a bear hug. "Missed you, kiddo. I just got you back, and you've gone and bloody left me again."

Uncle John rarely shows emotion, but I hear it clear in his voice. And then I see it shining in his eyes when I pull back to look at him.

I give him a sad look, wishing so badly that things were different, that I was different. "Missed you, too, Uncle John." I press a kiss to his stubbly cheek before he lowers me back to my feet. "But we're here now, so come on. Let's get this party started!" I force a big smile and lightness into my voice.

Petra grabs a hold of my hand and leads me over to our table, sitting me next to her. "So, what's good to drink here?"

"Drink?" Ben chuckles. "Are we not eating?"

"Yes, of course, we're eating." She gives him a look. "But the important thing is first—alcohol." She grins, making me laugh.

God, I've missed these guys.

And I try not to focus on the one person I'm missing most.

"I'll drive you back. It's on my way."

"You sure?" Uncle John checks.

"Of course. Seems silly, you all getting a taxi back when I'm passing that way."

We've been at the restaurant for hours, just eating and having a laugh. I haven't been drinking since I'm driving, but the three of them have put some beer away, and Petra is definitely merry.

We all pile into my car, and in no time, I'm pulling up to the front of their hotel.

I get out of my car, so I can say good-bye to them properly.

I'm just hugging Ben good-bye when I see *him*. He's leaving the hotel with his dad.

My heart stops at the sight of him. Everything else around me fades away.

The constant ache that I have learned to live with since leaving him intensifies, leaving me breathless.

I close my eyes on the pain, but I feel it the instant he sees me. Almost like he's touching my skin with his hands, I feel his eyes touch upon me.

I look straight at him, noting his shock at seeing me.

I move away from Ben, and my eyes follow Carrick as he walks toward me.

My body starts to tremble, my heart beating in double-time.

He stops a few feet away. He's dressed in jeans and a team T-shirt. He looks beautiful.

"Andressa…"

Hearing his voice saying my name is like having a glass of water in the arid desert, only to find that it's not real but a mirage.

"Hi." My voice is weak with everything.

"We'll leave you to it." Uncle John presses a kiss to my temple. "I'll see you soon, kiddo."

I don't watch them leave. I can't take my eyes off Carrick. We're both just standing here, staring at one another.

"I'll go get the car," Owen says.

Carrick gives a nod of acknowledgement but still doesn't look away from me.

Being here with him, looking into his eyes, I feel like I'm drowning and coming back to life all at once.

"How…have you been?" He takes another small step closer, but somehow, it's not close enough.

But then, nothing ever was close enough for me when it came to him.

That's always been the problem. I feel too much when I'm around Carrick. It's our greatest thing and my biggest downfall.

"Okay…I think. I mean…I don't know. You?"

Finally, he looks away, his gaze sweeping the floor. I hear him blow out a breath before he brings his eyes back to mine. "Same…I guess."

His hand is flexing at his side. He looks like he wants to touch me and run away at the same time.

I know this because I'm feeling exactly the same way.

Nothing has felt more difficult than this moment right now. I thought that the day we broke up was hard…horrific, but this seems worse somehow.

I guess because, back then, even though we were fighting…falling apart, he was still mine in a way. And now…we're nothing but two people who used to be together.

"I was going to call you." He clears his rough throat. "We need to talk"—my heart lifts a little—"about your car." Then, it deflates. "It's still in my garage, but I thought…I mean, if you're staying here, then I can have her shipped to you. Or if you are coming back home to England, I could drive it over to your place, or you could pick her up. I mean, whatever you want. Either way…just let me know."

My dad's car.

Carrick's and my car.

I feel a wave of emotions so strong that I don't know what to do with myself.

That car symbolizes everything that mattered in my life.

It was what finally brought Carrick and me together.

I have to let it go. It's the right thing to do.

Taking a deep breath, I hold my emotions back. "Thank you…so much. But I can't keep the car. It doesn't feel right, not now."

His brows draw together, and I can see a world of hurt in his eyes. "She's your car, Andressa. I bought her for you." His words are spoken softly.

And they punch me straight in the heart.

"She cost so much money, Carrick. Now that we're…no longer together, it would feel wrong of me to keep her."

He blows out a breath, pinching the bridge of his nose. "I can't keep the car, Andressa." His words are quiet, pained. "Even if you no longer want her, I just...I can't keep her. I can donate her to a charity auction or something. I don't know. Just tell me what to do, and I'll do it." He looks at me with pleading eyes, and there's a desperation in his words that says so much more.

Is he not over me?

It's wrong for me to feel a spark of hope that I have no entitlement too, but still, I feel it.

I so desperately want to reach out to him in this moment.

Keeping a hold of myself, I bind my hands together in front of me. "I'll keep her." I don't want to hurt him any more than I already have.

His eyes lift a little. "Where should I have her shipped to? Here...or your place in England?"

I still have my apartment. The lease was for a year, and it's not up yet.

Is that hope in his voice at the thought of me going back to England?

"It's...probably best to have her shipped here."

His eyes dim.

I wrap my arms around myself to try to ward off the chill I feel. But it's not going anywhere because it's coming from deep inside me. "Please make sure to send me the bill for shipping."

"It's okay." He brushes me off.

But I can't let him pay. He's done enough for me already.

"Please let me pay for the shipping, Carrick," I say softly.

"Jesus, Andressa!" he snaps. "Just let me do this one last fucking thing for you."

His impatience is driven by hurt.

I know that, and that's why I say in a soft, sad voice, "Okay, Carrick...okay."

The air is thick with everything. So much is left unsaid between us. It's hard to breathe. My whole body is aching for his. Memories are painting out in the air around us, killing me slowly.

I lift my eyes, meeting with his. It's there, that connection between us, the one that's been there right from the start.

His lips part, like he's just about to say something, but he's cut off at the roar of the engine as Owen's car pulls up in front of mine.

Breaking away from his stare, I glance at Owen's car. "I should...let you go." *God, this hurts—badly.* I don't want to leave him. But I have to.

I force my feet to move toward my car. "It was really good seeing you."

"Andressa..." His voice pulls me back, not that it would have taken much.

"Yes?" There's hope in my voice. I know it, and I can't help it.

"I just...wanted to..." He's struggling. It's hard to see, but it gives me that stupid hope again.

He rubs a hand over his hair as he blows out a breath. "I just wanted to say the garage feels empty without you."

Then, he's gone, getting in Owen's car, and they're driving away.

I watch the blink of the car lights disappearing into the traffic.

Steadying myself with a hand on my car, I breathe in deep, sucking back tears.

I unlock my car and get inside. I turn the ignition, the radio coming in midst of Beyoncé's soulful voice saying that she's "Scared of Lonely."

And I break down.

REVVED

It takes me fifteen minutes before I can compose myself enough to be able to drive home.

twenty-seven

🇧🇷 SANTOS, BRAZIL

"*BRIDGET JONES* OR *THE HOLIDAY*?"

I stare at the DVD cases in my mum's hands, not really feeling like watching either. I'm not exactly in the mood for a chick flick. I've apparently been in an "arse of a mood"—quoting my mum there—for the last few days…since I saw Carrick basically. I think these movies are her way of getting back at me.

Fingering my necklace, I say, "*Cars*."

"*Bridget Jones* it is." She gives me a saccharine smile.

My mum's not exactly a fan of *Cars*. I think I've driven her mad with it over the years.

Turning from me, she puts the disc in the player.

"I got some treats," she says before leaving the living room. She reappears a minute later with her hands behind her back. "When I was in town earlier, I went to that store that sells English food, and you'll never guess what they had." Her face is all lit up.

"Alcohol?" That's just my wishful thinking that she bought me some.

My mum's not really a big drinker, and she rarely drinks at home. But I could really do with a drown-my-sorrows beer right about now.

"English chocolate!" She pulls out from behind her back a big bar of Cadbury Dairy Milk and an even bigger bar of Galaxy.

Jesus Christ.

Carrick's chocolate.

I have to stop myself from bursting into tears.

Of all the chocolate in the whole of fucking Brazil that she could have bought, she buys his chocolate—not that she knows it's his chocolate. Still, it's like the gods have it in for me or something.

"I know how much you hate Brazilian chocolate since it's too bitter and how you miss chocolate from England, so I thought this might cheer you up."

"Thanks," I manage to get out. Flopping back on the sofa, letting my depression spread over me, I throw an arm over my face and sprawl out, my long legs taking up all the space.

On a tut, Mum lifts my legs. I move my arm from my face to see her sitting down, my legs still in her hands. Once she's seated, she puts my legs on her lap.

"Smile, darling. I hate seeing you so sad."

"I'm smiling." I force one showing way too much teeth.

She gives me a sad look but doesn't push on it. "Which one would you like?"

She holds up both bars of chocolate, unaware of my internal turmoil over that chocolate, which is raging on like a bitch.

And because I'm a masochist and I really feel like torturing myself, I take the Galaxy.

I try not to cry when I snap off a piece and put it in my mouth.

As soon as the chocolate hits my tongue, all I can think of is the last time Carrick kissed me. It was before his race in Singapore, and I could taste the chocolate on his tongue.

And now, all I can think about is how it felt to be kissed by him, to have him make love to me.

My body starts to ache for him. And I've got this pain in my chest, like someone's standing on it.

Will this pain of missing him ever go away?

"No."

What? Did I say that out loud?

I flash a glance at my mum, but she's looking at her phone.

She sees me staring. "Sorry, darling. Your Aunt Clara wants to borrow a pair of my earrings again. But I'm telling her no as I didn't get the last pair back. She went out, got drunk, and lost them!" she exclaims.

That makes me laugh, and I giggle at the thought of Aunt Clara drunk.

The doorbell rings.

We both look at each other.

"You expecting anyone?" Mum asks.

"Nope."

"I wonder who is calling at this hour."

Could it be Carrick?

My heart lifts and then deflates just as quickly when I realize I'm being stupid. He doesn't know where I live, for starters, and it's not like he has a reason to come see me. It's been two days since I bumped into him outside his hotel and nothing. If he wanted to see me, he would have come by now.

"It's only seven o'clock, Mum." I chuckle. "And we won't find out unless you answer the door."

"Guess I'm answering the door then." She gives me a look. Using the remote, she pauses the DVD, lifts my legs off her, and gets up from the sofa.

"Look through the peephole before you open the door," I call after her.

I don't want her to open the door to an ax murderer. But then, that might not actually be a bad thing. He could put me out of my misery.

I listen for voices to see who it is. I can hear low murmuring but nothing I can make out.

I'm just about to get up from the sofa when Mum comes back in the living room.

"You have a visitor." She moves aside to reveal Owen Ryan standing behind her.

"Owen—Mr. Ryan, what are you doing here?" Scrambling to sit up, I touch a hand to my hair, well aware of the mess I am. I can't remember the last time I showered, my hair is tied in a messy knot, and I'm wearing my *Still Plays with Cars* ratty old pajamas.

I'm looking less than awesome while Owen Ryan is standing here in his Savile Row suit.

But then, it's not like I have to impress him anymore. I no longer work for him, not that I ever impressed him when I did work on the team.

"I was hoping to talk to you," he says to me.

"Oh." I look at my mum.

"I'll make some drinks," she says. "Coffee okay, Owen?"

"Yes, thank you." He moves into the living room as my mum disappears down the hall to the kitchen. "You mind if I sit down?" He gestures to the chair.

"No, of course not." I'm forgetting my manners.

I'm just stunned to see him here. And I'm thrown because Owen's the closest thing to Carrick, and him being here is making me hurt all over again. Well, not that the hurting has ever stopped.

There's that awkward moment of silence there always is when you have no clue why someone's arrived at your home, unannounced.

So, I decide to break it with the most obvious. "Is Carrick okay?"

"Yes…and no."

"No?" The panic in my voice is evident. I sit up straighter in my seat.

"Carrick's fine…physically."

"Oh, right. Okay. Good."

"But Carrick *is* the reason I'm here."

"Right…"

I'm not sure if I want to have any conversation with Owen Ryan about anything, let alone Carrick. Maybe he's here about my dad's car. Maybe he's found out that Carrick wants me to keep it, and he thinks it's too much money to give to me. And he'd be right. It is.

"Before you start, can I ask, how did you know where I live?" I tuck my hands under my thighs. "Did my Uncle John tell you?"

He'd better not have, or he and I will be having words.

"No. I didn't ask John because I didn't want anyone to know that I was coming to see you."

"Why?"

"Because I don't want Carrick to know."

"Oh." I free my hands and wrap my arms around myself. "So, how did you find out?"

"It wasn't difficult. There's only one Wolfe listed as living here in Santos."

I freeze. He notices.

"Carrick didn't tell me about your father."

"Okay. So…how?"

"I had you looked into when you started working for Rybell…well, the moment I knew my son was interested in you for more than a roll in the hay."

A roll in the hay? I can't even…

So, Owen has known all along who I am, who my dad was. And honestly, I'm feeling a little pissed off at him for having me checked out.

I mean, who does that, apart from people on TV shows?

"You actually had me checked out?"

"Yes." He doesn't look ashamed of the fact.

"Why?" I exclaim a little angrily.

"Because I love my son and because I'm his manager. His career, to a big extent, is in my hands. You know his profile. Who he dates matters. Especially if she matters to him. It'd be big news. I knew you mattered, so I had to know if there were any skeletons in your closet that could potentially damage him."

I mattered to Carrick.

Mattered.

"And did you find anything?"

"No. But you know that already. But when I did find out that your father is William Wolfe, that presented a whole other problem for me. Not to Carrick's career. If anything, that would have been great press for him. No, what concerned me was *you*. Your dad's accident…I know you were there when it happened, Andi…and you were so young. It's bound to have affected you, left a mark. And Carrick doing what he does for a living…I foresaw problems. I know you've never had a boyfriend that has lasted beyond a couple of months. You have a tough exterior, and you're hard to get to know. And I know because of who Carrick is, if he cares about someone, actually lets that person in, then it's all or nothing with him. I figured you sat somewhere in the middle. Emotional attachments don't seem to be your thing, so I paid attention."

"I really don't want to talk about this," I snap, turning my face away.

"Andi…I didn't come here to upset you."

"Then, why did you come?" Swinging my eyes back, I glare at him.

"I came because what I said that night to you in the restaurant…I was wrong."

"Well, apparently, you were right. As you *foresaw*, I left him."

"No." He shakes his head. "I mean, I was wrong when I said that you should leave him sooner rather than later—before he got in too deep with you. I was wrong because he already was in too deep…still is. And I think you are, too."

"Are you foreseeing things again?" I'm being a bitch, but I don't care.

This guy has been nothing but an arsehole to me from the moment I met him, and now, I find out that he's been invading my privacy. I'm bloody livid.

"I deserve that," he says. "But no. I saw your face the other night when you saw Carrick outside the hotel. You're in love with him, and that was when I knew you'd left him, not because you don't care enough, but because you care too much, and you can't handle it. You think you can't be the person he needs."

Is this guy a bloody mind reader? Or a psychologist in disguise?

"Carrick has never loved a woman in his life—until you. And the way he loves you...that's not something you want to throw away. I've never seen him in a better place than when he was with you. And surely he's safer in that place than the place he's in now. He's not doing well without you. You not being around...I know my son, and it's killing him.

"It bothers me, what he does for a living, Andi. Of course it does, every time he's out there on the track. He's all I have, but I can't stop him from doing what he loves, and I wouldn't want to. Instead, I make sure that I'm there to keep him as safe as I possibly can.

"Don't stay away from him because you're afraid of what might happen. It's a waste, and I know all about wasting time. Don't make the mistakes I made in life. Don't live a life filled with regret. Because regret does ugly, terrible things to people, and I don't want that for you or my son."

All I can do is stare at him, stunned.

I'm taking it there's a lot more to Owen Ryan than I'll probably ever know.

"Here we go." My mum comes in with the coffees and puts the tray down on the table.

"I'm sorry, but I'm afraid I'm going to have to rush off." Owen gets to his feet. "I didn't realize the time."

"Oh, no problem," my mum replies. "I'll see you out."

I can't seem to move. I'm frozen in place.

"Oh, Andi..." Stopping, he turns back. "There's something I want to return to you." Owen puts his hand in the inside of his suit jacket, pulling out my access pass for the Prix.

I left it behind in Carrick's hotel room in Singapore.

"How did you get this?" I blink up at Owen. My hand curling around the pass, I take it from him.

"Carrick's been carrying it around with him since you left. I thought it was time you had it back."

And I'm left holding the pass, clutched to my chest, as my mum sees Owen Ryan from our home.

twenty-eight

🇧🇷 SANTOS, BRAZIL

IT'S HALF AN HOUR BEFORE THE RACE STARTS.

Thirty minutes before Carrick climbs into his car and pulls out onto the track at the Autódromo.

I'm pacing my living room, wearing a tread in the carpet. I have my Prix pass in my hand, fingers clutching around, while I chew on my thumbnail.

I didn't get a wink of sleep last night after seeing Owen. My mind has been reeling, bouncing back and forth on what to do.

Do I want to see Carrick? Of course I do. I want to see him more than anything in the world.

But I don't know if I can give him what he needs, if I can be what he deserves.

That's what's still keeping me here instead of me being on my way to São Paulo.

My mum comes into the living room, marching over to me and stopping me in my tracks. "Okay. Enough, Andressa. You need to go see him."

Eyes lowered, I shake my head. "I don't think I can."

"You're going."

My eyes shoot up to hers. She's got this determined look in her eyes that I don't see very often.

"I'm not standing back and watching you torture yourself. I've stood on the sidelines for way too long already, saying nothing, because I didn't want to interfere, but that's clearly what I should have done from the start. You need to stop pacing a hole in the living room carpet and go to him." My mum presses her car keys into my hand. "Take these and drive to São Paulo as fast as you can—but not too fast so that you're not being safe."

I let out a watery chuckle as tears fill my eyes. My voice weakens as I say, "I'm…afraid, Mum."

"Oh, darling." She takes my face in her hands. "There's nothing to be afraid of."

I let out a humorless laugh. "If only that were true. There's everything to be afraid of. I just keep thinking, if I could find a way to stop loving him, then it would be so much easier."

"I don't think you really mean that. You're just looking for an easy out, but easy doesn't come with love. You have to work hard at it, sometimes fight for it."

I stare into her eyes as I ask her this question, "If you could have turned it off with Dad, stopped loving him in the beginning, would you have?"

"Not for one second," she answers without hesitation. "I never want to know what life would have been like without loving your father. One thing I do know is that it would have been no life at all." Removing her hands from my face, she takes my hands in hers. "I heard everything Owen said to you last night—I might have been listening in a little—and he was right. I am so angry with myself right now."

My eyes widen. "Why?"

"Because it should have been me saying what Owen said last night. I should have seen what was going on with you. You're always just so strong, so sure of your decisions, so I let you be, but I shouldn't have. I should have pushed harder for you to talk to me. I knew you were hurting. I just didn't realize how badly, and I didn't know that you had left Carrick because you're afraid that what happened to your father will happen to him."

At the mention of my dad, tears spill over down my cheeks.

Mum wraps her arms around me, her voice washing over me, "Andressa, every time your father climbed in that car to race, my heart stopped beating until the moment he came back to me safely, and it was that way until the day he didn't come back. But that doesn't mean I would take back one single moment of the time I had with him." She leans back, staring into my face.

"Your father gave me one of the greatest gifts in the world—you. And not just that, he gave me a lifetime of love in the fifteen years that I had with him. I would rather have had that than nothing at all. I regret nothing. It took me a long time to come to terms with losing him, but life happens as it's meant to. We can't control it. Just like you can't control the fact that you love Carrick. Of course you will worry for him—whether you are with him or not. So, wouldn't it be better to be with him, to make those memories and have a life with him?

"Take the good with the bad. Learn to live with your fears. Because being with him…having the good, it makes the bad a whole lot better." She smiles softly. "And you know if your father could have chosen a man for you, it would have been a man like Carrick." She tucks my hair behind my ear. "This life—racing—is in your blood, and so is Carrick. So, go now, and get that man you love. Fix things, and then bring him back here because I want to meet the man who has my baby girl's heart."

"*Saia da frente, caralho!*" I yell, honking my horn at the idiot who is driving like a fucking snail in front of me. Basically, I just told him to move out of the way but in a not so nice manner.

I know. I'm being impatient, shouting at random people, but I can't help it. I need to get to the Autódromo. I need to see Carrick. I have no clue what I'm going to say to him. I just know that I have to tell him how I feel—that I love him and that a life without him is no life at all.

I've got to stop fearing the future and start living for today. And if I have to yell at a random stranger to get me to him that little bit quicker, then so be it.

My eyes keep flickering to the clock on the dashboard. The race is due to start any minute. I won't make it before it does, but that doesn't matter. I just have to get there.

"Finally!" I huff as the car moves over, allowing me to pass.

Shifting down to third, I press the accelerator hard, so I can speed up and gain momentum. I push back up to fifth the moment I'm flying.

Then, I hear my mum's caution in my ears. *"Drive safe."*

I panic over Carrick's racing, yet here I am, driving fast to get to him. I need to take it easy. I could get pulled over as well if I'm not careful.

I ease my foot off the accelerator a touch, but then "Back to December" starts to play on the stereo, and now, I'm cursing my mum for listening to a Taylor Swift CD.

Seriously, Mum?

Because Taylor is singing about how she's sorry for that night, how she wishes she could go back, make it all right…make him love her again.

My foot finds the floor again, speeding me up faster than I was before, propelling me down the road, toward São Paulo and to Carrick.

And if I get a speeding ticket, I'm blaming my mum and Taylor Swift.

Slamming the brakes on the car, I skid to a stop in the Autódromo parking lot. I'm out of the car with my pass in hand, and I'm running my way toward the entrance.

Once I'm in, I ask the security guard which garage Rybell is in, to which he directs me.

I start running again, reaching the paddock, and I catch sight of the giant screen, seeing the race well underway. My legs start to slow, my heart beating faster, when I see Carrick's name on the screen saying that he's currently in pole position.

Picking up speed again, I start to run toward the garage entrance.

I'm not too far from Rybell when scary thoughts invade my brain, slowing me to an almost stop.

What if he doesn't want to see me? I know he's not in there right now, but I don't want to ambush him in front of everyone.

Maybe I should just hang back here and watch the race on the screen until he's finished.

Stop being a chicken, Andi, and get your arse in that garage now!

I force my feet to move again, and I've only gotten two steps further when I hear the collective gasps filled with, "Oh God," and, "No," from the group of people watching the race in the paddock.

And I know. I just know.

My heart skids to a stop. *Don't be Carrick. Please not him.*

Spinning on the spot back to the screen, my eyes meet with the sight of a car in pieces on the track, flames coming out of the back of it.

And I'm flashed back fourteen years.

No.

I don't wait to see any more. I just start running. Toward Carrick.

My heart and mind are racing as fast as my legs.

Please don't be him. Please don't be him.

Reaching Rybell's garage, I burst in through the door. The whole team is there, everyone watching the screens, but no one is speaking.

"Tell me it isn't him!" I scream out the words in blind panic.

Everybody in the room spins toward me.

"Tell me it isn't him!" I yell again.

"Andi, it's okay." That's Ben. He's moving toward me. "It's not Carrick. He's okay."

I almost fall over from the relief. It's immense. I've never felt anything like it before.

"It's not him?" I'm breathless. I press my hand to my chest, trying to steady my racing heart.

"No. He's fine. Absolutely fine." Ben places his hands on my shoulders, steadying me.

"Thank God." I lift my eyes to his. "Then, who?"

His eyes dim, and my stomach sinks.

"Leandro Silva."

"Oh God, no. How…is he?"

He slowly shakes his head. "No one knows yet. They managed to get him out of the car. The medics are with him…but it doesn't look good."

How can I hate and love this sport in equal measure?

I hate that it takes great men from us, but I love the man who loves it beyond all reason.

My eyes lift to see Owen walking toward us.

"They're stopping the race," Owen tells Ben.

I see the shock on Ben's face, and it's mirrored on my own.

It has to be really bad if they're stopping the race.

"They need to clear the car from the tracks. They're bringing a helicopter in to take Leandro to the hospital. It needs to land on the tracks as they can't risk moving him."

"The race…when will it restart?" I ask Owen.

He looks at me briefly and then back to Ben. "It's not. They're stopping it for now out of respect. It's Leandro's home country. It wouldn't be right to continue…not until they know if he's going to survive."

Oh God.

My stomach drops, feeling hollow. Stopping a race happens rarely.

I only know of a few, and one was on the day my father died.

Oh God. Poor Leandro. And his family.

I know exactly what they will be going through because I've been through the same. My heart starts to ache for them.

But I also feel sick with guilt. Because even through the devastation I feel for Leandro and his family, I'm filled with relief that it isn't Carrick being airlifted out of here.

"Carrick will be in soon, so get the crew ready," Owen tells Ben.

"On it." Ben moves away across the garage, looking somber.

When something like this happens…even if it isn't one of your own, you feel it.

"So, you came."

I turn my eyes to Owen. "You didn't think I would?"

"Hoped, for Carrick's sake. Believe it or not, I don't know everything, Andi."

He gives me a half smile before walking back over to the desk where my Uncle John is sitting. He's speaking into his mouthpiece, probably to Carrick, but he looks over at me and smiles softly. A hint of sadness is in his eyes, and I know he must be thinking about my dad right now.

When I hear the roar of Carrick's engine as he pulls his car into the pit, my legs start to tremble, my heart beating in double-time. I'm not really sure how I'm still standing right now.

I'm scared as to how he's going to react with me being here. Especially with what's just happened out there, I might be the last person he wants to see right now.

My heart is in my hands, ready to give itself to him. I'm hoping he doesn't throw it away…throw me away. Because after the way I've treated him, I know I deserve nothing less.

I watch as Ben removes his steering wheel, unbuckling him. Then, Carrick is climbing out of the cockpit, and I'm pretty sure I'm going to throw up. My stomach is rioting. Hands shaking, I flex them at my sides.

Carrick's back is to me. He hasn't seen me yet. I can't move. I'm frozen to the spot.

He pulls his helmet off and then his balaclava, and he runs his hand through his damp hair, tousling it up. It makes me ache to touch him.

Then, he turns, and his eyes collide with mine. I see the shock reverberate through them.

I wait for what seems like forever—in reality, it's only seconds—to see what his reaction will be.

And I get nothing.

After his initial shock fades, his eyes clear and give me nothing. He just stands there, staring at me, waiting.

This is it. Here I go.

As I start to move toward him, everything and everyone disappears, and there is only him.

There has only ever been him. From the moment I saw him at Rybell, he's always been in my sight and on my mind.

Keeping his eyes on me, he puts his helmet down on the car.

I don't stop moving until there is less than a foot of space between us. And now I'm here, standing before him. My nerves are floundering, shaking and shredding my body and mind like I'm inside a blender.

"Hi." My voice is small, and seeing him like this, being so close to him yet still so far, makes my emotions crash down on me. My eyes fill with tears. I blink, and one runs from the corner of my eye. I quickly brush it away with my fingers.

I see his eyes follow the movement before coming back to mine, but he doesn't say anything.

He's just watching me with guarded eyes. But then, among that guard, I see the tiniest spark, and it makes what I have to say just that little bit easier.

Taking a fortifying breath, I part my dry lips. "Are you okay?" I want to make sure he's feeling okay after what just happened on the tracks with Leandro. That first, and then him and me.

"I'm not sure."

"Why?"

"Because I don't know why you're here."

Oh.

I blow out a breath, readying myself. "I'm here because…I wanted—no, I *needed* to see you…because I…" I'm stumbling, faltering. I'm ruining this.

Drawing my eyes away from him, I take another deep breath, and then I look back to him, trying to portray everything I feel for him through my eyes. "I came because I needed to tell you that…I love you. And I'm sorry. And I love you."

His expression gives away nothing. "You're sorry for what? Loving me?"

"No!" I rush to say. "I'm sorry for everything, for leaving you. I could never be sorry for loving you. You're the best thing that's ever happened to me."

His eyes and face are still giving me nothing, and I know it's not enough, what I'm saying. I need to give him more, say more. I just don't know what to say.

Why am I so bad at this?

My throat thickens as my desperation gets the better of me, and I burst into tears. I don't care that people are around us right now. I just care that I'm ruining my last chance with him. "I'm screwing this up," I whisper through my tears.

"I think you're doing just fine."

I barely get the chance to register what he said before my face is in his hands, and he's kissing me, stealing the breath I'm beyond willing to give him. My arms instantly wrap around his neck as he takes my mouth hard and deep, pulling my body against his. The feel of his lips, his body against mine, breaks me and then puts me back together, more whole than I ever was.

"I love you," I sob against his lips. "I'm sorry I left. I just…love you so much, Carrick."

Cradling my face in his hands, he brushes my tears away with his thumbs. "I love you, too, babe."

That only makes me cry harder.

Staring into my eyes, he says, "You wanna get out of here?"

I'm instantly reminded of Barcelona and the first time we slept together.

Swallowing a hiccup, I give him a watery smile. "Is that a trick question?"

"There's my girl."

Then, he smiles so beautifully that it makes my stomach launch a thousand butterflies.

Giving me one more kiss, he takes my hand and leads me through the garage, not saying a word to anyone.

When we're out the door and near the stairs to the driver's room, he says, "Wait right there. Don't move."

After a swift kiss to my lips, I watch him jog up the stairs, taking them two at a time.

Then, before I know it, he's coming back down. "Room key." He holds it up, shoving it into the pocket of his overalls, along with his wallet and phone. Then, he pulls on the ball cap that was in his other hand.

He takes my hand again, and we're walking out through another door. When we're outside, we quickly move across the paddock toward the main exit.

"You got a car?" he asks.

"My mum's." I dig the key from my pocket, holding it up.

He takes it from me. "I'm driving. I'm faster than you."

Then, I'm forced to part from him as we climb into my mum's car. But the minute we're inside, he grabs me by the back of the neck and presses a firm kiss to my lips, leaving me breathless and wanting.

Starting the engine, he peels out of the parking lot. My hand is in his the whole ride to Carrick's hotel. Thankfully, the hotel isn't far from the Autódromo, and in no time, we're pulling up front and getting out.

Meeting Carrick on the pavement, he takes my hand again.

Leading me into the hotel, he tosses the keys to the valet. "Park her up."

Then, we're in the elevator. Carrick presses the button to his floor. I can't wait for the door to close, so we can get upstairs, and I can finally touch him like I need to. But clearly the gods aren't on our side because a man appears outside the elevator, wanting to get in.

A low growl comes from Carrick, and then he says, "I'll give you everything I have in my wallet right now if you don't get in this elevator."

My eyes ping to Carrick in shock, but he's not looking at me. He's looking at the man. So then, I look at the man, interested in how this is going to go.

The man looks to be English. He's in his late forties, well dressed in a sharp black suit.

A hint of a smile touches Suit Man's lips. "You're Carrick Ryan, right?" It's not a question. He knows it's Carrick.

"Mmhmm."

The door starts to close, but Suit Man stops it with his foot. "My kid's a big fan of yours. Can you sign this for him?" He holds out the newspaper that was under his arm. "Do that, and I'll leave you in peace."

I hear a short burst of laughter come from Carrick, and then he reaches out and takes the paper. It's the sports section, and I can see Carrick's picture on the front.

"You got a pen?" Carrick asks Suit Man.

"Yeah." He pulls one from inside his jacket pocket and hands it to Carrick.

Resting the paper against the elevator wall, Carrick quickly signs his name across his picture and hands the newspaper and pen back.

"Thanks," Suit Man says, stepping back from the elevator. "My kid will be thrilled. I'll be in his good books for weeks."

Carrick chuckles low. "Well, give him this, too, and it might turn those weeks into months." Carrick pulls the cap from his head and hands it over to Suit Man.

"That's great." He taps Carrick's hat on his hand. "Thanks so much. And enjoy the rest of your day."

"Oh, I intend to," Carrick mutters low, jabbing the button for his floor.

The door closes, and we're finally moving up.

"That was sweet what you just did, giving him your cap."

Carrick turns his face to me. His eyes are blazing, and it makes my insides tremble.

"I'm not sweet, Andressa. I'm hard. Really fucking hard."

He takes my hand and presses it against his very present erection, making me gasp and my knickers instantly soak through.

Turning fully to me, he backs me up against the wall. Hands braced on either side of my head, he lowers his mouth to mine, lips almost touching. His breath brushes over my skin.

My body is quivering with need, and suddenly, I'm very breathless. "I can't believe you offered that man money not to get in the elevator."

Moving a hand, he runs it over the curve of my waist, pressing his hips into mine. "I haven't been inside you for two fucking months. I'd pretty much say or do anything to speed that up."

I don't get a chance to respond as my words are swallowed up by his hot kiss.

It's desperate and clingy on both our parts. His hands are in my hair, tilting my head back, so he can get better access to my mouth as he licks the inside of it. My fingers wind in his short locks, pulling on the strands, as I practically climb his body to get closer.

Two months of not having each other is pouring out into this one kiss.

But we have been apart. We haven't really talked about that or anything, and we probably should before we even think about having sex.

I break off, breathing hard. "Carrick...shouldn't we talk first?"

His brow lifts. "What the fuck do we need to talk about?"

"Us. The time we've been apart."

"Have you been with another man?"

"No!" I gasp, hurt that he even asked. Then, my heart sinks because I haven't even considered the possibility that he could have been with another woman. "Have...you?"

"No."

I breathe out my relief.

"You love me, right?"

I stare into his eyes. "You know I do."

"And I love you, madly and fucking deeply, and that's all we need to know right now. Talking can come later.

Right now, I'm gonna show you how deep my love for you can go—namely with my cock inside you."

"You're such a romantic." I giggle as I slide my hands down from his hair, wrapping them around the nape of his neck.

"You know it, babe." He gives a sexy smirk.

"And what you need to know is that I don't just love you, Carrick." I move my lips in close to his, so there's only a sliver of air between them. "I'm *in* love with you."

On a growl, he's kissing me again, devouring me.

The elevator pings our arrival on our floor. Carrick lifts me, so I wrap my legs around his waist on instinct. He carries me out of the elevator and down the hall. Key card in his door, we're in his suite and then in the bedroom. He lays me down on the bed.

Leaving me there, panting and horny as hell, he stands at the foot of the bed. He kicks off his shoes and removes his overalls. Not wanting to be left out of this race, I quickly remove my shoes and clothes.

Then, we're both naked, and he's on top of me. Skin on skin. I start to burn up like a fever.

There's no need for foreplay here. We're both more than ready because it's been way too long. Hands pinning mine to the bed above my head, he thrusts his cock inside me.

"Carrick!" I cry out, my eyes closing on the feel of him.

"Fuck," he growls, stilling inside me.

I open my eyes to his. They're fierce on me, his face austere, tight.

"Never again, Andressa. I'm not going without you ever a-fucking-gain."

"No," I whisper, swallowing down, my throat thick with emotion.

"Now, tell me you love me while I fuck you."

"I love you."

He pulls out and thrusts back into me hard. "Again."

"I love you!" I cry out.

His mouth comes down to mine, and he kisses me with bruising force as he thrusts in and out of me, his movements desperate, urgent, and hard.

"Don't…ever…fucking…leave…me…again," he pants, his forehead pressed to mine.

"I won't. I promise." Feeling and seeing the hurt I've caused him brings tears to my eyes. They run from the corners like a tap as a sob escapes me.

Halting, he pulls back, seeing my tears. Concern laces his eyes. "Jesus, Andressa, what's wrong? Have I hurt you?"

"No." I touch my hand to his face, reassuring him. "You're not hurting me. I'm just so…so-sorry for hurting you."

"Shh, babe." Turning his face in, he presses a kiss to the palm of my hand. "Don't cry. You're here now, and that's all that matters." Wiping my tears away, he tenderly kisses me. "I love you, Andressa." He starts to move inside me again, slower this time. "I love you so much."

We keep our eyes locked together during the whole time he makes love to me. Even when our orgasms rush and collide almost violently and it nearly becomes too much to bear, we don't break eye contact.

After we've come down from our high, framing my face with his hands, he kisses me softly, reverently. Then, slipping out of me, he moves, lying on his side. He brings me over to face him, and hooking my leg over his hip, he holds it there.

"I'll clean you up soon," he says. "But right now, I just need to be with you."

"I need to be with you, too." I can't ever imagine not being with him again.

He's staring into my eyes. I watch as he pulls in a deep breath and exhales it.

"Look, I know you said in the elevator that we should talk, but I don't want us to rehash all that bad shit. I want it to stay in the past where it belongs. All I will say is…being apart from you, was the hardest fucking thing that I've ever had to do. Those were the worst two fucking months of my life. I wanted to come after you so many times. I can't count the times I had my phone in my hand, ready to call you. I was even at the airport once, ticket in hand, ready to fly to Brazil and beg you to take me back, but I realized it would never be right between us if I did. You had to come back to me. *I* needed you to come back to me because I had to know that you wanted to be with me. That you feel as strongly for me as I do you. I had to know that you loved me, and the only way I would was if you came back. But I swear to God, Andressa, if you ever fucking leave me again, I'm chasing you, to the ends of the fucking earth if I have to. I'll never be without you again."

I touch my fingertips to his cheek as tears prick my eyes again. "You won't ever have to chase me. I'm not going anywhere, I swear. I'm so sorry I hurt you, that I let my fears get the better of me. But…you have to know that it's not going to be easy. Those fears I have over you racing…they haven't gone away. They're still here. I just finally realized that I couldn't be without you, fears or not. So, now, I just need to find a way to live with them. And I will," I promise him.

Cupping my cheek, he touches a thumb to my lips. "*We'll* find a way together. We're a team, babe. Don't ever forget that."

"*We're a team.*" I love the sound of that.

I smile as he brings his mouth back to mine, brushing his lips softly over mine.

"It's me and you, babe. You have to conquer something, we do it together. Okay?"

"Okay." I smile again before curling my fingers into his hair and crushing my lips to his. I softly whisper over them, "Team Ryan and Amaro forever."

twenty-nine

🇦🇪 YAS ISLAND, ABU DHABI

WE'RE HERE FOR THE FINAL RACE OF THE SEASON.

To win the championship, Carrick needs to win this race. He's on pole position as he came in first in qualifying, but everything rides on today.

I'm nervous for him. And about the race itself.

But I'm dealing. Kind of.

Okay, I'm shit fucking scared. But I'm forcing myself to stay calm. I will not freak out.

I'm not working today. Carrick wouldn't let me. I don't know whether that's a good thing or not, but he said to let Pete finish up this last race, so I'm not worrying over the mechanics of his car. He said he wants me to be relaxed. Well, as relaxed as I can be.

We'll get through this final race, and then when we go home to England, I'm going to start seeing someone, a therapist, to help with my issues over his racing.

If I want to be with him, I have to learn to deal.

Seeing a therapist was Carrick's idea, and I agreed with him. He said that he'll come with me to the sessions. He said if he understands my worries better, then he'll know how to handle me, if or when I flip out again.

I'm not sure how I feel about being handled, but I suppose I can't complain if Carrick is doing the handling.

One thing I do feel, oddly enough, is a sense of relief. I'm relieved that he knows how bad it got for me back then and why I left him. I just wish that I'd told him back then, so we wouldn't have lost those two months together. Hindsight is a great thing.

But it's all in the past now, and we're in a good place—a great place. We've talked a lot.

And spent a lot of time in bed.

That's definitely been fun, the making-up part.

Carrick got to meet my mum while we were still in Brazil, and they got along brilliantly. We all had dinner together—me, Carrick, my mum, Uncle John, and Owen. It was a great night. Owen is actually being much nicer to me these days, which is a good thing. He finally trusts me with Carrick, and that means something. Underneath the hard exterior is a good man who loves his son, as any father should.

I hear the announcements start to come up for today's race. It's not long before it's time for Carrick to go out there.

My heart starts to beat a little faster, so I take a calming deep breath.

Formula 1 is missing a man off today's announcement—Leandro. Thankfully, he survived his crash, but it was touch and go for a while. There was a lot of damage to his body, internal bleeding, but he managed to pull through, and now, he's on the mend. I'm not sure if he'll ever race again. For his sake, I hope he does.

Carrick and I went to visit him while he was in the hospital. Leandro didn't seem like his normal self, but he was still making jokes, so I took that as a positive sign.

Carrick's on the other side of the garage, talking with Ben, and I'm watching him. Well, I'm staring at his arse. It's a really nice arse.

Turning, Carrick catches me staring. A smirks spreads across his face, making my cheeks redden. But I up my game and give him a cocky look.

Leaving Ben, Carrick comes over to me. "You checking out the goods?" He places his hands on my waist.

"Maybe. They are good goods."

He gives me an offended look. "Only good?"

"Okay, the best goods—ever. That better?"

"Much." He smiles. Brushing my hair from my face, he says in a quieter voice, "You doing okay?"

"I'm a little scared. Announcements freaked me out a bit, but I'm coping," I answer truthfully.

I made a promise to him that I would always be honest with him, no matter what, and I intend to keep that promise.

"You remember what we talked about?"

"If I start to panic, sit down, take slow calming breaths, and drink some water. No running. Stay put, and wait until you're back."

His lips lift as he squeezes my waist. "Petra's staying with you, right?"

"Yep, she's my bodyguard."

I give him a look, and he sighs.

Carrick asked Petra to stay with me while he races. I got a bit pissy with him about it, not that I don't love being with Petra because I do, but I don't need Carrick getting me a babysitter either.

"I just didn't want you to be alone."

"I know. It's okay. I get it." I rest my hand against his chest. "I appreciate you looking out for me. It's good that she's here, so I won't be alone."

His brow furrows. "You're never alone, babe. You need to hear my voice, go sit with John and my da, and you can put an earpiece in. Okay?"

"Okay." I smile.

He returns my smile before kissing me.

I can taste his pre-race chocolate on his lips. *Delicious.*

"You taste good," I murmur into his mouth. "Chocolate...yummy."

"Carrick's chocolate kisses." He kisses me again, giving me another taste.

"Hmm...I like that."

"And I like you. A lot."

"Seriously, dudes. Enough with the kissing!"

I break away from Carrick to see Petra standing there.

"Jealous?" I smirk.

"Yeah. Totally. I really need a man." She lets out a faux-dramatic sigh. "Now, you, shoo," she says to Carrick. "I want some time with my girl. You have her enough as it is."

I stare back into Carrick's eyes, touching a hand to his face. "Good luck."

"Thanks, but you I don't need it, babe. Carrick Ryan, god of the tracks, remember?" He gives me a cheeky wink. "See you soon, babe."

One final kiss, and he's gone.

Sitting on the chairs with Petra, I watch as he pulls on his helmet and gets into the cockpit. Ben straps him in. Then, Carrick is pulling out onto the track, and I feel my heart start to race.

I reach for Petra's hand.

"He's just warming up. He's gonna be fine, Andi," she says softly. "He's gonna win this race, and then you guys will go back to the hotel and have a marathon sex session."

That makes me laugh. I turn to look at her, and she's grinning at me.

"Glad you're here, Pet." I give her hand a squeeze.

"Yeah, me, too."

"He's set to do it. The reigning champion is on the home stretch, set to take the gold home…"

I'm on my feet at the sound of the announcer's voice. My heart is beating faster, knowing that Carrick is almost there on the home stretch, so close to crossing that finishing line.

Come on, baby. You can do it. Come back to me safe.

It's been a tough hour for me, not that Carrick's racing hasn't been seamless because it has. But now, I'm watching him closing in the gap to the checkered flag, and my heart is in my throat, excited for him, but still nervous, and just needing him back here with me.

The flag is down.

He won!

Yes!

The whole team is on their feet, cheering and hugging each other. Petra and I are jumping up and down, screaming.

But I won't relax, not fully, until he's here with me and I'm in his arms.

My eyes are glued to the pit, waiting for his return. The moment I see his car pulling in, I'm running out of the garage to him. He's only just climbed out of the car when I'm jumping into his arms.

He hasn't even gotten his helmet off, but I just need to hold him. Need to remind myself that he's real. That he's here, and he's mine.

Tipping my head back, I press a kiss to the visor of his helmet.

I feel his chuckle rumble deep through his chest.

Freeing a hand from around me, he undoes the strap and pulls his helmet off. I remove his balaclava for him.

His hair's all stuck to his head. And he's never looked more beautiful to me than he does in this moment.

I run my fingers through his hair, ruffling it up. His eyes are bright with his win.

"You're here," he says on a smile.

I tilt my head to the side. "Did you doubt I would be?"

"Nah, not for a minute."

"Good." I smile. "Because I'll always be here, Carrick, waiting for you."

"And I'll always come back to you, babe," he says softly.

I touch my fingers to his mouth, tracing the curve of his lips. "So, you won."

"I did."

"Champion again."

"Mmhmm."

"Podium time soon. Trophy. Champagne spraying."

He loves that shit.

"Meh." He shrugs.

"Meh?" I look at him, surprised.

"Yeah, meh." He presses his nose to mine. "The podium can wait because I already have the greatest win of my life right here in my arms."

Then, he's kissing me, and I never, ever want him to stop.

epilogue

CARRICK

THREE MONTHS LATER

✈ BUCKINGHAMSHIRE, ENGLAND

I OPEN THE DOOR TO THE GARAGE and walk inside to see Andressa bent over her car, head under the hood, gorgeous arse stuck up in the air.

Sexiest fucking sight ever.

And this is exactly how I saw her a year ago today in the garage at Rybell. I knew right then, when she turned around and gave me all that sass, that my life was about to change, and I wasn't wrong.

Andressa is everything I never knew I wanted, and now, I wouldn't know how to live without her.

Soul mates—or whatever the fuck you want to call it—she's mine.

After we got back from Abu Dhabi, Andressa moved in here with me a few weeks later. People might think it was quick, but I don't give a shit. Life is too short to waste, and after not having her for two months, I knew I couldn't be without her ever again. I'd asked her to move in, and she'd said yes. It made sense, her moving in here anyway. She was never at her place, mainly because I wouldn't let her out of my bed.

Come on. Look at her. What man in his right mind would?

Living with Andressa is everything I knew it would be. We're not perfect by a long shot. We still have some stuff to work through—her fears about my racing and my issues with rejection—but we're getting there together.

We're happy.

When the press found out who Andressa was, that she's William's daughter, things got a little intense there for a while. Paparazzi were camped outside of the house for days, following us around and that kind of thing. I worried how she'd deal, but she was fine. But we did mostly stay home during that time. I didn't want her to be asked any questions about her father that could stir up painful memories for her.

I want her to be happy. And she is, but I'm not sure for how long.

Racing season will be starting up in a few weeks. We'll be flying out to Melbourne soon.

Andressa is back in her job at Rybell. She wouldn't have it any other way, and neither would I. There isn't anyone I trust more with my car than her.

But I know she's getting anxious in the run-up because she's told me. She always tells me. And I'm doing everything I can to reassure and help her.

She's seeing a therapist. She has been since we got back from Abu Dhabi. I've been attending sessions with her. She does one on her own and one with me, alternating weeks. I think it's helping. She says it is. I guess we'll find out how well in a few weeks, but no matter what, she's going nowhere.

I'm now confident in the fact that she won't ever leave me again because she's spent the last few months reassuring me of that. We're solid, but I was bruised up from the time we spent apart. We're giving each other the reassurances we need, and we're getting stronger every day.

Things can only go up from here. Well, at least that's what I'm hoping after tonight.

"Please tell me that you're my birthday present," I say, moving in closer to her.

Turning her head, she grins at me over her shoulder. I know she remembers that that's the first thing I ever said to her. I can see it in her beautiful eyes.

She moves out from under the hood, wiping her hands on a rag. Oil smudged on her cheek, she comes over to me.

God, she's fucking beautiful. I'll never tire of looking at her.

"It's your birthday?" she says, tilting her head with a sexy smile on her face, in that voice of hers that gets my dick hard.

She's playing along.

God, I love her.

At least I get to fuck her this time—unlike the first time when we spoke these words to each other. That nut took me fucking months to crack.

"It is."

Reaching me, she runs her fingers up my chest as she presses her body against mine, and I instantly want to fuck her.

Sliding my hands around her back and downward, I grab her arse.

"Guess I'd better make it extra special for you then."

There's a glint in her eye that's getting me all kinds of excited.

Removing the oil smear from her cheek with my thumb, I tell her, "You already do make everything extra special, babe."

The glint goes, and she gets that watery happy smile in her eyes that she always gets when I say soppy shit to her.

I love that look.

Bringing her lips to mine, she gives me a soft kiss, making all of me stand to attention, but then she's moving away all too quick.

"What time is it?" She looks around for the clock.

"Time for you to get your hot self ready." I give her behind a playful swat. "We have dinner reservations in an hour."

"Shit! It's that time already?"

"Yep."

"Sorry, baby. Have I been neglecting you on your birthday?"

"A little." I give a pout before kissing her again.

I'm playing it here, going for a sympathy shag. They're always the best as she goes to town on me when she's feeling guilty about something. And don't give me crap because you know you'd do the same.

"But you can make it up to me in the shower." I grin over her lips.

"I'm gonna suck you so hard," she murmurs.

Holy fuck.

Hands still on her arse, I lift her up, loving the way her long legs instinctively wrap around me. And I start walking out of there, carrying her back to the house. While I'm moving, she unzips her overalls, giving me a fan-fucking-tastic view of her tits, and I can see the McQueen necklace that I bought her hanging around her neck.

She never takes it off. She told me she kept it on the whole time we were apart. I'm just hoping there's something else she'll never take off either soon.

But definitely not her clothes. No, they'll be disappearing in a few seconds.

At the sight of her tits and the thought of her blow jobs, I pick up speed, practically running into the house, making her laugh.

I fucking love that sound. It makes my heart beat faster and my dick as hard as nails. But then, it doesn't take much because everything about her makes me hard.

I have her naked and in that shower in minutes. Another minute, and she's down on her knees, giving me the best birthday present a guy could ask for.

REVVED

We're in my car, and I'm driving. Andressa is in the passenger seat, her hand in mine. She looks stunning, wearing a short black dress that gives me plenty of legs to look at.

She's also not wearing any underwear. I'm pretty sure she's trying to kill me. I'm definitely fucking her in the restroom at the restaurant. I don't care what she says. There's only so much teasing a man can take.

Actually, thinking on it, I might get to be inside her before we even reach the restaurant—resting on the fact that things go as I hope they will.

Andressa thinks we're going straight to the restaurant, but there's a detour we have to make first.

I was feeling all relaxed after the spectacular blow job she had given me in the shower and the amazing sex straight after, but now, I'm all tense again. I've been feeling tense for the last few days.

I take the third exit on the roundabout, heading toward Heath and Reach.

"Babe, you took the wrong exit," she says, tapping her fingers against my hand.

"I meant to. I need to just nip into Rybell. I left something there."

"But we'll be late to the restaurant."

"We're good. We've got time."

We're meeting my dad, Katia, John, Petra, and Ben at the restaurant.

Andressa's mum is here, visiting. She wouldn't stay with us. She said we needed our privacy, so she's staying in Andressa's apartment. I think she just didn't want to be stuck under the same roof with her daughter and me going at it all the time. I have a hard time keeping my hands off my girl, if you haven't already figured that out.

We reach Rybell in no time. I park in front of the darkened building and turn the engine off.

My heart starts to pump in my chest.

"Shall I wait in the car?" she asks me.

"No! Come in with me." My words come out sharp, my voice sounding weird.

And she notices, her brow rising. She stares at me for a moment, and I can feel my nerves exploding like a motherfucking bomb inside of me.

Don't question me, babe, please.

Her face relaxes, and she lets out a laugh. "You scared to go in there alone in the dark?"

"Yeah, I'm shit scared of the dark. I need you to cover me in case any bogeymen jump out."

Letting out another sweet laugh, she frees her seat belt and gets out of the car.

Okay, that part was easy. Now, for the not-so-easy part.

Unlocking the main door of the building, I let us in, turn on the lights, and lock the door behind us.

"So, where did you leave—what was it you left?"

"It's in the garage. Come on." Grabbing her hand, I start leading her there.

I came earlier to set up. I'd given her some bullshit reason that Pierce needed to see me. What I needed was a little time to make this perfect.

Dad said he'd light the candles before going to the restaurant. I'm just hoping the fuckers haven't burned out. I want everything to be just right.

I push open the garage door a touch to see the flickering illumination.

Still good. I take a deep breath and push the door open all the way, leading her through.

I've set the garage up exactly as it was the day I met her, which wasn't exactly hard. All it needed was my car to be here and in the spot it was on that day with its hood up.

The only thing it's missing is her beautiful self underneath that hood.

Candles are littered everywhere in the room. Around the car, I set them out in the shape of a heart. And I've got "Dangerous" playing on a loop.

I'm a soppy fuck, but I don't care because it's worth it to see the look on her face right now. Her eyes are wide, and she has the biggest smile.

She looks the most beautiful I've ever seen her.

Breathtaking.

"Carrick…"

I seize the fact that she's lost for words. I'm not wasting time. If I do, then I'll lose my nerve and fuck this up.

I can't fuck this up.

Standing before her, I take her hands in mine and say what I've needed to say for a long while now, "From the moment I saw you in here, Andressa…you had me. I knew my life was about to change. And it has, beyond my wildest dreams. I used to think the only place I could truly feel alive was on the track, but I now know different. I feel most alive when I'm with you. You challenge me. You make me the happiest I've ever been. You make me laugh like no one can. You love me like I didn't know possible. But most importantly, you make me a better man."

My hands are shaking, my heart pumping. I can feel her hands trembling in mine. I'm just praying that's a good sign.

"I want to keep feeling this way for the rest of my life, so that's why I brought you here." I pull the ring box from my pocket.

She gasps. Pulling her hand from mine, it covers her mouth.

"I want to ask you in the very place on the very day that you changed my life if you'd consider sharing yours with me. Let me change your life. Let me give back to you everything you've already given to me." I drop to one knee and pop the box open. "Will you marry me, Andressa?"

She's staring at me and then at the ring, back and forth her eyes go. Her hand is still covering her mouth as a tear runs down her cheek, quickly followed by another and another.

My mouth is dry, my heart beating like a motherfucker. I've never been as scared in my whole life as I am right now.

"Andressa…"

"Yes," she whispers, moving her hand from her mouth.

"Yes?"

"Yes! A million times, yes!" She smiles big. And my heart explodes with relief, and pure fucking happiness.

Hands shaking like a bitch, I get the ring from the box, and I slide it onto the only finger it was ever meant to be on.

Then, I'm on my feet, pulling her to me. Claiming her mouth, I kiss her like it's not enough because it never will be with her. I'll always want more.

Pulling back from me, she stares at me with glittering eyes. "So…we're getting married?" She sounds like she almost doesn't believe this is happening.

My heart tightens in my chest. "Yeah, babe, we're getting married."

And I smile on the knowledge that I'm about to enter the most exciting race of my life, and there's no one else I'd want to be in it with than her.

Acknowledgments

ANDI AND CARRICK'S STORY hit me with the force of a freight train, and from the moment I started writing it, I haven't stopped, apart from sleeping during odd hours and occasionally eating things.

So, I have to thank my family—my husband, Craig, and the two lights of my life, my children, Riley and Isabella. They've put up with my absence and erratic behavior for the last few months without a word of complaint. And I know I tell them this all the time, but I'm still going to say it again. I love you all to infinity and beyond. The three of *you* make *me* a better person.

Andi and Carrick's story came to me when hearing a song for the first time. You've probably figured out which song. If you haven't heard me talking about it at any given opportunity, then it's featured heavily in the book—"Dangerous" by David Guetta, featuring Sam Martin. And I know they'll probably never see this, but I have to say thanks to them both—David Guetta, for his musical genius, and Sam Martin, for his voice. If it weren't for their musical talents, then Andi and Carrick would never exist to me as they do now.

I want to say a humongous thank you to Trish Brinkley. Trishy, when I came to you, bursting with this story and rambling like a lunatic, you burst into it right along with me. You've lived this story with me for the last few months, championing it and me. From the daily word counts to lending me your ear when I was having a meltdown or when I needed to run something by you or ask a random question or show you another paragraph or blurb, you were always there. Thank you for all of that and for loving Andi and Carrick as much as I do. You're the best friend a girl could ask for. I adore you.

And Shawn Brinkley, I owe you an honorary mention! Thank you for Mut! And for every other suggestion you send my way!

My gorgeous Sali Benbow-Powers—I literally threw this book at you with next to no time in which to do it, but as always, you jumped right into it with no word of complaint. I heart you. Your advice is invaluable to me, and you're always bloody right. I hate that! And I will get to Australia one of these days, so I can squeeze you in real life!

Christine Estevez, what would I do without you? You make my life a million times easier. Honestly, I'd be screwed without you! Thank you for fixing all the things I don't have the time to fix.

Surjit Harvey, that book…I will treasure it forever. You have no idea how much receiving it has turned things around for me. I truly treasure your friendship and our posh coffee chats!

Jovana Shirley, editor extraordinaire! Seriously, you take my words and weave them into magic, and no one can format quite like you can. Thank you for always doing an amazing job!

Najla Qamber, cover designer wonder woman! You literally took the image from out of my head and made it real. Thank you for that!

Lauren Abramo, my agent—We haven't been working together long, but in the short time we have, you have guided me and given me valuable advice. When I came to you with this book, telling you the route I wanted to take with it, you supported me one hundred percent. I can't thank you enough for that.

And finally my biggest thank you goes to *you*. Yes, *you*, the one reading this. Reader, blogger, reviewer—you've changed my life in a way I never thought imaginable. Thank you for taking a chance on me. Thank you for sticking with me and for supporting me. There aren't enough words in the world to describe how much it means to me.

about the author

SAMANTHA TOWLE is a *New York Times*, *USA Today*, and *Wall Street Journal* bestselling author. She began her first novel in 2008 while on maternity leave. She completed the manuscript five months later and hasn't stopped writing since.

She is the author of contemporary romances *The Mighty Storm*, *Wethering the Storm*, *Taming the Storm*, and *Trouble*. She has also written paranormal romances *The Bringer* and The Alexandra Jones Series. All her novels are penned to tunes of The Killers, Kings of Leon, Adele, The Doors, Oasis, Fleetwood Mac, Lana Del Rey, and more of her favorite musicians.

A native of Hull and a graduate of Salford University, she lives with her husband, Craig, in East Yorkshire with their son and daughter.

Printed in Great Britain
by Amazon